A MISPLACED LOVE

RENEE M. PALSTRING

Cover Design by Whimsy Book Cover Graphics

ISBNs

978-1-959414-02-5 (Hardcover)

978-1-959414-00-1 (Paperback)

978-1-959414-01-8 (eBook)

Published by Acorn Forest Publishing

CONTENT WARNINGS

A Misplaced Love is an adult romance novel that contains content that may upset some readers. This content includes graphic sexual scenes, graphic violence/death, some swearing and scenes of sexual assault.

To David,

For being there to listen to my 5th time working through an edit…and the 3 more times after that!

TABLE OF CONTENTS

CHAPTER 1

I jostled around the carriage as it rolled down the beaten path causing the nausea to worsen. I pushed my handkerchief, doused in lavender oil, closer to my nose. Inhaling the scent, hoping it would soothe my stomach.

"We're almost there, Your Highness. Would you like a few more drops of oil?"

"Please." I handed my kerchief to Lord Griffith, our hands grazing softly during the exchange. Under normal circumstances, this would have caused my heart to flutter, but the impulse to vomit was stronger and required all my energy to subside the feeling.

"Here you are, Princess Estelle."

I swiftly took the handkerchief and inhaled the floral scent, my stomach calming immediately. Lord Griffith, noticing my relief, smiled sweetly.

I did not like him seeing me in such a manner, but I was glad he was the one to help me through the sickness. No, it was more than that. I was glad he was the one traveling with me despite the horridness of this trip.

Four weeks ago, my father had announced that a union were to happen between me and the king of the rising country, Modare. A kingdom the world and I knew very little of until recently.

The country had existed for hundreds of years, much like Isara; however, it was small and wedged between two great kingdoms. Modare's past kings had not raged a war in years as they were content with their power and land, making them irrelevant to the rest of the world. And with Modare not having any valuable resources, power-hungry kings overlooked their existence. Thus, allowing Modare to stay the quaint, quiet, forgettable country it had been for a hundred years. However, the new King of Modare had other plans when his time of power came.

His rule had begun a year ago, a short time, and yet he had already taken over the countries that touched Modare's borders. Astra and Ula. Two respectable kingdoms, always at war with one another, but were ancient much like Isara. My father fearing Isara would be the next target had reached out to the King of Modare, offering me as a sign of peace and trust between our two kingdoms. And, finally, after many letters back and forth and the mention that with ties to Isara Modare's rise in power would be acknowledged quicker than without, Modare's king accepted my father's offering.

I remember that day vividly. I was walking with Lord Griffith, slyly asking him if he would join in this year's match-making season. He never got to answer as a messenger ran out, alerting me that my presence was required by my father, who then informed me I now had a fiancée.

My heart grew heavy, and my eyes dulled. The King of Modare had taken Astra and Ula. He had taken our allies' homes unprovoked. He was power-hungry, a tyrant. To be sworn to a man like that would cause no greater heartbreak. No, the greater heartbreak would be to lose the one you love, to know you'd never walk the gardens with them again, to never see them laugh, their smile. That's what really dulled my eyes that day.

I argued with my father for countless weeks, begging him not to send me, as I heard more and more about the King of Modare. The King had not allowed any outsiders to visit his newly conquered lands. Rumors spread of his raging temper, the servants who shivered before him, his iron fist. All of it adding to the terror and mystery surrounding his name.

King Titus the Conqueror.
Despite my pleas, my father's answer was always the same.

That this was my duty, my sole purpose as a princess. Marry a king and protect Isara from the inside.

I would run into the gardens and cry often. Lord Griffith always found me. He would give me his handkerchief and offer comforting words. My heart yearned for him. And so, I concocted a plan.

I asked my father for Lord Griffith to escort me to Modare. If I had to say goodbye to my world, I would at least spend the last of it in the company of my secret love. I would give myself and my heart to him before the journey's end. For that was the one thing I could do without hurting my kingdom.

The carriage came to a halt, throwing my body forward, my head flying to the wall across from me. I moved my hands in front, but my reflexes were not fast enough. I closed my eyes, my body tensing in preparation for the impact.

I felt a soft smack across my shoulders followed by the pressure of a hand on my back. My eyes fluttered open to find Lord Griffith's arm wrapped around me, his concerned eyes examining me from top to bottom.

"Are you alright?" he asked.

I nodded, feeling my cheeks warm.

He placed me back into my seat as my gaze drifted up to him.

His face was so close to mine, an inch more and our lips would have met. The thought made my body burn. Quickly my eyes retreated to the floor, my mind debating if now was the time to make my move.

We were alone, well, alone as we would ever get. This was my chance.

I gripped the fabric of my dress, opening my mouth, waiting for the words to come out but a restless neigh reminded me that the carriage had come to a halt. The doors would open soon.

I bit my lip in frustration. I had to speak swiftly, there was no time for murmurs. I needed to be decisive with my words.

I looked up once again, hoping a glimpse of his face would give me courage. But upon meeting his ocean blue eyes, the soft pink of my cheeks turned a bright red.

Though most Isarans shared this eye color, Lord Griffith's sparkled in the sun and pierced through the darkest days. It was as if I was looking into the ocean itself, wondering what lay in its depths.

I felt tears well up in my eyes.

In a day or two, I would never see them again. Now was the time to tell him. I once again opened my mouth to speak but was interrupted by the spring of the carriage door.

Lord Griffith edged toward the opening, glancing at the inn in front of us.

"Our last inn," he said with a smile as if to reassure me that the tiring journey would end soon.

My heart dropped in horror.

Our last inn?

I knew we were close, but not a day away.

If I was going to make my declaration it had to be tonight, no more excuses, no more stutters.

But when?

We had so few moments in which we were alone, away from the eyes of the guards who, no doubt, would report any scandal to my father. My head throbbed with annoyance. There had been many opportunities in which I could have announced my feelings, but the fear of rejection had held me back. Slowly this fear was leaving as we got closer to Modare, but it was replaced with the terror of never telling him, never getting to hear his reply, the fear of living in regret.

"Your Highness?" I looked up to see Lord Griffith eyeing me with concern.

Without noticing, I had dug my fingers into my hair, one of my tell-tale signs I was upset. I clumsily untangled my fingers from my dark brown locks, creating bumps in the sleek pulled-back braid. I groaned, attempting to flatten them.

"May I?" Lord Griffith leaned back into the carriage, blocking me from view of anyone who may pass by as I nodded.

I sighed, crossing my hands over one another, turning my back to him so he could have better access.

Though I enjoyed Lord Griffith's touch, it was embarrassing to have him help me with such feminine matters. Under normal circumstances, I would have called for my lady's maid. However, due to the recent change of power in the lands, Isara and Modare's council had deemed it safer to travel with our identities hidden. Meaning a small travel party, leaving room for only an attendant, driver, and two guards.

I hated leaving my lady maids back home, as they were not only good at their jobs but also dear friends. It had made this trip that much more difficult.

Lord Griffith had tried to make it less so by finding me a tavern maid at each stop. They would help me get ready after the night's rest, but none of them knew the proper hairstyles for a noble lady. Thus, their poor replications would easily become disheveled after an hour or two in the carriage.

The first couple of times this happened I would shyly attempt to fix the mess, but with the carriage knocking me about and only a tiny mirror to use, it deemed harder a challenge than I could handle. That is when Lord Griffith began to offer his hand in the matter.

He had grown up with two sisters and learned the basics of hair styling from them, not by choice, of course. I hated the idea, as it was a degrading job for a man of Lord Griffith's standing. I refused his help at first, but as the hairstyles worsened Lord Griffith became protector of my hair.

"Sorry to trouble you with such trivial matters," I grimaced out as his palms brushed past my ear.

He chuckled as he knotted the black ribbon at the end of my braid. "It's no problem, Princess. In fact, it's an honor to help you with something so *intimate.*" He leaned back admiring his handywork, his hands seeming to linger on the ends of the braid. "Is it to your liking?"

I patted my head, ensuring all the bumps were gone, twisting to get a better look in the small mirror that hung in the carriage. It was perfect.

I turned toward Lord Griffith. He sat, smiling proudly, his eyes aglow.

How I wished to pull him to me, kiss him as a reward, but all I could do was murmur, "Thank you."

"You're welcome." There was silence for a bit as we smiled at one another and admired his work, but the moment was interrupted as a guard impatiently coughed.

Lord Griffith gave a quick nod to the guard, signaling we'd be out in a moment, then turned to me, his face solemn.

"Now, I know I say this every time but still, it injuries me to address you so." Lord Griffith placed his hand flat on his chest and bowed as deep as the tight space of the carriage allowed. "So, allow me to apologize in advance for the belittling titles I will use tonight."

I shook my head in disbelief. I had heard this apology every day and every day I told Griffith it was not needed and yet he continued.

I did not mind being called a *Lady* or being treated as such. In fact, it was an appreciated break from the properness of being royal blood. But to Lord Griffith, referring to me as Lady Estelle was the greatest sin he would commit in his life. It was for my safety, and he was instructed to do so by my father but still, he chided himself over this trivial matter.

"Lord Griffith," I protested but was interrupted by the shaking of his head. He stepped out and offered his hand.

"Lady Estelle." He grimaced as the word *lady* swept across his tongue and out of his mouth. I would have felt bad if not for my heart setting a flutter.

I yearned to be *just* a lady. I would give up the jewels, my title, the luxury of it all just to be a lady. I would not be bound by my royal duties and could simply live day by day. My only duty would be to give my husband heirs. A duty I would welcome with open arms, especially with Griffith. The idea of his miniatures, our miniatures, running around made my heart soar.

In that world, I would be able to marry the one I loved. It was in these moments of pretend that I forgot why we were on this trip, and even though it pained Lord Griffith to refer to me as a lady, I fully enjoyed it.

CHAPTER 2

I wiggled my hips left to right in the creaky wooden chair—attempting to find comfort in the overly crowded tavern—shifting any time a patron stumbled toward me in hope to avoid any more incidents.

Upon our arrival, one drunkard had bumped into me, his ale sloshing out of his cup. Lord Griffith pushed him away, blocking me with his forearm, so the contents only drenched him. This happened twice more till Lord Griffith deemed it best for me to wait at one of the few empty tables as he inquired about rooms. I did as he said, but as I sat at the table alone, the already small room seemed to close in, the drunk patrons looming closer.

Having lived in the palace for the entirety of my life, I had not seen men drink to this excess. I hadn't seen much of anything really. Being in this environment, watching everything by myself, it brought about a sense of unease. However, this discomfort did not stop me from examining the room further, after all, curiosity always got the better of me.

Glancing around the room, I noted that this stop was not much different than other taverns. The walls were crafted from oak and lined with tapestries and ornamental steelworks that were slightly stained with drink. The door, located center of the front wall thus allowing the barkeep to fully examine each patron upon arrival from his perch, whined with age anytime it was forced to move. Bulky, wooden tables and chairs were scattered about in a pattern undiscernible to me. Their various scratches and nicks on them making each unique. Then, just left of the bar, a stairway sat leading to the boarding rooms on the second floor. Each step slightly bending and loudly squeaking as patrons ascended.

Despite examining the entirety of my surroundings, my curiosity was still not satisfied. I needed to watch the crowd. Thankful I had sat at a table that gave me a view of everyone on the first floor without moving my body, my eyes began to roam.

To the left, a group of men of varying ages held cards in their hands, faces unreadable, undistracted by the ever-growing pile of money in the center. Diagonally, a band of raucous men held their goblets high, singing an off-tune song as harlots sat on their laps. The women's fingers drifted across the men's chests then down just above their belts, forcing the men to meet their wolfish eyes. In response, one man grasped the breast of the woman in his lap. Immediately my cheeks heated at the sight, and I averted my gaze.

My eyes rested on the table directly in front of me, a rather safe sight. Here three men sat, smiling. Their attention directed to a fourth member who stood. His hands theatrically moved as words flew out of his mouth. The seated men began to laugh at his actions, in response he ran his fingers through his jet-black hair, devilishly smiling as he propped his leg up on the chair.

It was such a happy scene to behold that I could not help but laugh as well. The sound, uncontrollably loud, caught the attention of several other patrons. Quickly, I muffled myself, my eyes darting to the floor as I regained my composure. But I could not hold back my curiosity for long, as I wanted to see what this man would do next. I looked up once again, only for my gaze to be met by a pair of striking silver eyes. I stared back, lips parting, unsure how to react.

The man's gaze became softer the longer we looked at one another, then all at once, he put on a dashing smile and blew me a kiss. Shocked at this sign of affection my cheeks turned a bright red. I lowered my head to conceal it.

I couldn't help but wonder why my body was reacting this way. The only times, to my recollection, that I had blushed was due to embarrassment for myself, which rarely happened, and when I interacted with Lord Griffith.

So, what caused it now?

It was not embarrassment, that I was sure of. I had often caught men, while at court, infatuated with me and it would never bring a rogue to my cheek. So why, on this occasion, were my cheeks burning?

"Is it Lady or Miss?" a honeyed voice asked.

My heart skipped a beat as I looked up. The sliver-eyed man stood confidently in front of me, his aura overpowering mine. I looked him over once more in hopes to understand why he was so different from other men.

His jet-black hair complimented his sun-kissed skin as it slightly swopped over his forehead. His face was suitable, perhaps better than average, but other than his silver eyes there was nothing unique about him. *Surely*, eyes were not enough to make me feel this way. I continued my examination.

He wore a black vest over a white blouse that was halfway untucked from his onyx pants. He did not adorn himself with accessories beside his leather coin purse tied to his belt and, shockingly, a beautifully crafted broadsword.

The hilt was a sparkling silver with a blue sapphire as the pommel. The black leather grip was worn down, matching the callouses on his hands. The scabbard had a few scratches as well, but it did not diminish the sword's beauty. The locket and chape were a lighter shade of black than the rest of the scabbard, which blue sapphires danced upon.

My tilted as my eyes once again ran over his body, con-fused as how a sword like that belonged to someone who appeared...so...so inadequate in riches.

How had he acquired it?

My eyes drifted back to the hilt, in search of some sort of crest, but before I could reexamine the pommel his hand rested upon it.

"You have a fascination for swords, I take it."

I redirected my eyes to his.

"I would take it from its sheath, but some may see it as a threat." He smirked as the words rolled out and a glimmer of mischievousness sparkled in his eyes.

I looked around at the other men who held out their weapons, comparing the handywork. It looked as if no one cared.

I stared in silent confusion until his smirk grew and the meaning of his words hit me.

"Sir, I will not be subjected to such—" the man placed his hand on his chest and bowed remorsefully.

"I apologize. The drink has gotten the best of me." He took a breath. "If you would allow me to turn back time and start afresh, I would greatly appreciate it."

I let out an exasperated sigh. I never allowed second chances, but in this instant, I knew his rueful eyes would haunt me forever if I did not allow him this exception. And perhaps, continued talking would solve the mystery of the rouge that still hadn't left my cheeks.

I nodded and motioned for him to continue.

He gripped the pommel tighter in excitement. "Thank you. My lady?" His brow raised in question.

I shook my head, disappointed in myself. In my assessment of him, I had forgotten his initial question. A question that gave me a glimmer of hope that this might be a respectable conversation.

"Lady," I hesitated not knowing if I should give him my real name.

At our previous taverns, Lord Griffith had given false names to register for the rooms but with that gleeful smile—my stomach twisted at the thought of giving him a fake name.

The silver-eyed man cocked his head slightly in anticipation.

I opened my mouth to say Estelle then remembered the difference in his clothes and sword. Perhaps, he was a thief and that was how he managed to have such a luxurious blade when his clothes were that of a weary adventurer.

It was better to lie.

"Lady Eve." He smiled faintly as if knowing I was lying. "And yours?"

"Al, my lady." He gave a slight bow.

"Al?" I repeated.

"*Just* Al." One side of his lips moved upward, amused by my expectation that his name should be greater than Al.

I scoffed. He had no title, no sir, no lord, he was just Al. There went the idea that he was a knight. Al was not a respectable name, so coming from a well-off family wasn't an option either.

The sword had to be stolen.

He was a thief.

Perhaps my subconscious had made this connection earlier, had forced the blush on my face, some type of warning sign. It had to be.

The mystery was solved, but now I was faced with another problem; finding out which family the sword belonged to.

With its beautiful jewels, it had to be a family heirloom and would be greatly missed. With my strength I could not take the sword by force. Even with the aid of Lord Griffith and the guards' help, Al's men outnumbered us. If I were to find out the family's name, I could, at least, get word to them.

"Well, *just* Al, that sword looks rather mismatched for some-one of your caliber."

He grabbed the back of the chair and slid it out, taking a seat while rolling his eyes, smirking. "You wound me, Lady Eve. I came over to lay affections at your feet and you accuse me of being a thief." He leaned forward, propping up his elbow on the table, resting his head in the palm of his hand.

Affections? He had come over to lay indecent words in my ear.

My lips pursed together. If we were in Isara, he would've been thrown in the dungeon already, but I had no power in this tavern. He could turn and walk out the door without interference. If I wanted to see the crest on the pommel, I had to play nicely.

"I do not accuse you of anything. I am just stating facts." I smiled coyly, a sweetness in my voice.

"I see." He looked around the tavern then leaned in so that he may speak at a whisper. "And it seems you are a lady without company, a very dangerous game you play. Have you run away? If so, you may want to consider not telling people who you are. There are a million ways to make a pretty penny out of a darling thing like you." He leaned back, smirking once again, his eyes moving up and down my body as he drank from the cup he had brought with him.

Was he threatening me?

My body tensed and I could control my anger no more. "I have an attendant," I barked.

He titled his head. "Just an attendant?" His eyes raked over me once again, an eyebrow raised. "So, you are running away with a lover then?" He leaned further back in his chair, so the front legs came off the ground, allowing him to rest his feet on the table.

Lover. I wish.

I chewed on my bottom lip as thoughts of Lord Griffith leading me up the stairs crossed my mind. I could only imagine how his warm embrace would feel, his hot breath against my neck, our bodies intertwined till morning.

Please, gods, let me feel it tonight.

Al let out a cough, reminding me of his presence.

I glared. "No, we have two men traveling with us."

There was silence. I felt Al's eyes on me, assessing the situation. "*Interesting,*" Al murmured under his breath as he stroked his lower lip with his thumb.

Interesting? What was?

It was normal for a woman to be accompanied on a trip. Was he perhaps planning an ambush on us? Had he come over to collect information?

My eyes widened, wondering if I divulged too much information in my anger.

Al feeling my tension chuckled. "You seemed rather perplexed when I said lover, meaning you're not sure what you and your *dear* attendant are. That is what is interesting." Al slid his legs off the table and leaned forward, cupping his hands to his mouth so only I could see his lips. "So then, is it forbidden or unrequited love? If it's the latter—"

I snapped my head up. I'd had enough of this. I could deal with his vile words but for him to assume Lord Griffith did not hold feelings for me was a blow to my heart, my pride, and my courage for my upcoming declaration.

Al needed to leave.

"You…you…" I choked on my words, wondering if he might be right.

A voice boomed beside me, calm but edged with threat, "Sir, it seems my lady has become upset due to your company. I must ask you to leave us be."

I turned to my left and found Lord Griffith looming over us, hand on his hilt. His expression so hard that it stirred a fear in me.

Al stood up. "My apologies." He bowed once more. "I will take my leave but if you have an interest in hearing the rest of my monologue, do not hesitate to seek me out." Al gave me a wink before retreating to his table.

"My deepest apologies. The person before me had no regard for those behind him and talked so much the owner wished he was deaf." Lord Griffith sat two ales down before taking the seat Al had occupied.

"It's alright," I proclaimed as I dabbed my eyes. "I was in shock of his foul mouth, nothing more."

"Yes, but it is my job to protect you, in all manners of being." Lord Griffith reached out and placed his hand over mine, rubbing his thumb across the surface.

I looked down in shock. He had never touched me like this before. My heart warmed. He was so close. I could pick his hand up and kiss it, letting him know of my feelings. It would be perfect.

I lifted my other hand, that rested on my lap, stretching it to his.

"Here you are. Cheese, bread, and fruit."

Lord Griffith jerked his hand away as the chipper barmaid placed three monstrous plates on the table. "Thank you."

The barmaid smiled and nodded to Lord Griffith, allowing me to retract both my hands without notice.

Lord Griffith clapped his hands together. "Let's dig in. I took the liberty of ordering, I figured you were famished as lunch was quite small." There was a tinge of awkwardness in his voice.

"It was," I stammered out.

Did he know what I was about to do?

Lord Griffith held out his glass. "To our journey ending tomorrow. May you find the happiness you deserve and may we see each other often."

I clinked my glass with his, forcing the tears down.

CHAPTER 3

Lord Griffith and I stood at the top of the staircase alone, as the guards had gone to bed an hour ago. The cheers and songs of the tavern's guests, who were happy with drink, drifted up to us. A reminder that the party would go on for many more hours but Lord Griffith, despite my inclination to stay up and spend what little time we had left together, decided it was best for us to retire to our rooms.

"That room is yours." Lord Griffith handed me a set of keys "Mine is just down the hall if you need me." I looked to where he pointed, four doors lay between us. A respectable distance but close enough that he could quickly get to me if trouble should arise. "Just in case you wish to read tonight." I looked back to Lord Griffith who extended a candle stick to me.

"Thank you," I replied, blushing at the small yet caring gift. "Are you sure you wish to sleep now?"

"I am certain." I took the candle, my smile fading. "Though your friendship means the world to me, and I do not wish to see you go, you meet the king tomorrow and should be well rested. Don't forget as a queen you'll have more responsibilities with no one from Isara to take care of you. You must get your rest while you can."

I rolled my eyes. Through the past weeks, Lord Griffith had mentioned Modare once or twice but tonight he had brought up the king at least ten times. Constantly reminding me that I would be alone, that he wouldn't be around, how I would be Queen of Modare. It was as if he was ready for me to leave.

"I won't. Don't worry. I'll be on my own starting tomorrow; therefore, I believe I can watch out for myself tonight."

Lord Griffith's eyes became soft. "I know. I just wish—I wish I could stay with you."

My eyes widened. Could he be making a declaration?

Noticing my excitement, he stepped back and placed one hand on the back of his head, nervously chuckling. "To make sure you're protected but I'm sure Modare's guards are plenty capable. They did take over Astra and Ula." He took another step back avoiding my questioning eyes. "Well, goodnight then. If we're to stay up any longer, I fear I shall fall where I stand."

I parted my lips, giving room for the words to call him back to spew out, but he had already entered his room. I stared down the hall in silence, the last chance to reveal my feelings gone. Perhaps this was a sign that I should conceal them.

No.

I had to tell him tonight, or I'd live in regret for the rest of my days.

I marched off to my room, swinging the door shut behind me, filled with determination.

I would knock on his door and tell him of my feelings before the night was gone, but first, I needed to freshen up.

I set down the candle on the nightstand before filling the basin with water from the pitcher. I splashed the refreshing, cool liquid on my face, washing the impurities and oils away. Next, I took a piece of rough cloth, dabbing it in my rock salts and sage before applying it to my teeth, washing away the taste of ale and smell of stinky cheese.

I glimpsed in the mirror. Stray hairs jutted out from my braid. Some stood straight while others swayed to the side. A result of my carelessness while I washed. I couldn't face him like this.

I took my hand and placed it in the basin, dampening my skin. I transferred the water to my stray hairs hoping they would stay down with the weight of the water. Instead, they perked up even more with a slight curl. I growled at my reflection.

I hurriedly undid my braid in hopes that I was capable of redoing it but as my hair fell, I could not help but notice the natural beauty in it.

As a result of it being twisted, for most of the day, the strands now held the shape of a curl, beautifully framing my face. `

I tucked a strand behind my ear, wondering if Griffith would think the same. But seeing him in such a state would be inappropriate, borderline scandalous. For a woman of my standing, at least in Isara, to have her hair down like this, it was seen as unkempt, wild—at least that's what I had been told by my nursemaids growing up. However, with the lack of hair skills and the barmaids busy with the tavern's guests I was out of options.

I ran my fingers through my curls, trying out different parts. Finally, I decided that a left one would be best. I looked in the mirror once more, gathering my courage, reapplying some lip coloring that was made from strawberries, Lord Griffith's favorite fruit, as the final touch.

After locking my door, I took a deep breath and began the short but slow walk to Lord Griffith's room. My fist hovered over the dark wooden door before closing my eyes, taking a deep breath, and knocking.

There was a slight creak and then I heard his silky voice, "My Lady? Is everything ok?"

I opened my eyes to find Lord Griffith leaning on the doorway, his eyes drooping with sleep, his hair messily tossed to one side. The sight almost evoked laughter if it were not for his half-naked body that flexed before me.

His body was like a beautifully sculpted statue. His pectorals were comparable to the size of my head, his biceps bulging as he attempted to fix his hair. My mouth formed an O, and my mind became numb as I watched each individual muscle move.

"Lady Estelle?"

I looked up, snapping back into reality. His tired expression now turned to concern. "Yes. Everything is fine," I stammered out.

Lord Griffith's face filled with relief followed by a confused head tilt, waiting for me to speak.

By the gods! I had lost my mind to my nerves. I was so focused on finding the courage to knock that I had neglected to find the words to say.

Should I blurt it out? Or perhaps begin with a monologue? "Lady Estelle?" Lord Griffith questioned.

"I—I need help with my corset!" I nervously yelled out.

Not the line I wanted to start with but there was no taking back the words. I would have to go along with it.

"Your corset?" Lord Griffith repeated, his eyes filled with confusion as he rubbed his temple.

I wanted to slam my head on a table. Lord Griffith must think I am an incompetent fool for needing help getting undressed.

"Yes, my corset. You see the ribbons are so tight and tied so low I cannot possibly reach them." Lord Griffith extended his neck to look over my shoulder and down my back. I gulped, knowing very well I could reach the ribbons. I stammered more nonsense before Lord Griffith could see through my lie, "I normally ask a barmaid to help but none are available."

"I see," he paused, carefully choosing his next words. "I will help find someone, just allow me to—" He began to turn, reaching for his shirt.

"No!" I squealed. "I…want…I want…" Was I about to say this? Yes, I had to. It won't be the most romantic way but, "I want you to do it," I bumbled out.

Lord Griffith snapped his head around, eyes wide. "Your Highness!" The surprise in his heart overpowering his sense to keep using the fake titles. "That would be most inappropriate. I understand that you cannot find anyone but—"

I shook my head, placing my hand on his chest, feeling the beat of his heart. It, too, was beating fast like mine. Out of excitement or fear. I did not know.

I took a deep breath to stabilize my voice. I had intended to tell him about my feelings in a calmer, dreamier way but this was the way it had to be.

A nervous, awkward mess.

"I love you and…and…I want to be with you, if only for one night." My cheeks began to burn. Finally, the words had come out, the ones I had held back for years.

A sense of relief rushed through my body but now a new fear had risen; how would Lord Griffith react?

His pupils grew large as the words jumped off my tongue. We stood there in silence, letting Lord Griffith digest my words. After a while my hand dropped from his chest, finding comfort in clutching my skirts.

"Please, say something," I begged, tears on the verge of releasing.

Silence, this long, was never good.

"Princess Estelle, I can't."

His arm extended, reaching for my shoulder as a sultry voice came from inside his room. "My Lord! What is taking you so long? I will be charging you for this, but I rather charge you for something *fun*."

I took a step back as a single tear fell to the floor. The messy hair, the fatigue, his earliness to bed. It all made sense. He was with a harlot. I felt my heart shatter. I thought he shared my feelings. Instead, on our last night, our last adventure, he was with another woman. A woman, no doubt, he had just met.

He had destroyed my heart's desire, but he had also broken our lifelong friendship.

"I can explain," Lord Griffith stammered.

But what could be explained?

The damage was done.

He approached me, reaching for me once again. In a flurry, I dodged his hand, spinning around, beginning my run to the patio of the tavern. Behind me, I could hear the pitter patter of feet in chaos, clothes being ruffled and Lord Griffith's voice. I did not try to decipher the sounds that came from his mouth as the breaking of my heart was noise enough already.

The downstairs guests, still in high spirits, drank and danced wildly. It was the perfect, chaotic environment to hide. However, the tears pouring from my eyes would ultimately attract the attention of someone, whether their intentions be good or bad it did not matter, I desperately wanted to be alone.

I raced forward, crashing into a drunkard, forcing him to lose his balance and dump his ale on another man. Upon seeing the rage in the ale-soaked man's face I ducked into a crowd of harlots. He grabbed the unfortunate man, whom I bumped into, by the lapels and threw his fist, hard, into the man's gut. Another man jumped in, defending his friend, while another joined for the sheer fun of it and before I could blink, it had turned into a tavern brawl.

Chairs were being thrown and used as weaponry. Harlots stood on tables laughing and cheering for men they hoped to attract. Cups were thrown, and their contents sloshed on the walls. There was not a still patron in sight, save the barmaids who looked in horror at the mess they would later clean up.

The owner looked on in disbelief then made eye contact with me, his eyes cold. In that instant, I knew I was who he blamed, rightfully so, but in this moment, I was not equipped to handle him. I hiked up my skirts and ran through the door to the patio.

Once outside, the world became silent. I could not hear the music, the yells of the fighting men, or even the laughter of the harlots. All I could hear was my trembling breath and the tiniest pitter patter of my tears falling.

My legs began to shake. I stumbled to the far left of the patio, bracing myself on the railing. A cold breeze brushed against me, sending a shiver through my body.

It was about to rain.

I extended my hand, feeling the first drop. A cynical smile emerged on my face. At least the sky was crying with me.

The nearby door creaked open. I wiped my tears away and closed my eyes, not ready to see *him*. I needed the rest of the night to compose myself. If I were to face him, talk to him, I would fall prey to another crying fit.

"You caused quite the commotion."

My eyes flicked open.

This wasn't Lord Griffith's voice.

It sounded familiar, but I couldn't pinpoint its owner.

One of the guards? No, they would not address me this way.

I craned my neck to see who it was.

It was Al!

My heart fluttered as I saw his devilish smile. I didn't understand why. It had just broken, the only thing it should be capable of doing was grieving. Yet, something inside me wanted to run into his arms to seek comfort.

I gave myself a mental slap, as I noticed my body leaning forward.

No. I just wanted comfort. There was nothing *special* about him.

I turned back around, not wanting him to see the puffiness in my eyes. If I ignored him long enough he would leave me be.

"You don't look in the best of spirits," his sarcastic voice honeyed out. "Shall I fetch your travel companion? I'm sure he'd be more than happy to hold you, especially after seeing how he comforted you earlier," he offered with a sharpness in his voice that resembled jealousy.

I remained quiet, letting him tease. He'd get bored eventually and leave me alone.

The yelling from the tavern intensified. My body curled inward as a glass of ale was thrown out the window, barely missing my head.

Al's voice, void of any sarcasm, came from behind, a few steps closer. "You shouldn't be out here alone. I'll go get him."

"No," I growled, spinning around to face him. His eyes were wide with curiosity or maybe concern.

"Ah, a lover's quarrel? I suppose that answers my earlier question." His voice, once again, that sarcastic tone.

I spun around, debating if I wanted to hit him or cry. Sensing my anger, he held up a hand ready to block any action I chose to take.

"Steady now. I'm just concerned. You shouldn't be alone, especially in your state." My forehead crinkled at his words, but I allowed him to approach. If I let him stay with me, he was less likely to fetch Lord Griffith.

"I'm fine," I sneered, turning back to the railing, peering into the darkness of the night.

"You're clearly not and I intend to get to the bottom of it." He leaned his back against the rail, his eyes locked on the tavern door.

I scoffed, wondering what type of man he was to find amusement in my misery.

His eyes turned to me, examining my body.

"Your hair. It was in a braid earlier."

I patted my hair, feeling the flattened curls. I was a mess. I wasn't beautiful nor respectable.

"The braid fell," I said, keeping my voice flat

My hands trembled as I created three strands and intertwined them.

"Did he hurt you?" he growled out, as he laid a hand on the hilt of his sword.

My eyes widened.

Was my appearance that awry?

Al's brows narrowed, his grip tightening as I kept him waiting. He was ready to battle. If I didn't say something soon, Al would seek out Griffith and not to bring him to me as he originally threatened.

"No, no. Griffith would never hurt me." My eyes swept to the floor. My voice grew weaker with each word. "At least not in a physical way."

"Then what happened?" He faced me, not entirely convinced.

I turned my head meeting his worried eyes. He defied all the stereotypes of a thief. Or perhaps, he was invested in my problems so he could exploit me later. My face hardened. "None of your concern."

His eyebrows raised at the aggression in my tone, then his expression turned playful as if I had just challenged him. "But you see, I can't turn away from a maiden crying, let alone a beautiful one." I opened my mouth to speak, but he continued. "Now, I'll make a deal with you. I can go get your companion and find out from him or you can tell me exactly what's going on." He took a step away from the railing, walking backwards, hands out to the side, smiling devilishly. "The choice is up to you, but you have mere seconds before I reach the door."

I glared at him, contemplating if I'd have enough time to knock him from his feet and run to the sanctuary of my room before he or Lord Griffith caught me. It was a tempting idea, but the plan was unrealistic. I had zero combat training and whoever, whatever Al was, it was clear he did. I rolled my eyes as I told him everything, except, of course, who I really was and who I was marrying.

"I see," he responded, digesting the story.

Anger filled me. *I see.* That's *all* he could say.

He was a man, a thief. He was not governed by society. He could marry whom he wanted, sleep with whomever he wanted with no consequence.

So, no. He didn't *see.*

I opened my mouth ready to lecture when a burst of cold wind assaulted my limbs. My body shivered as a violent sneeze sent me a step backward. I grabbed my arms, rubbing my hands against my icy skin, pleading for my body not to shake again. I refused to give Al a reason to send me back inside. But hugging myself did little, so little that I was tempted to retreat until I felt the warm embrace of wool. I looked to my shoulder to see Al's dark blue cloak draped over my body.

"Thank you," I murmured.

He only nodded in response as he went back to resting his forearms on the railing.

I pulled the cloak closer to my chest, soaking in its warmth. The scent of pine trees and fresh rainwater wafted up to my nose, bringing forth comforting childhood memories of riding through the forest. My eyelids closed as peace and comfort fell over me.

"Where is she?" a voice thundered as the tavern door flew open.

My heart filled with dread. Lord Griffith. He had found me.

I frantically scanned my peripheral hoping to find a hiding spot. There was none. It was time to face him.

I began to turn, exhaling, trying to find my composure but was pulled back around to meet Al's eyes which shimmered with determination.

"Trust me," he whispered.

In one swift movement he covered my head with the hood of the cape, grasped my waist, pulled me flesh against him, and intertwined his lips with mine.

I squealed into his mouth, wiggled under his grip as shock overtook my body. But the more I moved, the tighter his grip became and so did the passion of his kiss.

My mother had told me, before she died, that my first kiss would be awkward. That I would be ill-prepared for it. That

I would, most likely, share my first kiss with a man I just met—my husband. She suggested the best strategy for that kiss would, simply, be to hold still. Allow the man to show me how to move, how to please him.

She told me I wouldn't like it. That it was simply part of marriage duties and must be tolerated. But this kiss was the opposite.

It was awkward and forced, but once I had stopped resisting, Al's kiss was anything but unpleasant. My body heated up, my hands tugged on the hems of his tunic, and my lips—my lips danced with his. I could feel the weight of my body pushing into him, wanting to be closer, demanding more. Al, as if responding to my needs, kissed harder till my body melted in his hands.

"You, there!" I pulled back, flinching at Lord Griffith's voice, my face turning a bright red.

Lord Griffith had seen our act of passion. No, he had seen my moment of weakness, my impropriety. If he caught me now, he would only look at me with shame.

Al pulled me into his chest, concealing my face from all angles. The wood creaked under Lord Griffith's heavy boots. I clutched Al's tunic, pushing my body into his. Al brushed the back of my head with his thumb, attempting to calm me.

"What?" His words were sharp. "You already ruined my fun with your companion. Must you ruin my pleasure now?"

"I am looking for that companion," Lord Griffith growled, clearly remembering Al.

"And why do you think I would know her whereabouts?" Al lifted his hand off my lower back, gesturing up and down. "As you can see, I am preoccupied. I have paid little attention to your companion since our meeting."

There was silence, for what felt like an eternity, tension filling the air.

"Let me see her face," he commanded, the words filled with suspicion.

"Absolutely not," Al hissed.

There was a pause, followed by the short sound of a sword leaving its sheath.

I gripped Al's tunic tighter. Lord Griffith was ready for a fight. And though my fear of seeing him was strong it didn't warrant combat. I could not bear to see either of them hurt.

With the sound of metal being so short, I knew Lord Griffith had not taken his sword out completely. There was still time before his rage got the better of him. I pushed away from Al, but he pulled me back into his chest.

"You see, you've caught us in a rather compromising position and my lady here, well, would rather keep her identity hidden." Al placed a hand on his sword. "Would you leave us be? For the sake of the lady's propriety?"

Silence again, as Lord Griffith debated. He was always keen on protecting a woman's honor. Maybe, he would retreat?

"There you are!" boomed a voice that was unrecognizable. "Your companion has caused much damage and I demand payment."

It was the tavern owner.

A door slammed loudly, followed by the stomping of boots and then a pause as he saw the standoff between Lord Griffith and Al.

"I don't care about whatever this is. But if you do not come back in and settle the debt, this instant, I will take my payment from your belongings. Rip your companions from their beds and release your horses into the storm."

"If you could just give me a minute, I will—"

"Now or my threat will be put into action," the tavern owner roared.

Al's chest shook as he muffled a chuckle.

Griffith's sword locked into his sheath before growling out, "Five gold coins. That is the reward if you bring me information on her whereabouts."

I remained quiet, listening as the two pairs of feet grew distant and the tavern door closed. Al's arms dropped, the warmth quickly leaving my body as he stepped away.

"He's quite intense," he said through laughs. My heart skipped a beat as I watched him lean against the railing. "I can see how you fell for him. With a ferocity to protect like that, I doubt any maiden would be immune."

My eyes lowered to the ground, remembering why I was out here in the first place. "And yet, he does not love any maiden. None that I know of at least." I walked forward placing my hands on the railing. The rain now a light pitter patter.

"Cheer up," Al suggested as he patted my head. "It's your last night before you marry that boring, sadistic old lord. Do something fun." He grabbed his chin with his pointer and thumb, pretending to think. "Didn't you say you wanted your first to be your choice? There's plenty of men here, take your pick." He motioned through the window, jokingly, at the drunks in the tavern. "That one there, he has quite the luscious beard. I mean if you can see past the crumbs in it. Or that one"—he pointed again at a heavily decorated man whose blonde hair reached his waist—"well, if you fancy a feminine looking male." Al continued pointing out the *attractive* features of each man.

I couldn't help but smile and laugh with him, momentarily forgetting about Lord Griffith and the horrors of tomorrow. But, perhaps, there was some truth in his joke. It wouldn't be Lord Griffith, but I could still choose in some way.

My eyes fell to his lips, still wet from our kiss. Our passionate, perfect kiss.

My stomach tightened, screaming for it once again. I wanted him. No, I needed him.

But sleep with a man I just met?

I was willing to do improper things with Lord Griffith because I loved him. But, this man, this possible thief, made me feel safe, happy even. That had to mean something. I bit my lip, almost breaking the skin.

"What about you?" My voice was meek, scared of another rejection.

His smile turned into a hard line. His eyes narrowed. "To sleep with?"

I nodded, taken back by his change of mood.

He positioned himself squarely in front of me, placing both his hands on the railing, trapping me. "You understand what you're asking?"

I nodded as his eyes glared at my bitten lower lip.

"I will be taking your purity. The thing you have been taught to protect till marriage." I would have thought Al didn't want me with all his questions and his explanations if it were not for his ravenous eyes, his hastened breathing.

I nodded again.

"I need to hear you say it," he growled as he held my chin in his hand, not allowing us to break eye contact.

My mouth dried as my heart began to thump faster and faster. "I—I understand."

He ran his thumb over my lip pulling it free from my teeth. My knees buckled at his touch. "And you want me to take it *all*, tonight?"

I gulped as his sultry voice pierced my ears. "Yes," I muttered out, my breathing becoming staggered.

His gaze lingered on me for a moment more, my body melting. The only thing holding me up were his fingers placed under my chin.

Did all possible lovers make you feel this way? Would my future husband be able to subdue me with just his gaze? Or was this only Al?

I gazed at him with anticipation, waiting for his reply, searching his eyes for an answer. Al smiled, releasing my chin. I stumbled forward. Summoning the remainder of my strength, I was able to steady myself. Al devilishly grinned as he fixed my hood, ensuring my face was still covered.

"It's a bit early for your legs to be giving out."

I patted down my skirts, my cheeks burning. "My legs are sore from traveling, that's all."

He smiled, his eyes dancing mischievously. "They'll be sore from much more than riding after tonight."

"So, you'll do it? You'll take me?" I asked, my voice a mixture of excitement and nerves.

"Yes, but on the condition that you don't fall in love with me."

My brows bunched together as I rolled my eyes. Al made my heart race, but fall for him? I wasn't afflicted with emophilia.

"I mean it. You'll get hurt. My heart is owned by another."

My head spun.

If Al had a lover then why would he fulfill my request? Was it unrequited as well?

He did not give me time to question him as he turned and ran to the stairs at the center edge of the patio, where a barmaid was walking up. Her boots were covered in mud and there was hay in her hair from the barn she had probably waited out the rain in.

Al whispered to her and pointed inside. I followed his finger to see Lord Griffith pitifully sitting in the center of the tavern, ale in hand, eyes struggling to stay open. My chest tightened knowing I had caused this, but I had my own goals to acquire. The woman nodded as Al plopped some money into her hand. Quite a bit, even too much for a thief to willingly give.

I would have to ask him about his profession in life later.

Or would that make tomorrow harder?

Al stood to the side as the women curtsied before heading into the tavern with the biggest grin I had ever seen.

"What did you tell her?" I inquired, as he came back to my side.

"Just watch," he said, gesturing to the window with his chin.

The woman walked to Lord Griffith and began to talk. His face filled with surprise, followed by relief. He stood up, rushing to the base of the stairs. The barmaid slid in front of him, not allowing him to pass. Griffith's face became hard, his mouth moved furiously. However, the women did not waver.

Her mouth moved just as quick, if not faster than Lord Griffith's as she waved her finger in his face. Lord Griffith's eyes lowered, subdued by her words, his brows pulled close together. The woman slid behind him, caressing his shoulder, his back as she whispered something in his ear.

Lord Griffith's head raised. His eyes ran over the barmaid's body, examining every curve. A playful smile appeared on his face as the woman grabbed his hand and led him up to the second floor.

My jaw dropped. He was already taking another woman to his bed, so soon after my declaration.

Griffith was a waste of room in my heart.

"I figured we couldn't get upstairs with him sitting there, so I asked her to distract him. But I didn't think she would do so in that way." I looked up at Al, his eyes wide, brows high. The shock on his face was apparent, funny almost. I muffled a laugh.

I wouldn't let Griffith ruin this. I wouldn't let him affect my mood. I was with Al, and he would give me what I craved—a chance to choose for myself.

Al held out his hand, smirking. "Shall we?"

CHAPTER 4

We had decided it would be best for Al to take my purity in his room, as this would make it harder for the maids to decipher which patron had lost her maidenhead. As the rumor of that could make any lady lose her place in society, but it was a risk I was willing to take.

The walk was long and slow, allowing my nerves to grow stronger. My body became stiff as Al closed the door. I wanted him, but it didn't make this any less mortifying. I had heard some women found the experience painful, void of any pleasure. I prayed to the gods that wouldn't be the case for me.

"I'm going to lock the door now. If at any time you wish to leave, the key will be right here."

Al placed the key, in plain sight, on a desk near the door. I rolled back my shoulders, more at ease, but my legs were still immobile.

My eyes followed Al as he crossed the room to a basin and a jug of water. He poured the liquid into the bowl, interrupting the flow with his fingers, testing the temperature. Such a simple task and yet I could not pull my gaze away. Something about seeing his glistening fingers, how they curved in the stream, how the water gracefully fell with his expert hands, stirred something inside me.

Al's eyes shifted to me, realizing I hadn't moved. "I'm just going to wash up a bit. Feel free to make yourself comfortable, sit anywhere." His voice was soft and reassuring.

Realizing that I probably looked like a frightening statue, I searched the room for a place to perch.

Our rooms were identical with the exception that mine was full of the trunks that I had brought from Isara, making the room feel painfully small, whereas the only personal item in Al's room was a small satchel which, of course, rested on the only chair in the room.

Not wanting to be rude and place the bag on the floor, I decided to sit on the bed. I was going to be on it at some point tonight, might as well get used to it.

I walked to the bed, feeling Al's eyes follow me. It felt unnatural to sit where another person slept, like I was invading a very intimate space, particularly this one since it belonged to a man.

My fingers grazed over the comforter, feeling the scratchy wool sheets, but that was typical for a tavern. I exhaled as my bottom sunk into the mattress. Al laughed as I wiggled, nervously, trying to get comfortable. I glared at him from across the room in warning. He held up his hands in retreat.

"I just find you cute. You're like a stray I found outside and took pity on, getting comfortable."

I opened my mouth to retort. Being compared to a dog was hardly a compliment. But the words escaped me as Al's tunic fell to the floor.

Unlike Lord Griffith, Al had numerous scars covering his sculpted body. Some small, some big. The most terrifying of all was on his back. It began at his left shoulder and ended at his right hip. The scar was two shades darker than his skin. It had been a deep cut, probably life threatening.

The sight had almost brought me to tears but not in a way of disgust. His body was ruggedly beautiful, the strength in it apparent with his bulging muscles.

I deduced Al was around my age and to have that many scars—he had been in some gruesome, violent battles. Battles that probably occurred because of the Tyrant King. I fought the urge to run to him, throw my arms around his body, ask if I could provide any comfort.

"It's rude to stare."

My eyes rushed back up to Al's face. He was smirking away. If he knew I was staring at his scars or thought I was admiring him, I couldn't tell.

I wanted to know more, how he'd gotten them and why there were so many. But I didn't have the right to ask. I looked down at my hands that now rested on my lap, away from Al and his scars.

"You can look now." Al's bare feet came into view.

I bit my lip as I raised my head. He had taken off everything, except his pants which sat loosely on his hips unlaced. His body glistened from the water he had failed to wipe off. The sight hastened my heartbeat, and my stomach turned with a hunger I had never experienced.

Al took my hands, pulling me up to him. My breathing hitched. I stood still, frightened at the thought of undoing my laces. Al, no doubt, had been with skilled women who knew how to seduce a man with a single glance, but I had never kissed one until tonight.

If I were to undress in my usual way would he laugh?
I shook my head. I couldn't think like that. I raised my hands to the back of my corset, fingers visibly shaking.

"Let me." Al's warm hands were on my shoulders, spinning me around then slowly they pulled at my ribbons. "If at any time you want to stop you must tell me." His voice was hard and direct, making sure I understood. I nodded. "Say it," he commanded.

"Yes, I understand," I stammered, feeling the corset fall to my feet.

"Good," he whispered in my ear. My body twitched as his warm breath caressed my neck. "Now, why don't you step out of those shoes."

Al, with both hands, grabbed my waist, steadying me as I kicked off my heels. I continued staring at the bed, wondering what would come next. I had little time to ponder as Al pulled me against him.

He collected my hair, throwing it over a singular shoulder, giving himself full access to the right side of my neck. His nails ran up and down, sending shivers through my spine. I inhaled sharply at the sensation. Al chuckled in response.

I wanted to scold him, but as his lips grazed over my neck, a noise, foreign to me, came out. I covered my mouth in hope to muffle the sound as it continuously grew louder.

"Let me hear you," Al growled, grabbing my hand.

"I've never—never made a sound like that before," I replied, embarrassed eyes meeting his.

Al smirked, pushing my sleeves off my shoulders, allowing my dress to fall, leaving me only in my stockings. He stepped back as he scanned me from top to bottom, biting his lip. "It's called a moan." His voice was so gravelly, so filled with desire that it almost brought me to my knees.

He picked me up and carried me to the bed, laying me down, softly, under him. Without looking away he began a trail of kisses down my body. Each kiss more tantalizing than the last. I wriggled under him, feeling tension form between my legs.

Once at my waist, he stopped, eyes glancing down. His hand expertly grazed my inner thigh till it was at my entrance. He swirled his thumb as if testing it.

I bit my lip not wanting to let out another *moan,* but as his finger entered me, I could not contain my voice. I covered my mouth once again, embarrassed at the sound. Al was back over me, his eyes on fire as he withdrew my hand.

"That is the most beautiful sound a woman can make, don't mute it," he ordered, his eyes ravenous.

My face turned hot at his words. I wanted to ask him questions, but my mouth had lost the ability to speak. The only sounds that I was capable of were gasps, whimpers, and those embarrassing moans.

Al sat up, placing something at my entrance. I wiggled wondering what it was. His fingers? No, those were now by my head. I gasped as Al pressed his forehead to mine, realizing it was his manhood.

"Are you ready?" He tucked my hair behind my ear, gently. "Once I start there is no going back." His voice was airy as if he was struggling. Struggling to hold back, to breathe.

I wanted him, I needed him to relieve the tension he had brought upon my body and somehow, I knew his manhood would bring that.

I nodded.

In one movement he was inside me. Only a bit of him and yet my moan filled the room as my nails dug into his back. The feeling was foreign and came with a bit of pain, but I wanted more.

"Are you ok?" he rasped; his face disgruntled as he fought off the urge to fully embed himself in me.

Al cupped my face, his thumb caressing my cheek while the other hand prevented him from squishing my body.

"Yes, it's just—different." Al's cock twitched inside me as if it were pleased with my response. I held tighter to his back at the foreign sensation. Al winced. My eyes widened, realizing how sharp my nails were. "How's your back?" I asked moving my hand to his shoulder, applying little pressure.

Al chuckled as he returned my hand. "Don't worry about it. I enjoy a tinge of pain occasionally." He kissed my forehead. "Do you want me to continue?"

I nodded, feeling the tension in my body rise.

Al slowly pulled in and out of me, adding an inch with each thrust, till he was wholly in me. He looked down at me once more, evaluating my emotions, making sure I was not in pain before he truly began bedding me.

It was slow at first but soon enough his own urges took control and before I knew what was happening, my nails pierced Al's back again, my legs wrapped tightly around his waist and my moans had turned into pants.

The tension growing in me became unbearable. I held tighter, sucking, biting Al's neck to satisfy my needs. I wanted more, I wanted to be closer.

Al, feeling every move of me, understanding what I wanted went faster, harder. Then, with one last thrust, the tension dissipated, and I was left with a convulsing sensation between my legs.

Al pulled me into him as he collapsed beside me. I rested my head on his chest, feeling it rise and fall as he caught his breath, and his fingers lazily trailed my spine.

Was all lovemaking like this?

Those tales I had heard, perhaps, they were made to encourage us to preserve our purity, because if I had known it felt like this, I would have taken a man to bed sooner. I wanted to ask Al, but my eyelids grew heavy. He kissed my brow once more and I drifted into a blissful sleep.

CHAPTER 5

My eyelids were heavy as I forced them open. My body was sore from last night's activities and my hair was a tangled mess. Yet, I felt refreshed.

I pulled the blankets closer to me as a cold breeze rushed over, but it wasn't enough. I wanted the warmth of last night. Al's warmth. I stretched my arms out, feeling for his body but only found an empty space. I sprang up, covers still wrapped around me, eyes darting around the room. He was gone and so were his belongings.

I had known last night was temporary, but my heart was heavy knowing he and his party were far away. I would never see Al again. I wanted to, at least, wish him farewell, a safe journey—have a proper conversation.

I jumped up, maybe they had just left. I could still catch him if I ran, to say goodbye, to thank him. But he had decided to leave before I had woken… perhaps, to make his leaving easier?

He, no doubt, had many dalliances like last night. It was best to trust him. Al knew what he was doing.

"Woah there. The horses seem agitated today," a voice boomed outside.

I strode to the window. The sun was rising, the birds were taking flight, and on the ground the guards were hitching the horses to a carriage—a peaceful morning.

I stood in the window, taking in the morning air, till panic overtook me.

The guards were hitching the horses to the carriage. Our carriage! Lord Griffith would awaken soon and be sending a maid to me. I needed to get back.

I ran around the room collecting my garments, hastily throwing them on my body. I didn't need to look perfect, just decent enough to get to my room without suspicion. I gave myself a quick look over in the mirror, patting my hair down before running to the door. I cracked it open, peering out, making sure the hall was empty. There wasn't a soul in sight. I breathed a sigh of relief before quietly shutting the door behind me.

I scurried around my room; undoing the covers, opening chests, and laying out the hygienic products I would have used before bed. I had to make it look as if I were here all night. My purity could not be questioned. I searched the room for more things I could rearrange when three knocks sounded on the other side of the door.

"Who's there?" I squeaked, not quite composed.

"It's me, my lady."

Lord Griffith? He never came to wake me.

"I've brought a maid, to help prepare you for today's journey."

I remained quiet. I was still wearing the dress from the night before. The maid would think nothing of it but Lord Griffith…he knew I needed fresh clothes to sleep, that I felt too dirty to relax, no matter the circumstances. I threw my hands into the nearest chest, desperately searching for my robe.

"My lady?" he called out. His voice was more concerned, louder than it was a second ago.

"A moment, please." I dumped the contents of a chest on the floor, my sleeping robe one of the last things to come sprawling out. I tore off my corset, leaving my underdress on, tightly wrapping the robe around me before taking a deep breath and answering the door.

"Good morning, my lady." Lord Griffith gave a stiff bow, averting his gaze.

It was improper for him to see me in my nightwear. I wondered why he came.

He held out his hand motioning toward the maid, the one Al had paid off. I cocked my head to the side.

How many times had he brought me his sleeping companion?
"This is Mary. She will be helping you prepare for today."

I curtsied, trying to find my composure. "Thank you." I studied Mary's eyes. "Pleased to meet you, Mary." I wondered if she recognized me.

She curtsied, much lower than I. "The pleasure is mine, ma'am."

There was silence as Mary raised her head. Lord Griffith's eyes on me, mine on Mary, and hers on the floor. I refused to look at Lord Griffith, despite his intense, pleading gaze.

"Well, we should get to it then." I motioned for Mary to enter. Once in, I gave a quick glance to Lord Griffith, his mouth open, ready to talk. "We're running late, later." I closed the door before he could even mutter.

"Ma'am are you alright?" Mary inquired as I spun around, my face twisted.

"Just annoyed is all," I replied, heading to the changing screen.

Just annoyed, I repeated to myself.

I would not shed tears for Griffith. I had seen his true nature. I wanted him gone, far from my side. I had Al to thank for that.

Al.

I touched my forefinger to my lips, tracing them down my body, reminding myself where he had kissed. My body grew hot, the temperature rising the lower my fingers went. If I closed my eyes, I could almost feel his touch. It would be a memory I'd cherish till my dying days.

"Ma'am, the bath is ready."

I jumped. Mary had been so quiet. I had forgotten about her presence. "Yes, coming."

I sank down into the lukewarm water, creating little waves that lapped against my breasts. The temperature was not as warm as I liked, but the freshness was a welcome feeling, especially after last night.

"Mind your eyes," Mary chimed as she poured water over my head. Her fingers massaged my scalp, spreading the bubbles.

I purred under her expert hands, closing my eyes for a minute before I scrubbed my body. But while she worked, I couldn't help but wonder if she saw Al leave or had any information about him. A last name perhaps? I leaned my head back, eyeing her, debating. If I asked then she would know I was the girl from last night.

Would she reveal my secret?

She stared back, puzzled. Then clarity overtook her. "No need to worry about that."

"That?" I spun around, water sloshing out.

"Your little adventure, with the gentleman last night." My pupils doubled.

"How?" I stammered out.

She let out a laugh as she walked to the changing panel, grabbing a towel and my robe. "It's obvious. I was paid to distract a lord and tell him his companion was safe. That same lord asked me to take care of a certain lady. The companion, I assume."

I slapped my hand on my forehead. Of course, it was blatantly obvious.

"But no need to worry, ma'am. Your secret is safe with me. I swore it to Al last night, and I make a note to never break an oath to him. If that man ever found out, well, there'd be hell to pay. I remember last time Al was here—"

Last time! Al visited here frequently. Perhaps I would see him again. "Mary. How often does Al visit here?"

Mary held out a towel while pity coated her eyes. "Oh, dear. You see, I promised I wouldn't," Mary tripped on her words.

I took the towel rubbing it against my skin before wrapping up in my robe. *My heart is owned by another.* Those were Al's words. He had no intention of seeing me again.

"I understand." I patted Mary's shoulder and headed to the vanity.

He knew I'd try to seek him out and prepared for it. He had warned me, and I still had succumbed to his charm.

I would not gain any information here. It was for the best. His heart belonged to another, and my body and soul were promised to someone else.

I would only have that one night with him.

CHAPTER 6

I lifted my lavender chiffon dress just above my ankles, as I descended the stairs. Careful not to reveal the symbol on the purple cloak I carried in my hand.

It had been weeks since I had seen the crest or even worn Isara's colors. We had hidden all things related to Isara deep in the chests. I hadn't been permitted to so much as wear purple while we traveled but now, in an hour, I would represent my country. So, when Mary asked what I would like to be dressed in, I pulled out the chest I wasn't permitted to open. Inside laid dresses of every shade of purple, accented with gold and silver thread.

Mary had gasped as I pulled out the chiffon dress I now wore. She had helped me put it on, her hands lingering longer than necessary, admiring the expensive fabric she'd never get to touch again. I chuckled to myself as I pulled out a box containing one of my many diadems. She had yet to be mystified.

This diadem was one of the simpler ones I owned. I wanted to seem innocent, non-threatening to the king. I held out the silver diadem, the crystals carefully embedded to look like glistening leaves—a sign of peace. Mary's hands shook as she reached out, unsure if she had the right to even look at the diadem, let alone touch it. After a few smiles and words of assurance, she continued to ready me.

I walked down the stairs, a picture of elegance, innocence, and secret power.

The tavern silenced as I reached the bottom of the stairs, Lord Griffith hastily stood.

I had forgotten the attention my presence commanded, but something was different. I felt more in control with each step. Last night was the first time I had not followed orders. A sign of the woman, no, queen I was about to become.

"My lady, you look…" Lord Griffith held out his arms taking me in, eyes bewildered.

He had forgotten how I normally looked as well.

I waved my hands over the food. "Pack it, I'm ready." Each word crisper than the last.

I was ready to get married. I had done the things I needed, but there was one last thing. Something I added last night. I wanted to make it very clear that I was over Lord Griffith.

I had loved him and perhaps a part of me still did, but he had made his choice last night. I also had to make sure I was ready to meet the king. I could not show him any wavering emotions. I had to show him the strength of Isara, of me.

Lord Griffith's eyes saddened as a maid came and wrapped the cheese and fruit in a cloth. He took the bundle with a nod, his eyes never leaving me. He knew I couldn't, wouldn't talk to him as a friend. Not today. Today he was simply my escort. He understood the roles we had to take on today. And maybe, just maybe, he was ashamed and regretful of his choices last night.

He dropped some coins in the maid's hand as we departed for our carriage.

For the first half, we traveled through the country. We only saw fields and tiny huts, giving little excuse to start a conversation. I was thankful for that.

Lord Griffith's sad eyes had not once stopped gazing at me, causing my hard heart to soften. I was sure that if he apologized, that little part of me that still loved him, wanted him to have an excuse, would rush back.

The carriage came to a brisk halt. I grasped firmly to my seat, careful not to fall into Lord Griffith's hands. That was the last thing that needed to happen.

We both peeked through the curtains. Blocking our path were four men on horses. Each one carried a shield and a sword. Their shoulders were covered by dark blue cloaks, the same dark blue as Al's.

I stiffened as a fifth man came forward holding a flag picturing two swords crossed under a shield that bore a silver crown in the center, Modare's crest.

Al was a part of Modare's army, he had to be.

Happiness and terror swept over me. I was likely to see him again.

"We are here to escort Princess Estelle and her party to the castle of Modare," the man holding the flag declared.

Lord Griffith waved his hand ushering them to lead the way.

The guards had come to greet us, we were close. I tied the curtains back as I watched the countryside turn into a humongous city. My stomach dropped. Modare had been a tiny country until their capture of Ula and Astra.

How was their capital this huge?

Almost as if he could read my thoughts, Lord Griffith responded, "When everyone ignores you, and money isn't going to war, monstrous cities can form without anyone knowing."

I glanced at Lord Griffith; his eyes were somber as he too took in the sheer size of Modare's capital.

"And so can their armies?" I asked, a tinge of nervousness in my voice.

He turned to me, a hand on the hilt of his sword, eyes filled with concern. "So too, can their armies," he answered in a tone I'd never heard.

It was in that moment I realized that this treaty, this alliance had to work. Why my father sent me away despite my protests.

Modare had been underestimated, unchecked, and unchallenged for far too long.

CHAPTER 7

The carriage rolled into the castle's courtyard. Guards were on every inch of the wall, wielding crossbows, and all adorned with *that* dark blue cloak. They stared, intrigued, at what their new queen looked like, all while keeping their grim, stern expressions.

The rumors were right. Modare didn't like outsiders.

Lord Griffith stepped out first, surveying the high, mighty walls as he offered me his hand. "Not the warmest greeting for a bride's arrival."

I kept my face unconcerned at the sheer size of their wall guard. It was a tremendous amount, far more than Isara's. A fact I would keep to myself.

From past reports, Modare had not allowed envoys from other countries to enter and vice versa since this new king had taken power. Putting us both in a state of mystery.

Once my feet were firmly placed on the ground and my hand out of Lord Griffith's, a flurry of servants raced out the castle's doors and lined the tall staircase. The last two to exit the castle approached us. The first was a man dressed in a midnight blue so dark that had it not been for the sun's glint shimmering off the material, I'd thought it black. Following two steps behind was a maid, about my age, dressed in the same color.

The man stopped three steps short of us and lead the mass bow that welcomed us. "Welcome to Modare, Princess Estelle." His voice echoed off the castle walls.

I gave a slight curtsey, letting them know they may be at ease. Lord Griffith slid between me and the man as he took another step forward.

The man cocked his head and let out a snicker. "I see travel has made you paranoid. But I remind you, you are in a friend's kingdom." His eyebrows raised. "At least that's what we assumed this"—he motioned toward me—"meant. Or were we wrong?"

Lord Griffith took a step behind me. "My apologies."

"So glad it was a misunderstanding." The man, this time, successfully approached and kissed my hand. "My name is Leo, Your Highness. It is my pleasure to receive you in the king's stead."

"And where is the king?" Lord Griffith interjected.

I gave him a wary look. It was apparent there would be consequences if we insulted Leo again. But it was odd that the royal family wasn't here to welcome us.

Leo stood up straight. "The king," Leo paused, emphasizing the title, "sends his apologies but his meeting ran late. We weren't expecting you for at least another hour."

Lord Griffith and Leo exchanged looks for what felt like an eternity. Silently challenging each other. I interjected. This was too risky.

"Apology accepted. Meetings are such a nuisance, but it will make the anticipation of meeting my future husband so much greater," I honeyed out.

Leo stepped back, theatrically holding out his hands. "Yes, it shall! Now, are these all yours, or are your companions' things mixed in?"

"The purple chests are mine." I smiled.

"No need to grab our chests, we will only stay for the night and be on our way," Lord Griffith chimed in, now composed into a proper diplomat.

Leo waved his arm, summoning the male servants. "Oh my, I suppose that letter didn't reach you before you set out." His voice was shrill as he attempted to hide his laughter.

"What letter?" Lord Griffith growled.

"The most previous letters between our two kings." I raised an eyebrow in question. "Once the princess arrives she is the only one allowed in. Security reasons." Leo shrugged his shoulders. "You understand."

"I do not!" Lord Griffith growled with such ferocity the servants froze. "I am to escort the princess to the king and see that she is received well. Then, and only then, will I leave." His hand turned white as he gripped the hilt of his sword.

I shuddered at the sound of bows raising above. The situation needed to deescalate. But how? Even I found this request absurd.

The treaty was not sealed till royal blood from Isara and Modare were bonded. If I walked in alone and the marriage fell through, if I was rejected by the king, I would have no power here. No power to protect myself if they decided to turn.

Our men, aware of the aimed bows, began to dismount and unsheathed their hidden weapons.

I had to think quickly.

Leo raised his hand, signaling the Modarian guards to put down their weapons. With the other hand, he pulled out a letter.

"A letter from your king." Lord Griffith snatched it in one swift movement, I peered over his shoulder. "He agrees to this request. He understands the tension between Modare and those who do not wish us to rise. He thinks, like King Titus, it best that we keep the castle's layout and its contents a secret. You never know where allegiances lie." One side of Leo's mouth moved upward in an awful gloating smirk of victory as Lord Griffith crumpled the paper.

My stomach twisted. Father was desperate for this alliance to work.

Was Isara really that weak in comparison?

"I need a moment alone with Her Highness, then I shall release her into your hands." Leo's forehead wrinkled in question. "She is my princess, but we have grown up together as friends. I merely wish to say goodbye."

Leo's eyes glimmered with curiosity, but as a servant whispered in his ear, his eyes became serious. "Make it quick, the king is ready, and he is not a patient ruler."

Lord Griffith made his way to the front of the carriage so that his voice was out of reach from Leo's and the servants' ears. I followed, reluctantly, unsure if this was a political or personal matter.

"Be careful, I don't trust them."

Political.

"Keep in touch, write your letters in code if things are amiss but do not let them know."

I gripped my cloak, now wrapped around my shoulders. He was still treating me like a child. "I know." My words sharp, his eyes bewildered. "I was trained for this, remember? You've done your duty, now I will do mine," I snarled out before stalking away.

Lord Griffith grabbed my wrist, effectively spinning me around, not caring who would see such a scandalous touch. "This is serious." He looked around to see if anyone was paying attention. "Your father did not want me to give you this task unless the situation was as bad as we thought." He gulped. "You are not just a means for a treaty, you are also our informant in case they decide to challenge us."

I stiffened. "But the treaty. My father, he has never used spies."

Lord Griffith drew closer. "Look around. They are ready for war. Treaties do not mean anything with this much power. Astra and Ula did nothing to provoke him, yet he took them as if they were mere towns. He wanted their land, more power. What's stopping him from taking Isara next? With a capital like this, we would, no doubt, fall too."

I stared into his panicked eyes. Panic for Isara, for her people, and for me. I nodded in silent understanding.

"Ok!" Leo clapped his hands forcing us both to look. "We must be leaving now."

I turned back to Leo, but Lord Griffith's strong arms grasped me tightly in a warm embrace. "I was going to propose." My eyes grew wide as I tried to jerk my head up, but he pushed it back down. "Then the decision was made for you to marry *him*. I was heartbroken, but we all have our duties. It was disgusting of me, but I used those girls to forget about you. I could not console myself any other way. I love you. Please forgive me."

I could hear Griffith's voice cracking; he was on the verge of crying. I threw my arms around him, hugging as tight as I could.

Why did he wait so long to tell me? Why was he telling me now?

My heartbeat grew faster. I had misjudged him, jumped to conclusions. I should've stayed and listened. I needed to kiss him. I needed to tell him I forgave him. I needed to tell him that we should just run, runaway together.

"Now, now. Friend or not, that is a bit too much affection for *our* future queen."

Griffith's arms slapped down to his side, his hard composure returning. "If she is hurt Isara will not hesitate to attack."

Leo hooked his arm around mine. "You wound our kingdom's honor. If it were not for my reputation with punctuality, we would draw swords. Good day to you Lord Griffith, have a safe trip back to your kingdom," Leo sneered as he steered me to the palace doors.

I glimpsed back, not breaking eye contact with Griffith. His eyes were sad and warm. Eyes of a bitter farewell and the release of a heavy secret.

The part of me that still loved him slammed against the chains I held her in, pleading for me to run back, to ask him more.

Why didn't he tell me sooner?
Why did he reject me?
Would I ever see him again?
The palace doors closed, and the chains stopped rattling.

CHAPTER 8

I had traveled to many countries and explored their castles. All of them were beautiful in their own way but none had challenged the beauty of Isara's until now.

The front entrance was a work of art. The floor was made of white marble, the walls made of the same but trimmed with sparkling gold. A double door, in the middle of two staircases with shimmering rails, was adorned with golden figurines of instruments and music notes accented with blue sapphires.

The staircases, both starting on each side of the double doors, curved as they climbed to the second floor. But before they could reach the top, they became one. Following the railing up, I saw a regal painting of the previous king and queen with their two sons beside them. The painting had to be about ten years of age as the sons were painted young yet the paint still shined and not a piece of it had been smudged by time. Next to it hung smaller paintings of queens and kings of the past, leaving no room for empty space.

Dangling from the ceiling was a chandelier made from sapphires, zircon, kyanite, and jewels I had never seen before.

My breath grew shallow as the sunlight ricocheted off them, sending out tiny rainbows that decorated the ceiling.

"Your Highness, Anna will take your cloak. We should make our way to the throne room."

"Anna?" I asked, forgetting about the girl who came out with Leo.

The maid glanced up at him as he motioned toward her.

"This is Anna, your lady's maid." She curtsied. "She has trained for multiple years and has received high praise from those she has served in the past."

"It's a pleasure and an honor to serve you, Your Highness," she chirped as she rose. Her arms extended to take my cloak.

I silently examined her accent. It was so familiar, yet I couldn't place my finger on it. It wasn't like any accents of the Modarians I had met. Perhaps, from a different region? No, Modare was too small to have a variety of accents.

"Your cloak." Leo motioned his hands once again as his foot tapped impatiently.

I sighed as I slid it off into Anna's hands, patting the embroidered silver shield protected by thorny vines. Vines that held up multiple flowers that had a gradient from deep purple to white. A flower that was known for its potent healing properties throughout the continent. A flower that only grew in Isara, an Isarilla. So beautiful and so helpful that my kingdom was named after it, that it decorated our crest. "Hold it dearly," I whispered to Anna who gave me a reassuring smile.

Leo looked at his watch, letting out an exasperated sigh. "This way!" he commanded as he steered me left.

My heels clacked on the marble as Leo hastily walked down the empty corridor. I glanced in every way possible, examining my new home.

There were hardly any blank spaces as paintings and giant windows filled the wall. I made a note to come back and examine each canvas as I was a lover of art. But my eyes stilled as I saw a beloved painting of an ocean. A painting I had seen many times when I visited Astra. My heart dropped.

How many of these paintings were stolen from the kingdoms they had taken?

"Your Highness?" Anna asked, her accent thick.

An accent from Astra.

I snapped my head to face her, my breathing hastening in fear and anger.

Was she a slave?

Perhaps she was a lady's maid to someone high at court. That would give them grounds to imprison her.

I reached out. "Anna you're from—"

"Quickly!" Leo screeched.

I retracted my hand, reminding myself I would have plenty of time alone with Anna to make sure she was ok.

I quickened my stride, trying to keep up as Leo turned the corner. The paintings were nowhere to be seen down this hall, but their absence was not missed as countless windows filled the corridor. I glanced out of one only to see a massive army—three times the size of my father's. My mouth parted as all the air in my body left. If we were to go to war, it would be a massacre, and not in our favor.

"How many times do I have to say this? We are in a hurry." Leo gently placed his hand on my back, pushing me forward as I froze in fear. "I promise, you will get a tour of the castle but for now we need to get you to the king."

The king. The Tyrant King. He who took over lands, stole family artifacts, kept slaves, and was to be my husband. He who would have full ownership of me, do what he desired to me, command me how he saw fit with no repercussions unless it affected Isara or the treaty. A shiver went down my spine as Leo stopped in front of an iron door, decorated with Modare's crest.

We were about to enter the throne room.

CHAPTER 9

The iron doors creaked open. A bellman announced, "Presenting Princess Estelle of Isara."

I peered inside, scanning for the reaction of his court, but no one was to be found. There were only guards who stood silently along the perimeter of the room with hard expressions. The steel of their polearms, which towered over each guard, glimmered as the sun ricocheted off the daunting weapon.

My heart quickened and my legs turned to lead. There would be no one here to witness this meeting except those loyal to him and only him.

Leo, as if noticing my hesitation, pushed me forward toward the throne. Where he sat. The Tyrant King.

His eyes weren't filled with villainous rage, he didn't reek of blood or wore the trinkets of those he'd murdered, at least not on him.

He slumped in his throne, filling it with his stout body. His cheek rested in his palm, expression aloof as I approached. He was only six years older than me, but the war had darkened the under of his eyes and given him soft wrinkles on his forehead.

I curtsied before him, wondering how this man took over Astra and Ula. "Your Majesty, I am Princess Estelle. I have come today to—"

He groaned, cutting me off. "Yes, I know what you are here for. Your father and I wrote *numerous, time-consuming* letters about it. No need to refresh the memories." He took a long sip from his goblet, the wine running down his beard.

My nose crinkled in disgust, but I continued to look upon him, my future husband.

"You must forgive King Titus. He's had several tiring meetings," Leo explained.

King Titus slammed his goblet on the armrest of the iron throne, silencing Leo who cowered three steps behind me. I held my head high, expression unchanging, but inside I was shaking.

King Titus took another sip of the wine, evaluating me.

"You are quite beautiful," he stated as his eyes came to rest on mine.

"Thank you, Your Majesty."

"I am glad to see your portrait was not exaggerated."

My eyes narrowed on the gut he had grown with drink. He was far from the image I had been sent back in Isara. I ground my teeth wanting to tell him so but remembered that I had to be a cordial, perfect princess. I needed to be appealing to this disgusting man who held so much power. I could not afford to displease him before we wed.

"The artist is known for capturing the reality of those he paints. He is well renowned in Isara," I replied, keeping my voice monotone, knowing I would not be able to hide the annoyance if I were to show any emotions.

"The reality of those he paints, you say? Does this include their character? If so, I would've loved for him to paint my past adversaries, it would have saved so much time."

My brow raised as my curiosity piqued by his odd words. Astra and Ula were very public countries. They did not have a history of hiding secrets, nor did they ever attempt to conceal when their country was in need. It was what made them so trustworthy. What was King Titus wanting to reveal? My lips parted but before I could utter a word, the iron doors opened once again.

"Ah, there he is," King Titus boomed, interrupting the bellman. Titus grinned ear to ear, raising his glass to whoever walked in.

I turned as the sound of boots came closer, curious as to who could make the Tyrant King smile.

My heart came to a halt, color drained from my face as I faced a second pair of silver eyes. The man—the man who made the king smile was Al.

He strutted in with a wide grin on his face, not a drop of fear as he approached King Titus. He no longer wore the simple clothes from the tavern. He was completely changed, apart from his sword. From the black leather pants to the sparkling golden buttons on his dark blue tunic, everything about him was profuse with elegance.

He was not a thief, not a guard. He was something more. I just didn't know what yet.

I gulped. My eyes darted to and fro, not sure if he recognized me or if he was just that good at pretending.

"My apologies for the tardiness. You know how it gets on the road," he jested, climbing the stairs to the throne without so much as a bow.

The tension in the room dissipated as King Titus rose, slapping Al on the back. Even Leo took a step forward, standing tall.

What sway did Al hold with the king?

"You must be thirsty." King Titus turned. "Wine, bring wine." The servant, I had failed to notice him upon entering, bowed with a smile on his face as he ran off to get another goblet.

I stood quietly, completely forgotten about.

"Now, we mustn't get too drunk. You have a bride to attend to." Al grabbed King Titus's shoulder, steadying him as King Titus swayed while downing the remnants of his cup.

"Bride?" Al jerked his chin toward me. "Oh yes, my bride! Isn't she beautiful?" Titus threw his arm over Al, holding him tightly.

Al took a sip of his wine, eyes softly trailing over my body. "Yes...yes, she is."

That stammer, he remembered me.

Would Al tell him?

If the king knew of my impropriety, if he knew what I had done with Al—the treaty would be over before it began.

I clutched my chest, batting my eyelashes, forcing the tears back in. Fear was taking over.

"She'll be a good wife for you. I'm certain."

I looked up to see Al's eyes on me. Those soft, understanding eyes. He wouldn't tell King Titus. Al was good.

Leo stepped forward. "Your Majesty." Titus turned, glaring. "The princess, if you approve, should move on to the examination."

Examination? No one had told me of such a thing. Perhaps it was to test my literacy, knowledge on kingdoms? Prove that I could offer more than just a womb.

Al's body stiffened as King Titus sat back on his throne. "Is the physician ready?"

A physician, so it was diseases.

"Yes, Your Majesty. Aeson is waiting in Princess Estelle's chambers."

King Titus leaned back, slumping once again in his chair. He flicked his hand, signaling that we were dismissed. Leo's hand was quickly on my back, pushing me along when Al spoke, his voice thick with honey, "Surely, we don't need to test her. She is of royal breeding after all."

Leo let out a sigh, turning, waiting for the king's response. "So much for staying on schedule," he murmured to himself.

"Royal breeding or not. Tradition is tradition," Titus grunted, waving the servant over to refill his goblet.

"They may see this as an insult. The examination can be mortifying for a young woman. Isara treasures their princess dearly."

"Enough!" Titus roared. "My head aches, and you are making it worse."

Al stood his ground, unaffected by King Titus's outburst. "But—" King Titus glared, a warning of his growing wrath, but Al did not look away.

This wouldn't end well. My fists tightened on my skirts.

And, maybe it was the need to repay last night's favor, to protect him, as he was still doing for me, or perhaps it was stupidity, but I found myself speaking.

"I don't mind being tested." Both men looked at me, bewilderment in their eyes. "I have been traveling through many towns. It is wise to see if I have caught anything. Plagues are far more dangerous than any army."

Silence. A slight chuckle. Then a storm of laughter as King Titus rolled back in his throne.

"You—you think the test—the test is for diseases." He wiped a tear from his eye. "Oh, you sweet girl. I almost don't want to test you because of this."

I glanced at Al. His lips were a tight line.

King Titus straightened. "The test, my sweet bride, is to see if your innocence is intact."

I stood silent, lips parting.

What had I done?

I was taught to protect my innocence, my purity, and if I failed I was to never let anyone know. I was to always say I was pure even if it was a lie. But no one had ever told me there was a way to test it.

My eyes darted to Al and for the first time since he walked through the iron door his gaze met mine. His eyes were void of joy or playfulness. I was doomed to fail whatever this test was.

"Take her. We're far behind schedule," King Titus commanded.

Leo grabbed my arm once again, leading me to my demise and the end of a short-lived treaty. I had failed my kingdom, my father, and Lord Griffith.

"Wait." Al's voice echoed through the room.

Leo released my arm, letting out an even louder sigh than before.

Al glared at the ceiling, teeth grinding. King Titus stared at him in anticipation.

"What now?" King Titus rubbed his temples, slouching further back in his throne.

Al bit his lip before exhaling. My eyes widened in horror as I realized what he was about to do. I shook my head, lunging forward. There was no reason for him to take the blame, for both of us to be punished. It only had to be me, just one of us.

"I am not pure, Your Majesty." I fell to the ground, ready to grovel.

King Titus, eyes filled with fire, turned to me. "Send her back." King Titus waved his arm. Guards approached, pulling me to my feet. "This treaty is over."

"Wait, please," I screeched, ripping my arms away from the guards, falling back down on my knees. "Please." Tears welled up in my eyes. Out of fear or embarrassment, I did not know. "It was a foolish mistake. My emotions were high and my head was unclear. I regret it with all my being." I did not look up, but I could feel the eyes of the guards, Leo, Al, Titus, every living things' eyes on me as I continued to beg, as I abandoned my royal decorum, my pride. "I cannot, *we* cannot throw away the treaty. We both can benefit from it."

The throne screeched against the floor as Titus furiously stood. "As a princess, your greatest task is to save yourself, so your purity can be used as a bargaining chip to aid your kingdom. Yet, you could not do that because of your emotions. A queen will have far more important, critical duties, and must face them in a manner of elegance. How do you expect me to give a pathetic, groveling princess this role? In the future, when you cause problems that will affect my kingdom and people, will you blame it on your feelings too?"

His words cut like a knife. The tears streamed down uncontrollably. I looked like anything but royalty, but still, I persisted, "Please, it was one night, one mistake."

"Take her away," he commanded with a voice so cold I shivered.

The guards grabbed my arms once again, my feet dragging as they pulled me to the iron door. All hope, gone.

I had failed. I would become a disgraced princess. I would be the reason for Isara's ruin if Modare ever chose to attack.

"It was me."

I spun around, my strength miraculously returning.

Al stood five steps away from King Titus, facing him squarely, with no shame.

"Care to elaborate?" King Titus growled, placing his wine down.

The damage was done, irreversible. Nothing he could say would change things. Him admitting his part in this wouldn't save me, it wouldn't save Isara. Why couldn't he just keep his mouth shut? He was the only thing that I could leave untouched from my mistake. I needed him to come out unscathed from this.

"No, he—" Al glared at me, the intensity turning me to stone.

"I was on patrol, I fancied her, so I took her to bed." His voice was flat, void of all emotion.

King Titus grasped Al's tunic faster than I could blink "You idiot. Do you realize what you have cost us?" He violently shook Al whose face remained unchanged, his voice rising with the question. "Do you?"

Show some fear. Maybe then, your punishment will be lessened.

Al gripped King Titus's wrist. "The treaty can still work. Let me marry her." My eyes widened.

Al was thrown backward but landed gracefully on his feet.

King Titus slouched back in his throne, gulping down the rest of his wine, resting his head in his palm. "You realize what that means? You won't be able to chase *her* anymore." Al grimly nodded. King Titus sighed heavily before speaking again, "Then we shall proceed." King Titus waved his hand, allowing Anna and Leo to retrieve me.

I stepped forward, evading their touch.

I appreciated Al's efforts to make the treaty work, but it would be void. The treaty required royal blood to marry royal blood.

King Titus raised his brow.

I stood straight, summoning the small amount of courage I had left. "I must marry royalty. I cannot marry a general," I stuttered out, still unsure of Al's position.

As the words left my mouth, the guards, Leo, and Anna all gasped in unison. I looked around at the perplexed faces then to Al's. His playful smirk was back, laughing at the shock in the room.

"You," King Titus stammered out with renewed rage. "You dare insult my brother, *Prince* Alexander of Modare, by calling him a mere general after his sacrifice so you may have *your* treaty."

A heaviness expanded in my core and my mouth dropped open. Al, no, Alexander was a prince?

I was dumbfounded as I replayed all our interactions, all the interactions between him and King Titus. How had I not seen it?

"There, there brother." Alexander patted his brother's shoulder. "You know I keep my identity secret when I travel." King Titus grumbled something under his breath that made Alexander chuckle.

"Leo, send a letter informing Isara about the change of grooms." King Titus glanced back at me. "Your father will know of your failures." I nodded, the only motion I could muster. "Get her ready, with haste, the court is waiting," King Titus uttered, his voice tired and somewhat relieved.

CHAPTER 10

Leo grabbed my arm and led me out of the throne room. Thoughts raced through my mind.

I was to marry Alexander—the man who I slept with all so I could say my first was of my choosing. Now, I was forced to marry him, stuck forever. He was stuck forever.

You'll get hurt.

My heart is owned by another.

The words rang over and over in my head. There was no hope in finding happiness in this forced arrangement. Alexander would hate me for taking him away from his love. At least with King Titus, I would've had a chance.

No. I couldn't think like this.

Alexander was a good man. He had protected me in the tavern, he protected me here. There may not be love between us, but there could be friendship. That was more than one could ask for in an arranged marriage

At least I knew Alexander would be kind, make our marriage duties bearable, maybe enjoyable. If I had to fulfill them with King Titus—I didn't want to think about it. His stout body, his beard drenched in wine—I gagged at the thought of him over me.

Maybe this switch wasn't so bad. I certainly would be able to relax more. My duties would be kept to a minimum as I would remain a princess.

A princess, not a queen.
My heartbeat stopped. I wouldn't be marrying the Tyrant King. I would be marrying the prince. I would never become Queen of Modare.

Would I still have enough power to keep my kingdom safe?
I clutched my skirts. My father would hear of my failings, of my shameful night. He would hate me.

No, I could still win back his approval.

I just needed to keep Isara safe.

I would be a spy just like Griffith had told me to do. I would prove I could protect Isara in another way.

Griffith. He would hear the news as well.

Would he think of me as a harlot?

Surely, he would.

Perhaps if I wrote him a letter, explaining why I did it, maybe, just maybe, he might understand. But a letter like that would show I held feelings for him. If that were read by someone other than Griffith—I shuddered at the thought.

"Here we are, Princess Estelle. Your private chambers," Leo's shrill voice exclaimed.

The door was opened, revealing a standard room for a royal.

A ginormous bed, a vanity, and a wardrobe filled the bulk of the room. Near the wall, opposite of the entrance, a chaise was perfectly placed near a window, so one could sunbathe in the comfort of the room or enjoy the warmth of the fire, only a couple steps away, in the cold months. A cozy, quiet place to escape the responsibilities of court. At least that's how I would've felt if it were not for the color of the canopy, chairs, and curtains. Everything was that deep rich blue. A *friendly* reminder that I was in Modare.

"I hope it is to your liking." Anna stared at me doe eyed, waiting for my response.

I took a glance around the room once more, skin crawling. Did it have to look as if Modare retched over it? Is what I wanted to say. However, I knew Anna, being my lady's maid, had oversaw the room's décor and I had no intention of hurting her feelings. Not after all the terrors Modare had given her.

"It's lovely," I stammered through a false smile.

Anna beamed, proudly. "Glad to hear it. We've added a few personal items for you to use, but please let me know if there's anything you desire. It may not be the same products that are found in an Isaran market, but Modare has quite the array of makeup, hairbrushes, soaps, and accessories."

I walked to the vanity, opening the various drawers. Inside, neatly organized jars filled with colored powder waited, colors I had never seen. Potions to cleanse or enhance the skin were packed in tiny bottles. Their aroma filled the air the longer the drawer remained open. I couldn't wait to see the products Anna had put in the bathroom.

I looked out the window. A beautiful garden sat just below, filled with rows of yellow, pink, and white roses. All the colors you could think of, except for red. That color was only found in a maze that was a short distance from where the other hedges sat. From the window, it looked fairly simple as it only required a couple of turns to get to the middle where a whimsical fountain waited. Another perfect, private place to waste a day away. I'd have to visit it soon.

I walked to the plush bed against the center of the wall, thankful the sheets were white. I grazed my hand across it, the buttery silk comforting my senses. I flattened my hand pushing into the mattress. It was a perfect mixture of firm and soft, ever inviting. A nap, I thought to myself, would be perfect right now. It would give me the energy needed to explore the grounds, write a letter to Griffith and my father begging for their forgiveness.

"Anna, could you wake me in an hour?" I sat on the bed and slipped off the shoes that had been pinching my feet all day. "I feel rather tired after the travels."

Anna's eyes widened. "But the wedding, Your Highness."

I looked at her with raised brows. "Can't we plan tomorrow?" I wailed, already spread across the cold silk sheets.

"Your Highness, the wedding is today."

I bolted up. Eyes wide, heart palpitating. "Today? Anna, I just got here. Isn't there planning to do? Tours? Things I need to do before marrying."

Anna moved to the foot of my bed; hands crossed resting on her dress. "King Titus has ordered that the wedding happen the day you get here, so the treaty can be enacted as soon as possible. It was discussed with your father."

I slid my legs off the bed, reaching for my shoes. "I must speak to the king right away."

I was halfway when Anna grabbed my arm. Her eyes filled with worry.

"With no disrespect, your time and his will be wasted. The court has been in the garden for hours, waiting. There is no backing out now. Please, trust me."

I stilled. I didn't care about wasting anyone's time. The changes that were happening already were far too overwhelming and to get married immediately after them, it was beyond what I could handle. But I couldn't say no to her, to those scared eyes. The gods would only know how King Titus would punish Anna for my disobedience, for her lack of skills to persuade me to *behave*. I sat back on the bed. Relief washed over Anna as she hastily pulled a rope next to the bed.

I closed my eyes momentarily, processing everything that was about to happen. I would be introduced to the court as the Princess of Modare, not Isara. They were taking my title, my lineage before it could even reach the Modarian's ears. Only Modare existed here, and my father had agreed to it. I wonder what else he'd allow me to be subjected to after he heard of my failure.

I opened my eyes as the latch of the door sprang loose. A flurry of maids invaded my chambers. I sprang up as two opened the door to the bathing room I had not seen. Another two carried in a long bag, used for protecting dresses, and hung it on the door of the wardrobe.

"Now then." Anna clapped her hands, gathering everyone's attention. "First things first, a bath."

In a blink of an eye, one of the maids from the bathing room stripped me down and had me in a freshly drawn bath.

I was barely able to enjoy the heat around my body as one maid dumped a bucket of water over my head and began scrubbing away.

"I'm sorry for the roughness, Your Highness."

I had no time to answer as another bucket assaulted me. I spat, trying to rid the taste of soap from my mouth.

"Out you get." Anna held out a plush towel. I rose, putting my naked body on display. Thankfully, the maids were decent enough to momentarily avert their eyes.

I wrapped myself quickly, unsure of how long they would give me. Sure enough, once I was semi-covered, the maids went back to *handling* me. One snatched my hand, leading me to the vanity, plopping me down as the other wrung the water from my hair.

Anna positioned herself in front of the chair, her bottom slightly on the vanity's surface. She pulled out a glass container containing an onyx-colored powder. Without a word, I closed my eyes as a thin brush assaulted my eyelid. I did not dare open them again while the sound of the drawer and glass containers clicked and clacked, opening with much haste.

No one spoke for what felt like an eternity. An impressive feat for the three sets of hands that attacked my hair, body, and face.

"All done," Anna mused. I opened my eyes only to find a hand blocking my view of the mirror. "Not yet. Let us get you dressed first."

I giggled at the playfulness in her tone before closing my eyes again. My heart warming as I realized this was something one of my lady's maids would have done back home

With my eyes fully closed, a rush of air hit my face as Anna's hand moved away.

"Ok. You can open them now."

The mirror was covered with a single white sheet. There would be no sneaking glances until she wanted me to look.

I stood up, still in my towel, and walked to my chests, the only purple in the room, to retrieve my undergarments.

"We've had some prepared."

I spun around. Anna stood by the bed motioning to something that laid on the sheets. My face went pale as my eyes focused on the vibrant red lace.

These could hardly be called undergarments. It was practically ribbons. I stared in disbelief.

How could she possibly think I would enjoy this? Even on one's wedding night this was too much. And red? A color associated with lust, impropriety. What was Anna thinking?

Anna, almost knowing the thoughts racing through my mind, shamefully stared at the floor. "The king—the king picked them out. Not directly. But he—well he—he made the criteria."

My breath shook as I sighed. I was to be shamed then. Not publicly. Never in front of the court, where rumors would spread and spread till they reached Isara. Where my father, depending on his displeasure with my eventful night, may take up arms to defend me. No. That wasn't the case. King Titus could care less about a war with my father. Any shame thrown upon me would be reflected on Modare, and that wasn't allowed.

But to take this away, the tradition of only wearing white. It was a message. There would be punishment, public or not, if I made any errors, or disobeyed.

This was a test to see if I would accept my punishment like a good princess. But how would King Titus know?

He wasn't the one undressing me tonight. Alexander would be.

Was he in on this distasteful joke, this message?

He couldn't. Al was sweet. Al had come to my rescue. He comforted me when I had no one else.

Al—Al had done those things. Not Alexander. Alexander was brother to the Tyrant King. I did not know him.

I slid on the disgusting red lace.

"Now for the dress," Anna mumbled, her eyes avoiding the shameful site of me.

I fisted my hands. King Titus would not have the dress showcase my failure. It would be too public. He could make it unpleasant to the eye though. I felt my skin break as my nails dug into my palms.

The most special dress of my life and it would be hideous.

The two maids, who had brought the dress in, unsheathed it from its covering and held it up.

My nails retracted. A smile drifted across my face.

It was stunning.

The dress was made of white chiffon. The full length off the shoulder sleeves flowed freely till they reached the wrists. Here they came together, creating a mild poof effect in the arms. The dress was covered in intricate lace designs of leaves and flowers, all of it silver.

"Do the thing," the youngest maid yelled from the bathroom.

Anna nodded, signaling another maid to open the curtains.

My eyes widened in awe as the maid holding the gown titled it in the sunlight, revealing the secret blue and purple shimmer.

My fingertips trailed over the lace flowers, the color changing from silver to blue then to purple. It was subtle but the statement was loud. I connected Isara and Modare. I couldn't have asked for a better gown.

"You like it?" Anna asked in hopes of redeeming herself.

I nodded, unable to form words.

I would belong to two kingdoms after today. I would be the bridge to ensure peace. I wouldn't mess up again.

CHAPTER 11

"Stand right here." Anna positioned me in front of the mirror, before grabbing the cloth that covered it.

The rest of the maids stood around me, gleaming at their hard work. I prayed to the gods that their skills were befitting of the gown.

"One, two"—I closed my eyes, not ready—"three."

I felt the rush of air from the cloth and opened my eyes. My lips parted in surprise.

Stunning. Absolutely stunning.

My cheeks were a light pink, creating the illusion of a continuous blushing bride. My eyelids were painted a lighter pink, accented with soft onyx wings, while my lips remained my natural color but were glossed as if they were candy, perfectly kissable. I tilted my head, examining my hair. It was half up, half down. White roses, woven into my soft curls, cascaded down.

I was the picture of innocence.

That night would be kept a secret in his court.

"One last thing." Anna grabbed the diadem I was wearing when I arrived. "Can't have you walking out there without this, Princess of Isara."

A soft smile brushed across my face. This was one of the last moments that title could be used, and Anna knew that.

She placed the diadem on my head, my eyes glistening. "I think I rather like you."

Anna giggled to herself. "Likewise, Princess."

"Is she ready?" a shrill voice asked from the opening door.

I turned to find Leo with covered eyes.

"Just finished," Anna mused, giving me one last look, one more smile before stepping away. "Good luck," she whispered.

I returned a faint smile as my stomach twisted into knots.

CHAPTER 12

I kept a tight grip on Leo's arm as he pulled me down the stairs to the second garden, otherwise known as *The Garden*. Not to be confused with the garden outside of my room, Leo had informed me. That was known as the Rose Garden.

With both gardens containing roses and on opposite sides of the castle the names for them were rather dull and confusing. It would be easy, for an outsider, to misunderstand which garden someone was talking about.

No doubt, this was a tactic to confuse Modare's enemies.

I'd have to tell Griffith about this.

Sunlight pierced my eyes as we came upon a giant archway. Red and white petals laid on the ground, creating the path to the altar.

I took a deep breath, my feet like stone as Leo pulled me forward. My heart pounded as if it were about to explode. I squeezed Leo's arm tighter with every step. I fought the urge to scream, to run. I had committed to being a better princess for Isara, to protecting her, to making this treaty work, but the idea of marrying a man that wasn't Griffith was still petrifying.

"Princess, you're making my arm numb," Leo whispered.

Too preoccupied with my own thoughts, his words ran out my ears.

For Isara, I repeated with each step, for Isara.

The path curved around a massive rose bush, revealing an army of nobles. All seated, all Modarians, and all their eyes on me. Sizing me up, searching for flaws, wondering if I was a worthy princess for their kingdom.

My breath hitched. My confidence faltered. My eyes lowered to the ground.

No, no, no! My head screamed, feeling the tears form.

I had to be strong, beautiful, someone they would respect.

I gathered my strength, thinking of all the things I needed to protect. Slowly my head raised, and my eyes focused forward. In front stood Anna—waiting to take my bouquet—the priest, King Titus, and Alexander. All of them stared at me. It took everything I had to not look back down.

Anna beamed with pride as her masterpiece walked down the aisle. Meanwhile, King Titus was the perfect picture of impatience. Neither of their expressions affected me. But when my gaze met Alexander's, my heart nearly stopped. His eyes were void of emotion as if his soul had left, leaving a moving carcass behind.

My heart is owned by another. The words rang in my mind.

This marriage, he didn't want it. I had ruined another's chance of finding happiness. Alexander would hate me.

If I had just been proper, did my duty, I wouldn't have hurt him. I bit my lip, stilling the quivering.

The ceremony was a blur. My mind was numb to the words of the priest. My body moved like a puppet. It wasn't till the kiss that I acknowledged the real world.

"Kiss the bride and show the gods she is yours."

Alexander's eyes met mine as both of us came out of a trance, simply to apologize for the touch that was about to occur. I made no movement as all my strength went to numbing my feelings, scared that if I let myself feel, acknowledge them, I would break.

The crowd sat in anticipation, their silence growing as Alexander grimaced as he looked upon my bruised lips. We were both at a loss for actions.

King Titus coughed, urging us to hurry up, commanding us to kiss. Alexander grabbed me firmly, his eyes empty.

There was no emotion, no movement as our mouths made contact. We were cold statues merely doing what we were sculpted for.

"And with that," King Titus grunted, raising our clasped hands in the air, "the treaty is sealed."

Celebration overtook the crowd. Many nobles jumped for joy while others hugged. A smile on everyone's face except a red-haired maiden in the back who stared at Alexander.

CHAPTER 13

My hand rested on the inner side of Alexander's elbow as he led me and the parade of nobles to the ballroom. We walked in silence, apart from a polite thank you to anyone who jovially wished us congratulations. Occasionally, Alexander offered a forced smile, hiding any trace of discontent. It was a gesture I could not rally myself to make.

We paused in front of the double doors that had greeted me when I first arrived. The gems still filled the hall with rainbows, despite the setting sun. Two servants stood by the doors, gripping the handles. The court huddled around impatiently, waiting to be let in. The anticipation building as the pitter patter of feet grew quieter. Finally, there was silence. King Titus looked back at the nobles then the servants and nodded. The doors opened, accompanied with a collective gasp when the golden ballroom was revealed.

Two tables, the length of the room, sat on opposite sides of the ballroom. Each table overflowed with gorgeous dishes and drink. In front was a much smaller table placed on a platform, so it was higher than the other two. It, too, was filled with platters of food and wine.

In the back two corners, a quartet of musicians played the most beautiful melody that made my feet glide across the floor. Made me want to dance despite the dreadful events of today. I closed my eyes for a moment, allowing myself to take in the scents and the music. All of it filled my heart with familiar comfort, ridding it of the horror and sadness for a few moments.

I looked behind me, waiting to see if anyone would start a dance. But to my surprise they dispersed, claiming seats at the long tables.

I suppose dancing would be later.

I hoped they danced here.

Leo, King Titus, Alexander, and I climbed the short staircase to the center table. King Titus and Alexander stood behind the middle two seats, placing Leo and me on the outer chairs. A placement I had no quarrels with. The less attention on me the better.

Alexander released my hand as King Titus raised his golden goblet. "Let the festivities begin."

We all raised our glasses, mimicking the king's motions. King Titus, seeing all the cups raised, drank from his goblet. We, too, drank until he stopped, emptying our cups.

I sat as did the others after King Titus lowered into his chair, the wine already clouding my mind. I didn't know if I should be thankful or worried. I wasn't prone to the effects of alcohol this quickly. Was the wine here stronger? I picked up the glass, sniffing the contents. The wine was sweeter here, but the alcohol smelled the same. I held my glass to my chest, questioning why the drink affected me so.

Boom!

The doors swung open as a troupe of acrobats danced in, bowing before the king. I stared in awe as their costumes of vibrant red, orange, and yellow decorated the room. King Titus gave them a slight nod and lowered his hands, motioning for the performers to proceed. The show was about to begin.

A fire dancer lit both ends of two staffs, twirling them around his body as the intense beating of a drum shook our hearts. The room collectively gasped as he threw a staff in the air. The performer backflipped as he waited for gravity to bring it down. I did not dare breathe as it fell, scared that the tiniest flicker of air would cause him to be burned, but sure enough, his expert hand caught it.

The fire dancer had barely finished his bow when a mesmerizing woman—dressed in a red two piece, that revealed her midriff—spun in front of him. The fabric from her fans grazed the floor as she stopped to bow to King Titus before truly starting her dance.

The fabric spun around her like the fierce wind of a storm and she, the center. Calm, elegant, peaceful. Barely visible but always looked for.

The music sped, becoming more violent as her twirling stopped. She slid toward the dais, flinging the fabric forward so they were mere inches away from our faces before she pulled them back.

I let out a delayed, petrified squeak as the fabric withdrew, reminding me of my inebriation.

Why was the wine affecting me so?

A whiff of maple and cinnamon apples danced up to my nose, the aroma ever enticing.

Food.

I was completely famished, having skipped lunch. I wondered when we could eat. I looked around. To my surprise everyone was digging in, enjoying the food before them, including the members of my table.

A blush ran across my cheek. I reached forward for the serving utensils next to the succulent pig. Anna raced forward.

"Allow me, Princess."

I gave her a nod, a slight smile as I shrunk into my chair, trying to appear invisible. Though I appreciated Anna's attentiveness, her fixing my plate made it even more obvious I had missed the start of the feast. I didn't need to give the people or King Titus any more reasons to deem me incompetent.

I looked around the table, wondering if anyone had noticed my blunder.

Leo and King Titus's attentions were transfixed on the dancer. Alexander's head was pointed forward; his eyes focused on nothing. His finger slowly circled the rim of his goblet, occasionally sliding off the edge and into the cup, reminding me of how he had played with me *that* night. I gulped, feeling a heat run through my cheeks.

Would tonight be as pleasurable as it was then?

I scowled at myself for thinking such selfish thoughts. Why should I even ask for such a night when I had taken everything from him? When Griffith still consumed my thoughts? After all, that night in the tavern was nothing more than just a favor, some fun for Al—Alexander. And for me, it was just misplaced revenge. There was no reason for him to pleasure me in that way again.

Anna slid an overloaded plate in front of me. "Here you are. I gave you a bit of everything as I wasn't sure of your tastes."

I attempted a smile, as I stared in fear at the mountain of food. "Thank you," I stammered out.

Anna curtsied and retreated to the back next to the other servants.

I surveyed the plate, wondering which dish to try first. An assortment of mystery meats sat in one section, while boiled potatoes took up another. A hearty meal, one that my nervous stomach was not willing to divulge in. I pushed the potatoes around to find an array of tropical fruits and some cheese.

Perfect. The lightness I needed.

A vibrantly colored fruit caught my eye, its outermost layer a beautiful red that transitioned to green as the skin came away from the inner layer. The center of the fruit was white with black speckles, the juice glistening on the surface. I licked my lips before taking a bite.

My lips pursed together as an awful, bitter flavor assaulted my tongue. I hurriedly spat the fruit in a nearby cloth.

Utterly disgusting.

"You're supposed to peel it." I looked over to find Alexander trying to hide his devilish smirk. He took the second slice from my plate, effortlessly peeling off the red skin. "Here."

My heart warmed as he extended the fruit. Our first pleasant interaction since my arrival.

Perhaps he didn't hate me.

"Thank you." I took a bite. A burst of liquid filled my mouth, and the texture of the seeds massaged my tongue as I chewed. A taste I had never experienced. I smiled, wondering what other flavors laid on my plate. "And this one?" I picked up a green fruit shaped like a star.

Alexander rested his chin on his hand, amusement dancing in his eyes at my ignorance, but I didn't care. I was famished. "That one you can eat as is."

The fruit had the texture of an apple with a sour aftertaste. Not the type to make you squirm, the one that made you pucker but just enough to spike your curiosity, to make your mind ask for another taste. I savored the flavor with each bite and before I knew it, I was on to my second slice.

"Did you not eat today?" Alexander's smirk had been replaced with a hard line. I slowly swallowed the piece in my mouth, averting my eyes from his. I shook my head. "Even at the inn?"

The inn—it felt like such a long time ago.

I had asked for the breakfast to be wrapped but with the unpleasantness between Griffith and I, I had failed to eat a substantial amount. I shook my head, no, once again.

There was silence between us for a while before my stomach growled, demanding more of the spectacular fruit. I looked down and found that only the cheese, meat, and potatoes were left. I grimaced.

The fruit had awoken my hunger, but my stomach was still too nervous to eat the rest. Not wishing to offend and abandon the food that filled half my plate, I stabbed a small piece of meat with my fork. It smelled delectable, perhaps I could stomach it. The taste was delicious, a perfect mix of spices, but as I chewed, my mouth began to salivate. Not in a good way.

I hastened my jaw, holding back the vomit that was rising in my throat. I swallowed my wine, using it to mute the intense flavors. Forcing *everything* down.

Leaning back in my chair, I let out a sigh of relief. My stomach still growling despite my almost sickness.

I eyed the platter of fruits between King Titus and Alexander, debating if I should summon Anna, but the heaping pile of meat discouraged me. I moved my fork, dispersing the mound to see if it was truly a terrible amount or if it was a mere illusion due to the stacking.

It was the former.

I picked up another piece, this time inhaling the scents to see my body's reaction. I placed it back down as I hid my gag. I could eat no more of what was on my plate, and I didn't have the courage to reach for the fruit and risk offending anyone or being seen as wasteful. The fruit I had eaten would have to tide me over till morning.

I set my fork down and pushed my plate away trying to feign fullness, but my eyes kept flicking to the glistening tray of fruit. Alexander sighed heavily and took my plate, switching it with his empty one. He reached for the platter of fruits, accidentally summoning several servants who dutifully rushed forward. Alexander waved them away. King Titus peeked over, debating if he should intervene, but his attention was quickly pulled as two more women joined the fan dance.

"It's going to be a long night, make sure you eat," he commanded, filling the plate in front of me with more fruit.

I looked at him with surprise, as he finished off my remaining food. He raised an eyebrow in question. "Did I read the situation wrong?"

I shook my head, stuttering out words, trying to figure out what to say. "N-no, I just—"

"Good. I made sure the cook wasn't looking to ensure she wouldn't be offended. Just relax."

I felt the rouge color returning to my face. He was still caring, tentative, despite my presence taking away his chances of being with his love. He was still Al from the tavern.

"A wonderful performance." King Titus applauded the troupe as they bowed.

My eyes widened. This night was moving far too quickly.

The rest of the nobles clapped with the king, the troupe beaming at their success. They turned to each table giving a graceful bow, theatrically leaving with spins while the applause still boomed.

King Titus sat back down as a merry song began to play. He chuckled to himself as nobles frolicked around the room to find themselves a partner. It was a mad dash as they tried to secure the first dance of the night with those they fancied. I smiled, remembering the nights my friends and I would do the same. An act that I would never partake in again.

I watched as couples took to the floor one by one, dancing fiercely in the space the troupe had taken up, the rhythm infectious. I wondered if Alexander and I might join. Surely the steps wouldn't be that hard to pick up.

"Lord Telin, happy you could make it to the celebration!" Alexander sat straight in his chair with a gleeful smile as a blonde-haired man approached carrying a slender silver box.

"I would not miss such a happy occasion, my prince." Lord Telin passed the box to Leo, now standing in front of the table. "A wedding present for the princess."

Leo brought the box toward me, lowering it as he lifted the lid. Inside lay a silver dagger, the hilt glistening with several blue sapphires, the pommel bearing the crest of Modare. My fingers glazed over it, admiring the craftsmanship, wondering why it looked so familiar.

"Thank you," I whispered, my eyes flickering up to Lord Telin in forced delight. I appreciated its beauty and the artistry, but I had never held a dagger, let alone used one. It was a useless gift.

"It's gorgeous, Lord Telin. The design, is it from the same man who forged my blade?" Alexander questioned, his head tilting to get a better look.

Lord Telin laughed. "You always have had a good eye. I had it made when I had yours crafted, just been waiting for you to be partnered up."

Alexander muffled a chuckle. "You've wanted to see me married for a while now."

"For good reason too. Maybe with a wife, you'll be more careful on your missions." Lord Telin, reaching over the table, slapped Alexander's shoulder, sending them both into a fit of laughter.

They were so friendly with each other, not a royal protocol in sight.

"Now, you two, this is not a friendly meeting. This is a wedding party. There are plenty others we must receive. Make haste with your greetings." King Titus slumped in his chair, trying to look aloof as possible, but I couldn't help but notice that one side of his lips were turning up.

"Yes, yes." Lord Telin gave my hand a quick kiss before bidding us farewell and offering another congratulation.

My eyes followed him as he descended, enthralled by his joyful demeanor but this didn't last long. My breath hitched as I spied the massive line, decorated in gold and silver boxes, that had formed. There was no hope of dancing tonight. No hope of leaving the table.

Each gift-giving went like Lord Telin's—an overly friendly greeting, lots of smiling, and talking. Some would try to strike up a conversation with me, though it never got far with King Titus's reminders that there were plenty more people to greet. Still, the interactions were a welcome change compared to the hostility and seriousness of this morning.

"May the gods let this one be quick," King Titus mumbled under his breath as a red-haired pair grimly approached us.

The man, in his forties, reached us first, while the woman, possibly his daughter, stayed three or four steps behind him. She glared at the ground, not looking up as she ascended the stairs.

"Congratulations on your marriage, Your Highnesses."

I looked to Alexander, waiting for him to speak first as he did with the past nobles. His jovial smile had once again disappeared. His eyes were narrow, focused on the woman.

Was she the one?

King Titus coughed, bringing Alexander out of his trance.

"Thank you, Lord Leon. Your congratulations means a great deal." Alexander's voice was flat, void of emotions. His eyes flickered back to the woman, now caught up to Lord Leon, whose gaze was still on the ground.

Lord Leon turned toward her as she came up the last step, her foot slipping beneath her. Her body fell, uncontrollably, forward.

There was a loud screech as Alexander jumped to his feet, extending his arm in case it was needed.

King Titus rose, softly pushing Alexander back in his chair. "Calm now, Alexander. I'm sure Lord Leon can catch his own daughter."

"Yes. My apologies," he said, his hand clenching into a fist on the table. "The wine seems to dim my senses."

Lord Leon let out a nervous chuckle. "It does it to us all." He looked to his daughter who had yet to speak. "I fear the wine has affected Veronica as well. We are just about to retire, but we had to give our congratulations."

The table grew quiet. All eyes were on Alexander and *his,* intensely on Veronica. Pleading. Pleading for her to look at him.

She was the one. She had to be. The one I kept Alexander from.
I examined her balled up body, trying to understand what their relationship was before. Alexander had told me his heart belonged to another, yet he still took me to his bed. I had assumed it was unrequited. However, her eyes, from the glimpse I caught as she bowed her head to the king, were full of regret. Not unrequited, maybe forbidden, maybe they had a fight that broke their relationship temporarily. Whatever the case, it was complicated and something I had no right to ask Alexander about.

My eyes flickered between Veronica and Alexander, wondering if I should intervene.

But what would I say? Apologize for coming between them? Let Veronica know I held no feelings toward Alexander? That would only make it worse. Make them feel hope. Not to add a declaration like that, in front of the whole court, would show a fracture in the alliance. I couldn't.

We needed to seem as strong as possible, even more so with the last-minute change of grooms. This wasn't a matter of hearts; it was a matter of politics.

I closed my eyes seeing the other nobles in line growing impatient, no, curious as to why this solemn presentation was taking so long. Talk of how the prince's heart was divided would begin. If it wasn't already. I had to break the silence.

"Thank you, Lord Leon and Lady Veronica." Wide eyes fluttered to me as if they had forgotten my presence. I licked my lips, knowing they were waiting for me to say more. "I hope we can talk more when Lady Veronica is feeling better."

Veronica's eyes flickered up with a glare so intense that I shuddered.

She wanted nothing to do with me. I was the villain in her world. I had no right to have her name in my mouth.

She parted her lips to speak, I'm sure vulgar words, as she clenched her fists and rushed forward. Lord Leon lifted his cloak, blocking her view and stopping the assault. I gulped, sensing the tension, spying the guards who had gotten closer, their hands on the hilt of their swords.

"Thank you, Princess Estelle. We would like that very much." Lord Leon paused as King Titus glared at him. His eyes turned apologetic as he muttered the last of his words, "But we will be leaving tomorrow, we are to visit the king across the seas."

"What? You're actually going through with it?" Alexander growled in utter shock.

King Titus placed a firm hand on Alexander's shoulder, reminding him to be calm, that several eyes were on us. "You haven't gone across the sea in quite a time, my friend. I wish you safe travels and good luck on your *business* there."

Lord Leon did not utter another word as he bowed, wrapping his cloak around Veronica, leading her away.

Alexander began to stand but was pushed down, aggressively this time, by King Titus. Alexander shot him a deathly glare, challenging him.

I held my breath, knowing I could do nothing to diminish the tension between them.

King Titus whispered in Alexander's ear. His grip tightened as Alexander clenched his fist. Alexander's eyes followed Veronica till she was out of sight, processing what King Titus had said, debating how to react. He bit the inside of his cheek, lowering his eyes.

The situation had been avoided, for now.

The remainder of the presentations were rushed. There were no smiles, no exchanges of stories. It simply consisted of introductions, congratulations, and the acceptance of gifts.

Alexander barely talked. We were lucky to see him nod as his gaze remained on the door Veronica had left out of. Leaving King Titus and me to do the bulk of the talking.

Hours passed before the line of nobles disappeared. I slumped in my chair no longer caring about how people perceived me as I enjoyed the much-needed break. Perhaps now I could venture down the stairs and join the dance.

I placed my hands on the table, ready to take my leave, when Titus stood and raised his glass once again, silencing the room.

"The night's end is nigh, so we must bid the *happy* couple goodnight."

Alexander pulled himself up, grievously. His expression was unreadable. His eyes were avoidant as he extended his hand toward me.

It was time. Our wedding night was to begin.

I placed my hand in his, struggling to find the strength to stand. I had already been with him before. My nervousness for the event should have been nonexistent. But with all the nobles staring our way, knowing we were about to partake in such an intimate event, my feelings were everywhere. Nervous, shy, sad, confused, I was all of them.

The crowd erupted in a cheer as the musicians blared their instruments. A perfect distraction, under normal circumstances, to help the bride not think about the act the couple was about to perform. To keep her nerves in check till they were in the quiet bedroom. But for me the noise rang in my head, making my thoughts louder, making the walk to the bedroom a yelling match.

CHAPTER 14

The door softly closed and the lock clicked into place, blocking out the music, freeing me from the chaos in my head.

I looked around to see purple chests in the corner. We were in my room, the room of choice for many couples when it came to marital duties.

I let out a sigh of relief. With us holding the duties here, Alexander would most likely leave after for the comforts of his personal room, allowing me the rest I needed after an eventful day.

Alexander strutted into the bathing room without a word. I stood still, feet like lead, not knowing what to do. Several thumps came from the bathing room followed by the sound of lapping water.

I suppose he wanted to freshen himself before the act.

I lowered my nose to my underarm. The smell of the lavender oil used earlier still lingered. I would be fine without a bath.

I twiddled my thumbs, not knowing if I should wait on the bed or undress. He had seen it all before, it didn't have to be too ceremonial. I'm sure he would appreciate my readiness as it would minimize the time needed for the joining.

I walked to the vanity, plucking the roses from my hair, allowing the curls to fall around my face. I looked to the mirror as I lifted my diadem off.

For Isara. I repeated in my head. It will just be a few minutes and then the marriage will be sealed, and the treaty officially enacted.

I stood, reaching for the laces on my dress. I fumbled for several minutes attempting to undo the knot with no prevail. I turned my back to the mirror eyeing it. It was triple knotted. I moved my hands upward, pulling the laces, attempting to loosen the corset in hopes I could slide it off just as Alexander had done at the tavern. It didn't budge. I slammed down in the chair, head in my hands.

Of course. They made it impossible to get out of the corset on my own. It was a husband's duty to undress his bride on a night like tonight.

I rubbed my temple, thinking of the intimacy that was about to ensue. The last thing Alexander wanted, after seeing his love, was to help me undress.

"I'll sleep on the chaise."

I lifted my head to see Alexander emerging, shirtless, from the bathing room. His scars glistened from the leftover water.

"On the chaise?"

He plopped down on the chair, patting his hands several times as if to show me what a chaise was.

I rolled my eyes.

"Yes, I know what a chaise is. I just thought you would return to your quarters after we were done."

Alexander tilted his head over the chaise as he leaned back, rubbing his eyes. "They've locked the doors for the night. Part of the tradition."

My eyes widened. We were to spend all night together? I had the will to consummate the marriage then be alone, not to interact for the remainder of the night.

Were we to talk after our tumble in the bed, get to know one another? That may be beneficial. It could help clear the air, allow me to apologize for getting him into this mess. But I highly doubted Alexander wanted to talk or do anything with me. Not after seeing Veronica.

I eyed Alexander. He was still slumped in the chaise with no desire to look at me.

Sensing my gaze, he lifted his head. "Well, I'll be going to bed now." I jumped up as he threw the towel that sat on his shoulders to the side of the room.

"But—but we still need to consummate the marriage."

Alexander froze, eyes remaining on the towel. "Seeing as how we got into this mess, the act of consummation has already happened, in my eyes at least."

There was a tightness in my heart as the monotonous words reached my ears. He was back to being Alexander, Prince of

Modare. He was no longer the man from the tavern. The man who chuckled at my ignorance. He wasn't Al. He was a man upset, upset by the situation he was only in because of his duty to the crown, a reason I could not blame him for.

He was here at least, he had said the vows, helped me keep the treaty. It was more than I could have asked for after everything.

We would have to, eventually, make an heir to strengthen the alliance. But today, everything happened so fast. I could not fault him or me for not trying tonight.

Alexander laid down as I continued my attempts at undoing the ribbons. I twisted my body every which way, trying to get a better angle, all attempts a failure.

I peered around the room looking for anything to aid me.

I jumped with glee as I saw a pair of scissors.

I grabbed them hastily and cut away the lace. I breathed in deeply, finally, unrestricted air.

I turned to the vanity, lips parting as I dropped the dress from my body. The red ribbon barely covered my nipples—I had forgotten all about it. I glanced behind me, checking to see if Alexander was watching. He was nowhere to be seen as he had already laid down, his eyes probably closed. Relief washed over me. We didn't both need any further reminders of why we were forced to wed.

I stared into the mirror, fingers grazing over the ribbon, over my shame. Yet as my eyes took in the sight of me, I couldn't help but admire how delicious my body looked.

A sleepy grumble came from the chaise. My body jolted, my hands frantically covering my chest, forgetting the fragile bottles within reach.

Shards of glass scattered around my feet. Their contents spread across the dark floor, making it impossible to see where they had landed.

I sucked in my breath, hoping that Alexander had slept through the sounds of the shattering glass. But sure enough, his head emerged above the back of the chaise.

"Are you alright?" Alexander asked, his eyes filled with sleep.

"Just a clumsy accident," I stammered out, looking for anything to cover my body with.

He stared at me, unaffected by my almost naked body, examining the situation.

I didn't know if I was relieved or saddened.

Alexander stood, making his way to the bathing room for his boots before slowly approaching the mess. His eyes moved across the floor searching for a clear path. He shook his head, realizing how many jars had been broken. It was impossible to get to me without stepping on a shard and vice versa.

Alexander let out a sigh as he walked to me, each step accompanied by the crushing sound of glass. "I'll carry you to the bed." He lowered his arms, waiting for me to crawl in. "The maids will clean this up in the morning." I glanced at his bare arms, my face warming at the thought of our skin touching.

Alexander groaned at my hesitation, sweeping me off my feet before I could decline. I held my arms tighter to my body as if the pressure would make me invisible. He kept his eyes forward, avoiding my gaze, my face, my body. Gently, he placed me on the bed, his forehead almost touching mine. I took a glance at his eyes, and for a moment, I thought I saw them graze over my body. He inhaled sharply before returning to the chaise without a word.

I pulled the covers up to my nose hiding the blush that grew redder. Then, the last candle in the room was blown out, and I drifted off to sleep.

CHAPTER 15

The clanging of glassware against wood nudged me awake. Slowly, I opened my eyes and stretched my arms toward the headboard. The smell of freshly baked bread and roasted pork danced up to my nose, beckoning me from the comforts of my bed.

I could have slept for another hour, but the call was too loud. I sat up.

"Good morning, Princess."

Anna stood over the table; eyes filled with light. She skipped over to the window, opening the curtains to reveal the rising sun.

I squinted, adjusting to the brightness as I looked around the room to see if Alexander was still here. There was no sign nor any evidence of his presence last night.

It was so early. What time had they permitted him to leave?

"Please come eat, Your Highness." Anna pulled out the chair at the table, motioning for me to sit. "King Titus has asked that I take you on a tour of the grounds. With Your

Highness's approval, I'd like to start early. That way we are done before the sun begins to beat down on the grounds."

Anna grabbed a purple silk robe that hung on the changing screen. The same one I brought from Isara, the one that I thought was still packed away.

I glanced around the room, noticing my chests were no longer in the corner. Instead, a stand stood in their place, all my diadems and jewelry neatly laid on it. I turned my head and noticed that the décor I brought was unpacked as well, strategically placed so it would not clash with the Modarian décor but still hung proudly.

"When did you—" I rubbed my eyes as a yawn cut me off.

"Unpack?" I nodded, sliding my arms through the robe. "This morning. Just an hour before you awoke." She turned to the bathing room, no doubt, to fill the tub.

I rubbed my head. *An hour?* Either Anna was extremely quiet, or the wedding had tired me more than I thought.

I took my seat at the table, taking note of the three plates in front of me. One had bread and cheese, a classic. The second held three pieces of thickly cut smoked pork, and the third, a pile of freshly cut fruits. Two porcelain teapots graced the table as well.

I opened the lid to one. The scent of freshly brewed coffee hit my face. I licked my lips. This was the perfect way to start the day. I opened the second pot. The aroma of roses filled the room. I closed my eyes, an involutory smile drifting onto my face.

"I wasn't sure which you preferred with the morning meal, so I brought both." Anna emerged from the bathing room, rubbing her hands on a towel.

"I usually prefer coffee, but this rose"—I waved my hand through the steam, pulling the scent to me—"it's so relaxing, like a warm embrace."

Anna poured the tea into one of two teacups. "It's the specialty here. In fact, these roses were raised specifically for tea right here in the palace."

I took a sip. The delicate floral flavor danced on my tongue, the fragrance stronger now that it was in my mouth. "I'd like to see those."

Anna let out a chuckle. "Well, you already have." My eyebrows raised slightly, as Anna pointed out the window to the Rose Garden. "Modarians love beauty, but they also value purpose. If they can combine the two, they always do it. It's a lovely concept."

A concept that the king didn't apply to himself.

I took a bite of the bacon, awakening the hunger inside me. My nervous stomach had subsided, and it was ready to consume everything on a plate. I took bite after bite, sipping the tea in between.

I threw the last piece of fruit in my mouth, licking the juices from my fingers, staring at the plates I had quickly emptied. Embarrassment rushed over me as I remembered Anna was still in the room.

This was not the behavior a princess should exhibit. I needed to explain myself. I needed to explain that I wasn't normally this way but with the lack of food the previous day, I couldn't help myself. But as I found her, her focus was elsewhere. She stared out the window to the distant horizon, deep in thought.

Anna's brows were soft, her lips twisted into a melancholy smile, her hair shimmering as the rising sun drifted over her face. Such a beautiful, painful image, one the painters of Astra would rush to draw. That is, if they still had patrons to support them.

Astra was renowned for their artisans, for them to diminish would be the loss of Astra's culture, history. Perhaps, that's what Anna was thinking of. Not the painters per se but Astra. All that she lost and still had to lose.

This sweet girl, she didn't deserve to lose anything else, and she wouldn't, not if I could help it. I wasn't queen, but I still had some power. I could make some of her wishes come true. I just needed to know them. Soon. Soon, I would ask her.

I walked to the bathtub almost filled to the brim, bubbles coating the water's surface. I stripped off the few remaining garments and settled into the deliciously warm bath.

I rested my neck on the rim of the giant tub, basking in the relaxing bathing oils. This was my first proper bath in weeks, and I was going to enjoy it.

I remained like that, eyes closed, listening to Anna's footsteps till the water was lukewarm.

My eyelids opened slowly, finding a sponge on a table within arm's reach. I went to work lathering my body, competing with the lowering temperature of the water. The intoxicating scent of the oils not helping my speed.

Eventually, the water became cold and my body clean. I had no further excuse to stay in the tub. I reluctantly stood. The splashing water summoned Anna who raced over with my robe. Her smile, once again, graced her face.

"Besides the tour, is there anything else for today?" I asked as we walked to the vanity.

Anna held my damp hair and softly stroked it. "Nothing too demanding. The king has invited you to dine with him tonight, but he understands if you decline. A tour can be a tiring thing."

My brow raised in suspicion. The one inviting me to dine should be Alexander, so we may strengthen the alliance, not King Titus.

"Will Alexander be joining?" I asked, assuming it was a *family* affair.

Anna froze. Her gulp was audible. "Well, the prince set off for a hunt this morning."

My eyes flashed to Anna's through the mirror. Hunts could range from a day to weeks, depending on how far the animal got or how greatly someone wanted to avoid their *problems*.

"How long?"

"A week," Anna mumbled. My eyes lowered to the ground.

A week. He had left so soon. Before the sun had risen.

His avoiding eyes from last night flashed in my mind.

He had no intention of spending more time with me than necessary. But he had been kind during the feast; the fruit, the plates. Was his kindness a farce so he may see the true extent of my ignorance, so that he may find amusement in it, so he could suppress the grief that consumed him?

My body heated at the thought. The thought that he could find joy in belittling someone but a part of me understood. He needed to grieve; everything had been stolen from him but to be gone for a week after we just wed. This would make the treaty look weak. The other kingdoms wouldn't take peace meetings with Modare easily. It would seem as though Isara didn't honor our side of the treaty, giving Modare an excuse to attack.

Maybe that was their plan all along.

The plans of the treaty had been made public months ago. Some kingdoms, by my father's request, had already met with Modare and created their own treaties.

To my knowledge, it was only a handful of kingdoms, but it was the ones that were the biggest threat to Modare. Depending on what those treaties entailed, Modare may not have the need for any more peace meetings, thus, no longer a need for Isara.

They simply needed to pretend they were trying to honor the treaty till it was beneficial for them to turn against us.

Neither King Titus nor Alexander could be trusted.

CHAPTER 16

My feet ached by the time we reached The Garden for afternoon tea. Anna had shown me every inch of the castle, well, every inch that was a respectable place for a princess to roam; from the library to the ballroom, then several sitting rooms where ladies of the court often gathered for tea.

Everything had been mesmerizing, even the simplest objects. The curtains were made with silk from across the seas. The metal of the candelabras were mined from the highest mountains that were once thought unreachable. Never had I seen such beautiful, rare things, even in Isara.

"Please, have a seat, Princess Estelle." Anna pulled one of the two seats out from the cream table underneath a blue canopy laced with gold ribbon.

I sat, licking my lips as I examined the beautiful tiny cakes and sandwiches that decorated a three-tiered platter.

"I hope everything is to your liking." I nodded to Anna, who, somehow, stood strongly on her feet. She beamed. "Then, with your permission, I shall take my leave." I glanced at her in confusion. "Just for an hour or two, for lunch. Philip and Eric will wait on you until then, with your approval, of course." Her words rushed out as the worry that she had insulted me consumed her.

I blushed, with the lack of company I had become dependent on Anna to fill the quiet void. I wasn't ready for her to leave me. I stared at the mountain of treats. There was enough for three or more people.

"Would you like to join me instead?"

She stepped back. Her eyes were wide.

"Eric or Philip, please fetch another set of plates," I ordered, refusing to take no as an answer.

Both men looked at one another in surprise before the blonde one set off to fetch the set.

I knew the request was a bit absurd, but there was no one to judge, as the nobles were still weary from last night. And though it went against decorum, the rules I had been taught, I needed the company.

It was selfish to take Anna's free time, but I also needed to get closer to her. I needed to find out how to help her with this transition, her grief for Astra.

Anna stood still, puzzled.

"Come. This is more than enough food. It will just go to waste unless you help me."

Anna, seeing the determination in my face, curtsied and sat down. "Thank you, Princess Estelle."

As she sat, the blonde-haired servant placed a teacup, plate, and spoon in front of Anna.

"Thank you, Philip." He gave a swift nod, not sure how to wait on his fellow servant.

Anna stared at the treats, her mouth salivating as mine did. I moved a couple sandwiches to my plate before grabbing one and taking a petite bite of it. Anna did the same. We chewed and swallowed, our lips turning up in a smile at the delicious flavors.

"Such a simple sandwich and yet I feel like I am at a feast."

Anna laughed, licking her fingers. "Greta outdoes herself every day."

"Greta?" I repeated, the name foreign to me.

"The castle's cook. She's spectacular. She can cook anything with a flick of her wrist."

I smiled as she grabbed another sandwich, her rambling continuing, her growing comfortability, apparent.

I glanced at Philip and Eric who aloofly starred in our direction. If we talked in a whisper, they would not hear us.

"Anna." Her eyes widened as she slid the last bit of sandwich into her mouth. "Your accent, is it from Astra?"

Anna dabbed her mouth with a white napkin trimmed with blue. "Yes, Your Highness. You have a good ear." She slid the napkin away from her mouth, revealing a worried expression.

I grabbed her hand that rested on the table, offering her my strength. She should not need to fear her origin.

"Anna, I'm sorry about your home. I visited it often. It was a beautiful country."

She gave a brief smile before sliding her hand back into her lap, her eyes following it. "Indeed, it was."

She was so shy, so quiet. I needed her to know she could trust me.

"Anna, I'm sorry it fell. Isara, we should have been there."

Anna's wide eyes met mine in horror.

"Anna?"

"Your Highness, please, I—" I titled my head in confusion as she struggled with her words. "You shouldn't talk like that. You're a *Modarian Princess.*"

I offered her a smile. Breaking down her walls would be harder than I thought. I needed to make bold moves to earn her trust.

"Anna, I do not wish to be here, same as you. Let us be allies against this tyrant king, this conquering kingdom."

Her pupils dilated, her lips parted, and her chest stilled.

"Tyrant king?" she stammered out.

"Yes." I looked back at the men, making sure they weren't watching. "King Titus."

"Princess Estelle." She held her hand over her heart as if she were finally summoning the courage she had suppressed for only the gods knew how long. She trusted me. "Don't—don't speak of King Titus like that."

I shrunk into my body, confused at her protest. "There's nothing to be afraid of Anna. I'll protect you."

Her lips pursed into a hard line. "There's nothing to protect me from. Everything that was a terror has already been destroyed."

Her eyes held mine with such passion it was clear she wasn't sputtering lies out of fear. This is what she truly believed.

"King Titus, he is not the most charming king, but he is a king of the people. The lies spread about him were from the cowardly nobles of Astra and Ula. They will do anything to get their land back, start any war."

I stared at her in disbelief. I had met the king and queen of both kingdoms when I was little. They were kind, their people happy, and there had been a festival every time I visited.

"Anna." I reached for her. "You've been here far too long. They've manipulated your mind."

Anna violently shook her head. "Your Highness, I say this with only respect and with the hope you do not accidentally offend someone who matters, but you don't know what you're talking about. Astra—Astra needed to be taken."

I jolted up. The treachery in her words was too immense. She had betrayed her kingdom, her king, and queen—Isara's friends.

Anna was my last hope of having someone here, someone to trust. If she betrayed her *happy* kingdom like this, she would do the same to me.

I was completely alone.

I stormed off.

"Princess Estelle, please, let me escort you back."

I turned on the brink of tears. "Do not follow me." Anna's shoulders curved inward. "Only come to my room to inform me when I am needed and to bring me my meals. I wish to be alone."

Anna did not speak as she nodded.

CHAPTER 17

Lord Griffith,

By now you have, no doubt, heard about the change of grooms. I do not know if you have heard the reason for this change. If you haven't, I am sure you will know soon, but if you have…I am sorry. It was a moment of weakness that will haunt me till the end of my days. I only hope that you and my father can forgive me.

I have written to my father as well. The letter was sent yesterday. I fear he will not respond, the same fear I have with you. I pray to the gods that you both can find enough forgiveness in your hearts to respond, but if not, know that I am taking your last pieces of advice to heart and will stick to them. I will make Isara proud.

After you left and I met King Titus I got a glance of their army. It is vastly larger than Isara's. I was in awe when I laid eyes upon it, a feeling I am in a constant state of. My room seems to be the only place I can relax.

I face the Rose Garden, one of two gardens. It is wonderfully placed as it is positioned at the back of the palace, perfect from the prying eyes of anyone who arrives. It is, thankfully, a decent distance from the training grounds. I can finally take midday naps without hearing grunting and the loud clanging of swords.

I have been eating my meals in my room as the prince has gone away on a hunting trip. My maid should be here soon. I shall write again after I explore the castle more, perhaps then my letters will be more entertaining.

Your Friend,
Princess Estelle

CHAPTER 18

I t had been a week since I sent my letters. By now, they should have reached my father and Griffith, filling me with anxiety. I was unsure if they would even write back or if Griffith would recognize the small map I had drawn with my words.

I had tried my best to share as much information regarding the castle as possible without being too obvious, in case Modare was monitoring my letters. Still, I didn't know if it would be blatant enough to Griffith's eyes or be too apparent. Part of me hoped it was the latter, at least then I could feign innocence that I was too naïve to spy, that this was not a role of a princess. If it was the former, I would be useless to Isara.

I stretched out on the chaise, taking a deep breath, letting the rays of sunlight warm my body. Griffith would have said I looked like a kitten, made fun of me, scolded me on my improperness. I smiled at the thought. A foreign reaction to me nowadays.

After the grievous incident with Anna, I had shut myself in. I never left my room. I declined the numerous invitations from the ladies of the court and barely talked to Anna when she delivered my meals.

It was lonely, but I was in a court of lies and treachery. I didn't know how to handle it, not without Griffith's guidance. Something I would never receive again if his anger, his disappointment got the better of him. Feelings he deserved to have.

The sound of wood hitting porcelain came from the breakfast table.

I looked out the window to see the sun rising. Anna had brought me my morning meal. A normal occurrence. However, this time she hadn't knocked. Or perhaps I hadn't heard her, and she had quietly entered assuming I was still asleep.

I stilled my body, debating if I should let her know that I was awake. It wouldn't matter though. I still had no desire to speak to her or anyone. At least with this, we'd avoid the forced salutations.

The clacking ceased. I waited for her footsteps, but none came. We sat there in silence for a minute. My heartbeat grew faster.

What was she doing?

I sprang up, unable to sit in the quiet any longer.

"If you have a need for me, Anna, then quickly say it and be gone," I commanded with a whine of irritation.

My body froze, and my pupils dilated as a pair of silver, striking eyes met mine.

"Very rude way to talk to someone, even if you did think they were a servant."

There he was, slouching in the chair, his feet resting on the table, a cup of rose tea in his hand.

"Alexander," I stammered out, straightening my back, completely unaware of his return.

"Come," he ordered, pouring some tea into a second cup.

I stood, knowing it wasn't a request.

At my approach he returned his feet to the ground, his eyes locked on me.

I sat in the chair across from him, avoiding his gaze as I stroked my braid, trying to tame the flyaway hairs.

"Eat." He pushed a plate of eggs, smoked ham, and bread toward me. I grabbed at my stomach, lowering my eyes to see the golden buttons glistening on his immaculate dark blue tunic. I hugged my robe tighter, trying to conceal the wrinkled nightgown I had worn for the past two days.

I peered down at the food, the sight of it twisting my stomach, the smell causing my nose to wrinkle. It had been like this all week, my body rejecting the food placed before me, it was no surprise that it would do the same today. In fact, with Alexander's surprise visit, I was certain the feeling would be stronger.

The past week I had been debating, debating if Al was real or fake. I had come up with so many questions, but now that he was in front of me, I could not form the words. I could not tell if I was angry or sad, if I wanted him to leave or to stay. But

I did know, by Alexander's unflattering eyes, that whatever I wanted, I would not receive till I obeyed his order.

I picked up the ham and nibbled on it. To my surprise the saltiness had been lessened, the juices calmed as if Greta was asked to subdue the flavors, but still, I ate slowly, scared that nausea may overcome me. I could have sworn I heard Alexander sigh with relief as I finished the slice in my hand and reached for a second one, but when I looked up his gaze had fallen to a second plate I had failed to notice.

I watched him eat, the silence between us deafening. "I didn't know you were back," I mumbled, unable to take any more of it.

"I arrived ten minutes ago," he replied, not looking up.

I swallowed involuntarily, lodging a piece of meat in my throat. I violently coughed as I hastily drank my tea, thankful it had cooled just enough to not burn as it slid down my throat. Alexander offered me a napkin with worried eyes.

"Ten minutes ago?" He nodded "And—and you came here? Didn't you want to rest or clean yourself after the travels?"

Alexander patted his lips with a cloth. "Are you insinuating that I smell or look disheveled?"

I shook my head. He was perfect, the evidence of travel absent. He had probably stopped at an inn the night before to rest. "No, it's just—" Alexander's brows rose. "The first thing you did, when you came back, was visit *me*?"

"Yes, a husband should check on his wife after being gone."

His wife. The words, the ownership rolled off his tongue effortlessly, nonchalantly as if he hadn't abandoned me. It was then I knew what I wanted, how I felt.

"I assure you, I am completely fine despite your absence." I reached for a slice of an apple, my volume rising as I forgot my role as the obeying wife a princess should be.

"That's not what I've heard," he stated, refilling my teacup.

He was keeping tabs on me. I raised my chin, rolled back my shoulders, and glared.

Alexander continued in a monotonous voice, unaffected by my attempted hostility, "Anna told me you haven't come out of your room since your little tiff. That you've barely eaten anything."

My hair stood on end.

If Anna had informed Alexander what I said about King Titus, Modare, or that I had wished Isara would have aided Astra—those words of treason, treaty or not, would give them grounds to punish me without repercussions.

My hand trembled, color draining from my face. There was nowhere to run, no one I could turn to for help.

"Estelle, I understand your reservations. I do. But talking about how you don't want to be here—it will just make the transition, the treaty harder."

I dug my nails into my hand, hoping the pain would stop the trembling.

"I just want my kingdom to be safe."

"It will be, but the treaty needs to be strong, and for that, we need to trust one another."

Alexander reached for my hand. I jolted up, my nerves, my rage getting the better of me.

"*Trust?* How do you expect me to trust that brother of yours, the king? And how will he trust me? He'll never trust me after what I told Anna."

Silence.

"What you told Anna?" He lifted his brow.

My heart nearly stopped beating. Alexander didn't know the full extent of Anna and mine's conservation. She had protected me.

Alexander continued his inquisitive stare. His eyes glued to mine, watching my panic grow.

What was I to say? I didn't know what Anna had told him. If our stories didn't align, one of us would be punished.

My legs shook as my strength depleted.

I keep messing up. I was right to have locked myself away this week.

Just as my knees were about to buckle, Alexander let out a sigh and broke eye contact.

"All Anna told me is that you had a fit about not wanting to be here, that you had locked yourself away, and you wouldn't talk to anyone. She only came to me because of her growing concern for you."

Tears filled my eyes. I still didn't understand why Anna sided with Modare, but she had saved me. I was too quick to judge her.

"If there was anything else, that is between you two, but be careful from now on. If the wrong words were to be heard, if it were made too public, Titus would have to act on it. Regardless of if he wanted to or not." Alexander gestured to the chair. "Sit, calm yourself."

I stared blankly at Alexander, processing his words.

"Estelle," he growled, "sit before you fall."

I wobbled back to my chair; thankful my knees didn't give out, thankful for Alexander's unpredictable kindness.

"We want this treaty to work as much as you. We need to stand as a united front." He sipped his tea calmly. "You can no longer hide away."

I felt my strength return as my blood began to boil.

"Hide away? That's rich coming from you," I sneered.

"I wasn't supposed to wed last week, next month or even this year, Estelle. You had months to prepare. I needed time away to get in the right mindset." He paused, pivoting his eyes to the ground, his voice calm. "I needed time to get over her."

Over her? The red-haired girl?

I chuckled to myself. He had laid with me before our marriage while still in love with her. That was proof that his heart was black enough to stay in the luxuries of the castle after the marriage to protect the treaty. He was just making excuses.

"You seemed over her that night in the tavern."

"You asked me to bed you." His voice was strained as if he was holding back.

"I did, didn't I? But I didn't ask you to pretend to enjoy it. You seemed quite enthralled by the activity all on your own." Alexander stared at me with cold eyes. "I would wager that you took me to bed, not for my own goals, but simply because you are a selfish prince who doesn't understand that there are consequences for his actions. You don't understand how your leaving made us look, the treaty look, how taking me to bed would betray your so-called love. You act like you were the one who was wronged, not her."

Alexander jolted up, gripping the sides of the table effectively shaking it. "Don't talk about things you know nothing about," he barked.

A shiver went down my spine as my body froze, my breathing hitched for a moment, but anger clouded the common sense that screamed for me to stop my assault.

"You cannot bear to be faced with the truth, and you plan to silence me by instilling fear with your animalistic behavior? You're just like your tyrant brother of a king."

Alexander slowly released the table with a heavy sigh and begrudgingly walked to the door. "He's not the tyrant you make him out to be, and neither am I."

I remained quiet as he made his exit.

CHAPTER 19

That night, Anna did not come and help me with my bath. A maid I had never met came instead. She was quick with the job and barely spoke, which I appreciated as I was still shaken from Alexander's visit. I had let my anger get the best of me. I had said hurtful words and would, no doubt, be punished for them.

Despite this, I couldn't help but wonder where Anna was. I wanted to see her, to apologize, to thank her. I had half a mind to seek her out, but with night's rapid approach, it was best to leave her be until morning.

Even if she rallied behind Modare, she had kept my thoughts a secret. Anna could be someone I trusted, not entirely, but enough that I could call her a friend in this foreign kingdom.

My thoughts weren't just filled with Anna though. Alexander's last sentence echoed in my mind. *He's not the tyrant the rumors make him out to be.*

Both Anna and Alexander had said the same thing. Could it be true? No, he was brash, wine filled when I met him. He had been ready to fight. Even the servants and guards were on edge.

Anna had clearly been brainwashed, stuck here too long. And Alexander had been raised to be loyal to King Titus since birth. He would always back him despite the truth.

Yet, Alexander had spared me, shown me kindness after I alluded to speaking ill about King Titus. If he was completely loyal to him, he would have taken my treasonous words to his brother immediately, let the king decide on how to act and yet he didn't.

Was there a part of him that was really Al? Or was this an act to win me over so they could easily use me as a pawn later? Fill me with sweet lies about them wanting peace. Make me lower my guard, reveal things about Isara or other kingdoms so the conquering would be easier.

It was a sound strategy.

Whatever it was, I wouldn't trust him or King Titus. I would be civil, show my face, attempt friendship, but I would still gather information.

Two can play the game.

CHAPTER 20

The door slammed open, waking me from my deep slumber. I sat up waiting for my blurry vision to clear. Alexander marched toward me, wrapped in a pitch-black cloak, void of any shade of blue.

My body tensed as he threw a bundle of tattered clothes at me.

"Get dressed."

I picked up the pieces one by one—a cream blouse, a black corset, and a dulled red skirt. *Peasant clothing.*

"Where are we going?" I stammered out, as Alexander checked the hall.

He turned toward me. "You'll see when we get there."

His eyes held mine, waiting for me to get up. Tension filled the air. I had pushed him last night and now he was sneaking me out in disguise. My gut twisted, told me to run, to get away. But I knew better than to go against him in the castle, where everyone would be on his side, so I obeyed.

I hid behind the changing screen, pulling the fabrics on. Frantically, I looked around the screen for anything that I could use to defend myself if the need should arise. There was nothing besides a pile of wedding presents.

Wedding presents!

The dagger gifted to me by Lord Telin, it could be of use. I eyed the pile, searching for the slender box.

"Can you please be a little faster?" Alexander aggressively whispered.

"Getting dressed, for a lady, is no easy feat."

I stumbled through the gifts as Alexander groaned.

There it is!

I opened a silver slender box, revealing the beautiful dagger.

Now, where to hide it?

My hands stumbled over my body, patting the clothes I wore, looking for a place for the weapon. Everywhere I thought of would be too obvious or allow the blade to fall with the slightest jostle. I had far too little experience with weaponry for this. I rested my hand on my thigh, feeling the trimmings of my stocking. My eyes widened.

I lifted my skirts and pinched the top of my stocking pulling it away from my flesh and slid the dagger in. The metal sheath was cold against my skin. I dropped my skirts and shook my leg. The dagger did not fall nor even move. It was perfect.

I flattened down my skirts before emerging from the screen.

"About time." Alexander tossed me a cloak that was twin to his. "Keep the hood on even as we walk through the palace."

I nodded, barely having time to fasten the cloak and shroud my face with the hood before Alexander took my hand and dragged me down the dark corridor.

Alexander pulled me through the hall, careful not to make a sound, to be seen. He paused at every corner, checking to see if anyone walked the halls before continuing. There was no one, save the occasional servant readying to wake the castle. Upon hearing their footsteps, Alexander would press me into a corner and cover my mouth. He made sure any sound from me, voluntary or not, would be muted.

We continued like this till we reached the kitchens on the first floor. He held a finger over his mouth as he cracked open the door.

The clanging of pots echoed in the empty hall, followed by Greta barking orders.

"Almost there," he whispered to himself with a soft smile, like this was some sort of game.

We sat in the hall watching servants pass through the kitchen, the sun slowly entering from the windows. There were several moments in which the path to the door was clear and yet we didn't move. I eyed Alexander, wondering what he was waiting for. As I turned, I noticed he was counting.

"…eight, nine, ten." The count increased as a servant passed.

He gripped my hand tighter. "Be quick," he ordered, as he hauled me to another door.

I looked to and fro for any passing servants. There were none, save the ones in the kitchen that were too busy to notice us.

Alexander had memorized his own servant's paths, their routines.

Why?

He snuck out often enough to memorize this information. He was hiding something, something King Titus didn't like.

Alexander pushed the door open, quickly letting it shut behind us, knowing the clanging of pots would hide the sound.

"It should be smooth sailing from here," he declared, a victorious smile growing on his face as he noticed my deep breaths.

Alexander walked forward, releasing my hand. He cocked his head, gesturing for me to follow. My nose crinkled. He was letting me decide if I kept going after *all* that work.

I didn't understand.

I glanced back at the castle. Just a couple steps and I'd be safe from whatever Alexander was leading me to.

Anyone sane would have turned back, and perhaps it was the week of being alone, the need for someone, something to change, or his irritating smile, but I found myself moving forward with curiosity.

We followed a small dirt path passing several racks filled with swords, javelins, shields, and other weapons I didn't know the names of. I carefully examined every training tool we passed, taking note of what they had more of, hoping to correctly guess their weapon of choice so I could later inform Griffith.

We passed a group of dummies made of dried hay. Next to them was a small building with several windows, perhaps a stable. I took it all in till we reached a massive iron gate.

I leaned my head back, trying to spot any guards at the top.

"The shift change is happening." I looked to Alexander who was next to a small door, key in hand.

I raised a brow. If timed right, anyone could pass through without detection—perfect information to send to Griffith.

The door creaked open as Alexander opened it halfway. He motioned for me to follow before locking it closed.

"Not much further now."

He walked toward the woods, far from the castle walls. Shivers ran down my spine.

Whatever stupid feeling that made me follow had departed. Only fear and embarrassment from my foolish decision were left.

Maybe that's why he let me choose.

It was too late to turn back now. I was trapped out of the palace, the only way back in was lying in Alexander's pocket.

I gripped the dagger through my dress, assuring myself it was still there before following.

I stayed five steps behind him, making sure whatever happened I had time to react.

My feet turned to lead as I stared into the darkness at the forest's edge. Alexander glanced over his shoulder, making sure I was still close.

"Don't run now," he ordered, a hint of humor in his voice before disappearing into the woods.

I didn't dare follow, too scared of the fate that waited for me because of my stupidity.

I waited for him to call me, to force me into the woods, but no sound came except for a soft neigh.

Alexander emerged from the forest on a beautiful black stallion. His hooves dented the earth with each step, his ebony mane dancing in the wind. I reached out to stroke his snout but was rejected by the beast who let out an annoyed neigh and stomped his hooves in warning.

"Shadow isn't a fan of new people." Alexander chuckled to himself as he lowered his hand to me. "But he'll still let you ride him, with my permission."

I glanced at Alexander's hand then his smile.

What game was he playing?

He could've easily killed me by now, there were so many chances. Why wait any longer? Perhaps he found pleasure in playing with me, messing with my emotions as I did to him last night. I wasn't certain. But I knew I couldn't be caught out of the palace walls alone.

I grabbed Alexander's hand letting him pull me up behind him, wrapping my arms around his waist. The closest we'd physically been since the tavern.

"Will you tell me where we are going now?"

"Just hold on," he playfully ordered as he softly kicked Shadow's sides.

I gripped tighter as Shadow took off. The wind whipped through my hair as our surroundings became a blur. It was a crime not to enjoy this, but my nerves were still there. They poked my brain, reminding me to be on my guard as I still had no inkling as to what was happening. But the feeling was too enticing. I closed my eyes, resting my head on Alexander's back. Weirdly, it felt comforting, safe.

"Here we are."

I opened my eyes to see the edge of a bustling town.

"Where are we?"

Alexander, already dismounted, grabbed my waist and lifted me off Shadow. My legs wobbled, sore from the long ride.

"We're about two hours from the castle," Alexander answered, one hand remaining on my hips, the other hand on the reins.

"Two hours!" I spun around as if I could see the distance we traveled.

"Welcome to Asla, formerly known as The Middle."

"The Middle?" I repeated back, the words lost to me.

I turned back to Alexander who was already walking toward the town.

"Alexander," I called, running after him, the sound of faint music reaching my ears.

Alexander handed Shadow's reins to a stable boy, dropping a generous amount of silver coins into his hand.

"I told you to wait," I wheezed as I clutched Alexander's sleeve, hoping that would keep him stationary.

"I did. I waited for you right here," he chimed with his signature devilish grin.

"Why exactly are we here?" I gulped, composing myself.

Alexander pulled his sleeve from my hand. "There's an ale that I've been wanting to try."

"Pardon?" I exasperated. "You brought me here for an ale?"

"And music." He shrugged, gesturing toward the outdoor tavern.

My lips parted. "You aren't going to murder me?"

Alexander jerked his head to me, forehead wrinkled in confusion. "Murder? Gods, Estelle! You think so lowly of us."

"With last night's talk, it made sense. Then this morning with you sneaking me out without anyone knowing—it's a perfect way to get rid of me in secret."

Alexander came closer. "I gave you so many opportunities to leave though, yet you still followed."

I avoided his inquisitive gaze. "I was too scared to run."

Alexander grabbed my chin, turning my face to him, allowing him to study my eyes. "No. A part of you trusts me. Even if you can't admit it to me or yourself." He stood straight, releasing me. "This might work after all," he whispered to himself before strutting off.

The barkeep, recognizing Alexander, brought a plate full of cheese and fruits followed by the ale Alexander had dragged us here for without so much as a request.

"It's good to see you again! It's been a while, old friend."

"It's good to be back." Alexander grasped the barkeep's forearm.

"I see you've brought a *lady* friend." The barkeep tipped his hat to me. I smiled in return. "Idin at your service ma'am."

"I had to show her the best ale in all of Modare."

"You flatter me too much."

"I only speak the truth."

Idin smiled at Alexander, placing his hand on his chest, giving a slight bow before departing.

"You come here often?"

Alexander took a swig of his ale, smiling at the taste.

"As often as I can," he replied, admiring the trio on stage as they played their merry song, his eyes sparkling.

I took a sip of the ale, the taste making my lips pucker. I placed the wooden cup down, staring at the contents. This was hardly worth the effort of this morning.

My eyes wandered, looking for something special—anything that made this town different from others. There was an abundance of happiness and joyful music, but that could be seen anywhere. It just had to be created.

"I come here when the politics, the battles get to be too much." I turned to Alexander, his eyes still on the performers. "To remind myself that it's all worth it, that to give them peace I must go through those hardships."

I stared at him, puzzled.

"That's why you were looking around, weren't you? To figure out why I come."

I nodded.

Alexander leaned in, speaking as soft as he could. "You know of the tension between Astra and Ula? Their never-ending battles?"

I nodded. It was basic knowledge known to all the kingdoms.

"This town sat on the border of them, it was supposed to be a gray area for those who didn't want to partake in their feud."

My brows furrowed together as I recalled my lessons. *The Middle.* I had a vague memory of it. Both Ula and Astra had agreed to this gray area so that peace could be attempted. I had been told the idea had succeeded by both countries' rulers. They still, of course, had their problems but they were lessened because of *The Middle.*

"That idea only lasted for a short time as more people began to abandon their own countries for The Middle. With both countries' cultures, ideas, and tactics merging, better ideas and crafts formed. It became a coveted land."

Alexander paused as the trio's song ended, waiting for the next one to begin.

"This town was attacked relentlessly. The master was always changing."

I stared at him in disbelief. I had never heard of such things.

"The people were tired of it and soon sent someone to Modare to plead for help."

Alexander stared into my eyes searching for any emotions.

"And that's how the war started." His eyes darkened as if it was just as a terror for him as it had been for Ula and Astra.

Thoughts raced in my head as I recalled all my lessons, my visits with Astra and Ula. There had been no signs, no mention of what Alexander spoke of.

"I know it's hard to believe but it is the truth. Kings and queens can hide so much when they want to, but the truth is always revealed by the kingdom's people. Just ask Anna, she was one who escaped to The Middle."

"Why didn't you tell anyone? Why did you let the other kingdoms assume you were just power hungry?" I questioned, my voice stale.

Alexander ran his thumb over the handle of his ale. "We've been out of contact far too long. No one would've believed us. We'd be marked as liars, peace treaties would've been harder to achieve." Alexander took a sip of his ale. "Sometimes it's better to be feared and made the villain."

Alexander leaned back in his chair, watching my eyes waiting for my reaction.

I looked around, listened to the voices, some were from Astra others Ula. The people were happily talking, laughing, and dancing. A sight I never thought possible.

Perhaps what Alexander and Anna were saying was true.

"So, you don't want to take over the other kingdoms?"

"No. We will fight who we must, to protect our people, but we do not wish for more power or land." Alexander leaned on the table, his face inches from mine. "That is why this treaty is just as important to you as it is to us. We do not want any more bloodshed."

I gripped the handle of my mug as his honest eyes burrowed into my soul. I bit my lip, debating all that I had seen, debating if this was a trick.

If it was, they could have easily brought me in a carriage, there wouldn't have been a need to sneak me out. And the controversy that this truth exposed, it would cause the other kingdoms to question their trust in Modare, Astra, and Ula. Everyone would have to choose a side, making Modare vulnerable. Telling me this, if this was a trick, seemed counterproductive.

I took a deep breath before speaking, hopeful this wasn't another foolish choice, but I wanted to believe it. "Don't make me regret trusting your story."

Alexander sighed with relief, his shoulders rolling back as the tension left them.

"Thank you."

"I trust the story. Not you, not completely."

He smirked, raising his glass to mine. "You will, eventually."

His happiness was so contagious. I couldn't help but return the smile as I clinked my glass with his.

I really did trust his story. I trusted Anna's words. I trusted the sight I saw before me. But I still needed to be wary.

CHAPTER 21

It was dusk by the time we got back to the castle. The gate we had used was now guarded by four soldiers. There was no hope in sneaking back in. Though it would have been meaningless as the lack of our presence in the castle had been noticed.

"Here we go," Alexander whispered behind me as he saw Titus emerge from the castle, storming toward the gate.

Alexander dismounted, helping me down, as a stableboy took Shadow's reins.

"I gave you explicit orders," Titus growled.

"I know." Alexander raised his hands up in the air. "But we got quite a bit of bonding done."

"I would have you whipped if it didn't bring shame upon our family."

Alexander grabbed Titus's shoulder. "She believes us."

Titus fell silent, his eyes freezing on me. His breath almost halted. I gave a slight nod, silently telling him what Alexander said was true, breaking Titus's shock, his disbelief.

"Escort her to her room then come see me. Regardless of your victories you still need a scolding."

Alexander gave a cheeky smile. "Of course, my king."

"He's as pleasant as always."

Alexander laughed as we climbed the stairs. "Well, no one reacts well to secrets being exposed, particularly to a princess who could easily share them. And especially when the person sharing the secrets was told explicitly not to."

My feet halted, the ceased pitter patter of them summoning Alexander's eyes. He had gone against his brother; an action I did not think he was capable of. I raised a brow.

"You wouldn't have changed your attitude otherwise, and it was becoming quite taxing."

I rolled my eyes; he hadn't even spent time with me, with my *taxing attitude.* But I suppose he had heard about it from Anna. Still, what he did was dangerous. "But revealing something like that, you said it yourself, it's a dangerous truth."

"A truth I decided to trust you with. Don't disappoint me."

Alexander escorted me the rest of the way in silence.

"Here you are."

Alexander gave a shallow bow and headed to wherever Titus waited, completely trusting that I wouldn't use this newfound truth against them.

He was right, there were some lines I wouldn't cross. I would give Griffith other information.

CHAPTER 22

I woke up, the sun at the peak of the sky. I stretched my body, feeling the soreness of yesterday's ride, wondering why the maids had not yet woken me.

I stood from my bed, legs shaking, reaching for the rope to summon a servant. Instead, I found a note tied to it.

I told the maids to let you sleep in. After yesterday's activities, you deserve it.

Bells aren't working. You'll have to tell someone in the kitchen you're hungry.

-Alexander

I rubbed my temple, wondering when Alexander had come in. *How had I not awoken?* Everyone was so quiet and sneaky here.

I inhaled deeply as my stomach growled for food. The smell of sweet breads and mutton filled the air.

The kitchen was void of Greta's yelling, unlike yesterday morning. There was little movement as everyone was en-thralled with their own tasks. One maid sat at a table and hemmed while another picked leaves off a stem and then there was Greta, calmly stirring a pot.

I took a step in, waiting for anyone to notice me.

Nothing.

I wasn't sure what to do. Announce myself? Stand in silence till someone looked up? That would take a while. I looked down at my shoes, contemplating. A cough would do the trick.

"Oh, Princess Estelle."

That sweet voice. Anna.

She stood, with puzzled eyes, next to the doorway holding a basket full of cheese, fruit, and steaming bread.

"Is there something we can help you with? We didn't hear the bells go off," Greta asked in her high-pitched, plump voice. Her eyes on me and whisk in hand.

"I thought the bells weren't working today."

"Not working! Why I never—they certainly are. These bells are how I know if anyone is hungry and there won't ever be a hungry person in this castle while I'm in charge of the kitchens." Greta pointed her whisk at the back wall, lined with chimes, flinging some soup onto the poor maids at the table.

Alexander, what was he up to?

I rubbed my neck as Greta's voice rose while she continued her speech on the importance of sustenance.

Oh, how I wish she'd stop, but I couldn't open my mouth to interrupt her. Something in her tone and mannerisms commanded respect, no matter how high your status. Never before had someone beneath my station had this effect on me or treated me as such.

"Greta, I'm sure *Princess* Estelle just misunderstood."

Greta scowled at Anna. "Well, misunderstanding or not, she now understands about the bells." Greta handed her whisk to the maid who was hemming, cocking her head to the pot. "I have a delivery to check on. Anna, make sure the princess is taken care of."

Greta gave a clumsy curtsy before heading through a hallway off to the side.

"Sorry about that, Your Highness. Greta is very...passionate sometimes." The maids nodded in agreement. "How can I be of service?"

I frowned at the bluntness of her question. I had hoped for a little more conversation after the awkwardness of Greta.

"Or if you need someone else, I could fetch them?"

Someone else?

I was so stupid.

Our fight. This week I had ignored her. How could I forget?

I needed to make things right.

"Oh, I was hungry is all."

But how do I make things right?

"Would you like anything in particular? I can have it up as soon as I deliver this basket to the training grounds for Prince Alexander."

"No, nothing really, just my usual."

Anna curtsied, offering a small smile, ready to depart. However, as she rose, her right leg quivered, sending her center of gravity forward.

The two maids threw their arms out, barely catching her in time.

"Anna," I called out, the concern in my voice evident.

I stepped forward helping her to a chair.

"Just a sprained ankle is all."

Was this why she was gone for the past two days?

"Anna, you shouldn't be walking on it. Have you seen a physician? We must send for one at once."

Anna shook her head. "I have. Walking in increments is supposed to help the healing. I'll take a break once I finish delivering this and getting you your breakfast."

Here was my chance.

"Absolutely not. You'll take a break now. I'll deliver this." I gestured to the basket.

The two maids looked at one another in deep concern.

"I can't possibly let you do that, Your Highness."

Anna stood, making a grab for the basket, but I was quicker.

"Then you will let me accompany you in case your ankle decides to give out."

Anna opened her mouth to rebuttal, but she was too slow as I made my way to the backdoor.

She followed with a sigh and a suppressed smile.

The training grounds reeked of sweat, as men wrestled one another and others swung their sharp steel.

"This really is no place for a princess," Anna whispered.

"So I've been told all my life, but right now, I am just a woman helping a friend."

Anna shook her head, smiling. A good sign she was getting comfortable around me again.

"Anna." I chewed on the inside of my cheek. "I wanted to apologize."

Her feet slowed as she turned to me, wide-eyed.

"Alexander, he told me about The Middle—Asla. He showed me." I stopped walking, completely, turning so my body faced her squarely. "It is the opposite of everything I know. But seeing it—"

Anna stared at the ground. Considering her next words. "We were tired of the kings' feuds. They acted more for themselves and not for the happiness of the people."

I nodded at the truth I was blind to when I was a Princess of Isara.

"I know. I understand that now."

"Thank you."

I gave her a nod as we returned to our walk.

Our relationship wasn't the same, but it was on the path of healing.

We approached the edge of the training grounds where the stables and a fighting ring sat.

Alexander stood, sword in hand, a shield in the other. His white blouse was drenched in sweat and clung to his body. Swiftly, he raised his shield as a morning star came overhead, the clang sending shivers down my spine as sparks flew.

The hit should have knocked Alexander down, but to my surprise, he let out a nerve-racking battle cry. He threw his body into each swing until he knocked his opponent out of the ring.

Alexander stood ferociously over the man as both caught their breath.

"Estelle."

I gasped for air at the sound of my name. At some point, I had forgotten to breathe.

"What are you doing out here?"

"I…I…" My brain went numb as I stared at his sheer, wet blouse. Every crevice of his body was fully on display.

"The princess insisted on escorting me," Anna explained, passing the basket to Alexander.

"I see. I suppose yesterday wasn't enough for you." I raised a brow. "Perhaps I should have visited you after my meeting with Titus." His mouth turned up in that annoying smirk.

I scoffed. He was back to being the man I met at the tavern, full of himself and ready to tease.

"I did it for Anna's sake," I sneered, refusing to fall prey to his flirtish attitude.

"It still bothers you? You should have Aeson check it again."

My sneer softened in surprise at Alexander's concern over a servant that was not directly his own.

"It only hurts a bit. I should be fine soon. I'd hate to burden Aeson with something so trivial."

Alexander eyed the hem of her dress as if he could see through it.

"Take the rest of the day off. Prop it up, take a cool cloth to it, do what you must. I'm sure Princess Estelle can manage on her own and if it continues, see Aeson. That's an order."

Anna blushed at his concern as did I. I didn't expect him to be so *caring*.

"Yes, Prince Alexander, I will, just after I serve Princess Estelle lunch."

Alexander glanced in my direction. I shrugged, letting him know I had already tried.

"Is Samuel's portion also in the basket?"

Anna nodded.

"Samuel will escort you back, and Estelle and I will have a picnic out here."

"Your Highness," Anna protested, but Alexander held up his hand stopping her from continuing.

"I have things to discuss with my wife, and I'm sure Samuel would enjoy eating lunch out of the heat for once."

Alexander turned, waving over a black-haired, slender man.

"Samuel, escort Anna back to the castle. Ensure she rests until night falls. Then you both are free, if you are feeling up to it, to help with nighttime preparations."

"Yes, Prince Alexander." Samuel quickly bowed to Alexander then held out his hand, motioning for Anna to lead the way. "After you, Anna."

Anna gave Alexander and me a brief curtsy before walking away. But as she turned, I couldn't help noticing the soft pink forming on her cheeks.

"Come, Estelle, I'm starving." Alexander motioned toward a patch of grass under an oak tree. Far enough away from the ring and the stables that the clanging of metal wouldn't ring in our ears.

"What was it you needed to talk about?"

Alexander dug into the basket, placing the contents on a cloth.

"Nothing. Just wanted Anna to rest."

I stared at him with wide eyes, my silence pulling his attention away from the basket. He let out a singular laugh as he saw my bewilderment.

"I thought after yesterday you no longer thought us cruel."

My lips parted, annoyed with my own transparency. "It's a mindset that will take a while to change."

Alexander shrugged as he tossed some cheese into his mouth.

I picked up a slice of bread, slowly tearing off pieces and placing them into my mouth. We sat in deafening silence, both of us unsure what to speak about.

I wished things were easier, simpler like it was with Griffith. But our relationship was anything but that. Back at the tavern, I had thought I would never see Alexander again. I was forward, telling him what I wanted, how I felt, and not worrying about the repercussions, the protocol. When I got here I was a whirlwind of emotions—ignoring him, avoiding him, distrusting while also trying to be submissive. Now we were past the shock. Now was the time to solidify the standard of behavior.

I looked at Alexander, wondering if he felt the same and how he planned to act.

Alexander let out a heavy sigh, stripping off his shirt then throwing it over a low hanging tree branch.

My cheeks turned a bright red as he plopped down on the ground, his hands supporting his head.

"Just be yourself." I tensed. There he was, reading my mind again. "You're too stiff, too focused on protocol. We're stuck with each other for life, no sense in pretending around one another. It's already exhausting enough around the other nobles."

I bit my lip. I had followed protocol all my life. The only person I was ever myself around was Griffith.

Griffith

He should have received my letter by now. Maybe even written back if he had chosen to. If he had, the response should arrive in three or four days. That's when I'd know if he still thought of me kindly. I didn't know what I would do if he thought of me otherwise. When I was around him, I felt there was nowhere safer. I could be in his presence and not be expected of anything. We could sit in silence or talk for hours. Either way it was soothing. With Alexander, maybe it was too soon to tell, but with him, I felt nothing similar. The more we talked, the more smart remarks piled up—waiting to be said aloud.

"There is such a thing as trying too hard to relax."

Talking about smart remarks.

I looked down. Alexander had one eye open, the other closed as he tried to block the sun with his hand.

A sharp tongue was not what a princess, let alone a wife to a prince, should show, but I couldn't think of any other response, couldn't calm myself enough to act *properly*. I reached up for his shirt, tossing it down on his chest. "It's rather hard to relax when you're half naked."

Alexander snickered, pulling on the shirt. "You realize you'll have to get used to it."

I hugged my knees tighter.

I know.

He would have to visit me during the night at some point. They weren't power hungry tyrants, but they were still of royal blood, and royalty always needed heirs.

"How long do I have to prepare?" I rested my chin on my knees in case I needed to hide any tears that spilled.

"Prepare?" Alexander asked sleepily.

"Till your next night visit." I kept my eyes focused on the stables, but I could feel Alexander's alert gaze on me.

"You don't have to make it sound so dreadful."

From the corner of my eye, I saw Alexander sit up, rubbing the back of his neck.

"Remember at the tavern?"

I dug my nails into my flesh, ready for him to tell me how good he had made me feel, that I had been the image of ecstasy. But this was different. Back then it was good because it had been my choice. With his expert hands on me now, I'm sure my body would still respond in that manner, but my mind and heart would be screaming.

"I told you that if you ever wanted me to stop, all you had to do was say so. That still applies now." I loosened my grip, eyes bolting to his. "Having heirs is not that important for a secondborn. We can go the rest of our lives and never have to do *that*."

My eyes softened at his words. My lips moved but no sound came as emotions flooded me.

All my life I had been told I was to make heirs, and when that time came, I was to never protest. A thought that had scared me all my life.

I should have been relieved, so many noble women wished to hear Alexander's words, but for me, it was another failure. I did appreciate them, and I wanted to accept them but because of the treaty, I couldn't.

If rumors spread about our lack of trying, the strength of the alliance would be questioned. Isara's words would be deemed unreliable. Modare's peace talk would be less likely to succeed. I had weakened the treaty enough; I would not allow more damage.

"We should. It's our duty." I clenched my legs tighter to me.

Alexander laid back down. "With a reason like that, I don't think I could *rise* to the occasion."

There was silence as he waited for my reaction to his distasteful joke, but I would not, could not, muster any counter for it. I was scared that if we veered from this topic I would not have the courage to speak on it again. Alexander shrugged before continuing.

"I'll pretend with you though. Once a month I'll come *visit* you. I'll stay the whole night, make it more believable, but I won't touch you."

Alexander stared up at me, an eyebrow raised in question.

Most couples, the man would stay for an hour or so, till the act was done. If he stayed the night, that would be an entirely different level of affection. No one would question it. His plan could work.

"How's every first Friday?" I asked, my voice barely audible as I shyly accepted his proposal.

Alexander sat up, pouring wine into our cups.

"As long as you don't get mad when I beat you in cards." He handed the cup to me, the devilish smirk evoking my own playful side.

"I don't think I'll have many opportunities to get mad, but when you do win, I'll try not to."

We clinked our glasses, drinking deeply with a newfound comfortability with one another. But as I listened to Alexander ramble on about bridge, I couldn't help but notice the fluttering feeling in my stomach.

CHAPTER 23

Princess Estelle,

I had heard of the news shortly after leaving the castle, it was the talk of the tavern. It took all my strength not to run back to the castle to ensure you were safe, to ask about the reason for the change. However, I knew if I did it would insult King Titus. It wasn't till I arrived back to Isara that I learned why it happened.

I admit, hearing the news at first sent me into a shock but I do not hold ill feelings toward you. We all make mistakes from time to time. You were in a panic. You didn't know how to properly handle the situation. It is I who should be sorry. I should have been there for you, so you did not need to seek comfort by the means you did.

Your father did not take the news well. I fear it will be a while till he writes back. But I know his love for you has no bounds and he will forgive you soon.

Unfortunately, our allies are more reluctant to talk to King Titus because of the situation. Do not guilt yourself over it, I sense this reluctancy would have happened either way.

I am glad to hear about your view. I can almost envision the castle.

Is the prince treating you well? How do you fill your days?

Your Friend and Loyal Subject,
Lord Griffith

P.S. I hope you find joy in the parcel I have sent along with this letter. I wish it to give you hope in these changing times, that it will remind you that no matter how far away you are some things will never change.

As if seeing the words of forgiveness in the letter wasn't enough, I ripped open the brown paper revealing a tiny jewelry box. My fingers shook as I pulled off the lid.

Tears filled my eyes as I held up the golden gladiolus pendant on a thin gold necklace. A flower that represented hope and strength. The notion was beautiful but that was not why tears fell.

This pendant was the symbol of Griffith's family and had been handed down throughout the generations to those who married the family heir.

We could not be together now, but his heart would always be mine and mine, his. We would find a way through this.

173

CHAPTER 24

I twirled the pendant between my forefinger and thumb as Anna braided my hair in preparation for tonight. Alexander's first night visit since we talked in the training grounds.

Though he told me he wouldn't touch me, my heart felt as though it might burst. We'd still be trapped with each other till morning, forced to talk or sit in silence till the sun rose. I still didn't know how to act. I wanted to be a proper wife, a princess. I wanted to be even tempered, genteel, but anytime Alexander opened his mouth I lost composure. It also didn't help that I was supposed to spy, not trust him nor Titus. And yet, even though he set me aflame, I couldn't help but feel a false sense of comfortability. My feelings, my personality were all in shambles. This didn't even include my greatest fear about tonight.

If Alexander changed his mind, I would have to…I would, but I wouldn't be mentally prepared. The thought of that scared me more than anything.

"There we are, absolutely perfect." Anna rested her hands on my shoulder and offered a small smile in comfort noticing my heightened nerves.

"Thank you, Anna. The braid is lovely," I sighed out. It wasn't a lie, everything Anna had prepared tonight was lovely, from the white flowing nightgown to the soft pink powder she had used on my eyes. I was a dream, too much so, it scared me.

"Princess Estelle, would you like me to wait till Prince Alexander arrives?" Her concerned eyes met mine in the mirror. I nodded silently, reaching for her hand, gripping it in thanks.

Anna may trust Alexander and Titus, but she knew that as a woman, a visiting night could be daunting. I appreciated that.

A soft knock made Anna and I perk up from the chaise where we had been sitting, waiting together.

It was time.

Anna gripped my hand once more and offered a smile, the only comfort she could provide. I nodded my head, telling her I was ready. A complete lie, as I still had no clue how to act when I met those silver eyes. But at this rate, I knew I would never be ready.

"Anna," Alexander softly spoke as if he didn't want to spook something.

"Your Highness," Anna replied before the door clicked in place.

I kept my eyes to the window, not bothering to look back, as the soft, slow sound of Alexander's boots came closer.

"No hello?" His voice came from behind causing me to grip the fabric of my nightgown. "Estelle?" My hair stood on end as his voice grew closer.

I should say something. I should do something but here I was, still mortified. I heard the chaise creak, felt it shift as his hands rested on it then came a burst of hot air on my neck. I jolted at the sensation, jumping out of the chaise and swinging around to find Alexander devilishly smirking.

"What was the purpose of that?" I asked, wholly uncomposed.

"You looked like you were thinking too hard, again." Alexander walked around the chaise before plopping down, resting his arms on the back and his ankle on his knee. The white blouse, he had failed to close, shifted so the opening at the top revealed a large portion of his tan skin. "Like what you see?"

I bit my lip, embarrassed that my eyes had lingered long enough for Alexander to notice. I reached for Griffith's pendant around my neck, once again rubbing it between my fingers. I should only have eyes for him.

"Is that a new necklace?" Alexander asked as he began to shuffle cards he had pulled from his pocket.

I stiffened at his question. I had not expected anyone to notice the new piece that adorned my neck apart from Anna, but I knew she wouldn't ask anything of it. Even if she did, it would be easy to explain that Griffith was *just* a dear friend, and this was a wedding present. Alexander, however, well he was there that night. He knew the truth about Griffith, a fact I had forgotten about. If he wanted to, he could destroy me with that fact alone, and if he knew that Griffith admitted his feelings for me, his true feelings—I shuddered at the thought.

My hands fell to my side, acting as if the necklace was just a mere trinket. "It was a gift."

"From whom? I didn't see anything like it during the present ceremony." I shifted my weight back and forth on my feet as I thought of how to answer. Prompted by my delay, he spoke again, "Is it from *him*?"

"Him?" I repeated back.

"Your attendant from the tavern, the one whom you—"

"Yes," I yelled before he could finish his thought. His hands froze and I felt a chill around me. "It is nothing though. Just a wedding gift."

Alexander looked up from the cards, his eyes as serious as the time he thought Griffith had hurt me. "Glad to hear that is the reason for this *present* and it isn't an apology full of regret for his choices that night."

I flinched at the sharpness in his voice. It was like he was warning me.

"Of course not. I—that night was a mistake for multiple reasons. My asking of him for that favor, it was one. I do not hold feelings for him any…any…" My jaw clenched shut, unable to speak further. I knew I should have, but my heart wouldn't allow me to utter such lies about Griffith, not when he had finally announced his feelings after all these years.

Alexander's eyes softened as if there was a glimmer of sadness, but I couldn't tell as his eyes moved back down to the cards. "I see…that's good. I was worried about the treaty for a minute. If you two were involved with one another, again, that would be quite the scandal and no matter how many *visitation nights* we set up, the people and other kingdoms would see us as divided." My eyes widened as I tried to mumble out a response. "Which is why I plan to keep those *extra* details about the tavern to myself. The less people who know, the better. That includes Titus."

I froze at the mention of King Titus's name. This would be the third time Alexander, to my knowledge, kept something from his brother—someone whom he seemed so close, loyal to—all to help me. I didn't know what to think of it or feel, other than the urge to reveal just a bit of truth, so if it was brought to his attention he wouldn't be blindsided.

"I write to him." Alexander stiffened. "Just because he is a dear friend, and as a reminder that I am a Princess of Isara." Which was the truth but not the entirety of it, not after Griffith sent me this necklace. We held feelings for each other, wanted to be more than just friends, but that was a detail Alexander, anyone, couldn't know.

"I see." Alexander licked his lips. "You should keep doing so then. Just be careful it doesn't become something more. I don't want to see the treaty or *you* hurt because someone misinterpreted your friendship."

Relief washed over me.

Alexander let out a sigh as if he was transforming back into the playful man he was before he saw the necklace. "Now come, sit, I want to see your skills," he teased, holding up the overly shuffled deck of cards, motioning at the empty space on the chaise that was far too little. If I sat there, we would be on top of one another.

I began to mutter some protest but couldn't find the right way to decline his invitation. There wasn't exactly anywhere else to sit beside the chairs at my table, which was on the opposite side of my chambers.

"Don't tell me you're too shy to sit this close to me. Come, Princess. Our bodies have been much closer before."

His lude comment snapped me out of whatever consumed me, and my sharp tongue returned. "Just because we've been close before doesn't mean I wish for it now. I find being next to you absolutely—" My eyes widened as I realized that I was a princess insulting her prince. I sucked on my lips. I needed to have a pleasant demeanor, one that would not start quarrels, one that would help strengthen the alliance between Isara and

Modare. I needed a demeanor that would please Titus and Alexander.

He was too infuriating.

Alexander let out a laugh. "There we go, that's the woman I know, who rudely assumed I was a thief."

"I didn't know who you were back then." My voice returned to a calm tone, one expected of a princess.

Alexander stood, leaving the cards on the chaise as he headed for my bed. My forehead wrinkled as he pulled off the top sheet and grabbed a couple pillows. "And now, you're back to using *that* tone." He frowned as he laid out the blankets on the floor, throwing the pillows on top so they faced across from each other. "I really prefer if you'd just be yourself. It's too exhausting. Get mad if you're mad, happy if you're happy but stop being this"—he waved his hand at me—"character. I know you don't trust us entirely but trust us enough that you don't have to keep your personality guarded." Alexander sat on one of the pillows and began to deal out cards. "It's not like we'll null the treaty if you scream at us occasionally. In fact, being your real self is probably what will make us like you more and make us want to keep to the treaty." Alexander patted the pillow across from him, gesturing me to sit.

I came forward, biting my lip. He really wasn't like any other royal male or lord. Back in Isara, I was quiet, acted how I was supposed to. I prepared for the time when I was to be bounded, to ensure I would not upset my future family until the fear of being separated from Griffith kicked in. That set off uncontrollable emotions that made me do uncontrollable things. And though I knew it was the right thing to return to my normal decorum, it felt good to have tiffs. Outbursts.

I continued to stare at Alexander, watching him deal out the cards. I didn't understand him or anyone in this court. From Anna telling me I was wrong to Greta lecturing me in the kitchens, everyone seemed to do what they wanted.

"Why are you being so kind to me?" The question left my lips before I could think.

Alexander, done dividing out the cards, set the excess down. "Maybe because you're my wife?" He picked up his hand, rearranging his cards. "The goal of the game is to try and get as many high pairs as possible before you or your opponent decide that cards should be shown, whoever has the most pairs with the highest value wins. You can take the card your opponent discards or you can take from this pile, then you discard your own," he explained, unaffected by my question.

"I appreciate you telling me this, encouraging me to do so, but it doesn't make sense. Especially after I separated you from the one you love." Alexander froze. "Aren't you upset?"

"First, I believe everyone should be given the opportunity to do what they desire, be who they want regardless of my feelings for them and their position in life. I've always hated, Titus too, royal protocol. Remember, I was the one who encouraged you to seek comfort in the tavern and I didn't originally suggest myself. That's proof I wasn't encouraging for my own gain." I bit my lip. "Second, V-Veron-"—Alexander swallowed hard as if the name he almost spoke pained him—"*she* was erased from my heart when I went on my hunting trip. I did so because I am your husband, and I will act like it. *At least that's one of the reasons.* I do not need to lust after anyone else, even if all we do is play cards, or at least try to." He threw down a two of hearts.

I looked down at the pile of cards but couldn't bring myself to pick one up. There was more that needed to be said about both subjects; Veronica and Griffith. But Alexander was short with both as if he wanted to put the whole situation behind us. Start new. I should be happy, but I couldn't help but mumble one more thing.

"I'm sorry, for everything."

He sighed deeply. "Everything that happened, it was for the best." He glanced at my necklace then dropped back to his cards, so his eyelashes hid them. "Well at least for me, for you—I hope that I, we can make you happy here." My eyes widened once again. I was even more confused. My lips parted to say more but Alexander cut me off. "Estelle, can we please play? It's going to be a long night if you keep asking questions like this."

I stared down at the cards then back at him. He was focused on the cards in his hand. He would say no more on this topic and maybe that was for the best, maybe we did need to put it behind us.

"Ok." I reached for the card on the top of the pile.

"Thank the gods."

I smiled, readjusting my cards, knowing that the *ok* I said was more than just an agreement to finally play. It was an *ok* to venture into this arrangement as friends, to let myself be me. Of course, I would keep Griffith informed because this was a friendship with Alexander, not Titus who controlled the armies. I would not act anymore with Alexander.

CHAPTER 25

Lord Griffith,

I am overjoyed to hear from you. I had almost lost hope since it had been a month since my last letter. I had feared I lost my greatest friend. You have given me much counsel over the years, and I hope you can continue to do so even through these letters.

It weighs on my heart to know of my father's feelings. I wish in some way I could explain to him how I felt, the feelings that provoked me to make my mistake. But I shall heed your words; I shall give him time to recover.

Prince Alexander has surprisingly turned out to be a pleasant character, as well as King Titus. The latter, however, is an acquired taste.

They are not the tyrants or the conquerors we thought them to be. They are of the people. I trust them to hold to the treaty.

I know, still, you would tell me not to trust entirely. I am first and foremost the Princess of Isara before a Princess of Modare.

My schedule is quite like my days back in Isara.

I wake up, at a decent time, to breakfast in my room.

The food here, Griffith, I wish you could've tried some before you left. It is divine. So much so, mornings have turned into an excitement.

I typically go to the training grounds, after the morning meal, to watch Prince Alexander spar then have a picnic. The picnics tend to be intimate; once we sit the men disperse into other training areas. They mostly practice swordsmanship, which is fascinating to watch.

The soldiers here are extremely talented, but none are as talented as the prince. I have yet to see anyone best him. Though, against you, it may come to a stalemate. It is a fight I would love to see. Perhaps you could join the Spring Tournament. I hear the prince is competing.

The Spring Tournament is just before the Spring Festival. It is very similar to the one in Isara. I believe it falls on the same days as well.

After this, I tend to go read in the library or the gardens, if court isn't being held. Which, surprisingly, I am required to attend. But it is good to see how the king handles business. It encourages the idea that they are good.

I have supper with the king and the prince if they aren't busy with their meetings about future actions with the other countries. I'm hoping I can join those soon.

The only changes are really when the prince does his monthly visits. I don't have supper with them on those days. I tend to eat in my room, alone, to prepare. Though the prince is kind about them

I still feel rather nervous when they happen. Even now I know the next one is not but a month minus a day away, but my stomach knots at the thought.

I have rambled enough for the day. If I write any more, I will be late for horseback riding with Prince Alexander.

How are the preparations going for the Spring festivities in Isara?

Princess Estelle
P.S. Thank you for your gift, I will treasure it dearly.

CHAPTER 26

My brown boots sunk into the ground, flinging mud up with each step. The wet dirt almost reaching the oversized navy-blue tunic that ended at the mid of my thighs.

Several times I had tried to hike it up, thinking it was a dress. Luckily, the ebony pants prevented any indecent flesh from being revealed. Well, that and Anna's reminders to not fiddle with it.

I had never done anything that required this attire or even been allowed to own anything that shared a resemblance with it. However, after Alexander and I's last ruinous riding trip, he had ordered me six riding outfits from the seamstress. All of which required pants.

I had tried to convince him to let me wear my normal dresses, that it was merely a bad day's luck when I had fallen off the horse and not the fault of my dress that got caught on a branch. Regardless, Alexander refused to let me anywhere near a horse unless I wore something *safer*. So here I was, trudging through the mud in a man's outfit.

I could only imagine my father and Griffith's face if they saw me now.

"There you are! I was starting to think the mud would keep you away."

"More like this outfit." I lifted the sides, fanning the tunic.

Alexander circled me, examining the clothing. "This could be tighter." Quickly he hooked his finger through my belt, pulling me close, unfastening it, only to pull it taut against my waist.

I gasped for air as I playfully slapped his arm away.

"You said it was for safety, not to suffocate me."

He gave me a shrug. "Better to be tight than loose and snag on something."

I rolled my eyes. He was starting the bants before we had even mounted. I didn't mind though. It was Alexander's way of being playful and it had slowly turned into my way too.

It was a way to forget the tension caused by the numerous visiting diplomats, to forget about the eyes that were always on us, waiting for us to slip. This teasing gave us reprieve from the perfect roles we were meant to play. It was much like my chats with Griffith, but this was different. It was more *freeing*, I hate to admit.

"I told you already. I was distracted. Never have I fallen off a horse before. Your money was wasted on this"—I gestured to the outfit—"new wardrobe."

Alexander stroked a restless Shadow's snout. "This will make you a much better rider. If you're not constantly worried and restricted by your dress, you'll be able to do things a lot quicker and more efficiently."

Samuel emerged with Lady, a present from King Titus after he was informed of Alexander and mine's frequent rides. She was an olive branch of sorts.

King Titus and I had come to at least trust one another now. Well, at least respect each other. Our relationship was still strained, but I no longer thought of him as a tyrant. Just as how he no longer thought of me as a useless princess. On occasion, he even asked for my input when court was held to hear the people's complaints.

King Titus's full personality, his being was still a mystery to me though. His presence was not one I looked forward to being in. However, the way he was with his people? He was compassionate, just. He listened to their concerns wholeheartedly. The people's problems were never too small to dismiss. He truly did care. The brutish behavior I had seen when I first arrived was only ever used on strangers, those who were simply villainous, or when his wine ran dry.

Regardless, I kept Griffith informed—particularly the castle's surroundings and my schedule.

"When I see it, I'll believe it," I responded to Alexander.

He chuckled, pointing behind me. His eyebrows raised, his head cocked slightly, as if to say there's your proof.

Anna had thrown her skirt over her arm, revealing her white stockings splattered in mud. Every step was filled with anger as the earth tried to steal her slippers repeatedly.

Guilt struck me as I saw the struggle she faced while I had walked here with ease, so much so that I hadn't noticed how far she had fallen behind.

I inched forward to retrieve her, but before I could take two steps, Samuel handed me Lady's reins.

"I'll retrieve the basket and escort Anna back, Your Highness. No need to worry."

I gave him a thankful smile, though I still felt it my duty to retrieve Anna. But I knew better than to take this chance away from him, well Anna. I had not asked her about her feelings, but after I had noticed a rouge form on her cheek, on multiple occasions that involved Samuel, I had an inkling she fancied him.

"I give it until the second day of the Spring Festivities."

I looked over to my left at Alexander and Shadow.

"Until what?"

"Until one of them admits their feelings."

Samuel had reached Anna, now holding the basket in one hand and his other hovering close to her in case it was needed. I smiled at the budding romance between them.

"I think it will be before. A kindle like that doesn't take long to light."

Alexander took a step toward me. "Such romantic words from you. Are you feeling well?" He placed a hand on my forehead.

I swatted it away before leaning in so our noses were inches away. "I'm a romantic when it comes to those who deserve it," I sneered.

His surprised facial expressions cooled as his hand slid to the lower of my back, pulling me in. "Am I not deserving of it?"

My cheeks grew a bright red, my heart thumping. My eyes darted to his lips.

It's a game of chicken. It's just a game of chicken. He plays it all the time.

I stared at him, faking calmness. But as I began to feel his warm breath on my neck, I spun out of his grasp.

Alexander let out a chuckle. "I win again."

"Honestly, you have the humor of an adolescent boy," I yelled, hiding my blush behind Lady.

I knew he didn't mean anything from these games. They were just a way to irritate me, sometimes to show that our relationship was *real* to those nearby. I never knew which reason he was doing it for which is why I allowed it. But sometimes my heart pounded too fast, and my mind would guiltily think of *that night*, forcing me to run away.

I gripped the pendant around my neck.

Alexander reached over to pat my head, to reassure me that everything was a joke, but was interrupted by a messenger sprinting towards us.

"Prince Alexander! Prince Alexander!" the messenger screamed on repeat. "Prince Alexander, your presence is expected at the throne room, as well as Princess Estelle's."

Alexander and I stared at one another with wide eyes.

"Vropan!" we yelled in unison.

Vropan had been one of the hardest countries to convince to attend a meeting. We were foolish to forget this day. Even as Isara's official allies, my father never fully trusted them. They loved war and always looked for excuses to wage it. Negotiations with them had to be strategic and slow. Our actions perfectly calculated and the alliance between Isara and Modare needed to appear strong. If any country was looking for weakness in our alliance, it would be Vropan. Our presence was undeniably required.

"Ready to put that outfit to the test?" Alexander pulled himself onto Shadow.

I nodded, as I locked my heels into Lady's stirrups.

"Will you need Anna to help you get ready?"

I watched as Anna saw me mount Lady, her eyes filled with horror. She hated riding. It would take longer to get dressed without her, but it was doable. I'd spare her from this. I shook my head, no.

"Samuel, escort Anna back. We'll see you both when this torture session is over."

They nodded shortly before Alexander let out a deafening hyah.

He peeked behind him, once he had a five-foot lead, with that challenging half smile I so often saw.

I should be worrying, calculating for this meeting, yet a competitive fire stirred inside me. I kicked my heels, asking Lady to go fast.

The wind rushed by my ears. My tunic flapped in the breeze. We were gaining speed; one we had never reached before. I tightened my thighs around Lady, scared I would fly off, but I refused to slow. Alexander had won too many of these challenges lately. It was time to end his streak.

I looked ahead; we were only a couple of feet behind. Alexander leaned forward, his head crouched behind Shadow's neck. I mimicked the motion. Instantly, the wind ceased to exist as Lady's neck blocked it.

I still had so much to learn.

We were one foot behind them.

Faster, faster. We can't slow down.

I leaned forward, my gaze shifting to see where Alexander was. A deep neigh came from the side. I turned to see Alexander's wide, mystified eyes beside me. Our eyes locked till he was behind Lady and me. I smiled in victory.

"Estelle, slow down," Alexander yelled.

My eyes darted to the front. We were a couple of feet away from the castle. I gasped, pulling on Lady's reins hard. She reared in response. My thighs tightened, clutching for dear life. Her hooves came down with a great thud. I let out a sigh, somehow, I had stayed on. My heart thumped as I patted Lady's neck, a smile emerging from the exhilaration of it all.

"Estelle, you shouldn't be going that fast. You're not—"

Alexander trotted up beside Lady and me. His face was filled with panic. It was my turn to tease.

"Do not feign worry, it can't hide the soreness in your pride." Alexander began to protest but I didn't allow it. "You're just mad we won, despite your cheating." I dismounted Lady, nuzzling her snout. "We're the superior pair, aren't we?" Lady let out a soft neigh as if she was agreeing. "I can't wait to do that with you again," I whispered to her.

Alexander's feet planted on the ground as he waved over two soldiers sparring. "I should have never recommended you stop wearing dresses."

"You are such a sore loser. I can't wait to see how badly you'll react when I beat you again. I noticed that without the excess fabric flying around, I can reach an entirely different speed. There's an outfit from the seamstress, it's a bit tighter, not the most feminine, but it will have less drag and—"

"Not such stupid outfits now, are they?" Alexander leaned on Shadow with the biggest grin.

My bottom lip pursed out. Even when I managed to win a round, he won the game.

Alexander flashed his signature smirk at my clear irritation.

I bit my lip trying to think of a quip, but none came before the two soldiers reached us. Alexander's smile grew wider as he realized his victory.

"How can we be of service, Your Highness?"

"Get these two some water then take them back to the stables."

The soldiers bowed before taking Lady and Shadow's reins.

CHAPTER 27

I yanked my boots off as I sped to the wardrobe. I needed something regal, nothing too innocent or sweet, but something that demanded respect.

I pulled out a blue dress that Alexander had gifted me a couple of weeks ago. It wasn't whimsical nor covered in gems. A simple dress, perfect for this meeting. I hung it on the changing screen before striding over to my excessive collection of heels, but my mind halted me. The dress couldn't be purple nor blue. Choosing one color over the other would send the message that I favored one of the kingdoms. I walked back to my wardrobe. Over three-fourths of my closet was unusable. The colors that remained were pink, red, and black.

I rubbed my head. Maybe I needed Anna after all, she was always good at helping with this. But I didn't have time to wait for her. I needed to decide now.

I stared at the three colors, wondering what would be best. Pink was too girlish. Red was too sensual. Black, it was a dull color, but it was a color that would allow me to be taken seriously. I could always spruce it up with accessories.

I dug through the dresses, finally settling on a black dress that's bust was embellished with gold embroidery. It was a tad revealing for what I wanted as the sleeves did not begin till it was past my shoulders, leaving the area above my bosom bare. Nothing a necklace couldn't distract from though.

I stripped the dirt ridden clothes off, wiping myself down with a wet cloth.

"Are you still getting dressed?" Alexander inquired from behind my door.

"Almost done."

I hurriedly brushed my hair, smoothing the strands that had been misplaced by the wind. Luckily, Anna had done a simple half-up, half-down today, an easy style to mend.

"I'm coming in."

My pupils grew wide as I stared at my naked reflection in the mirror. "Don't you dare!" I barely finished the last word as the doorknob twisted. I grabbed the dress and leaped behind the changing screen. Quickly I pulled the dress over my shoulders.

"Couldn't you have waited just a couple more minutes?" I hissed.

The screech of a chair echoed in the room. "Figured this would make you hurry. I don't want to be so late that we miss their arrival. Titus would have a fit."

I chewed the inside of my cheek. Alexander had no shame. A fact I had come to terms with a couple of weeks after I first arrived, but it didn't make it any less annoying.

He constantly came to my room without permission. I was lucky if he even announced himself before entering, always using the excuse that it would hasten me. But we both knew it was to irritate me, his favorite way to amuse himself.

I reached for the lacing on my corset. The ribbons were like butter in my hands.

"You're taking longer than normal to get ready. Are you sure you didn't need Anna?"

I yanked the lace through the second eye. "I just need to lace the dress up."

Alexander made a grunt of approval.

I had made it to the third set of holes when the clock chimed noon. We had thirty minutes till the Vropanians arrived. I hastened myself, which proved counterproductive as the ribbon slipped from my worried hands. My gut twisted as I felt it fall out of each eyelet.

I let out a groan. This was proving more difficult than I thought.

"Everything alright?"

"The ribbon, it just fell." I shook my head, refocusing my attention. "Looks like I'll have to start again. If you just give me one second of—"

"Let me," Alexander's silky voice whispered in my ear.

I craned my neck to see him behind me. His eyes were focused on my bare back.

I clutched the fabric tighter to my breasts.

"I can do it," I mumbled, feeling my cheeks warm.

"It's faster this way," he replied, already pulling the ribbon through the eyelets before I could step away.

I gulped, turning my attention forward, trying to pretend it was Anna at my back. But as Alexander's calloused fingers grazed my bare skin, I could not ignore the immense tingles that ran through my body. I whimpered at the touch. Praying to the gods he didn't hear.

My body tensed, preparing, waiting for the next accidental graze.

Visions of that night, the night in the tavern appeared in my head. The way his fingers delicately unlaced my corset. How his lips softly kissed my skin as it was exposed.

I bit my lip at the thought. I wanted to feel that again.

I shook my head. *What was wrong with me?*

My heart belonged to Griffith, and it would only belong to Griffith.

I hadn't touched another—besides hands—since the tavern. That night had been delectable and, no doubt, my body craved a touch like that again.

This wasn't my heart responding. It was just my body's natural response to a touch that was a prerequisite to a martial night, nothing more.

"Not too tight?"

"No," I breathed out, still fighting my urges.

Alexander slowed as if contemplating the meaning behind my tone. "Sorry about this. I'm almost done," he said, his voice sounding defeated.

Sorry.

My heart dropped at the word as did my previous thoughts.

Alexander made quick work with the rest of the corset, remaining quiet throughout the process, even as I adorned my gold tiara and Griffith's necklace. It wasn't till we exited my room, with ten minutes till their arrival, that he spoke.

"Shall we?" was all he said as he offered his arm.

CHAPTER 28

"Where have you two been? We were supposed to strategize before they arrived."

I looked over to Alexander who faked a yawn as King Titus furiously paced in front of the throne. It took everything I had not to snicker. Any thoughts of the awkwardness that had just occurred dissipated as Alexander continued to mock Titus.

"You two, are you listening?"

Titus faced us, nostrils flaring. Reminding me of the king I once faced the wrath of.

"Yes, brother. We hear you. Do not fret. With your politically blessed brain, I'm sure we will have them as allies by the end of the week."

I nodded in agreement as Alexander calmed King Titus.

Through the past meetings I had attended, I had learned that King Titus was the brains behind the scenes. Not to say Alexander wasn't intelligent, in fact, Alexander oversaw battle plans, strategies, and the training of the troops. He was the one who devised the plan that allowed Modare to take two countries at once. A feat that was virtually impossible. King

Titus, on the other hand, was well educated on imports, exports, the culture, and the needs of other countries, knowledge that was needed to have the upper hand when creating a treaty. His only downfall was his temper and his acquired personality. Which is why Alexander attended all the meetings and put his charismatic personality to work.

"It should, as long as you two act like the love birds the treaty needs."

"You mean the love birds we truly are," Alexander corrected with thick sarcasm. He threw his arm around my waist, embracing me tightly. Overdramatically, he pressed his lips to my cheek.

I rolled my eyes, pushing him away.

"That doesn't seem fake at all," I scoffed at Alexander.

He smirked as he saw the irritation he had awakened in Titus and me.

This man never ceased to be a brat.

The iron doors creaked open and Alexander's shoulders squared, and his smirk sunk into a polite smile.

"Introducing, Lord Visimar of Vropan," Leo announced, his arms opened wide as he walked toward the throne, stopping with a deep bow.

A tan man in black leathers strode in behind him, void of any green—the color of Vropan.

He placed his hand on his heart as he slightly bowed his head.

"Your Majesty, first and foremost, it is a pleasure to step foot in this beautiful palace to talk of peace." His voice was thick with honey. "My king has sent me with a list of his wishes and hopes so that they can be added to this possible treaty. I look forward to sharing them with you." He rose, examining our faces, twirling the tips of his mustache.

"It is an honor to receive you," King Titus replied, his voice monotone. "You must be tired after your travels, perhaps—"

"There is no need."

I glanced at Titus as his eyes narrowed. Cutting him off was one of his biggest triggers. Alexander, noticing the tension, stepped forward.

"That is fine. We shall proceed to the study then." Alexander offered a smile to Visimar and Titus.

"Wonderful," Visimar replied with glee. "I want to get done as soon as possible, so I can visit some brothels in the evening."

I closed my eyes, hiding the disgust in them.

Titus scoffed but made his way down the stairs, leading the way to the study.

"This is going to be an interesting meeting, isn't it?" Alexander whispered to me.

"It always is with Vropan. Good luck with keeping King Titus calm."

Alexander shrugged. "At least this is the last meeting for a while."

I nodded in agreement. "I'm just happy I don't have to attend the rest of it; I'm looking forward to an early night." I flashed a smirk at Alexander, pleased I got to flaunt this small blessing before heading off.

Alexander stopped his descent midway down the stairs. "Did you already forget about tonight?"

I tilted my head.

"My night visit," he calmly replied.

"Oh," was all I could murmur as my pupils dilated and my heartbeat quickened.

This would be his second visit since we decided to have marriage duty nights. The first—after we got past the awkwardness of it all and I decided to open myself up—was amazingly pleasant. We had spent the night playing cards then getting to know one another even further. It turned out we had quite a bit in common. The conversation was so intriguing that we didn't even notice the sun beginning to rise. In truth, I was looking forward to the next visiting night but now…

I had cravings for him. It was only the one time, but the thought of being alone with him for an entire night, with the possibility that those *urges* may occur again…the thought terrified me. I didn't want to do that to Griffith; I didn't want to ruin the friendship that Alexander and I established this past month.

"Estelle?"

I blinked a couple of times, getting out of my head.

"Yes. Sorry. Just thinking of how I lost track of time. It flies so fast nowadays."

"You've been acting odd all morning."

"It's probably the fatigue from all the ambassadors' visits," I stated, unconvincingly.

"Estelle, if anything is wrong you can tell me."

There was something wrong with my body, but I wasn't about to give Alexander another thing to torment me about.

"Everything is fine." I offered a reassuring smile. "Now, catch up before your brother rips Lord Visimar's head off."

Alexander sighed, not at all convinced, but he knew my warning was real. "I'll see you tonight," he uttered before racing off.

CHAPTER 29

"Are you sure you don't want me to wait till Prince Alexander gets here? With the meeting, it could be hours."

"I'll be fine Anna. You've worked enough for today, go get some rest." I kneeled on the bed as my nightgown flared out, creating a perfect circle around me. "Plus, I have some reading I want to get done."

My eyes darted around the room for the book I had picked up from the library this afternoon, but there was no sight of it.

"This one?" Anna picked up the leather-bound book, turning it in her hands, examining the title.

I held my breath knowing the words she was reading. *The King's Rose*. A romance novel. A genre I typically didn't read—nor did the other noble women in Isara—as the idea of a love marriage being possible was a frivolous notion amongst us. But in my haste to figure out the cause of these *urges*, I grabbed it from the library.

"I didn't know you had an interest in romance novels." Anna walked the book over to me.

"I don't. I mistook it for something else." I traced my hands over the letterings, hoping the answers I needed lay in this fictitious tale. "I realized what it was after I returned to my room, and my stubbornness never allows me to return a book to its home till I have finished it."

Anna thumbed through the book with a half-smile.

"It's quite an enjoyable book. Chapter ten made me into a bit of a romantic."

"You've read it?" The words raced out of my mouth as my heart sped.

The plot of the book was fairly like my own life. A woman forced to marry a king has to try to figure out how to live and complete her political mission, all while denying her growing feelings for him. Of course, the latter did not apply to my situation. I harbored no feelings for Alexander. Just physical desires.

I bit my lip, hoping Anna wouldn't pick up on the overlapping details.

"I've forgotten much of the plot. It's been a while, but I remember I enjoyed it."

I slumped into the pillows, a rush of air leaving my body as a soft smile emerged.

"Well, I best be off, Your Highness."

Anna curtsied, bidding me goodnight. I nodded in return.

I curled into a ball underneath the warmth of the blankets. The pillows held my body at an incline. The scent of lavender oil from the bathing room circled around me, lulling me to sleep. It wasn't long till the leather binding slid from my hands.

I jolted out of bed, awoken by a thundering clang. I peered around the room, searching for the source of the sound, but to my avail, I found nothing out of place.

I shrugged away the mystery, blaming the sound on a clumsy servant in the hall. I laid my head back down only to meet the dulled corner of an object.

A book? I questioned, my mind still hazy with sleep.

I rubbed my eyes, placing the item on the nightstand.

I hadn't fallen asleep with anything in my bed since I was a child. My head pulsed as I tried to think of the reason for this odd occurrence.

The night visit!

I looked up at the clock that was barely illuminated with candlelight.

"Nine," I squealed.

Never had a meeting run this late. They were typically over by lunch and if they ran past that then dinner. My mind ran wild, thinking of all the worst reasons the meeting could go this long, but worrying would do nothing. I placed my hand on my chest, forcing my breathing to slow. I needed to remind myself who the meeting was with—Vropan, the snakes of the continent. Of course, it would take a while, I needed to have faith in Titus and Alexander.

I laid my head back down, pulling the satin sheets to my chin. Already my heart was calming. I could easily drift back to sleep, but Alexander would tease me for ages if I wasn't able to stay up as he did.

I willed my body to sit up. My hand reaching for the book, my eyes squinting as I tried to read its contents with the small flame by my bed. The darkness of the room was too powerful. I needed a brighter light.

I begrudgingly tossed my legs out of the warm bed, making my way to the center of the room. There, a torch big enough to hold a flame that would illuminate the entire room hung by chains from the ceiling.

It hung, twice my height, above the ground. I let out a sigh as I moved a dining chair under it, shaking the seat to ensure it was stable enough to climb.

I stood atop it, arms reaching up. To my distress, I still couldn't reach the torch. I bit my bottom lip as I stood on my toes, willing them to stretch, trying to overcome the two inches that kept me from the blinding light.

I tilted my candle down, the flame barely touching the torch. Instantly, a fire erupted and the room illuminated.

I climbed back down, blowing out my candle stick, marveling at my tiny victory, watching the light spread. But as the light spread to the corners of the room, my mouth went dry, my stomach dropped, and every inch of my body shook.

A figure of black stood, his brown eyes glaring at me from behind the ebony mask he wore. His body glimmered with daggers.

I needed to run.

I was ten steps from the door, five steps from him. There was no way I could make it out before he caught up to me. My eyes darted around the room looking for anything of use when I spied the rope that rang down to the kitchens. I could pull it in time before he reached me.

I took a step back, putting the chair between us, hoping he wouldn't notice.

"Do not move," he snarled, unsheathing his sword.

I threw my candlestick, striking him in the head, racing for the rope.

Please let them hear, please.

I had pulled the rope five or six times before the man's hands wrapped around my waist, pulling me to the window. I clawed at his hands, gagging as pieces of his flesh wedged under my fingernails. I let out petrified screams, hoping anyone would hear. My throat burned then he shoved a black ribbon in my mouth. I thrashed my body harder, attempting to free myself, using it as a weapon. Pain flashed across my cheek. The force of his hand sent me to the floor, leaving me dazed, allowing him to effortlessly pin me down, and bind my hands then my feet.

Tears streamed down as I realized my efforts were futile, that I had failed to escape. Soon I would be taken to gods know where, be held for ransom or be killed.

What would become of the treaty?

I closed my eyes, the ribbon muffling my sobs as my body was lifted off the ground and heaved over a shoulder.

"Let her go," a murderous voice commanded. My eyes darted to the source. There, Alexander stood in the doorway with rage filled eyes.

The two stared at one another, both trying to predict each other's next move. The masked man backed away to the window. I screamed in terror as my body fell to the floor, as a warm liquid dripped onto my cheek then to the wood, revealing the bright red color of it. I looked up to see a dagger impaled into the palm of the intruder's hand.

"Do not attempt to touch her again," Alexander growled, each word coming out sharper than the last.

Alexander drew his sword, advancing toward the masked man who in turn pulled out a dagger.

My breathing hitched as I watched Alexander swing his sword. I had seen him battle before, seen him take on men twice his size. He had stayed calm, collective but now—now his eyes were aflame, his teeth gritted, and his swings led by pure fury.

Their metal clashed over and over as I lay on the ground helplessly whimpering, wishing I could help.

"They're in here," Anna's voice sounded, accompanied by stomping feet.

"You're a dead man," Alexander spat as sparks flew from their blades.

The masked man reached into his pocket, throwing black soot in Alexander's eyes before kicking him to the ground. His scream pierced my ears as a dagger sliced into his dominant arm, a river of crimson flowing from the gash.

I wormed my way over, desperate to help, but the masked man grabbed my bindings and pulled me to my feet.

I looked at Alexander, blood staining his tunic, his hand barely gripping his sword. He was too injured to fight, and yet he still rose from the floor, moving toward us.

I was thrown over the masked man's shoulder, my eyes locked on Alexander's to tell him goodbye when an arrow flew past my ear and into the masked man's back. The sound of his pain was deafening as he dropped me once again to the floor, my head taking most of the impact.

"Princess Estelle," Anna shrieked.

Anna raced forward, placing my head onto her lap. A guard followed to break my bonds. I sat up and brought my fingers to my throbbing head, only to feel a sticky substance—my own blood.

"Please, don't move," Anna pleaded, pressing a handkerchief on my wound.

"You there, send for Aeson. The rest of you, start searching. Discreetly! We do not want Vropan to know of this."

Titus.

"Let me see," Titus commanded.

"It's just a scratch," Alexander replied.

A pair of leather boots came into sight. I followed them up to Alexander's eyes which were filled with worry and relief.

"Just when we think you won't cause any more problems." Alexander half smirked as he helped me stand. My eyes shot to his arm as he winced.

His tunic was covered in blood, making it near impossible to see the source of it all, if it were not for the makeshift bandage made from another's shirt, indicating where the wound was. The fabric slowly changed from white to red, meaning the bleeding had reduced, but it still sparked concern in me.

"Your arm," I whispered, rejecting his help, worrying I would cause more pain.

"I've had much worse," Alexander reassured me before attempting to grab me again. Too dizzy to dodge his grip, I allowed him to guide me to the chaise. His hands never leaving me till my bottom was safely seated, as if one more fall might kill me.

Anna took the seat next to me, continuing to apply pressure as she wiped away the blood that dribbled down with her other hand. Alexander leaned on the wall, refusing to take his gaze off me even as Titus examined his shoulder.

"I came as fast as my legs would carry me."

A bearded man hobbled into the room, his forehead wrin-kling at the sight of the blood drenched floor, his aged lines becoming more evident.

"Aeson." King Titus bowed his head.

"Yes, yes, yes." Aeson raised his hand and flicked away the king's greeting. "Now, who is bleeding more?"

"I believe the prince should be taken care of first," Titus replied.

Aeson stood between us, sucking his lips, moistening them, taking long glances between us.

"I think"—his lips popped out of his mouth, sending out little droplets of spit—"I'll tend to the girl first."

Anna withdrew her hand revealing the slow bleeding gash on my head. Aeson limped toward me, grabbing my chin with his thumb and forefinger.

"There's a bit of swelling." Aeson tilted my head upward, his mouth slightly parting as he examined the wound closer. "You'll need stitches, but I don't see any long-term effects. If anything, a minuscule scar."

Aeson waved over a young man who stood quietly in the corner. He ran across the room, placing a large wooden box on the floor next to the now kneeling Aeson.

"If you could lie down, Your Highness, so your wound is facing the ceiling."

I slipped down in the chaise, carefully minding my dress as I felt the attention of several concerned eyes.

Aeson's thick fingers rummaged through the box, carefully moving tiny, corked glass bottles filled with varying-colored liquids. It was a wonder how he kept them all organized.

"Here we are."

Aeson pulled out a folded white cloth, carefully placing it on the floor before revealing the sharp, metal instruments.

"What's that for?" I inquired, pointing to a bottle filled with brownish liquid, trying to distract myself from his tools.

Aeson looked up from the needle he was stringing.

"To sanitize but mostly for the pain." Aeson extended the bottle to me after dampening a cloth with the liquid. "You're going to want to drink this."

I hesitantly took the bottle before sipping the contents. I coughed violently as the liquid burned down my throat. I covered my mouth, hiding my gag as the bitter flavor washed over my tongue.

"Not a rum person, I suppose." Aeson shrugged his shoulders, taking a drink as well. "Now, just stay as still as possible. This should take but a few moments."

My eyes flickered to Alexander who held his arm. "Can't your assistant do it while you attend to the prince?"

Aeson turned his head slowly, mumbling something about patience under his breath, glancing at Alexander's arm.

"Has it stopped bleeding?" Alexander nodded. "Clean it up, then pour this over it." Aeson tossed the bottle of rum over to Alexander who caught it flawlessly with his good arm.

"Can drinking it also be a part of the treatment?"

Aeson shook his head, holding back his laughter. "As long as I get a replacement by tomorrow morning."

Alexander raised the bottle in the air toward Aeson. "That I can do." Alexander drank from the bottle till only half the contents remained.

Titus breathed heavily as he watched Alexander wipe the rum dribbling down his chin. "That is all? He is the prince, Aeson. His health is of the utmost importance."

Aeson let out a heavy sigh, shaking his head as he rolled his eyes. "As a physician, I will treat who is in the worst condition first, not whom the king deems more important." King Titus stepped forward, opening his mouth to retort but was cut off as Aeson stood. "Titus, Son of Malachi." Aeson's booming voice filled the room. "If you wish for me to look at your brother then let me do my job. If you cannot be quiet for one second, make yourself useful and fetch Alexander a fresh shirt."

There was silence as Titus stared begrudgingly toward the stone-faced physician. Neither of them budged. Then, after my blood began to dribble onto the chaise, Titus stormed out of the room, cursing under his breath.

"Now then, back to business." Aeson knelt to the ground, smiling.

My eyes widened as my lips parted in shock. Aeson had not used titles, nor showed the decorum one needed when talking to royalty. He had not faltered nor hesitated when going against King Titus's wishes. And even more surprising,

King Titus let him do so without punishment. In all my life, I had never seen such a person.

"Now then, where were we?" Aeson fiddled with the needle and string once more, this time without interruptions. "This will hurt, but please try to lie still."

Aeson's fingers were warm as he positioned his calloused hand under the gash, making the skin taut. I closed my eyes as I felt a stinging wetness sweep across the wound, a slight bubbling, then the cold metal of the needle grazed over my skin. I bit my lip trying to find a sound to distract me. I could hear crickets chirping from outside, the wind rustling through the trees. It was a symphony of nature. I listened closer, finding the softer sounds. The ones you can only hear in the midst of night once the world has gone to sleep. My mind drifted off, forgetting the coldness of the needle, but it was quickly recalled as a searing pain forged its way through my skin.

I clutched the chaise, curling my knees to my chest.

"It will be over shortly."

I gave a minuscule nod as my lips quivered, a soft whimper escaping as the string followed the needle.

I could no longer hear the symphony, no longer focus on the distant distraction. The tears welled up as the needle stabbed my skin again.

"Will I be in your way if I sit here?" Alexander inquired.

"Just don't block the light," Aeson replied.

The chaise creaked as Alexander sat, his warm lower back touching my stomach. "It's almost done, I promise," he mused in my ear.

I clutched the chaise harder as the string pulled through a second time, but instead of the soft fabric, I felt Alexander's hand laced in mine. My eyes fluttered open to find our fingers tightly entwined, his knuckles turning a blush pink color. I loosened my grip and retracted my hand, but he pulled me back.

"Squeeze as hard as you need."

The needle stabbed a third time, forcing my eyes shut again and my toes to curl. This spot was more tender than the last two. I gripped Alexander's hand tighter as if it could somehow subside the pain.

"You're ok," Alexander cooed, his free hand tucking my hair behind my ear. "You're ok."

My body unclenched; my toes uncurled as his hand grazed from my neck down to my lower back, the pleasure of it, distracting me from the pain.

I focused on each of his fingers delicately grazing my night dress, the thin fabric allowing me to feel every minute movement. If his fingers went slightly left, if he applied more pressure, or if he simply slowed even by a millisecond, I could feel it all.

This was the distraction I needed. No, it was more than that, this was comfort.

"And we are done."

My eyelids fluttered open at the sound of scissors snipping away the excess thread.

Aeson sat on the ground placing the cloth back in the wooden box, the glass bottles clinking as he made his way to the bottom.

"It should heal within a week. I'll visit you then to take them out."

Aeson chuckled to himself as my eyes widened in horror.

"It will not be nearly as painful, that I promise you."

I let out a sigh of relief.

"Can I have my hand back now?"

My cheeks ran red as I released Alexander's hand. It had been such a comfort I had forgotten to let go.

He rubbed it back to life, staring down at me. "I honestly thought you were going to break it at some point."

I scowled at him, but not for long as I realized he was naked from the waist up. No wonder he was so warm to the touch. I hastily sat up, sliding to the opposite end of the chaise.

Alexander grinned with his devilish, playful eyes, noticing the rouge on my cheeks.

"Now, let's fully examine you." Aeson plopped in between us, preventing Alexander's taunting from going further. "It's closed up on its own, mostly." Aeson moved Alexander's cleaned arm every which way, carefully examining the wound and Alexander's face. "You should be fine." Alexander grimaced as Aeson lifted the arm up. "It hurts more than you let on."

"There might be a little pain," Alexander admitted, rubbing where his collarbone met his shoulder. Aeson raised an eyebrow in warning. "He may have taken a jab at my shoulder."

Aeson tenderly touched where Alexander rubbed.

"You are not permitted to train nor fight till I say otherwise."

"Aeson, I have the spring tournament to practice for."

Alexander yelped as Aeson struck his shoulder. "It will hurt a lot more and for far longer if a sword hits it."

"You could have just said that."

"Would you have listened?"

Alexander tilted his head left to right, debating with himself, before shaking his head.

"Here you go." King Titus marched to Alexander, handing him a white blouse despite his own being torn.

I suppose that's where the makeshift bandage had come from.

"Alexander is to not hold any weapons till I say so. The wound has caused more damage than he lets on."

King Titus's nose flared. "Again?"

Alexander shrugged off the question, leaning back in the chaise.

I looked between all three sets of eyes, two silently staring and the other gazing off into the distance. The aura of royalty dissipated as there was only concern.

"Your Majesties!" A guard sprinted in, bowing deeply for his interruption. "We managed to track down the intruder."

Titus and Alexander straightened their backs, their regal auras returning while my eyes grew. With all the worry, I had failed to take note that the intruder had escaped despite the arrow in his back.

"Well, where is he?" Titus boomed.

The guard's shoulders curled inward. "He's dead."

"What?" Titus stepped toward the guard.

"He was shot with another arrow, Your Majesty. A foreign one."

Alexander stepped forward. His lips in a tight line. "Not one of ours?"

The guard shook his head handing over a black arrow.

Alexander snatched it away, examining everything from the shaft to the feathers. "I've never seen this material used in an arrow before."

Titus grabbed the arrow from Alexander.

"Blackwood? This is only found across the seas. A very expensive, rare material."

Alexander's brows furrowed together.

A shiver went down my spine as Titus's cold eyes met mine. "Someone very rich wants you dead."

My hands shook at his words; my palms turned clammy. Assassination attempts were not uncommon among royals, but this was the first attempt on my life.

Why now, would someone want me dead?

"Did you search the body?" Alexander snarled at the guard, his calm composure slowly coming undone.

"Yes, yes." The guard frantically patted his pockets looking for an item. "Here it is."

The guard held out a piece of parchment splattered in blood. Alexander snatched it from his hands, reading intently.

"Double the guard," he whispered.

"Your Highness?" the guard replied, unable to hear clearly.

"Double the guard," Alexander roared, striking so much fear in the guard he fled from the room.

My eyes widened. In the months I had been here I had never heard Alexander use such a terrifying voice. A voice filled with fear, anger, and the intent to kill.

"Let me see." King Titus approached Alexander, carefully, as he took the crumpled parchment.

"It's a map," Alexander spoke, his voice so low I could barely hear, and yet it was filled with so much fury.

King Titus's breathing hitched upon seeing the parchment.

"There are some errors, but it's a map of the castle," Alexander continued to explain. "It even has private rooms marked."

"This was a very well-planned assassination."

Alexander nodded. "Look at the back."

"She will be alone tonight. Make your move while the prince is at the meeting," King Titus read aloud.

My body stiffened. The intruder knew everything.

He had known the layout of the castle, that the guards would take their leave tonight for Alexander's visit, and that Alexander would be late. They had private information—information that an outsider couldn't obtain without the help of someone inside.

I jumped as Anna grasped my shoulder. Her eyes flooded with concern.

"Do you think this is Vropan's doing?" Alexander asked murderously.

Titus shook his head. "They were with us all day so were their attendants." King Titus paused, stroking his beard, thinking. "But I will send a spy to observe them until we know more." Titus turned to me. "You will be escorted everywhere you go. Whoever did this will strike again. They aren't just after your life; they want the treaty to fall."

"That's all?"

King Titus turned to Alexander. "For tonight, yes." His voice was deathly calm.

"We should patrol the grounds, look for the owner of the arrow," Alexander growled as he closed the space between them.

"We cannot let Vropan know there was a breach. It will show we have weaknesses in our defenses, weaknesses they will look for."

Alexander, nostrils flaring, glared at King Titus who remained calm. Silence filled the room at the rare sight.

"I'll go alone then. They won't have the opportunity to strike again if they are dead."

My stomach twisted at the thought of Alexander patrolling in his condition.

Alexander was halfway to the door when King Titus roared his name, stalling Alexander long enough for the king to run in front of him and push his arm into Alexander's chest, effectively stopping him from leaving. King Titus whispered in his ear and gestured to me. Alexander looked back, ferocity in his eyes. I shivered at the sight. Once more, King Titus whispered in his ear. Alexander's eyes calmed; his shoulders dropped. He took a breath, calming himself.

King Titus retracted, releasing Alexander, knowing that his words had taken effect.

King Titus turned to the door, motioning everyone to leave apart from two guards. I watched the many pairs of feet disappear into the hall, unable to focus on anything else.

"Anna, how long will it take to clean the room?" Alexander asked calmy or at least tried to.

Anna cautiously spoke to Alexander as she examined the mess. His anger had scared us all. "If I were to wake one or two more maids I could have it done in two hours. By myself, twice the time."

I scanned the room. Blood was splattered on the walls, the breakfast table was turned over, and fabric was shredded.

"I see." Alexander exhaled. "Worry about it in the morning."

Anna and my eyes snapped to Alexander. I didn't want Anna to stay up nor did I want her to wake the others, but I certainly didn't want to, couldn't sleep with the hundreds of reminders of my almost assassination.

"Estelle, you'll sleep in my room tonight."

His expression was solid as stone, unwavering. This wasn't a request, but an order. My stomach flipped, invading his space, sleeping in his room felt wrong. It was rare, almost unheard of if a woman visited her husband's chambers. I would have protested if it were not for the fear of evoking Alexander's wrath once again. A wrath that could not compare to King Titus's on the day of my arrival.

Anna draped a thick dark blue robe over my nightgown, ensuring I looked modest to anyone that I might encounter on the long walk to Alexander's quarters which lay on the opposite side of the castle. An area I was completely unfamiliar with. Afterward, Anna reluctantly bid me goodnight.

The guards followed closely as we made our way to Alexander's room. I hardly noticed them as I listened to every sound, stared at every dark corner, wondering if it was safe.

Alexander stopped in front of a pair of iron doors. He opened them without a word revealing his dimly lit room.

The layout of his chamber matched mine entirely, apart from the vanity and chaise. In place of these items was a desk covered in thick parchment paper each adorning the crest of Modare, the other was a table hosting a map covered in little figurines. Even in his private quarters, Alexander worked. He was always prepared to protect Modare and her people.

Alexander led me further into his room, closing the doors behind us. The guards positioned outside.

"I'll sleep here." Alexander gestured toward a dark blue armchair, I had failed to see, next to the bed. "Should I leave a candle lit tonight?"

I nodded, still too shocked to speak.

Alexander slowly blew out each candle, watching my expression.

Darkness took the room as I remained standing next to the last light. My eyes surveyed every corner again and again, making sure nothing stood in the shadows.

"It's safe, I promise," Alexander assured me as he led me to the bed.

I slid off my cloak and hesitantly climbed into the sheets Alexander held open for me, still searching.

Nothing. There was nothing here. I will be fine.

I wrapped the velvet sheets tightly around me. My eyes slowly shut as they weighed heavy with sleep, then there was a creak.

I sat up. Frantically, I looked for the source of the sound. I couldn't see anything in the dark corners of the room. My breathing hastened, and my body shook.

Comforting warmth spread across my cheek as a callused hand caressed it. "You're ok," Alexander whispered.

"I thought I heard the window open," I whimpered.

"Estelle," Alexander cooed, enveloping my shaking hands in his. "What can I do to calm you?"

I stared into his concerned eyes, the warmth of his hand reminding me of the distraction he provided an hour earlier.

"Lay with me." I gulped, not caring if he'd tease me. "Just for tonight."

Alexander's eyes softened as he raised my hands to his lips. "I will. Tonight and any night you need."

Alexander pulled back the covers, settling himself beside me. He glanced at me then the arm he laid on top of my pillow in invitation. I slowly laid back down, resting my head on his surprisingly comfortable bicep. I nuzzled into his chest, inhaling the scent of pine. His fingers ran through my hair then to my back. I pushed my body closer to his, drifting to sleep, feeling completely safe in his arms.

CHAPTER 30

Lord Griffith,

I'm sure my father has received a letter from King Titus inform-ing him of the attempt on my life.

I would like to tell you not to worry about me, but I cannot bring myself to do so.

Evidence points that there was more than one person involved. I am scared. How do I even attempt to return to normalcy when I know that the mastermind is still out there?

Everyone in Modare has tried to help me move forward, tried to make me feel safe yet the nightmares still come.

I wish you were here.

Princess Estelle

CHAPTER 31

The carpet was drenched in blood, splintered wood from broken furniture laid across the scuffed floor. The delicate canopy over my bed had been shredded. Feathers jutted out of the gaping holes in the mattress. Holes that could only be made with something sharp, like a knife. I needed to get out of here. I turned my feet to the door, ready to run, ready to find safety then came a piercing scream.

My head turned just in time to see a woman's body fall to the ground. Cold and lifeless. A shadow towered over her, dagger in hand, blood dripping from it, falling onto the victim's lavender dress as if it wanted to be reunited with its owner.

I backed away slowly, thinking there was nothing I could do to save the unknown woman. After two steps she groaned, pleading, begging for help.

She was still *alive*.

The shadow knelt beside her, entering the light, slowly revealing the many arrows impaled in his torso. Despite this, he moved elegantly with no sign of distress. He knelt next to the woman, titling his head, examining her. She pressed her arms into the floor, attempting to crawl away. My body shook uncontrollably as I realized I had seen this fiend before, the man in black, the one from that dreaded night.

The woman let out a cry as he pulled her dark brown hair upward, giving him access to her neck. Her eyes fluttered open, revealing her dark brown eyes, my dark brown eyes.

I was watching myself being murdered.

I willed my legs to move, but my feet were shackled to the floor. The dagger glinted as it rested on my neck. I screamed for help, for him to have mercy, but no sound came. The dagger moved, blood dribbling down. I clawed at the chains, trying to free myself, screaming till my throat went numb. The light was leaving my other self's eyes as a pool of blood formed around her. Then, when her body no longer twitched, and all the blood had stopped flowing, the masked man released his hold on her. The body fell into the redness, the liquid splashing, and the masked man smiled as if he were a boy that had just watched a stone fall into a lake. I whimpered and his head raised. His eyes widened as if he was seeing me for the first time. He stalked toward me, manically laughing. I was next.

"Estelle, Estelle! Wake up."

An alarming voice came from above. I cried in terror as the world began to shake. Then, with a jolt, my eyes flicked open.

A single candle illuminated a room, the bed that I sat up in, my bed. Hot tears streamed down my face, a cold sweat on my brow as my hands shook uncontrollably.

"You're ok," a voice cooed.

I jumped as warm calloused hands caressed my back. I took deep breaths as Alexander's face came into the light.

It was all a dream.

"A nightmare?"

I nodded, wiping tears away.

"Do you need anything?"

I straightened my back, attempting to look strong. This wasn't the first nightmare since the incident, but it was the first time someone had witnessed one.

"I'm fine," I mumbled unconvincingly.

Alexander's eyes drifted down my body, pausing on my shaking hands. His eyes stayed, unwavering, as his breathing grew shallow. Quickly, I covered my hands, pleading with them to stop.

"It's ok to still be scared," he uttered, his eyes softly returning to mine.

I breathed out, putting on a mask. "Me, scared? Not at all." I smiled up at Alexander whose lips were a hard line. "Really, I'm fine." I stared out the window, avoiding his concerned eyes. The stars were shining brightly. "What are you doing up this late?"

"I could hardly stay asleep with your screams invading my room."

I gripped the sheets, ashamed. Alexander was already tired from evaluating and replanning Modare's defenses. He shouldn't have to experience more fatigue because of me. I needed to get a hold of these nightmares, more so than ever, now that his room had been relocated across from mine. Everyone's had after the attack, for security reasons, riddling me with even more guilt.

"When I came to check, the guards seemed unphased. These nightmares happen often, don't they?"

I bit my lip refusing to answer.

"I'm here for you if you need anything."

I remained quiet.

Alexander stood with a nod, taking the candle with him, respecting my wish not to talk.

The light began to fade as I stared toward the window. The beating of my heart turned into a pound as imaginary shadowed figures stalked toward me.

I gripped the blankets, grimacing as words rushed from my lips, "Wait, please." Alexander turned to me without hesitation. "Can you stay with me? Like the night of the attack."

Alexander gave a single nod before walking back to my bed, setting the candle on the nightstand as I made space.

Comfort and warmth swept over me as his arm wrapped around my waist, pulling me flush against him. I breathed deeply, inhaling the comforting scent of pine, easing my heartbeat into a slow, calm pace.

I hadn't felt comfort like this since my talks with Griffith back in Isara. No. I felt more comfort now than I ever did back then.

My stomach twisted as I clutched the pendant to my chest.

CHAPTER 32

I begrudgingly opened my eyes, as they were still heavy with sleep. The bed was warmer than usual. Something weighed down on my side, another object between my legs, making it impossible to wriggle out of the bed. I waited for my vision to clear before searching for the cause of my immobility.

A blob of black, that looked like hair, came into view. I willed my eyes to focus, slowly the details became clear.

Alexander.

His arms were tightly wrapped around me, and my fingers were entangled with his blouse while his leg rested between mine. I released his shirt, placing my palms on his chest, pushing him away, wiggling out of his grasp. The warmth left my body.

I had slept so soundly that I had forgotten he had stayed.

But what was I supposed to do now?

My eyes trailed over Alexander. His cheek squished against the pillow. His lips parted as deep breaths flowed in and out. He looked so peaceful. It wouldn't be right to wake him.

I scooched farther away.

I'd read my book while I waited for him to wake.

I had almost reached the edge of the bed when his arm flopped over me and pulled me back to him. I pushed away his arm as his nose nuzzled my neck, but his grip only tightened.

"Alexander," I growled, grinding my teeth.

He replied with a mumble of sorts and a short snore.

He was still asleep.

"Alexander," I repeated louder, trying to wake him. I would not have his eyes open with me in his arms, fully awake. The amount of teasing that would ensue…I didn't want to think of it.

I grunted as I tried to move his arm with no avail as his dense muscles outweighed all my strength.

What to do?

A loud knock came from my door. I froze. Anna could help me, but at the expense of embarrassment for both of us. I hesitated to reply.

"Prince Alexander." The voice was deep with no trace of femininity in it. I listened closer as it rang again. "Prince Alexander, are you in there?"

It was Samuel.

Alexander groaned, rolling onto his back, *magically* waking to Samuel's voice. His eyes shifted left and right assessing his surroundings as if he, too, had forgotten the events of last night.

He dragged himself to the door, opening it ever so slightly so his body blocked the view of the room.

I listened closely, trying to decipher their mumbles.

Something about Anna, breakfast...

Their voices were too low to decipher any details.

The door cracked open further, revealing a sliver of Samuel on the other side. His eyes met mine briefly, and red flooded his face as his gaze darted away. I sleepily looked around, trying to figure out the cause of his embarrassment.

I gasped, gripping the blankets to me, as I noticed the lacing on the front of my sleeping gown had come undone, revealing the tops of my breasts. The fabric was mere inches away from my peaked nipples.

Panicking, I looked to the chaise then the vanity, desperately searching for my robe.

Alexander began to turn around. My heartbeat hastened. I looked to the ground, hand on my bosom. I could only imagine the teasing he was about to do. But as I gave up hope, I saw it, my robe.

I snatched it off the floor, frantically trying to throw it on. But as I put one arm in a sleeve, Alexander turned around, a breakfast tray in his hands.

He chuckled as his devilish smirk emerged.

"Why so embarrassed?" He sat on the bed, placing the tray between us. "Let me remind you, I've seen much more of you before."

I cinched the robe tightly around me, examining the mountain full of meat, bread, and fruit, highly concerned if this was his routine breakfast.

"I didn't know if Samuel was about to come in."

Alexander's eyebrows rose as he purposefully misinterpreted my words.

"So, it's fine if I see it then?" Alexander's hand lurked toward the ribbon keeping the robe closed, his eyes glinting with mischief.

I slapped his hand away, glaring at him as he chuckled and raised his hands in surrender. "Sorry, couldn't resist. You know I love a good tease."

I aggressively bit a piece of bread, attempting to instill fear. Alexander only smiled and followed suit.

"Anna will be here soon," I grimaced, looking at the rising sun.

"Is that your way of politely telling me to leave?" Alexander took a sip of tea. "You know, when you share such an *intimate* night with someone, you shouldn't rush them out. It's only polite."

"There was nothing intimate about last night. Stop your teasing."

"One would think it that way, especially with how close you were when I awakened."

I rolled my eyes, ignoring his teasing. I didn't understand why he had to be like that. "If Anna comes in while you're here, it will be very," I hesitated, searching for the right word.

We were married. There was nothing shameful about *this*. It was a good sign for our union, at least for the public eye.

So why didn't I want Anna to see?

Perhaps the secondhand embarrassment that I would feel when she walked in on us half-dressed snuggling? No. We were awake now, not even touching. As a maid, she was used to such sights. My nose wrinkled as I searched for the answer, twirling the floral pendant on my neck.

Griffith.

Anna wasn't a gossip, but the more people who knew about *this,* the more likely it would spread. A rumor that Alexander and I slept with one another for more than just *duties*. A rumor that may reach Griffith's ears.

"Don't look so worried. I told Samuel to instruct Anna to come late and to do so for the next couple of days as well."

My eyebrows rose.

"Since I'll be sleeping with you from now on."

"Excuse me?" I squealed, almost spilling my tea.

"You didn't scream again." Alexander stared at me with serious intent.

My eyes darted down. "I told you. The nightmares are nothing."

"No." His voice was thick with concern. "I've seen your eyes the past couple of days. You've been walking around with them half open. These nightmares happen often and probably more than once a night."

I bit my lip, avoiding his gaze.

"This morning, you've had the most energy I've seen in you for a while. You didn't have another nightmare after I laid next to you. Did you?"

I raised my head meeting his eyes.

"Estelle, let me help."

I dug my nails into my palms, my eyelids closing.

I couldn't do this to Griffith. But I needed this. I needed Alexander. I needed the comfort of last night.

This is nothing more than a means of survival. A way to protect my sanity from the nightmares, the shadows that haunted me at night. Griffith would understand. Right?

I breathed out, eyes opening. "Only until the nightmares go away."

CHAPTER 33

Princess Estelle,

Things are busy at the castle. We are undergoing investigations of our own. Do not worry about us. We have all the information we need. Your help is not required, nor will it be in the future.

I have heard that the prince has moved his chambers closer to yours, that he comforts you when nightmares occur. I am glad he is there for you when Isara and her people cannot.

I believe my job as your confidant has ended, that you have found friends who can better help you. Just as I have found my services are better to Isara if focused on those here. I will always serve the Princess of Isara when she needs me most, but for now, I believe it is best for us to focus on the matters that stand in front of us.

Lord Griffith

CHAPTER 34

My knees dug into my chest as blankets laid over me, blocking the sun. The wax from Griffith's letter scratched my chest as I sobbed.

Why hadn't I been stronger?

If I had just dealt with the nightmares, none of this would've happened. I had lost my best friend and my only connection to Isara.

I needed to find a way to code a letter, apologize. I needed to explain why I had Alexander in my bed.

I reached for the pile of parchment on my side table, trying to pull ideas from my head. I needed words only he could understand.

I pushed my quill into the parchment. The ink flowed, creating a blob. No words came.

Your help is not required, nor will it be in the future.

Griffith didn't even want to communicate with me for the information I gained as a spy, nothing I could say would fix this.

I crumpled the paper, throwing it across the room as tears dropped. As I fell back onto the chaise, I clutched the pendant Griffith had gifted me with love.

I should send it back, but this…this was now the only reminder I had left of what we shared between us.

"Your Highness, are you still asleep?"

Anna.

I wiped my tears, peaking at the clock, nine. It had been two hours since Alexander departed, and the letter was delivered.

"Princess Estelle?"

Anna's footsteps grew louder as she dove deeper into the room.

I rubbed at my face, trying to remove the stains that began at the corner of my eyes and ended at my chin.

"Your Highness," she chimed over me in concern. "You've been crying. Are you in pain?" I remained quiet, unable to explain. "I'll fetch Aeson."

My heart dropped. Aeson couldn't help this pain. No one could. I was the only one who could heal myself. Bringing Aeson would only bring this sadness to light and cause people to look for what caused it.

I reached for Anna's arm, barely catching it before she was out of reach.

"I'm fine, Anna, just tired."

Her eyes of worry cascaded over my body, looking for any signs of harm. I waited, knowing she would find none then her gaze froze. *The letter in my hand.* I crumpled it behind my back as if the action could rid Anna's memory of the parchment. But it had been seen, and with the crest visible, she would know it was from Lord Griffith.

"Is everything fine back in Isara?" she asked, pausing between words, tip-toeing around the sensitive topic.

I sat up, letting out a sigh.

It was no secret that Griffith and I had kept in contact, as Anna was the one who delivered most of the letters until Alexander had started sleeping with me every night. Now, Samuel delivered them when he came to ready us for the day. But still, I needed to select my words carefully. As far as I knew, Griffith and mine's relationship, our past relationship, was still a secret—apart from Alexander knowing I had once loved him. Information he hadn't shared. I was confident he would keep it that way, just as he had promised. Which meant that if the secret got out, it would be the fault of *my* sneakiness.

"The castle has gotten busier than ever since the"—I gulped. It had been weeks, but the event still haunted my mind—"the incident. Letters from home will be scarce."

Anna's eyes shifted to the floor, carefully selecting her words—a thing everyone did around me nowadays, even Titus. It constantly reminded me of the injured animal I was.

I wanted things to be normal, to be treated as such. But I knew it wouldn't, not while the memories of the running blood and my bounded hands still haunted me at night. No amount of sleeping potions kept the nightmares away, only

Alexander did that. He was the cure for my trauma but the poison for Griffith and me.

"Princess Estelle." Anna's hand gently unfurled my fist, massaging the indentations caused by my nails. "The letters may be scarce now, but they will return in time."

Anna continued to massage my hand, offering up a soft smile.

Her smile was so kind that I couldn't help but offer one back, but in my heart, I knew the letters would never return.

"Perhaps some fresh air may do us some good." My eyes stung as Anna flung open the curtains, revealing the bright sun. "How about a layout in the garden?"

I gave Anna a quick nod, sending her into a flurry of movement. I felt a small bit of warmth in my heart as she began to ramble on and on about the spring weather, the blooms of the flowers while she hustled around the room.

Perhaps the letter was true in the aspect that we needed to focus on the things in front of us, find happiness there.

CHAPTER 35

"You two are just now heading out for the day?"

Alexander sauntered out of his room, sword in hand, his bedhead from this morning groomed.

My eyes shot to his sword. "I thought you were supposed to be resting."

"And I thought you had a well-rested night." He leaned in close, examining the puffiness no amount of powder could hide.

I took a step back, biting my lip, my breath halting. I couldn't let Alexander know that I was saddened by one of Griffith's letters. To others who didn't know our history, my excuse was plausible, but Alexander...he knew of our past. He would see through my lie; see that Griffith and I wrote for more reasons than what I had claimed in the past.

I had to be careful. I needed to act like usual. I couldn't let him see the sadness that I was suppressing.

"Maybe if you didn't snore, I would have." I teased; the only thing I knew would make his examination end.

"It is you, princess, who is the annoying sleeping companion. Always moving around and seeking warmth by my side. It is a wonder how I stand straight every day."

I rolled my eyes. His monstrous body simply took up too much room. I would never seek him out, even my subconscious wouldn't, for my heart belonged wholly to—my fingers reached for the pendant around my neck. The presence of Alexander's eyes grew stronger on me.

"I suppose you're right since you carry around a sword you're not even allowed to use. Perhaps you should stop visiting my bed before your deliria worsens." The words rolled out, frantically wanting to change the subject as I felt my heart crack, my hand dropping, and my eyes meeting Alexander's.

Alexander's face was solemn for a second as my gaze met his, then he let out a hearty laugh. "You have a particularly sharp tongue today. You really must not have slept well. But you would get worse sleep if I wasn't there." I rolled my eyes but knew his words were true. We had tried a couple of times to sleep separately, but each time I woke screaming, searching for him in the dark. "Aeson just cleared me, so no need to worry about my mind or the cold you would've felt tonight if I took your prescription."

I sucked on my lips. His teasing had gotten so much worse since we started to share a bed. My tongue became sharper as a result. It was an extension of the game we played. Now it wasn't used just to distract from the pressure of the foreign diplomats. It was used to distract from the real reason he slept in my bed. A way to keep my mind off the nightmares he protected me from. My lips parted, ready with my next remark when a voice grumbled behind Alexander.

"To do basic training movements, you're still not allowed to raise your sword against another."

I peered around Alexander, spotting Aeson hobbling out of Alexander's room.

"They're basically the same." Alexander shrugged and smirked, but that quickly dissipated as Aeson held his cane above Alexander's shoulder then allowed gravity to bring it down.

"Why would you do that?" Alexander rubbed his arm.

"If you think that hurts, imagine a sparring sword coming down on you."

Alexander's bottom lip jutted out as he bit the inside of his cheek.

I let out a chuckle, the first of the day, catching Aeson's attention. "Where are you two going?"

Anna and I stiffened, and my mouth went dry.

Upon my first meeting with Aeson, I had thought him a kind old man, who occasionally stood up to Titus and Alexander. However, after he took my stitches out, I learned he was more of the grumpy grandfather of the castle.

He said and did whatever he liked because he knew no one would stop him. He was more frightening than Greta when she was in a foul mood.

I frantically looked around. I had been so consumed with Alexander and mine's banter, I had forgotten what Anna and I were doing and the sadness that had caused this venture.

"We're going to read in the garden," I finally spoke, gesturing at the basket resting on Anna's arm, containing a handful of books and a blanket.

"So, nothing too important." A statement, not a question.

"I thought you would be glad we were reading."

Aeson examined the basket. "Are you reading about medicine?"

"No," I answered softly, knowing that the books were romance novels. Despite my original disgust of them, I now found them captivating.

"Politics?"

I paused then followed with a no.

"History?"

I shook my head.

"So, pleasure reading?"

Anna and I looked at each other once again, a blush forming on both our cheeks.

"You two will keep an eye on Alexander today."

All three of us gaped at one another, urging each other to conjure an excuse. But none of us dared to challenge Aeson.

"Well, get a move on. I'll send Samuel to check on all of you once he's done helping me with my herbs. Thank you again for lending him to me." Alexander gave him a brusque nod.

I glared at Alexander through my lashes.

How could he offer up poor Samuel to the claws of Aeson?

Aeson let out a cough, calling back everyone's attention. "With that, I'll take my leave."

We all gave him a respectful bow, remaining quiet till he was no longer visible.

I positioned myself in front of Alexander and Anna. "And what if we don't follow his orders?"

"Last time I disobeyed Aeson, I was diagnosed with a rare illness. The only cure was an elixir that tasted like dirt and swamp water," Alexander replied.

I threw my hand over my mouth hiding the gag.

I had wanted to be alone, alone as one could get after almost being murdered, to process my feelings. But the idea of drinking the foul liquid for however long Aeson saw fit was not worth the solitude.

"At least we still get to breathe the fresh air," Anna piqued as we laid out the blanket.

"Yes, with the smell of sweat wafting around us."

Anna giggled as we plopped down while Alexander, already in a fighting stance, faced a straw figure.

Despite his meek opponent, his focus did not differ from when he sparred with a real threat. His arms trembled slightly as he held the broadsword, making the weakness he gained from his time off apparent. His breathing flowed in and out of his body, steadying himself. Then, with one hit, the straw head fell to the ground.

"I oddly feel bad for the dummy, being hacked away like that, such a slow death to have," squeaked Anna.

We were going to be here for ages.

I stood up, my violet-blue dress flapping in the wind. "Must you really chop off its limbs one by one? Can't you just stab it and say it's dead?"

Alexander lowered his sword, glaring at me. "It's harder than it looks."

"Yes, I'm sure straw is *very* hard to cut through."

Alexander swung the sword in a circle, warming his wrists, wrinkles forming on his brow.

I was getting on his nerves. We wouldn't be out here long. I smiled.

"Come on, you should be able to flick your wrist and—"

"It's not that simple," Alexander grumbled, his body fully facing me. "Come here."

I looked back at Anna. Her eyes were wide with worry. I hesitantly took a step forward, knowing the fire in his eyes, a fire so compelling I could not do anything but his will.

"Here." Alexander held the blade in his hand, so the hilt was closest to me. I opened my mouth, tilting my head, ready with excuses. "You said it was easy, then you try."

I gripped the hilt, slowly taking the weight as Alexander let go. He had just taken his hand away when the sword came crashing down. I braced myself ready to hear, ready to feel the metal collide with the ground, but calloused hands gripped mine, sharing the weight.

"Too heavy?"

I looked up to find Alexander peering down at me with that annoying smirk. He took the sword from my hand as I gave him a shy nod, sheathing the blade.

"Guess I'll be going back to my reading then."

"Not so fast." He grabbed my forearm, flinging me back to him, our chests touching as they often did at night. "Try this." He pulled a dagger from his boot, placing it into my amateur hands.

I titled the blade, so the sun shimmered off it. This was the second time I had held a dagger. The first was when I had thought Alexander would take my life, now a laughable memory.

Alexander grasped my hands, tightening my fingers over the handle. "Hold it tightly." He took a step back, circling me, his voice commanding yet alluring.

Alexander forced his foot between my legs, spreading them inch by inch. "Keep your stance wide." He forced my non-dominant arm up. "Use this arm for balance while the other swings."

He circled around me once more, nodding his head every so often, his eyes inspecting every piece of my body.

"Perfect."

A shiver went down my spine, as the word left his lips. Something about that word, the way he said it inclined me to believe he was referring to more than just my form.

I shook my head, it wasn't possible. What Alexander and I had was merely platonic. Not to mention, my heart was still healing from Griffith.

"Now," he whispered, his voice slithering into my ear from behind, "do you know where to aim?"

My body stiffened. *Aim to kill.* I couldn't even raise my hand to a fly. "I don't think this is a skill I ought to learn."

I lowered the blade, but Alexander caught my hand. Slowly, he forced it back up, his breath hot on my ear. "I want you to be prepared if it happens again, be able to buy time till I get to you."

"I…I…" My throat went dry, as images of the blood splattered room jumped into my mind, memories of how I laid there defenseless not knowing what would become of me.

He leaned in closer to my ear, his chest hot against my back. "Please, it will keep me at ease if you know how to defend yourself if only a little."

My stomach tightened as blood rushed to my cheeks. After all these weeks of sleeping together, I never had the inclination that the intrusion had affected him nor that he thought of me in his free time.

I peeked at him, his eyes pleading. I didn't want to see him like this.

"You just want an excuse to leave my bed," I teased, hoping to lighten the air.

"You really think I want to return to my bed?" he growled as his fingers tightened again, his temple touching mine while his lips brushed the cuff of my ear.

My body tensed. *He wasn't teasing me back.*

"Alexander," I whispered, turning to face him. If there was any confusion on what our relationship was, it needed to be addressed.

He shushed me as I turned. "Later," was the only word he uttered. His eyes were fierce, fiery, taking away my breath. I gulped, turning around, unable to face them.

I raised the dagger, no longer relying on Alexander's strength to hold it.

"The first and most obvious spot is here." He slowed his words as his thumbnail glided, deliciously, across my neck. "The next area"—his hand pivoted so his thumb touched the top of my throat, and his pinky touched the base of my neck while the others sat between them. Slowly, he dragged them down till they were between my breasts—"come from under and plunge the dagger upward."

My body shivered, as the warmth from his breath tickled my ear.

"Then"—his fingers grazed down to my abdomen.

I shut my eyes, calming the heat that was rising in me.

This was wrong. My heart belonged to—

No.

It didn't.

Not anymore.

Griffith had relinquished my heart and moved on, suggesting I do the same. Maybe this was what I needed to look to, move toward. But Alexander, he was my friend. I couldn't ruin that.

"Don't let go of the reins!" a deep voice boomed followed by a terrifying neigh.

"Look out!"

I opened my eyes in time to see a brown horse racing toward us, his hooves chipping away at the earth. I held up my arm, curling into a ball as the beast stood on his back legs, ready to feel the weight come crashing down.

An arm shielded my head as my body flew sideways, effectively softening the impact to the ground. I peeked through my eyelashes in time to see the brown stallion's hooves dent the earth with force, force that would've killed.

Four stable boys circled the horse, throwing lassos around its neck, battling its strength.

Alexander grimaced beside me in a ball, clutching his shoulder.

My eyes shot up in a panic, surveying the training grounds. The stallion panted, drool dribbling out of its mouth. Two stable boys held the ropes, leading him back to the stables, leaving two watching.

"You," I barked, pointing at the one who looked the most fit. "Fetch Aeson." The boy's eyes shifted to Alexander who remained on the ground groaning. "Now," I roared, sending the boy off with fear.

Anna raced over, kneeling next to us.

"Let's get him to the blanket," I commanded.

Anna and I stood on his sides, carefully pulling him to his feet, the motion causing him to whimper.

"Do you think Aeson is going to ban me from practicing again?" Alexander moaned out as we leaned him against the tree.

I kneeled beside him; fists clenched. "You get hit by a horse and that's what you're concerned about!" My voice rose with every word.

"Not hit." He shifted himself, letting another groan escape. "We dodged it last minute, I just fell on the wrong shoulder."

My fists shook as the urge to slap him heightened. This was no time for his smart remarks.

His eyes ran up and down my body. "Good. You're not hurt."

The anger subsided in me as I met Alexander's soft gaze. He had no concern for himself, only relief for me.

When did my safety become more important than his own?

"You idiot. You're the Prince of Modare. You should've—"

"And you're my *wife*. I will protect you, always. No matter the risk."

My heart stopped at his words, his serious eyes.

"Where is the stupid Prince?" Aeson gurgled as he dismounted a horse.

"Here we go." Alexander straightened his back, concealing his pain.

"I heard a horse beat you." Aeson pursed his lips together as he moved Alexander's arm in all directions, looking for any signs of pain. "I thought I told you to stick to the straw."

"I got bored."

"Well, you're lucky, everything looks fine," Aeson mumbled, his eyes perplexed.

"So, I'll still be able to compete?"

"As long as there isn't any pain."

Alexander shook his head no, smiling, convinced he had fooled Aeson.

"Oh, there is pain, he's just good at hiding it." I flicked Alexander's arm forcing a groan out of him.

He cursed under his breath, glaring at me, as Aeson gave me an approving nod.

"I suppose you won't be competing after all." Aeson rummaged through his bag.

"Aeson, I compete every year." Aeson ignored him as he continued his search. "It was a mere fall. I'll be fine."

Aeson turned from his bag in a huff. "If you compete in combat while that arm is still injured, I can guarantee your sprain will turn into something beyond what I can heal. So, you will not be cleared as long as I am your physician."

Alexander smacked his lips, brows furrowed.

"Now"—Aeson reached back into his bag— "I can offer this ointment. It is known to quicken the healing process."

Alexander reached for the jar greedily. "I can reevaluate you, a couple days before the tournament." Alexander grinned ear to ear. "But," Aeson warned, his voice now stern, "there is no guarantee I'll clear you, but you do have a better chance if the ointment is applied today."

"Thank you, Aeson." Alexander stood, too swiftly. Pain enveloped his face.

Both Aeson and I rolled our eyes.

"You'll need the aid of Samuel or me. The ointment needs to be massaged on the back of your shoulder till it dries, about twenty minutes.

I chuckled at the thought of Aeson massaging Alexander's back. Such an *intimate* affair.

"I'll have Estelle do it."

My jaw dropped and my eyes bulged. *I would not.*

Aeson looked me over, nodding his approval. "Do it sooner than later today. I suggest you do it in your bed chamber as you need to lay on your stomach, out of the sun, for the best results."

"What? I—" But it was too late, Aeson was already hobbling away, dragging Samuel with him.

"Since you enjoyed intervening so much, I figured you'd like to help." Alexander stood next to me, holding his shoulder with one hand and the jar with the other.

"You are absolutely—"

"Princess Estelle, if you don't wish to apply the ointment, I'm sure I can step in," Anna whispered, her face tomato red.

"No, it's fine Anna," I replied, unable to subject her to the torment of Alexander. "Enjoy the air."

Anna nodded, appreciative of my rejection.

I focused on the desk, trying to stop the blush rising to my cheeks, trying not to think about Alexander's bare skin as he laid on the bed.

"You realize you'll have to look while you're applying the ointment," Alexander seethed. "If it's not properly applied and I can't compete, I will blame you."

I scooped the slimy salve out of the jar, smearing it onto Alexander's shoulder. "If Aeson says you can't compete, it won't be my fault."

Alexander let out a groan of relief as I rubbed in the cool ointment.

"It will be. You're the one who flicked me."

"You were hiding the pain. If I hadn't, Aeson would have let you compete."

"Exactly." Alexander flinched as I rubbed a tender spot.

"You just flinched at what is supposed to be a caring touch. You need to be on bed rest." My voice rose, frustrated with his hard-headedness. "It would be careless if you did anything otherwise."

"As a second son, carelessness is my job," he replied, his tone feigning boredom, angering me more.

"Alexander, you cannot think like that. You can't just say, I'm the second son and do whatever stupid thing you want. Carelessness doesn't just hurt you. It also hurts those who love you."

He remained silent, *finally* subdued by my words. I nodded in approval, hoping my harsh tone had gotten through to him. He needed to be more careful. If anything happened to him…

"Estelle," he whispered. "Will my carelessness hurt you?" He tilted his head up.

Of course, I would care.

I rolled my eyes before finding his. My stomach dropped. The intensity in them was far too great as they anxiously waited, pleaded for an answer. I inhaled sharply as I realized what he was truly asking. My hand slowed as my heart fluttered, a part of me wanting to give him the answer he craved.

When did I come to care for him like this?

I had been so preoccupied with Griffith that I had been blind to the budding feelings for the man before me. The man, who granted me a wish, pulled me back to the light when I had given up, shielded me from danger, and now enveloped me in warmth and safety.

Was it too soon to move on?

My eyes shifted down to his lips. It'd be so easy to lean in and kiss them, to forget about Griffith, to find love in this forced marriage. But I was too scared, too scared to fall for another, to lose another friend if this—whatever I was feeling—didn't work.

Tears welled up in my eyes. I blinked rapidly, commanding them to cease. I needed more time. I touched Griffith's pendant, now a painful reminder to protect my heart.

Alexander grabbed my hand, bringing it to his lips as if to apologize. "It's alright, you don't have to answer."

I looked to his eyes, which were darting away from the pendant, filled with defeat but understanding.

He had misunderstood my reaction. This isn't what I wanted. I had to explain.

"Alexander, I—"

"Prince Alexander," a shrill voice screeched, so unique I instantly knew its owner, Leo.

The door opened without invitation.

"Prince Alexander, King Titus requests your immediate presence. He would like a—" Leo's eyes met mine as I sat on the bed over Alexander's half-naked body. "Oh, was I interrupting something? I can come back later, I just have to—" Leo backed away, lowering his eyes from the scene.

For once, he could read the room.

"It's fine. We were just finishing up." Alexander sat up, pulling his shirt over his head, avoiding my gaze.

"Ah, I see, well…"

Leo clearly didn't walk into many scenes like this.

Alexander, still avoiding my eyes, donned his belt and jacket as he gave Leo time to collect himself. I wanted to tell him what was going on, that my heart, my head, all of it was confused. Still, I cared for him nonetheless.

"King Titus would like an injury report before your journey to the docks, to greet the nobles who will be attending the Spring Festival."

Alexander hopped around the room pulling on his boots. "This couldn't have waited till the day I left?"

"We just got word that the Ambassador from Pineton will be arriving tomorrow."

Alexander let out a sigh. "Which means I have to leave today."

"Precisely."

Alexander placed his hands on his hips, surveying the room. "Have Samuel pack two jackets, five pairs of pants, and shirts. Nothing too regal, just my travel clothes."

Leo nodded, opening the door for Alexander to leave.

"You're leaving now?" I involuntarily screamed as I hastily stood.

Leo's eyes widened in surprise as Alexander turned toward me, his body like lead. "I'll be back in a week, I'm sorry. Aeson has been making a stronger sleeping potion for you. It should be ready."

A sleeping potion?

My forehead wrinkled. He thought my outburst was out of concern for my nightmares. This misunderstanding was too great. It was now or never. It didn't matter if Leo was here.

"Alexander."

"You're going to be late," Leo shrilled.

I glowered at Leo, effectively quieting him. "Alexander, we need to talk."

"We'll talk in a week during the Spring Festival." Alexander pulled me into a sorrowful, understanding hug. "Try not to get into any trouble," he mumbled into my hair, swiftly pulling away, giving me no time to speak.

I watched till he was out of sight, the warmth leaving with him.

CHAPTER 36

"What do you mean delayed?" I shrieked, spinning around.

Anna grabbed my shoulders, turning me back to the mirror, allowing her to place the silver ornaments in my braid.

"Apparently, there's an ambassador that decided to come last minute."

Anna waved the last silver ornament around my braid, contemplating where to place it.

"How absurd? Ambassadors should know their plans better."

Anna shrugged her shoulders, finally placing the silver butterfly in between two flowers.

I had been counting down the days since Alexander had left. Not because of the nightmares, those had subsided as Aeson's new sleeping potion proved to be potent against them. I was counting down because I missed his teasing, his smirk, our talks before bed. And above all, I had missed him. I had been unaccepting of my realized feelings, too stricken with grief over Griffith that I was unable to tell Alexander when he left, but now, it was all I wanted to do.

"Which cloak would you like?"

I stared into the mirror, inspecting the light blue chiffon dress decorated with silver gems resembling the many blooming flowers of spring. The color was bold at the bottom but as my eyes moved up, the color softened till the fabric turned sheer at my arms. Any cloak would hide the dress's beauty.

"None. I think I'd rather be cold than conceal this design," I replied, as I stood, allowing my leg to pop out of the slit.

Anna smiled, nodding in agreement.

"Does nobody keep track of time in this castle?" Leo's shrill voice sounded from the door.

I did not turn to look at him, as I was still angry about his last interruption.

"Princess Estelle, you are late! The tournament has begun."

I looked in the mirror tucking in a stray hair. Missing a tournament was the least of my worries, in fact, being late was a blessing.

"King Titus—"

Curses.

Another grueling lecture was coming and not from Leo. I nodded to Anna who followed closely behind as we sped past Leo, who was left with a baffled expression. As we rushed down the halls, the applause from the tournament—being held on the training grounds—echoed through the castle and vibrated through our hearts.

"King Titus." I bowed deeply, showing the respect the people expected.

He grunted, slightly bowing his head, allowing me to join him.

I took a seat in the chair that sat lower. A serf quickly handed me a silver goblet filled with fragrant wine.

"I'm sorry for—"

King Titus held up a hand, silencing me, as a flag was dropped. Two horses rushed at one another as their riders—one dressed in yellow and the other green—lowered their jousts. Wood flew upwards as shield and joust collided. A simultaneous groan, from the crowd, drowned out the thud of the yellow rider who had fallen from his horse. He clambered to his feet, unsheathing his sword. A squire tossed him a metal shield. He clanged them together, challenging the green knight. The green knight, accepting it, threw down his joust and shield to take hold of a flail. He raised it above his head, arrogantly prancing around the arena, calling for the people's cheers. Their screams grew louder and louder as he circled. Then, when the screams could no longer rise, he charged on his horse, successfully swinging his flail into the yellow knight's shoulder.

My hand shot up to my mouth as his screams of agony rang in my ear, his distraught face reminding me of Alexander's injury.

"I take it you didn't attend many tournaments in Isara."

I looked over to King Titus who was respectfully clapping while the green knight completed his celebration lap.

"No, never had a taste for them." I took a long drink from my cup as the squires cleaned the arena for the next round.

"Finally, something we can agree on."

My eyes flickered to King Titus in shock.

"I see you still think I'm a violence loving king."

My lips parted, unable to speak. I knew King Titus was not a tyrant king; however, I still saw him as a brash, unrefined man. I imagined watching a tournament would be his favorite thing. But, I suppose, I never truly got to know him as I avoided him on most occasions.

King Titus grunted as I shamefully lowered my eyes.

"You can go if you wish. There only needs to be one of us here."

King Titus drank deeply from his cup as he toasted to the next set of knights, avoiding my eyes.

I should have been thankful for the invitation and taken my leave, but my legs couldn't lift me. Modare was to be my home for the remainder of my life, and in these past months, I had lived as if I would return to Isara, that this was only temporary. I believed that one-day Griffith and I would be together. It was only a week ago that this irrational idea ended.

Maybe it was time to truly see who King Titus was.

"And let you be tortured all alone?" I raised my glass signaling for more wine.

King Titus turned to me with raised brows as the serf poured till my cup was full.

"How do people even find this enjoyable? It's the same thing over and over again," I slurred to Titus as he hiccupped.

"I have absolutely no idea." Titus took a sip of wine. "I've been asking Alexander about it for years, and none of his answers ever make sense."

I threw my head back, groaning at his name. "That man would not stop talking about how he was going to compete despite his shoulder." I signaled for my fifth glass of wine. "So irritating. I swear he would've competed without Aeson's approval."

Titus let out a laugh. "That's why he's not here."

I leaned over the armrest, placing both my hands on my warm face, waiting for Titus to divulge more information.

"He would have competed without a doubt, either snuck in as someone else or just showed up on the field before we could stop him. Then, he would've ended up like Sir Rolio—" Titus gestured to the yellow knight whose arm was now in a sling—"completely immobile for months. Absolutely careless."

"Agreed. I tried to tell him that he needed to take better care of himself as he is in line for the throne. He could be king one day and he simply…" I sat silent as Titus's face turned somber. My sobriety returned, realizing what I'd said.

I had spoken of his brother becoming king, a grave insult, as it inferred that Titus would die before he sired children.

"I'm sorry. The wine…" I set the devilish cup down.

"He should be king," Titus whispered.

"Titus," my voice trailed off as his whisper continued.

"He loves this country and would do anything for it. He is always the first to grab a sword and head out the gate. I hate it." Titus placed his goblet down.

I fought the urge to reach for Titus's hand as tears welled up in his eyes.

"I've almost lost him before, back in the war."

Images of his back, the scar that I had seen flashed in my head.

"He insisted that one of us had to be out there, that it had to be him. He was slashed in the back, by a cowardly Lord from Ula, when he went to help an old man who had gotten caught in the battle.

"The Lord would've killed him despite the old man pleading if it were not for one of our dear friends, Lord Leon, who stabbed the villain down. He was quick to bandage Alexander, quick to bring him home. He was so close to the brink of death though. We truly thought we'd lose him."

The next round began, but neither Titus nor I paid the knights any attention as the flag was dropped.

"He was out for a week, and we began to lose the war. I didn't know what to do, I couldn't think. Every choice I made led us closer to defeat. Then, by some miracle, he woke up and went straight to work. He revised battle plans, rebuilt our defenses, and sent out the troops. He put hope back in the people's hearts. We started winning again because of him."

Titus gulped, forcing the tears back down that crept out of his eyes.

"I tell him to stay time and time again, to be careful. But he just repeats that he is the second son. If he was king, he would stay behind these walls. He would've been strong enough to rule alone. He loves this kingdom so; nothing would cloud his rule."

I sat silently in my chair, not knowing what to say. Never had Titus shown a glimmer of weakness, and now, I knew his greatest fear.

"Except you."

I straightened my back at the change of tone in his voice.

"You are the only thing he values more than Modare." My eyes widened. "You aren't just important for the treaty anymore." Titus's eyes met mine, his body stiffening as he realized the truths, the weakness he drunkenly revealed. "I will make sure you are safe, that peace remains between our two kingdoms. But know this, I will always put Alexander first before that treaty or you."

I inhaled sharply, realizing the depth of Alexander's feelings that I was blind to, the power I had over him.

CHAPTER 37

I collected the blush pink tulle of my dress, hiking it up as I stepped out of the carriage. My cloak grazed the steps as the footman lent his hand to me. A sparkle in my eyes as my feet hit the lush grass. Everywhere I looked there was color; pinks, yellows, blues, greens. I spotted it all as music filled my ears. The smell of fragrant flowers and fruits flooded the festival grounds that sat just before the shimmering lake.

"Welcome to Lake Inanna," Anna trilled behind me.

"It's beautiful." I beamed. My eyes frantically moved, attempting to take it all in.

I wanted to experience it all. The maypole dance, the food, and the wine. I even wanted to watch the games of croquet. I had no idea where to start.

"Shall we visit the royal tent first? Perhaps Prince Alexander is there already."

Alexander.

Finally, after a week, I would answer his question. A soft smile emerged as a rose pink formed on my skin. I nodded to

Anna, unable to speak. She led me down the hill to the dark blue tent that overlooked the festivities.

"King Titus." I curtsied deeply, knowing nobles from various countries were attending the festival. Titles and manners were necessary today.

Titus nodded, gesturing for me to join him on the brightly colored pillows and blankets placed artistically on the grass. I smiled in thanks but inside my stomach flipped. There was no sign of Alexander. Disappointed, I picked up my dress allowing it to flare out as I sat on a golden pillow.

Titus grunted at my theatrics, reaching for a piece of fruit from the table the blankets surrounded.

He was back to his sober, grumpy demeanor, but I did not take it personally as I used to.

He had opened up yesterday. He had regretted it, but some part of him trusted me, and I would follow suit.

I looked out into the festival grounds, wondering where Alexander was but was distracted as a sweet scent drifted up to my nose. I looked over to find Titus slicing a peach in half, the juices dripping down his hand. My mouth salivated.

"Stop looking like we don't feed you," Titus said, handing me half of the peach.

I flashed a smile in thanks before letting the sweet liquid drip down my throat. I let out a groan as the flavor danced on my tastebuds. Every bite was more satisfying than the last. I did not stop eating till I had completely devoured my half.

"Are you going to stay here for the whole festival?" His voice feigned annoyance.

I looked over at Titus who was still savoring the peach. I bashfully looked back into the crowd.

"Not planning on it, just…" I wanted to enjoy the festivities; however, the tent—if Alexander had not arrived yet—would be the first place he would go. And if he was here already, the tent had the best view of the grounds making him easy to spot.

"You should visit the painters. They're over there by the flower fields."

Titus pointed left, to the outer rims of the grounds, past the maypole dance. The worst place I could be while looking for Alexander. I began to protest, but Titus's eyes narrowed, forcing me to take my leave.

"Where to first?" Anna peeped as she left her spot just outside the tent.

"King Titus suggested I admire the painter's work of the flowers."

"A good suggestion. It is always amazing to see them at work, but a rather dull choice considering the many other activities."

I shrugged, slyly smiling at Anna. "We'll go for a couple of minutes, long enough so he knows I took his suggestion."

We walked through the plethora of nobles, each one bowing as I made my way through. Occasionally, one would invite me to participate in the dance or join their group to promenade.

Their sweet smiles tempted me to give in, but I could feel the presence of Titus's eyes on me. As I did not want to see him so offended early in the day, I rejected them all. Then, finally, after much temptation, Anna and I reached the painters at the edge of the meadow.

"Your Highness." One bowed, setting off a chain reaction as all the painters acknowledged my presence. With a soft smile, I gave several curt nods in all directions.

There were about ten painters in a line. Each one was engrossed in their work, elegantly grazing their brushes on the canvas. I scanned each painting, occasionally complementing the work when an artist stepped aside to allow full view.

All the art was beautiful, but by the time I reached the end of the line, the music and laughter were all too enticing. I turned back to Anna, who understood, by my glance, that I was ready to leave.

We had taken about three steps when Anna's sweet voice whispered beside me, "Samuel."

I turned to see him, beaming, as he set a box of paints on a table in the middle of the painters.

"Anna! It's good to see you, again."

Samuel walked briskly to Anna giving her a swift hug. My eyebrows raised with a curious, fascinated smile.

Their romance had progressed since I last took notice.

They looked at each other at arm's length, awkwardly smiling. I couldn't help but chuckle at their infatuation with one another.

Samuel's head bolted up at the sound of my laughter. A red flashed across his cheek as he bent deeply at the waist.

"Your Highness," Samuel stuttered out.

"It is good to see you, Samuel."

"It is a pleasure to be in your presence after a long trip." He slowly rose, his eyes flickering to Anna. The words secretly for her. I would have to tell Alexander of their progression.

My eyes grew wide. Samuel had gone to the port with Alexander. If Samuel was here, then…

A sharp hollow sound came from behind, louder, and louder it grew then all at once it was silent.

Anna and Samuel both bowed as a recognizable neigh rang in my ears.

"You're back," I whispered, turning to find Alexander holding Shadow's reins.

"I told you I'd be back for the Spring Festivities. I just didn't say which day."

My heart fluttered as my eyes welled up. I had never been so happy to see someone in my life. I threw up my arms as my body uncontrollably leaped forward. My head like a magnet to his chest.

"Your nightmares must have been really bad," he teased as he hugged me with his free hand. "Thank you, Samuel," he mumbled as his second hand joined his first. "You cry when I leave, and you cry when I come back. Such a complicated woman."

My head shot up. "I am not," I disagreed, my pitch high, almost a shriek. I uttered a cough, returning it back to a respectable pitch, "complicated."

Alexander smirked, letting me go to unpack several paintbrushes from the satchels that hung from Shadow. "I meant to be here when you arrived, but the painters had forgotten some things. I offered to fetch them, but only because I thought I'd be back in time." A painter came forward, taking the supplies gratefully.

I stared at Alexander sweetly as he continued to pull more and more supplies from the satchels. The warmth had returned. I wanted to be in his arms, fully feel it as I told him of my feelings. But I couldn't possibly do it here, in front of everyone.

"Samuel, could you take Shadow back? I want to take a walk around the lake before the sun sets."

"Of course, Prince Alexander." Samuel mounted Shadow, taking off at a trot.

"Will you join me?" Alexander held out his arm.

A pink blush raced across my face at the thought of holding one another in front of so many nobles.

"It will be good for the treaty," Alexander whispered.

My heart dropped. Alexander had made the attempt to turn our friendship into something more and I, like a fool, had given all the signs I didn't want it. So of course, my blushes would, to him, be because of the love I rejected. He thought

I blushed because I knew he was no longer acting, that these sweet affections he doted on me were real.

I grabbed his arm, my lower lip pouting. I *needed* to tell him. "Anna, could you give us some alone time?" She nodded, smiling sweetly as she retreated to the blue tent. "It'll make us look more in *love*," Alexander whispered so only I could hear.

His words were like daggers to my heart. I knew that they were not of malicious intent. That they were, in fact, to ease me. To let me know that despite his feelings, he would not push unnecessary affections on me. That they were only for our ruse.

We strolled to the lake, quiet at first as the number of eyes on us grew, everyone observing, admiring, and questioning.

"They're like wolves waiting for an opportune moment to attack."

"That's what we get for inviting other countries. Everything is always political." Alexander gave a quick nod to the ambassador from Vropan as he walked past.

"True. But some of these stares"—Alexander's eyes flicked to me, his eyes running up and down my body, debating if he should finish. He bit his lip scowling at himself as he knew he couldn't keep the words to himself—"are just admiring you—your beauty."

My cheeks once again matched the color of my dress. "Thank you." I bit my lip, looking down. We were finally alone. Now would be a good time as any to confess my feelings. "Alexander."

The mention of his name made him freeze. His face went pale as if I was about to scold him.

"You must be excited for the festival," he sputtered out, changing the topic before I could say more. "How does it compare to Isara's?"

My lips pursed together; brows furrowed. What in the gods' names did he think I would scold him about? His compliment? Perhaps. But I welcomed his flirtations now—a fact he wasn't aware of.

I let out a heavy sigh. In all my life I had never been so obtuse.

"Estelle?"

"It's rather fun, very similar in fact, besides the lake. Anna told me the festival closes with fireworks as everyone watches from boats." My words were long and airy as I reworked the courage to tell him my feelings.

"It's a magical moment. I hope you enjoy it. Even Titus starts to smile once we board."

I turned to Alexander; his brow raised waiting for one of my jokes about Titus. I couldn't resist.

"I think that will be more magical than the fireworks."

He chuckled, leaning in to whisper in my ear. "I'll be sure to point it out tonight then."

A shiver ran down my spine as his hot breath unintentionally caressed my ear then my neck. I leaned in as the urge to kiss him grew, but he pulled back.

"How do you close the festival in Isara?"

"Well, we light lanterns. Each one is unique as they are personally handcrafted by each noble." I looked over at Alexander who attentively listened. "Then, when the moon is high, and the stars are bright, we release our lanterns into the night sky."

A melancholy smile appeared on my face as I thought of the fond memories from past years. This had been my favorite part of the festival, but last spring, I had snuck off before it had even begun, for a chance of being alone with Griffith. He had left early, and I thought if I found him, we could spend time alone together. I never did though, but back then it was all worth it to me.

I was so stupid.

If I could see those lanterns one more time, I would give anything to send my lantern up with my father's. A father who I still craved forgiveness from.

My hand clenched into a fist, nails piercing my skin.

"That sounds wonderful. We'll have to visit Isara next year for it," Alexander whispered, his voice gentle and soft as he saw the sadness in my heart.

I cynically laughed. "I don't think my father would welcome me back. He still hasn't written to me since my failure."

There was silence as Alexander selected his words carefully.

"I'm certain he will. If not, we will show him what he is missing and all that you have done for both kingdoms."

I gulped, holding back my sorrows.

"I'm sorry to interrupt, Your Highnesses."

A young girl, perhaps of ten years, with blonde flowing hair and blue eyes, skipped up to us, too young to see the somber aura around us. I wiped my tears, composing myself as Alexander hid me behind his broad back.

"The maypole dance is about to begin again, and I was wondering if the princess will join? I've never seen a princess dance before, and I've heard they move like fairies."

She continued her nonsensical ramble as Alexander peeked over his shoulder to see if I was composed. I coughed, clearing my throat, making sure I would sound cheerful before emerging.

"I'm not sure that I'm as graceful as a fairy, but I certainly shall try." I looked at Alexander as the girl applauded and looked back at her friends who shyly watched from afar. "Will you come?"

"I have one more thing I need to attend to but go enjoy yourself. I'll be back before it is over."

I nodded, taking the little girl's hand as she led me, giddily, to the maypole.

The girl released my hand before handing me a pink ribbon. I smiled in thanks as I took my position on the outer circle with the other women. I held the ribbon tightly as the men stood around the base of the maypole.

I gave a quick nod to those around me as they excitedly curtsied. Then I took in my surroundings, taking note of pebbles and cracks in the earth to avoid during the dance but as I did, I realized a crowd had begun to form. My heart fluttered as I realized all eyes were on me. It had been a while since I danced. I would be rusty. Maybe I shouldn't have agreed. I began to loosen my grip on the ribbon, scanning for someone who wanted it instead, but then the music started.

The tune was slow, melodic as if it was a waltz. One, two, three, I repeated in my head as the outer circle walked clockwise, spinning on the third step, as the men stood still. A splendid way to start the dance as it allowed for partner pairing to be random.

The music picked up. Our walking turned into a skip as we spun our bodies around, flinging our dresses in time with the beat.

The men moved forward, some eyes filled with terror while others were filled with hope, knowing that partners would soon be chosen by fate herself. There was no dread in the outer circle as we were too busy spinning in place, unable to see who approached. Then the music stopped along with our feet.

A man of 20 years stood in front of me. His eyes were filled with intimidation as he stood before me. I let out a chuckle, curtsying as he stiffly bowed. He extended his free, slightly shaking arm as the music began again. This time merry and upbeat. We skipped around in a circle, our ribbons intertwining then reversed the motion to untangle them. A smile burst across my face as I bent down to run under his ribbon before moving on to the next partner.

I curtsied again as the beat of the drum vibrated through my body. This time it was a man in his forties. With a proud smile, he took hold of my hand.

I looked at the maypole; half of its length had been covered in gold, pink, blue, and yellow ribbons. There wasn't much left of this dance.

I got to my last partner, as the circle of people got tighter and tighter. The music sped up, far faster than anyone's feet could move. But as the music reached its peak tempo, we all released our ribbons, allowing the wind to take them. We spun till we were back to the outer circle where the ladies had begun.

I tried to come to a halt. My feet staggered, trying to remain beneath my torso as it moved every which way with dizziness. I looked around and saw others doing the same, some had even fallen to the ground. I let out a laugh, slowly lowering my bottom to the grass.

I braced my arms behind me, trying to stabilize the spinning world, watching the many colorful ribbons carefully be undone for the next dance.

"Looks like the maypole got the better of you." Alexander's hand wrapped around my upper arm, taking most of my weight as I stood.

"I forgot about the spinning."

I leaned on Alexander, focusing on the horizon as the world finally came to a halt.

"Come, the sun sets soon. We need to be next to Titus for his speech."

I nodded, still giddy from the dance.

"Cutting it close," Titus grunted.

I took a seat on the same golden pillow as before, reaching for the remaining fruits that had escaped Titus's appetite.

"But we're here and on time." Alexander took a seat opposite of me, as Anna and Samuel served us wine.

Yellow, orange, and red filled the sky as dusk began to fall. Servants lit torches, illuminating the paths to boats and carriages. The nobles slowly gathered around the royal tent, excitedly waiting for Titus to give the closing speech.

Titus rose from the ground, Alexander and I followed but stayed one step behind him, so we made a triangle.

"Spring is a time for life to begin anew, for flowers to bloom, for the animals to birth, for new love to be found. It is a time for new beginnings." He paused, as everyone leaned in to hear his captivating voice, even me. "In this festival, we gather to celebrate all that spring is, but in this particular year, we celebrate a new beginning for our kingdom. With Isara and Modare united we have opened our doors and made new friends. So, before we head to the boats, let us raise our glasses to Prince Alexander and Princess Estelle. To thank them for birthing us this new opportunity."

My lips parted, surprised at Titus's kind words. He had said them for the public, to better our image. But as he turned and raised his glass to Alexander and me, I could see the sincerity in his eyes.

The crowd dispersed. Some headed to the boats while others, particularly young couples, escaped to the dark corners where they could not be seen. I looked at Anna with wide eyes.

"It gets rather romantic once the fireworks start." Anna peeked at Samuel before returning her eyes back to me. "It's an unofficial tradition to spend it with the one you yearn for. It is best to stay in the light tonight, or you may stumble upon an improper site."

I blushed at Anna's words, but not for the reason she thought. My eyes darted to Alexander. Would he come with me if I asked? To the dark?

"Shall we?" Alexander inquired looking at Titus and me.

"I've had enough for the day. I'll watch from my carriage as I return to the castle."

Titus drudged away before we could retort, leaving Alexander and me looking at one another nervously.

Alexander led me to the last boat on shore. As we got closer, I realized the boat was more like a luxurious raft with wooden railings.

The rowers, equipped with long sticks that could reach the bottom of the lake, opened the gate. I stepped onto the wooden platform, carefully, as it bobbed in the water. The heat of Alexander close by as he held out his arm in case I slipped.

Once on, I fully examined the boat. The design was simple. Built-in benches, decorated with plush pillows, created a U along the front of the boat, their backs making the railing I had seen from shore. In the center, a table held a platter of fruit, wine, and a couple blankets, to help combat the cold night air.

I stood still, not knowing where to sit.

"Over here has the best view."

Alexander headed to the left corner of the boat. I followed sitting close but a respectable distance away.

The boat jolted as the rowers used their sticks to push us offshore and into the water. I looked back as Anna and Samuel waved us goodbye and the land fell away. I gave them a quick wave right before the rowers shut a curtain that acted as a door, giving Alexander and I complete privacy.

My body shivered in nervousness. There was nothing to interrupt us now. I had no excuses.

"You must be cold, here." Alexander unfolded a blanket and wrapped it over my sheer cloak.

I smiled nervously. I didn't understand myself. Alexander had insinuated that he had feelings for me. Titus had told me of the power I had over them because of Alexander's love, yet I was scared, scared of the rejection I might face.

Griffith had been kind. He had given me hints of his affection, but when I confessed he had turned me away. He had done so to protect me back then, but that awful feeling still haunted me. I never wanted to experience it again.

Perhaps his question from last week was his attempt to rile me up. He did love to tease. If Alexander rejected me, I couldn't just run away. He was my husband, I belonged to Modare.

Was this worth the risk?

I jumped—sending my body and the blanket backward—as an explosion sounded, and red and gold splattered across the sky. I looked up despite the scare, admiring the magnificent light show that had begun. A warmth spread across my back.

"Are you that scared that you need to curl up to me?"

I looked behind to see my body flush against Alexander's chest, my bottom an inch away from his lap. His smirk widened as my cheeks grew a deep red.

I made a movement to scooch away, but his broad hand wrapped around my waist to my front, resting on my stomach, keeping me in place.

"One second. I want you to see them take off."

I stilled. "What take off?"

I eyed the shore, but there was only darkness.

"I don't—"

"Give it another second." His words were quiet, mysterious.

I squinted into the darkness. A light popped up on the shore, then another and another till there were a hundred. They drifted into the water, quickly approaching the boats. I stood, leaning over the railing as I tried to see what they were.

Lanterns. They were floating lanterns.

"We couldn't find the material that would allow them to fly so we made them float instead. I hope you still like it."

The lanterns surrounded our boat, hiding the water. It was as if we floated on them, like we were sailing in the sky.

"When did you," my voice trailed off as I noticed that Isara and Modare's crests decorated the lanterns.

"While you were dancing, I had a talk with this year's planner. He was terrified at first, but he got it done. It did cost quite a bit for the rush though."

"Why? Why do all this for me?" I questioned. My voice was soft, weak from his kindness.

"You seemed like you missed home."

I took my hands off the railing, clutching my dress. My heart was ready to burst, but I still couldn't bring myself to tell him. I didn't want to ruin whatever this was.

"Lord Newly, I highly advise you not to do that!" someone yelled from the darkness.

There was a splash followed by laughter, signaling that no one was in danger. But the splash was close enough that it sent a tiny wave, powerful enough to rock our boat.

My body swayed as the boat climbed the swell. As we hit the peak, my heel slipped on the damp wood, sending my body backward. I threw my hands up, grasping for the railing, but I was too late. I braced myself for the hard wood floor, instead, I only found warmth.

A strong, calloused hand gripped my forearm, pulling me up, sliding it around a torso. A bulging bicep pushed into me, supporting my back, while the hand rested on my side. My head was softly but firmly planted into a warm soothing chest.

"That was a close one."

My heartbeat sped, as I looked up to find Alexander's lips inches from mine.

"Be careful of your footing, Princess," he teased.

One side of his lips curved upward, creating that annoying, irresistible smirk. I looked down, hiding the blush that so frequently visited when Alexander was around.

My breathing thickened as I realized how entangled our limbs were. I could feel every curve, every bulge of him and I knew he could feel the same.

A fire was rising between my legs. The urges I had felt when he helped lace my dress now consumed me.

"Alexander," I whispered, my head still down.

He let out a nervous chuckle, his hands slowly leaving my body. "Here, you should sit in case—"

"I don't want to sit," I squealed out.

Alexander froze.

I didn't want his hands to leave me. I didn't want to feel the cold. I wanted him. I wanted to tell him how I felt.

If there were consequences, then let it be so.

I slid the hand on Alexander's waist to his chest, so it sat parallel with the other. I could feel his eyes on me, curious. My fingers played with the fabric of his tunic as my stomach fluttered.

"I need…I need to tell you something. I—" The words struggled to come out as fear and the thirst I had ignored for so long took over.

"Is everything alright? Do you feel sick?" he questioned moving his head closer to assess my face.

I bit my lip, raising my head, meeting his eyes. He looked back at me with concern, but as he stared deeper, his eyes narrowed, and a hungry fire ignited as he realized what I was trying to say.

He tightened his hand around my waist, attempting to pull me closer, but our bodies could move no more. His other hand caressed my cheek, stopping at my chin. He held it with his thumb and forefinger, pausing, looking for any indicator that I wanted him to stop. Then his lips were on mine.

He was gentle, his lips barely caressing mine, giving me the opportunity to pull away if I wanted. I wanted anything but that.

I pushed into him, nipping at his lower lip.

"Estelle," he groaned. His voice was raspy under his staggered breath. He exhaled, trying to calm himself, rubbing his nose on mine, "tell me what you were trying to say."

"You already know," I breathed out as my urges took control, and my brain went numb. I wanted more of his kisses. I wanted him on me. Talking would be for later.

"Estelle, I want to hear you say it." His breathing had turned ragged. His bulge twitched against his pants. He was trying to do the proper thing by discussing these feelings, but that was not what our bodies needed right now.

"Later," I hissed, stepping back. I undid the ribbon to my cloak and let the sheer fabric fall to the ground, revealing my bare collarbone and the top of my exposed bosom.

Alexander's chest stilled as his eyes raked over me, hungry.

"Please," I begged.

"Fuck," he growled, the last of his restraint breaking.

Within mere seconds, his lips were back on mine, possessive, forceful. His grip was tight as he picked me up to lay me down on the bench. His lips never left mine. His fingers trailed my collarbone sending delicious chills throughout my body as his leg rested between my own, leaving them slightly spread.

I threw my arms around his neck, pulling him closer, feeling a smile form across his face at my need. No doubt, already planning on how he'd tease me about it, but I didn't care as long as he would quench the thirst in me.

His fingers slowed as he moved his lips off my mouth and onto my neck. His tongue flicked against my skin, evoking a moan.

Alexander's hand muffled the sound. "Hush, I don't want them to hear you." He looked at the curtain. "Those are reserved for my ears only."

My stomach clenched as a tingling sensation made its way between my legs. I bit my lip as another moan tried to escape.

"That's my girl."

His fingers grazed my neck in a line, lower and lower they went, his lips following. I wriggled underneath him at the slow, tantalizing sensation.

His lips reached the top of my bosom, there, he began to suck as he clawed at my bodice. He pulled it lower till my bare breasts were at the mercy of the cold air. Alexander rested his chin on my chest, staring at me with devilish eyes as he rubbed my peaked nipples with his forefinger and thumb. I arched at the pleasure, at the hunger in his eyes. Alexander devilishly laughed before filling his mouth with my breast.

I brought a hand to my mouth, muffling the agonizing moans that I so desperately wanted to let out.

His fingers advanced down while his mouth stayed on my bosom, alternating between breasts, licking, biting them. I closed my eyes as his hand reached my knee, where the fabric of my dress was bundled. He curved his hand inward, his hand slipping under the fabric. His fingers trailed up my inner thigh, making their way to my entrance.

My breathing hitched as he danced closer and closer. The heat I had felt forming before, now blazing, almost painful, as my want, my need for him grew.

"Please," I begged.

He laughed between my breasts. "So greedy and you haven't even told me why you want me."

He rested his chin between my bosom, once again. Our eyes locked as his fingers circled my entrance.

"Alexander."

"Estelle, I refuse to fully take you till I hear it first," he growled as his eyes darkened.

"I...I..." The teasing was too much. I had lost my ability to speak.

Pulling pieces of my brain back together, I formed the letter l. Alexander froze as he looked over the railing.

"Damn it."

He pulled himself off me, searching for my cloak.

"We'll be at shore soon," he explained as my brows raised in question.

I peeked over the railing and gasped as the shore, which still hosted numerous nobles and servants, came into view.

I yanked the top of my bodice, willing it to come over my bosom.

How had he gotten it to come down?

I looked to Alexander for help, but he was too busy patting down his own clothes, adjusting his pants, attempting to hide the beast we had awoken. I grunted as I yanked with all my force, successfully getting the bodice back in place.

"Just need this and no one will suspect a thing." Alexander wrapped my cloak around me, tying the ribbon with a single knot. "That way it's easier to get off later."

My eyes averted to the ground unable to take in his sexual prowess. But my heart fluttered in happiness knowing we would continue.

The boat jolted as we washed ashore, and the curtain opened. Outside, Anna and Samuel waited, but they weren't looking at us. Their attention was wholly on one another.

Anna held her hand up to her mouth, hiding her giggles and the blush that consumed her face. Samuel theatrically threw his hands around, telling a story, biting his lip, hands running through his hair as he noticed the intrigue in Anna's eyes.

"About time that blossomed," Alexander said as he took my hand and led me out the boat.

"I suppose the lanterns made everyone show their true feelings today."

"I still want to hear you say it," Alexander whispered into my ear before kissing my forehead as we stepped off.

"You're back," Anna stated, finally noticing we had come ashore, her eyes darting to Alexander and mine's interlocked fingers. Her brows raised as an *about time* smile appeared.

"We are," Alexander replied as I was too busy exchanging glances with Anna.

"Shall I summon the carriages?" Samuel asked.

Alexander gave me a starved look before replying, "Please, we're in a hurry to get back to the castle."

Both Anna and Samuel blushed at the apparent hunger in his voice, at Alexander's eyes that raked over my body, planning what he'd do to me once we were alone.

Samuel darted off, giving Anna an apologetic nod as she had to stay and watch our embarrassing lustfulness. I squeezed Alexander's hand, reminding him we weren't alone.

He coughed, composing himself, calming the animal inside him.

"Anna, you and Samuel should enjoy the festival in town." She tilted her head. "Once we're in the carriage, you two are dismissed for the night."

Anna's eyes darted to me. I gave her a reassuring smile, letting her know it was fine.

"Thank you, Your Highness. I'll let Samuel know." She took off to the line of carriages.

Alexander smiled, turning back to me once she was out of ear's reach. "I'm going to ravish you tonight."

I gulped as the heat returned between my legs. His teasing was unbearable, but I couldn't let him win. I leaned in so our lips were mere inches away. "Just like at the tavern?"

He smirked at my tease. "No, nothing like the tavern. Back then I was granting a favor for a desperate girl, tonight," he paused, kissing my neck then grazing up to my ear, "I finally get to make love to *my* wife."

"Alexander." I turned my head, extending my neck so our lips could meet. I wanted him and he wanted me. I was stupid for being scared.

"Prince Alexander."

We looked up from our almost kiss. Alexander's hands grasped my waist tighter, scowling at the interruption.

"A message from Lord Leon."

Leon.

The name sparked a distant memory that I couldn't quite recall, a feeling of unease. I shook off the feeling as names had been a blur the past months. This one was probably not special, just another Lord's name I had met in a haste.

"He apologizes for the lateness, but he said it's urgent."

Alexander's brows furrowed together as he took the letter, stepping away to read it.

"Tell him, I'll be there soon." The messenger, who still was catching his breath, nodded before sprinting off into the distance. "I'm sorry Estelle, but I need to go handle this."

I held his hands as agony washed over his face and kissed them. "It's fine. I'll wait for you in my room."

He smiled sweetly as Anna and Samuel both returned.

"Samuel, change of plans. I'll need Shadow as I have an errand to run. Anna, could you please escort Estelle back to the castle."

They both nodded, unquestioning of the sudden change.

"Will I be needing a horse as well, to accompany you?" Samuel asked.

"No. You're dismissed for the night once I have Shadow."

Samuel nodded as Anna's bottom lip pursed out.

"Anna, walk me to the carriage then you are dismissed as well. I don't want to keep you from the town's festival."

"Really?" Anna squealed.

Samuel's lips transformed into a massive grin.

I nodded, smiling at their excitement.

"I may be late," Alexander whispered in my ear.

"It's fine. They deserve this." I kissed him on the cheek, hoping to improve his mood. "Now, quickly, let us be off. The sooner you are gone the sooner you can join me."

CHAPTER 38

The door closed behind me as I made my way to the vanity. I sat before the mirror inspecting my appearance, inspecting the face of a woman who had found true love in her husband—in the man who I had questioned since I got here. The man who ruined my chances of being queen. The man whose brother was my country's biggest threat. And yet, I loved him. I trusted him with all my heart. Maybe that night in the tavern was the gods answering my pleas, the plea to be with the one who was my soulmate.

I smiled in the mirror, removing my diadem. As much as I wanted Alexander to undress me, the thought of wearing all this finery for one more second seemed unbearable.

I undressed, examining each of my nightgowns. They were all respectable. A fact I had appreciated before, but now I wanted something…something scandalous. Something that would arouse him as soon as he walked in.

A speckle of red at the bottom of my drawer caught my eye. I pulled it out, wondering what it was. My face turned a bright rouge. It was the nightgown from the marriage night.

The one I was made to wear so I would know the shame I had brought upon myself.

I held the satin fabric in my hand then up to my body. It wasn't shameful any longer. I pulled on the undergarments, tying the ribbons loosely. I looked in the mirror. At a glance, one would think I was completely naked, but the fabric covered all my intimate parts. Creating an alluring, seductive look.

I laid on the bed, trying out different positions, wondering what would be most appealing to Alexander when he arrived. I felt foolish, wondering where my propriety had gone but I didn't care. Nothing in our relationship had been traditional or perfect, but this could be.

After many different poses, I decided I would sit on the edge of the bed, my arms behind me so I sat at an incline, allowing my body to be open and every detail of it exposed. I couldn't wait to see how Alexander would respond.

I tapped my foot, eyeing the candle I had lit when I arrived. Only half the stick remained. I knew he would be a while but not this long. I allowed my body to fall back onto the bed, curling my feet to me. The night air had invaded the room, and with such little fabric on, I began to shiver. I wormed under the blankets.

He would knock before entering, allowing me enough time to get into position. Waiting in the comfort of the blankets would be fine, I thought. But as the weight of the blanket warmed my body, my eyelids grew heavy, and I fell fast asleep.

I slept soundly that night, but I couldn't help but hear a mumble.

"I won't let this come between us, you're my love now. My real love."

My mind was lost between the dream world and reality. I could not decipher where the words came from.

CHAPTER 39

N ails softly grazed my bare skin as I lay on my stomach, the sensation waking my body. I groaned with pleasure as it turned into a massage.

I opened my eyes to a sunlit room. Blinking to adjust my eyes to the light, I turned my head. Beside me, Alexander lay, shirtless, smirking.

"Good morning."

As my mind was still clouded with sleep, I didn't question his appearance and simply scooched closer to him.

"Sorry, I got here after you fell asleep."

I gasped. "Sorry, I fell asleep. I tried to stay awake but—" Alexander ran his fingers through my hair, politely quieting me.

"I got here when the night was half done."

"You should've woken me."

Alexander kissed my forehead. "I couldn't. You were sleeping so soundly, but I wanted to be here when you woke. I hope you don't mind."

I shook my head.

"I will say, I am sad I got here so late." He lifted the covers, peering under them. "It seems you had something planned."

I blushed, remembering the red undergarments I wore.

"Don't worry, they didn't go to waste. This lace," his words were guttural as his eyes ran across the ribbons, "teased me late in the night till early in the morning, asking how I'd rip them off you."

I gulped, feeling my body heat up. "And did you decide?" Alexander nodded. "Show me," I commanded, tired of waiting.

Alexander threw his arm around my waist, pulling me closer till our bodies were flush against one another. His nose nuzzled mine as he tucked my hair behind my ear. "I will, but there is one thing I want to hear from you first."

"And what's that?" I coyly asked as I slid my arms around him.

"You know what it is," he growled into my neck.

My body shivered as he began to kiss me, his kisses trailing lower and lower. His hands wandered just outside the red satin that barely covered my nipples.

"I won't give you what you want until you say it. I'll just keep playing with you."

"You haven't even said it yourself," I teased.

Alexander froze, his eyes softening. "I've thought it for so long now, I forgot that I've never said it." He chuckled at himself.

Alexander repositioned his body, so his lips floated above my forehead. He kissed it softly, then my nose, and finally my lips. He hovered over me, staring deep into my eyes.

"Estelle, you have made me feel more deeply than I have ever thought possible. Before you, I thought I knew love. And when that was taken away, I thought I knew hurt. But I didn't. It is with you that I truly learned what it feels like." Alexander stroked my face.

His eyes glistened as he poured his heart out to me. I threw my hands over his neck pulling him in for a kiss before confessing myself. "I don't know when it started, but I have had those same feelings for you. I think I was fighting with them for a while. I couldn't let go of my past love. I couldn't let myself become this vulnerable for Isara's sake, but I can't stop it anymore. I love you too."

I could feel Alexander's smile forming as his lips met mine. His hands were firmly on me, protecting me from any force that would try to take me away. His lips went back to my neck, beginning that agonizing trail to my entrance, his nails clawing down my sides.

I wiggled beneath him, moaning his name as I became wetter and wetter.

Finally, his mouth was on my hip then in the middle of my undergarments. He moved his fingers to both sides, sliding them off.

I opened my hands, ready to embrace him, thinking he was repositioning to insert himself. But he stayed below, his hands on my thighs, spreading my legs.

"Alexander?"

I heard him chuckle at my confusion. But before I could speak his name again, his tongue was on me, circling my entrance, adding to the wetness that was already there.

My body arched, my entrance pulsing. The pleasure was too immense. I attempted to close my legs, but Alexander's calloused hands gripped my thighs, pushing them *much* wider. I gripped the sheets, trying to ground myself as his tongue flickered. My moans grew louder and louder.

"Alexander, please, I need you inside me," I pleaded between pants.

He looked up, wiping his mouth, smirking as he looked upon my flushed complexion. "Whatever you wish, Princess."

He was in me in seconds, his cock sliding in effortlessly. He smiled above me as the muscles from his forearms bulged beside my face. The thrusting was slow at first, allowing me to fully feel his length. I wiggled underneath him, demanding more. The tension between my legs grew. He smirked to himself before speeding up, plunging deeper till he could go no further.

Everything he was giving me, I could barely handle it, yet I wanted so much more. I lovingly bit at his forearms, moaning his name into them.

"Is it too much?" he asked, sweat dripping down his face.

I shook my head, no, breath staggered. "I just want you closer."

Alexander caressed my cheek, lowering his body so it was flush against mine.

"Better," I groaned, wrapping an arm around his back and the other through his hair as he resumed his thrusting.

I whimpered as the tension grew unbearable. I clawed at his back while my other hand pulled at his hair, the pleasure awakening animalistic tendencies buried inside me. Alexander's breathing thickened.

"Estelle," he moaned.

I wrapped my legs around his waist. He nipped at my neck, following it with a kiss.

"Alexander," I whispered repeatedly.

The tension grew each time I said it, so did the volume of my voice. My hands gripped tighter as the tension burst, and I felt euphoria. Alexander let out a finishing groan, and both our bodies went slack.

Alexander rolled over, knowing his weight would squish me if he lingered any longer. I attempted to roll to him, but my strength was gone, taken by the pleasure. He pulled me to him, resting my head on his chest as his hand softly ran down my arm.

"I didn't think it could get any better than that night in the tavern."

Alexander laughed. "It's always better when you share feelings with the person."

I turned on my stomach, my strength partially returned, resting my chin on his chest. "And when did you start having those feelings?" I asked as I drew various objects with my finger on his pectorals.

"Like you, I think I was fighting them, or just being oblivious to them. I'm not sure." His fingers weaved into my hair, massaging my scalp. "I thought I loved another before you came. It was complicated."

I stared up at him, remembering the red-haired maiden from our wedding. I wanted to know more but the disdain in his voice—I knew better than to pry, or I would ruin this bliss.

"That night, when you walked into the tavern, I was immediately drawn to you. It took me by surprise. I had been trying to find someone else, someone I could move on to, to test my feelings. I wanted to see if they would finally subside for the woman I thought I loved. I tried with many others, and none caught my eye in the slightest. Till you. It was then I knew I had to talk to you.

"I hadn't planned on being intimate with you. I merely wanted to see if I could connect to another, and I did. I was going to leave you alone afterward, not complicate things for you further but then you asked for me to take you.

"My feelings were torn as I still had a love, but I knew I needed to rid her from my heart. And the best way to do that was to replace her, show myself I could connect to another. I knew there was a possibility that it may end badly for you. I didn't care at the time. But when morning came and I saw your beautiful, innocent face I was stricken with guilt. I knew if I had stayed one minute longer, I would have taken you with me, save you from whatever fate you may have. That was something I couldn't do. Not while I still loved *her*. It would've been unfair to all of us."

I kissed his hand in forgiveness as a shadow crossed his face.

"The day you arrived, the day you were to marry Titus, I walked in ready to meet the Princess of Isara and I found you. My heart stopped the moment I saw your golden-brown, fear-filled eyes. At that moment, I knew I had messed up entirely.

"When it was decided I was to marry you, my heart sank, but I also felt a rope pulling it back up, pulling it to you. I didn't know if it was merely an attraction or perhaps the start of love. Whatever it was, I didn't dare climb it, meet you halfway. I didn't want to figure it out while I still grieved over the woman I loved. So, I left to sort out my feelings, to fully forget her. I owed it to Modare. I owed it to myself to give my heart a chance at finding *real* love. And I owed it to you, for taking away your future."

I tightened my fist knowing all too well the feelings he had gone through.

"I came back, ready to give it my all but you…you had locked yourself away. You weren't trusting or willing. I knew it was my fault. I had failed to think about you when I concocted my *healing* plans. You too had just been heartbroken, and the title of queen had been taken from you when it was within your grasp. You were scared for your future, for Isara's future. I had to do something.

"I asked Titus if I could take you to Asla. He didn't want you to see the lay of the land. It was the major advantage we had with our enemies—that none of them had maps of Modare. We didn't know if you'd make a map of what you saw, use it against us, especially with you being so distraught, resentful toward us. But it was the only idea I had. It was my only hope of seeing your smile return, of gaining the slightest bit of trust from you.

"Once you began to trust me, and we started spending time together, I felt that tether grow tighter, stronger. I craved to be in your presence, to hear your laugh, to tease you. But I couldn't bring myself to see the feelings hiding behind my *fondness* for you.

"But that night, when the assassin came"—his breath halted at the memory—"I've never lost my composure so quickly. I've been trained since birth for combat, for war. I've been trained to handle situations like that, but that night, after you were safe, I wanted to punish everyone; Vropan for having that meeting go so late, the guards, and myself for not getting there sooner. I wanted to capture the man and kill him with my own hands, kill him slowly, torture him."

I shuddered.

"That's when I realized if anything happened to you, I would be broken. I needed you in my life."

Alexander stared at the end of the bed, his face grim, the silver in his eyes dull.

"Alexander, you couldn't have prevented it."

I grabbed his chin, turning him to me so our eyes met, so he knew my words were true.

"I will always be by your side. Nothing, no one, will take me away." The stormy gray drifted away, the silver returning. "Plus, with those dagger lessons you'll be giving me, I doubt anybody would even try."

Alexander let out a laugh, bringing the back of my hand to his lips. "Yes, you'll be such a terrifying spectacle." His lips grazed to the palm of my hand, his tongue trailing to my wrist. I felt my insides flip, the tension rising between my legs once again.

I could stay in this bed all day.

A loud knock came from the door. Alexander glared, but before he could turn whoever it was away, the door swung open, and Anna hysterically rushed in.

"Princess Estelle, my deepest apologies for the lateness," she squeaked.

Alexander and I stared at Anna as she came to a halt in the middle of the room. She turned her head every which way, searching for me.

"Princess Estelle," she whispered.

I held my breath, hoping she would give up, leave Alexander and me to our bliss, and to avoid this embarrassing encounter. She turned back to the door, but our eyes briefly met.

Anna walked closer, her shoulders relaxing, but they didn't remain that way for long, as she noticed the second body.

"Your Highnesses," she stammered, her eyes shooting anywhere except the bed. "I did not think it was a bedding night, I…I…" Anna stumbled over her words, her cheeks apple red.

I felt the rose blush spread across my own face as I debated on what to do. Alexander was, indeed, my husband in title and now he was mine in love. There was nothing to be ashamed about. However, having Anna or anyone walk in on our tangled naked bodies…it was…well…it was awkward for all.

"Anna," Alexander's instructive voice sounded, "wait outside."

"Yes, of course," Anna somehow managed to stutter out, giving a quick bow as she briskly walked to the door.

Alexander sighed as he heaved himself out of the bed, his naked body fully on exhibit.

I bit my lip as I took him in, *all* of him.

Alexander laughed under his breath. "Don't worry. You'll be seeing a lot more of it tonight."

Alexander sheathed himself away, loosely tying his trousers, attempting to hide what we could not tame.

"We shouldn't let Anna wait any longer." Alexander handed me my robe.

I gave a reluctant nod as I stood. Alexander's eyes ogled me as I took the robe from his hand, his lips plump from this morning's kisses.

It was my turn to play.

I slowly turned, taking away his pleasurable view, and wrapped myself leisurely in my robe.

"You're so beautiful," his words came as a whisper in my ear. His arms wrapped around me; his hand splayed across my stomach.

"What happened to not keeping Anna waiting?"

He stilled, smiling into my neck. "A stupid idea on my part but you're right." He let out a sigh as he let go. "But tonight, I'm going to admire what's mine, without interruptions."

My stomach twisted in excitement.

"I need to attend some meetings today, but I'll see you at the dance."

I nodded, unable to say goodbye. I knew it would be for a short while, but I wanted him wholly to myself. I wanted to remain locked in this room for hours.

Alexander kissed my forehead and turned for the door, allowing Anna to enter.

"Your Highness," she uttered, avoiding eye contact with Alexander as he departed.

Anna turned to me, her cheeks now a light pink. "Princess Estelle." She curtsied again. "I'm sorry for the disruption. I did not know it was a visiting night."

A sly smile crept across my face as I made my way over to the vanity. "It wasn't a visiting night. Well, it wasn't a planned one."

Anna's eyes grew wide, as her grin stretched from ear to ear. "Princess Estelle, are you and the prince—well, are you," she trailed off, wondering if this was too personal to ask.

"Yes, we are." I bit my lip, trying to contain my smile. "I suppose arranged marriages can end happily ever after, after all"

Anna clapped her hands together. "Your Highness, I am so happy for you. I was hoping this would happen, I always," her voice trailed off again as she remembered her place, but I kept smiling to let her know she had done no wrong.

"Thank you, Anna."

She beamed back at me. Her eyes were filled with happiness and her complexion was glowing.

"Enough about me, what about yourself Anna?"

"Your Highness?" Her eyebrow raised.

"You and Samuel."

"I…I…"

I turned toward her. "I've seen the looks between you two, don't deny it now."

Anna looked to the floor, trying to hide the smile forming on her face.

"I—he kissed my cheek last night and he, well, he said he would like to take me out again."

"Anna, that's wonderful! Last night really did bring out everyone's emotions."

Anna nodded, still smiling.

I tied my hair up, readying for my morning bath, as Anna filled the tub. Things were falling into place for all of us. We were all getting our happily ever after.

CHAPTER 40

Anna passed me my fan as we reached the archway to the Rose Garden, an odd but intriguing place to hold a ball. The festivities were fairly similar to last night, but on a much smaller scale, as this event was only for high-ranking delegates and nobles.

I took a step past the threshold, taking in the whimsical tunes, the smell of Greta's food filling the air—enticing everyone to the buffet table—yet it did not shadow the sweet, delicate fragrance of the roses. Canopy tents were strategically placed on the outer rims of the festivities, discouraging any foreign diplomats to wander farther than need be.

I scanned the canopies looking for Modare's crest. If Alexander were here already, that would be the best place to look for him.

I spotted our banner on the opposite end of the festivities. I lifted one side of my forest green dress, thumbing over the pink fabric petals that looked as if they had fallen from the roses that bloomed just above my waist and grew toward my bosom, the same roses that dotted my iridescent sleeves. The dress was heavy as I made my way to the canopy. A part of me wanted to drop it, allow it to drag behind me, but it was far too beautiful for that.

"All you'll find there is a grumpy king." My body stiffened as my feet turned to lead at the all too familiar voice—a voice of the past.

I slowly turned to meet the deep blue eyes I had once loved. "Griffith," I whispered.

"It's been a long time, Estelle."

I stared into his melancholy eyes as a wave of emotions crashed over me. I wanted to run into his arms, not as a lover but as a friend. I wanted to cry, to shove my head into his chest so I could fill my senses with that all too familiar scent of Isara, of home. At the same time rage filled me, my fingers curling into a fist. Why had he ended things so abruptly? Why was he here now? After my heart had finally moved on. Moved on to Alexander.

Before I could process my feelings, Griffith was closing the space between us. I clenched my fist to my heart, closing my eyes as overwhelmed tears filled them.

Griffith's arms clamped around me, shoving my head into his chest, his chin resting on the top of my head. I heard Anna's muffled gasp. I could only imagine her confusion. She had no idea what Griffith looked like, to her he was a stranger that I seemed perplexed by. It was only a matter of time before she would call over a guard.

I wedged my hands between our chests, creating a respectable space between us. His hands fell to his side, noticing the gazes his hug had attracted.

"Sorry. I've just missed you," he whispered so only I could hear.

He took a step back, bowing deeply, making sure the crest of Isara was obvious to those watching as if being a fellow countryman justified his intensive hug.

"Words cannot express how grateful I am to be in my Princess's presence once again. Please forgive me for my abrupt, undignified affection. I have overstepped," he spoke loudly, so his words drifted over to those surrounding us. His bow was so deep I thought his brow might hit the ground.

I gave Griffith a curt nod, allowing him to rise without further suspicion as I took on the role of a perfect princess. A role I had forgotten I played with my previous love.

Griffith rose. His focus on me, waiting for me to say anything. I searched his eyes, looking for answers as I couldn't decide what to ask first.

"Your father sends his love."

My pupils dilated. "My father? But he hasn't written since—"

"We have much to talk about, Princess Estelle." Griffith's eyes shifted past my ear. "Privately."

I turned to see Anna who was waiting for my orders. Her eyes were filled with concern.

"It's alright. This is Lord Griffith. He serves my father."

Anna reluctantly curtsied. "I'll be at the tent if you need me."

I smiled at the protectiveness in her voice as she retreated to our banners.

"Shall we take a stroll around the festivities?" Griffith asked, offering his arm.

I nodded, resting my hand on the top of his as we followed the outer perimeter of the garden.

Once the curious eyes retreated, Griffith began to speak.

"I've missed you," he mumbled, making sure the words only reached my ears.

The words stabbed at my heart. "Your last letter said otherwise."

Griffith smiled as a group of nobles passed, not allowing the words to break his composure.

"You don't know—"

"Tell me about my father," I roared out. I had enough of his excuses. He had hurt my heart once before, and I had allowed him to wound it again. I would not allow a third time.

Griffith's eyes wavered, the harshness of my tone breaking his composure. "What would you like to know?" he asked in the voice of the loyal lord who had served me and my family all these years.

"He sends his love, but I have not received one letter since I arrived in Modare."

"He's been busy," Griffith replied with the sincerest of voices, a voice filled with apology. For himself or my father, I did not know nor did I care.

"Or is it that he just needs something now?"

"Estelle—"

"Princess Estelle," I barked back.

Griffith halted, turning to me, his face deathly serious. "Your father has been busy collecting information, making sure you are indeed safe here."

"Well, I am safe, as you can see." I gestured toward my unscathed body.

Griffith reached for the scar on my face. "And what about the attempt on your life?"

I pulled back, slapping his hand away before his thumb could brush over my skin.

"Titus and Alexander are handling it."

Griffith surveyed our surroundings. I did the same. We had walked to the outermost part of the grounds. There was no one within earshot.

"That's exactly my worry," Griffith's eyes narrowed, his voice like ice. "Don't you think it's strange? No one has known the layout of the castle for years, no one has attempted to break in, but now that the Princess of Isara lives within their walls, there is a successful breach."

"I don't like what you're implying," I snarled as rage boiled inside me.

How dare he accuse my family of such treachery.

My family.

The words rang in my head. Titus and Alexander, they were my family now. They may be rough but underneath they wouldn't hurt anything, anyone, me.

I lifted my foot, readying myself to walk away, away from Griffith, away from his foolish accusations.

"Princess Estelle." He squeezed my hand, a touch I had once craved so much. "Please, see reason. I know you are mad from my previous letter, but do not let that cloud your judgment." I pulled my hand away, brushing it against my dress as if I could rub away this unpleasantness. "I stopped writing because I believe they have something to do with the assassination attempt. I think that they are looking for an excuse to get rid of you. They have all the connections they need now. There is no longer a need for the treaty.

"You wrote to me with our history, if anyone realized we were more than friends it would give them grounds for execution. You must understand."

"You don't know anything," I hissed, my voice a deathly whisper.

I wouldn't listen to his words. They weren't true. Alexander knew at the tavern that I loved Griffith, and still, there were no repercussions. Alexander loved me, and I, him. Griffith's words were far from the truth. He didn't know anything.

"I know that I love you, that necklace you wear is proof of that." Griffith stepped forward. "And the fact you still wear it tells me you still love me."

I twirled the pendant in my fingers as I so often did before when I yearned for Griffith, but that was not the reason I still wore it. Now, it was just a reminder of home, a token of the days of old, a piece I wore out of habit. But if Griffith saw it as more than that…

I ripped the necklace off and forced it into Griffith's open hand that had been reaching for me. "I will say this once more. You don't know anything, and you never will."

Our eyes met for a second. Griffith's eyes searched mine, pleading that my words were not true, but I held steadfast, and his gaze dropped in defeat. I turned away, ready to leave this unpleasantness.

"Estelle." My gut twisted as he forgot my title once again. "Your father sent me to get you out."

I turned toward Griffith, looking at his desperate eyes with shock.

"I leave at midnight, while everyone is distracted by the fireworks. I can't force you to leave with me but for your sake, consider it. Please."

"There you are," spoke a warm voice from behind.

Alexander.

I wiped my eyes of the tears that I had unknowingly shed. Not because I was scared or frightened. But because I had longed for those words for so long from Griffith, *leave with me.* I had dreamed up a hundred different scenarios where we would run away together and now I felt nothing. Not satisfaction, not pleasure, not happiness. No. I did feel something, sorrow for Griffith because at that moment he knew he had lost me, so much so he was resorting to using my father as an excuse to keep the conversation going, to get me to leave.

"I see that you have already run into one another." I turned my head, hearing his voice closer, expecting Alexander to be standing right beside me. Instead, he stood a respectable distance away, as if he was the one who wasn't allowed to lay affections on me. "I hope it was a wonderful surprise for you." His voice was even as he looked between Griffith and me.

"It was good to see—hear what I am missing back in Isara. It makes me less homesick." My words were sharp as I sneered at Griffith.

Alexander's eyes darted between us, sensing my hostile energy. His eyes ran up and down my body then he paused on my neck. "You're missing your *necklace*."

I rubbed at my empty neck where the pendant rested mere seconds ago, surprised Alexander noted it. "Yes, I must have lost it while we were walking."

Alexander began to turn. "I'll let the servants know to start looking for it. It was, after all, a *precious* gift from what you've told me."

"No, that's not necessary." My eyes found Griffith who sucked in his lips. I wanted these words to hurt him. "It was a mere trinket."

Alexander's eyes grew but soon that devilish smile appeared on his face. He closed the space he had created between us immediately, slid his hand around my waist, and pressed me into his body, possessively. I leaned into it. "Then at least let me buy you another one, replace what used to lay on that delicate neck of yours."

Griffith ground his teeth at Alexander's words, making Alexander's grin grow. It was like he had wanted to help me anger Griffith. But why? Alexander didn't know the meaning of the necklace, that his words basically were a way of saying he had replaced him.

"It's been an honor to catch you up on everything, Princess Estelle, but I must take my leave. There is a certain diplomat from Vropan I wish to talk to."

I gave Griffith a curt nod, dismissing him as he bowed and kissed my hand. "Like always, we'll have the flower in full bloom."

I rolled my eyes at his message, his way of telling me the getaway carriage would still carry Isara's flag.

I stared into the distance till Griffith's body was lost in the sea of nobles. Alexander's hand loosened as he let out a sigh. His shoulders sank in as if he just released the weight of the world.

"Are you alright?"

Alexander's relieved eyes turned bashful, his fingers running through his hair.

"I wasn't sure how you were going to react when you saw him."

I continued to stare. An eyebrow raised.

"I thought it may bring back your feelings for him," Alexander rambled. "I wasn't sure if you were only falling for me because he was no longer an option or—"

"Is that why you kept your distance?"

Alexander remained silent, looking up at the sky, pretending he didn't hear.

"Alexander," I said his name with a force that made him look.

"I wanted to give you two a moment more, but people were growing curious. I know what he means—meant to you."

I stilled. Alexander knew that the necklace was a gift from Griffith, probably noted I wore it every day. He had connected two and two together. He had thought I was still in love with Griffith despite everything that had happened the past couple of days, and though it hurt him, he had let me continue to speak to Griffith alone. He hadn't held me close because he knew that it would hurt Griffith to see his love being held by another man, which in turn, would hurt me. That is if I was still in love with him. Alexander would've kept doing so too, acted like nothing had happened between us if I hadn't referred to the necklace as a mere trinket.

Before I could think, my feet were moving, running to embrace him.

"You are mine, and I am yours. No one will change that."

I felt a smile spread across his face as his lips caressed my neck in thanks. "Be careful with those sweet words, or I may have to take you in this field."

I pulled back, looking deep into his beautiful silver eyes, shaking my head in loving disapproval. I would never leave this man for as long as he loved me.

"Dance with me?"

I looked toward the middle of the garden, next to the maze, where nobles were taking their places for the next dance.

"Do you think we'll make it in time?"

"Only if we run."

Alexander grabbed my hand, pulling me as we ran to the group of nobles.

We stood amongst the row of couples but their laughter, their presence faded from existence as I gazed into those captivating silver eyes. I wasn't sure whether the dance would be slow or if it would be a jig, but I knew if I was with Alexander everything would be fine.

CHAPTER 41

The dance left us all breathless. I stood still, trying to compose myself, scanning the row of nobles, looking for Alexander. I had lost sight of him midway through the dance as it required us to trade partners every couple of steps. I looked every which way, standing on my toes, searching over the sea of people, but he was nowhere to be found. Perhaps, he had retreated to Modare's tent. It was, after all, a few feet from the dancing.

I began the short walk but only saw Titus, Anna, and Samuel as I reached the tent. Anna and Samuel were huddled together, their faces perplexed, while Titus sat on his throne looking more annoyed than usual. I wondered what could be amiss as all faces turned to me.

"Has anyone seen Alexander?" I asked, the question slowly leaving my lips.

Anna and Samuel's necks snapped toward one another, avoiding eye contact with me. Titus took a sip from his wine—a tell-tale sign he was choosing his next words carefully.

"I believe I saw him heading to the maze," Titus sighed out.

I looked toward the hedges that I so often gazed into from my old bedroom. Many nights, when I couldn't sleep, I had looked out and mapped the maze, memorizing the shortest path from the entrance to the center where a fountain lay. It was an easy feat to accomplish as it was two lefts, a right, then a left again.

Curiosity stirred in me as I looked at the vines climbing the archway.

What could Alexander be doing in there?

As if Titus read my mind, he responded, "If you're so curious, you should go find him instead of standing there like a lost doe." His words were condescending, but in his tone, I could hear a sliver of disappointment, pity even.

My eyes angrily flashed toward him. I would've said more if it were not for the heightened tension of Samuel and Anna. Not at Titus's insult, no, they were used to his foul mouth. It was at the idea of me going into that beautiful, thorny maze.

I needed to know what was going on. I needed to know the cause of their concern.

I gave a curt nod, lifting the hem of my skirt, and drudged off to the maze of roses.

CHAPTER 42

I stepped through the archway, the smell of roses intoxicating as they surrounded me. I took a deep breath, truly appreciating their scent. If I had known it smelled like this, I would have visited sooner. I continued through the maze, running my hand gently across the velvety flowers, using the sensation to distract me from the growing knot in my stomach. I made sure not to damage the roses, made sure my fingers didn't stray to the stems where their thrones waited for something to prick.

One more turn and I would face the fountain. My stride hastened, my fingers still on the roses. I was at the corner, all I had to do was turn and I would see it. There, I was certain I would find Alexander as there was no other seating in this maze. I took one step forward but quickly retracted my foot as a stinging pain shot through my finger. I looked down, facing my hand toward me. Blood dribbled to the ground as I plucked a single thorn out.

"Enough Veronica," a voice roared. Not just any voice, Alexander's. It was near, just around the corner.

I clutched my finger to my chest, trying to stop the bleeding as I peeked around the hedge. Alexander stood, one hand on his hip and the other rubbing his temple, blocking his eyes.

I would have emerged from my hiding spot, to ask him what was wrong, if it were not for a beautiful, disdainful voice.

"You said you loved me."

Alexander's body turned, revealing the brightest red hair that belonged to only two people in this court. The lord I had met on my marriage night and his daughter, Veronica—Alexander's past lover.

"It wasn't real." His voice grew quieter with each passing word. "To you or me."

Veronica fell to the marble bench, tears in her eyes.

I began to leave, allowing them the privacy they much deserved. Alexander was mine. I was confident of that. But he was also once Veronica's, and they never had the chance to properly end things, to say their goodbyes.

"Veronica, don't cry." Alexander's feet scuffled through the fallen leaves. My gut twisted as I imagined his arms wrapped around her, comforting her. I hated it, but it was a line that I was ok with them crossing. "You're just going to make everything harder."

"Kiss me," she pleaded.

"Veronica."

"Kiss me and you'll see. I made a mistake, Alexander, you must know I loved you. I still do."

I spun on my heels. That was not a line I was ok with being crossed. I peeked around the corner. There was no way Alexander would kiss her. He loved me. He was loyal to me. He may feel bad for Veronica, he may want to comfort her but a kiss—he had been worried about me and Griffith. He would never—

My heart dropped at the sight of their intertwined lips, Veronica's slender hands caressing his face. Her body curled toward him as mine did this morning.

This wasn't the goodbye I thought they would share. No. This wasn't a goodbye. This was them reliving the romance they once had. The romance that Alexander wanted. He said it himself, he had tried to find another, but he always went back to Veronica.

I clasped my hand over my mouth as an audible sob broke from me.

Alexander's eyes met mine. He pushed Veronica away, but it was too late. I was already running.

I would not be subject to another betrayal, another heartbreak. I had too many this year. I was done, done with love.

But where would I go?

Griffith.

I wouldn't return to him, but I could use him to get back to Isara.

I looked around the festival. The servants were extinguishing the flames. The fireworks would start soon. I had about ten minutes. I picked up as much of my dress as I could carry, no regard to how much skin I showed, and ran.

I could hear the faint sound of feet running after me, but I didn't dare look back. Alexander was faster than me, but with my head start, I had a chance of getting to the carriage before he caught up. I just needed to focus.

A few nobles, that had not yet gathered in the middle, stared at me in confusion as I rushed by. My eyes lowered, hiding the tears that ran down my face. I ran along the castle walls, shoving puzzled guards out of the way.

I was twenty steps away from the front gates. I could hear Griffith telling the driver to wait a couple more minutes. I was close.

My throat burned. My legs shook, but I continued running. I was almost there. I would make it. I would. I—calloused hands clamped around my wrist, pulling me back, pulling me into a chest.

"Let me go," I screeched. I shoved my free hand against his chest. Alexander's lips remained in a tight line as his eyes watched me pitifully, guiltily. I tried to pry his fingers off one by one, crying.

Maybe Griffith would hear. Maybe he would come running.
No. He couldn't. That would start a war. This could start a war.
"Let me go," I wailed as I kept struggling, my voice growing weaker with each passing second, becoming less hopeful.

"Estelle, let me explain," Alexander pleaded.

"Let's go," a voice sounded in the distance, Griffith's voice, followed by the sound of running hooves.

I was too late.

My body went limp. My chance of running away, gone. I slid to the ground, Alexander's grip loosened, and I watched the purple flower grow smaller and smaller.

Alexander's eyes followed mine. "You—you were going to leave with him," Alexander whispered, shocked.

Alexander's hand had completely left my wrist. I looked back at him as his eyes focused on the last spot the carriage was visible from. His posture had stiffened, his brows were drawn together as his eyes filled with a depth of pain I had never seen before. But I could care less. He was the first to break us.

I pushed my hands against the plush grass, somehow managing to stand on my tired legs. My feet began to move toward the servant's door nearby.

"Why?" Alexander grabbed my upper arm as I stood parallel to him.

"Why?" I mockingly said back. "Why did you kiss her, Alexander?" I shrugged off his hand, my voice breaking but out of anger.

"So, you'd leave me because of some silly kiss? You'd go back to Griffith? You'd go back to the man who not only has broken your heart once but twice now?"

My brows furrowed together.

Twice.

How did he know?

"You've been monitoring my letters," I whispered.

"I've done no such thing." His nose crinkled.

"Then explain to me why you know it's been twice."

"You wear your emotions plain as day, Estelle. Like with that necklace, I can see right through you all the time."

Tears began to fall once again. How could he keep lying after I had caught him? I clutched my dress. Everything was fake. Griffith was right.

"Stop telling lies," I growled, cutting him off.

I headed for the entrance to Greta's kitchen.

"Where are you going?" Alexander's voice boomed from behind.

I took a step forward. "Why do you care?" I roared out so loud that if the fireworks had not already started the party would have heard me. "You've got what you need." I gestured behind me as if we could see the crowd of delegates and nobles. "They've met with you. You've made your alliances. You don't need me anymore. Stop acting like you're in love with me."

Alexander whispered my name, advancing toward me as my hysterics continued.

"Just show your true self. You and your brother, just admit that you're not these wonderful rulers that—just admit it, you used me, you both did.

"You only care about yourselves. I should have listened to Griffith. I should have never trusted you. You're just as the rumors say you are. Who knows if that story about Asla was even real, if Veronica truly broke your heart or you were just playing the victim."

Alexander's arms reached for my waist, but I slapped them away.

"Whatever it was, you deserve all the heartbreak that you said she gave you, real or not, you deserve all of it and so much more."

I was breathless by the time I was finished. I waited for Alexander to say anything, for him to retort, but the man in front of me said nothing. His eyes were void of emotion. He simply nodded, solemnly, before walking away, leaving me alone in the night.

CHAPTER 43

I pulled the covers over my stinging eyes, grazing the puffiness caused by last night's tears as the sun peeked through the windows.

I didn't know what time it was, and frankly, I didn't care. Many diplomats were to depart today and I, like the rest of the royal family, was expected to wish them a safe journey as they returned to their respective kingdoms and territories. But that was not my problem, not anymore.

The Moadarians had used me enough for a lifetime. They had their treaties, their alliances. Now, the only question was, what would they do with me? Now that Alexander's real love had returned, would I be subjected to watch them promenade the castle for the rest of my life? See my husband with his mistress every day? Perhaps, they would send me off to a country home they rarely visited. It wasn't unheard of amongst royals. Or would they allow me to return home? I would see Griffith every day, but that was better than facing this humility.

I shook my head, returning home wasn't an option. If they were to send me back, without producing an heir, it would be like we never wed. A repercussion I hadn't thought of last night when I had tried to run. But was it really? Griffith and my father had wanted me to leave.

A knock came from the door. "It's me, Anna, Your Highness. Permission to enter?"

I grimaced at her request. A request she only made because she had learned of Alexander's and mine's successful love marriage. Successful, until I discovered the lies.

A shiver went down my spine. Had Anna known? She couldn't have. That had been genuine excitement yesterday.

"Princess Estelle?" Anna called again this time at a higher pitch.

I coughed, a failed attempt to clear the sorrow from my voice. "Enter."

Anna cracked open the door, examining the room, looking for any sign of Alexander. The news of our fight hadn't spread around the castle, not yet. Anna, once certain Alexander wasn't here, carried on in her normal way—placing my breakfast tray on the table then filling the tub with warm water and fragrant oils.

Anna came to the foot of the bed, wiping her hands on her apron before holding out my robe.

With glazed eyes, I looked at the fabric, silently debating if I should even get up. I had no intention of leaving this room, but a morning bath, soaking in those fragrant oils, did sound enticing. It was a much needed comfort after last night. I willed myself to stand.

Anna gasped. "Your Highness, I am so sorry. I should have come last night to help you undress but King Titus, he—"

I looked down to find myself still in the forest green dress, the bottom splattered with dried mud. I reached up, feeling the fallen braids and crushed roses I had destroyed in my sleep. The smell of them evoked a gag.

I held up my hand to Anna. "Whatever Titus said to stop you from coming, it was the right call. I wanted to be alone."

Anna's eyes grew as she stood speechless. Her mind clearly racing through the scenarios that might have occurred last night.

I stood and made my way to the bathing room, ripping the flowers from my hair as Anna followed behind to unlace my dress. I should've held still, but those questioning eyes, I couldn't be near them. If she asked what had happened, I was sure the tears would fall once again.

I stepped into the steaming water, exhaling as I sunk into the comforting warmth taking in the aroma.

Lavender. Not roses. Thank the gods.

Anna dipped a sponge into the water before scrubbing my back. My silence was the only indicator she needed to know that last night had been a terror for me. To what extent, she did not know. But she knew me well enough that granting me silence would be a comfort.

Anna set the sponge down, silently preparing my towel for whenever I chose to end my soak. As she waited, she began to tidy up the room. I watched as she opened the curtains further and made the bed. I wondered if I should stop her. Once she was dismissed, I would undo her hard work.

The water went cold. I had half the mind to ignore it if it were not for Anna beginning to dust everything a second time.

I stood, the water lapping at my calves. Anna's head turned at the sound, her feet rushing toward the wardrobe. "What would you like to wear today? I was thinking about the silver dress. You'd be like a dove of peace for the diplomats."

I wiped my body down as Anna rustled through the clothes. She really did have a knack for finding the meaning in clothing. Wherever they sent me, I hoped I could bring her.

"I'm feeling rather ill today, Anna. Just a sleeping gown please."

Her lips formed an O as she threw the silver dress back into the wardrobe and quickly looked for sleeping attire. I grimaced at her worry, but I wasn't prepared to tell her the truth. Not yet. I couldn't even think of last night without tears welling up.

She walked the gown to me, holding it in the air so I merely had to pop my head through. I gave her a grateful smile before retreating to my bed, pulling the sheets to my chin.

"Would you like me to fetch Aeson?" she asked, her body tensing and brow wrinkling as she placed the breakfast tray on the bed. "Or perhaps some porridge?"

"No, Anna. That won't be necessary," I replied, scooching away from the tray, lessening the chance of it spilling.

I could feel Anna's eyes on me, full of concern. "Would you like me to fetch Alexander?"

I stiffened at his name, my brow furrowing. "Please don't mention him," I answered coldly as I tried to hold back my tears.

Anna pursed her lips in a line and nodded in understanding. She didn't need further explanation. I remembered her face from last night, Samuel's and Titus's too. They had all seen Alexander walk into the maze with Veronica. They all knew it may cause strife, but they didn't know to what extent.

"I'll be back up to bring you your lunch. Please ring the bell if you have need of anything else."

"Thank you, Anna," I whispered.

I lay in my bed watching the shadows move across the room as the sun changed positions in the sky. I listened to the occasional cajoling bird, anything to make the time pass. But pass to what? Tomorrow would be the same and the next day after, well, until they decided what to do with me.

Anna brought me lunch and hardly uttered a word. She knew my sickness was more emotional than physical. By now, the castle would be talking. I debated asking her if Alexander was already parading around Veronica or if he was waiting for all the delegates to leave. But the sane side of me knew better than to ask and kept me quiet until Anna left.

The room grew dark then reilluminated as the moon took the sun's spot, and the clouds drifted away, revealing the twinkling stars. I pushed the covers away, bringing my feet to the cold wooden floor. I reached my arms up to the ceiling, releasing the tension from the balled-up position I held all day before walking to the window. I sat on the ledge, resting my forehead on the glass that had cooled with the night.

A knock came from the door.

It was dinner time.

Anna, not waiting for my response, opened the door, tray in hand. My nose crinkled at the familiar scents; garlic, chives, saffron, and lamb

"Greta noticed you hadn't eaten much today. I told her you were feeling under the weather, so she attempted to make a dish from Isara." Anna placed the tray on the table, lifting the silver covering. "She hopes you like it."

Enticed by the aroma, I walked to the table. A shy smile brushed across my face as I investigated the bowl.

Lamb stew, a meal I had many times in Isara. It was a comfort food of sorts. The cook back home always made it when I was feeling down as did many mothers when their babes felt ill.

The chair creaked as it took my weight. I leaned my face over the bowl, the steam warming it, the aromatics dancing around my nose. I took a bite.

It tasted like home.

The sweetness of the carrots calmed the gaminess of the lamb. The garlic and saffron mixed together to create a complex fusion of flavors. The savory broth warmed me from the inside. I took another bite then another and another. I didn't stop until I finished the entire bowl.

"I'll have to tell Greta you liked it," Anna's voice came from behind, slightly relieved.

I turned to see piping hot steam emerging from the tub. I stood, giving Anna a grateful smile.

"Before you get in, Princess Estelle, shall I brush your hair?" she asked timidly.

I looked at her with confusion. She typically tended to my hair after my bath. I shrugged, walking over to the vanity, sure Anna had a reason. Perhaps It was a new trick she had picked up or—I sat in the chair, my lips parting at the ghastly image in front of me. My eyes were puffy, a light black underneath them. Red streaks formed at my eyes and ended at my chin. And on top of my head, sat a bird's nest of hair.

"Nothing a quick combing can't fix," she reassured, keeping her voice soft as if she were scared that I would break at any moment.

I stared back at my reflection as Anna took a brush to my head. I was a creature from the woods. I hadn't seen myself like this since the week after the marriage when Alexander had left.

I was—I couldn't become her again. That girl I was after the marriage, waiting around, hiding in my room. I wasn't living. I wasn't helping my kingdom. Today would be the last day to mourn, to have this pathetic demeanor. I was a Princess of Isara, and Modare had wronged me.

Why should I be the one to hide away?

Tomorrow I would stand in pride despite the horrendous things I would see or hear. For I represent Isara, and we do not take kindly to backstabbers.

CHAPTER 44

I was up before the sun had risen before Anna had knocked on my door. I wasn't healed completely, but I wouldn't let them see me cry.

"Princess Estelle?" Anna's voice came from outside.

"Come in."

"She entered, looking puzzled at the fully drawn back curtains, at the sight of me sitting in front of the vanity. "You're up early, Princess Estelle."

I rose from my perch, letting my robe sweep behind me as Anna placed the breakfast tray on the table. I took off the lid to see chicken porridge and some fruit.

"Gretta insisted on making it, in case you were still feeling *ill*."

I smiled at the sweet gesture. "Tell her, thank you, but I won't be needing comfort food for a while."

"Glad to hear," Anna chirped as she left to prepare the bath.

Her happiness was genuine, she truly thought I was ok. Little did she know the storm I was about to become.

"Anna," I called while I scrubbed my skin, noticing she was already in the armoire. "Could you prepare a purple dress?"

I watched as Anna thumbed through the clothes finding every color; blue, white, yellow, green, pink, and black. It wasn't till she was at the back that she found any purple.

"Is there a particular one you'd like?"

I leaned over the tub, peering into the depths of the wardrobe. "That one, the one with the silver embellishments." Anna tugged the dress out.

It was a shade of purple I hardly ever wore, even in Isara. I found the lightness of lavender more playful, and inviting but, this was the true purple of Isara. A deep, rich, royal purple. Staring at the color, I didn't understand why I never wore it. It was mesmerizing. It wasn't vibrant nor was it dull, it was bold. And on this dress, it was a magnificent piece of art.

The skirt consisted of two layers. The first was a silk underlining that could be seen under the top layer. The top layer, which was made of sheer tulle, made the dress sparkle without losing the darkness of the purple. The bodice hugged tightly, making the boning of it apparent. The dusty purple of the top complimented the skirt perfectly. Silver embroidery started just below the navel, climbing up and out till it covered the bust. From there, the embroidery joined together and departed the dusty purple fabric, so the loose straps of the dress were only solid purple.

How could I not see the beauty of this dress before?

How could I forget I had it?

I had been wearing blue for far too long.

"Anna, could you please bring the rest of the dresses I brought from Isara to the front? I have a feeling I'm going to be wearing them much more nowadays."

Anna nodded, turning her back to me, trying to hide the concerned expression on her face.

I'm sorry, Anna, but this isn't my home.

I had Anna do my hair in a braided crown, allowing full view of my winged eyes, my tearless face.

I smirked at the image in the mirror. With my diadem, I looked like the queen I was meant to be.

"Come, Anna, let us walk through the garden."

Anna curtsied as she raced to open the door, her demeanor completely changed into a loyal servant instead of a friend.

This look gave me power.

We walked through the halls that lead to the garden, passing the nobles who preferred to spend their days in the castle rather than their own homes—nobels that I normally smiled and waved at. But today, I held my head high, my face unreadable. They all bowed and remained that way till I passed.

I felt in control, for once in my life, in control of—

Two bodies stood at the threshold. One old and brittle—Aeson. The other, strong, quick, and despite everything he's done, deliciously handsome—Alexander.

I hesitated to walk forward, my head tilting to look behind me, looking for an escape. But before I could find one, a cough summoned my attention. Aeson held his hand to his mouth, eyes darting between Alexander and I as if he was alerting both of us of each other's presence.

Alexander's eyes turned to me, I looked away, not knowing the meaning of his gaze. It was still too painful to be around him.

"We can finish this later," Alexander spoke, his voice like ice as he stiffly walked away from Aeson and past me without a word.

I felt my ankles pivoting, to watch the irresistible man who hurt me walk away, but I still had respect for myself. I gulped and held my head high once again, walking with the intent to pass Aeson without so much as a hello.

"You're not doing that to me, young lady," Aeson scolded, holding out his cane, blocking my path.

I stopped parallel with him, only turning my head to speak. "Doing what?" I cajoled.

"You know exactly what. The whole court knows exactly what you're doing with"—he gestured toward me, his nose crinkling as he tried to find the right words—"this style."

"There's nothing wrong with—"

"Tea in the garden," Aeson yelled. "Anna, run to the kitchen and have them prepare something. Estelle, walk with me till it is ready."

Anna looked at me with those doe eyes, not sure what to do. No one really knew what to do when it came to Aeson.

"Now." He shooed her off with his hand. "Come, Estelle, help an old man walk," he grumbled, extending his arm for me to take.

Begrudgingly I took it, unable to refuse.

Aeson led us over to a table, one that Anna and I used often for our own luncheons, the one that sat amongst the many flowers.

"You and Alexander seem to be having quite the little tiff."

I scowled at his words.

Tiff. This was much more than a measly argument.

"You two had finally made progress in your relationship. What happened?"

My brow raised. "If you know about the *tiff*, I'm sure you know what caused it, Aeson."

Aeson exhaled, letting out a small laugh. "The hostility in your tone doesn't suit you, *Your Highness*, but if you wish to get to the point, I will oblige. I have heard about a problem with a certain red-haired maiden."

"Then you know Alexander's heart lies with someone else."

Anna along with another servant rushed over with trays of tea and cake in hand. Aeson waited for them to set the table before continuing.

"You think it does, my child, but—"

"I know what I saw, Aeson," I gritted through my teeth.

Aeson took a sip of tea, his lips pursed as he reached for the sugar, unaffected by my tone.

"You may interpret what you saw however you wish, but at least let me tell you the history of those two." I leaned back in my chair; arms crossed. "Once I do, I won't bring it back up again. I simply wish to convey all the information that is known by others, facts you do not know because you weren't here."

A small price to pay for Aeson not to intervene again. I poured myself a cup of tea, silently allowing him to begin.

"Veronica and Alexander have had a long history with each other. A history that is known to many in the kingdom."

A history no one thought to mention.

"Alexander never had much interest in romance as he was focused on wars, battles, and strategies. He didn't see the need for a woman in his life as he would constantly be at risk. After the war with Ula and Astra and he had returned home, he became the prey of every woman in court. They were taken with stories of his heroics. He denied every single one. He wanted to focus on the post war meetings, the treaties that needed to be made. Every single maiden respected his choice, all except one."

"Let me guess, a certain redhead named Veronica."

Aeson let out an exasperated sigh, smiling at the snark in my voice.

"She would follow him around the castle, making sure she was always in his thoughts. There was even talk of her sneaking into his chambers. The prince still denied her, at least from what spectators saw. However, those of us close to Alexander knew he was falling for Veronica. We just didn't know why they weren't making their relationship public. Until, one day, they were caught in a compromising position that ruined Veronica's reputation."

Seems like deflowering nobles was Alexander's hobby.

"Alexander, of course, offered to take her hand in marriage. Not just out of pity. He loved her, wanted her. He would have married her much sooner if she had let him. But, Veronica, she wanted to be more than a princess. She wanted to be a queen.

"She came before Titus to plead for her innocence, for her honor, for her purity to be restored. She asked that Titus let it be known that her being found alone with Alexander was only a malicious rumor started by a jealous courtesan.

"Alexander had already asked for her hand, so her plea was unexpected. A waste of Titus's time. Titus was ready to dismiss her till she revealed the letters.

"Veronica had been exchanging words with a king in the far east, slowly gaining his *favor*. The letters dated back to a year. A letter for every week. There was never a break in between talks, even during the time span when she was with Alexander.

She claimed she could become the king's wife. She promised she would ensure a meeting between him and Titus."

I looked straight ahead, trying not to falter, trying not to acknowledge the pain in my chest. Veronica had used him, used him as a safety net in case she could not win the king. I bit my lip. Alexander had used me too; I had to remember that.

"Titus, as a king, pardoned her. As a brother, he wanted to banish her for hurting his little brother. We all saw what she had done, even Alexander, but he was too enchanted with her. He courted her for months, showering her with presents, showing her what a prince could do. She would play with him, but she never offered her heart. Eventually, he did try to move on, multiple times, but she would pull him back. She always succeeded until you came along."

"I only succeeded because she was gone. Now that she's back we can see that his heart still lies with her." I bit into one of the cakes, redirecting my rage.

"Estelle, did he not run after you? Did he not—"

I stood up, slamming my hands on the table, making it apparent we were done talking. "He ran after me to keep the peace between our kingdoms. He wants to keep playing pretend. He wants me as a safety net for when she finds the next king to flirt with. I've heard enough, Aeson."

I turned, heading back for the door, Anna scurrying to her place behind me.

"You're just as stubborn as him. It will be both your down-falls," Aeson grumbled.

CHAPTER 45

"What would you like to wear for the luncheon today?" Anna called from the wardrobe.

I leaned over the tub, looking inside. All my royal purple dresses were out at the wash leaving only the lighter ones.

"The darkest shade of purple you can find."

Anna sighed. I knew it was the wrong choice of shade and color for the first day of the matching season, but I was still determined to be the unapproachable Princess of Isara. This façade would keep the cheerful court members away, preventing them from asking about how Alexander and I were. He was the only person I still couldn't be around, couldn't discuss without my mask falling.

"This was the darkest shade I could find."

Anna held out a lavender dress. I grimaced as I stared at the chiffon material, at the dress I had worn when I first arrived.

"I suppose that that will do," I grieved out, knowing that the other dresses were far more whimsical and would make me look even more approachable than this one.

Anna silently nodded. A tinge of pain in my chest. I hated being cold to her, but I couldn't easily switch this act on and off.

A knock came from the door. Anna cracked it open to see who it was.

"Samuel."

I sank lower in the tub. Samuel's presence could only mean one thing—a message from Alexander. He still resided across the hall and could have easily come to ask himself, but my anger kept him away. Or maybe Veronica did that. I wasn't sure. Either way, we had turned into strangers.

"Prince Alexander would like to know if Princess Estelle would like to be escorted," Samuel's voice was slow, the words struggling to escape his mouth as if they were terrified of my boiling blood. "Or would she prefer to meet at the luncheon?"

There was silence as Anna looked over to me. I did not move as she knew my answer already. Nowadays, she only pretended she was giving me time to decide.

"Getting ready is taking longer than expected. She shall see him there."

"Of course."

They both let out a sigh as Anna closed the door.

"Are you sure you don't want to walk with him? It is a matching party. It would give the nobles something to model their own—"

I stood from the tub, splashing some water onto the floor. "I won't be here much longer Anna. You know that."

She grew quiet at the phrase I so often said. The first time she had asked what I meant by it, but I had only replied with *you'll see soon.* It was only a matter of time before Alexander sent me away so he could better enjoy his mistress, officially claim her. But it was taking longer than I expected.

Eyes turned toward me as Anna and I entered the ballroom. I held my head high and walked straight to the dais where Titus sat with two empty seats beside him. He let out a small laugh as he saw the nobles take several steps away before bowing.

"King Titus." I lowered into a curtsy before ascending the steps.

"Princess Estelle," he calmly said in greeting, accompanied by a nod.

I climbed to my seat.

"I had heard there was a change in your personality, but I didn't think it would be so drastic," Titus whispered to me, taking a sip of wine.

"Well, when you've been through enough betrayals you tend to have a change of heart."

Titus let out a single laugh as Anna poured me some wine.

I observed the crowd, watching the many young singles pair up as a new dance began. Others, in particular a cackle of young women, stood in a corner, staring at us, at Titus. It was his turn to wed. I wondered if he was planning on marrying a princess from another kingdom. Not that it mattered to me, I would be out of here by then. I didn't care unless it affected Isara.

I continued to survey the crowd, noticing heads turning toward the door, watching Alexander walk in, Veronica on his arm.

I breathed in, straightening my back, raising my head.

So, it begins.

Our eyes met briefly as they both continued their walk to the dais. Alexander was unreadable whereas Veronica smiled brightly.

I bit the inside of my cheek, gritting my teeth as they approached closer.

Alexander came to a halt, stepping to the side as Veronica bowed to Titus and me.

"Your Majesty, Your Highness. I have been gone from court so long, it is a pleasure to finally bow before you again."

I didn't speak as she looked to the floor, waiting to rise, neither did Titus.

I glanced at him, confused. He rested his face in his palm, a picture of boredom.

As a brother, he wanted to banish her. The words echoed in my head. Alexander may have been faking his affections for me, for the treaty, but at least Titus's dislike in Veronica was real. Perhaps I should hold Titus in a better light.

Alexander, noticing neither one of us was going to allow her to rise, tapped her waist. He leaned in as she glanced at him, talking softly enough so others could not hear. Veronica rose shyly but kept her eyes down as she retreated to a table of drinks.

Alexander climbed the stairs. "You could have dismissed her," Alexander spoke, his words directed to Titus.

I drank deeply from my chalice.

"She returned to court as a lady, not a queen as promised. She deserves punishment."

Alexander scoffed, placing his hands on the table, leaning toward Titus. "The entire court knows of her failure, that is punishment enough. It is already hard for her to be reintegrated into our society. Your displeasure with her does not need to be made public further. You'll only make it harder on *us*."

Titus leaned across the table, stopping mere inches from Alexander, his eyes piercing. "Her problems are hers alone. Not mine, not yours. Stop using them as an excuse to avoid your own."

They stared at one another, challenging.

Alexander stood up, exhaling. Titus nodded toward me and for the first time in days Alexander spoke directly to me, "Will you dance with me?" The words were bitter in his mouth.

I raised a brow, looking him up and down. I didn't have a brother to make me play nice. "No," I flatly replied.

"Estelle," he growled with annoyance. "Can we at least—"

"More wine, please." I held up my glass without breaking eye contact. No, we couldn't just pretend.

Alexander stood over me, his fists clenched together. People were beginning to stare.

"Lord Leon and Veronica look as if they require your aid. Go to them." Titus glanced between me and Alexander. "You two can sort this out privately later," Titus replied, his voice void of emotion.

"I thought you said it was *her* problem, not ours."

"Lord Leon has done so much for you, for the kingdom. He still is a friend of ours and though you should not aid her, it will aid Lord Leon to do so."

Alexander turned with a huff, heading toward a worried red-haired man standing next to Veronica.

Lord Leon.

His name had been mentioned the night of the boat ride. Back then I didn't remember who he was but hearing the name and seeing its owner now, I felt like a fool.

Veronica had arrived the night that Alexander and I kissed. He had been late to bed because her father summoned him. Alexander had put her first. Why did he even sleep with me? Tell me his feelings? Did he know Griffith was going to be at the garden? Did he know there was a risk I would go with him if Alexander hadn't fooled my heart the night before?

I felt the tears well up. I looked toward the ceiling, blinking rapidly. No one could see me like this. If they weren't going to send me away soon, I had to take matters into my own hands.

"Send me back."

"What?' Titus replied, lines forming between his brows.

"Send me back to Isara. You've made your connections with the other kingdoms. I've done all I can do to kindle a relationship between you and them. There is nothing more I can do. So, allow me to return to Isara, even if it's for a little bit," I gritted out, holding back the tears.

Titus looked at me, I focused on the ceiling.

Please don't look too closely.

"Damn *woman*, complicating everything," he scowled so low I almost didn't hear.

I tightened my grip on my skirts. If Titus said no, I wouldn't know what to do.

"I need you to stay for the remainder of the month, only to show the visiting nobles the unity of Isara and Modare. But after, if you still desire, I shall let you return. We'll say you were homesick, and you can visit for half a year," he whispered. I flinched at the care in his voice.

Had he noticed my watery eyes?

"Thank you."

"But you need to tell him that you're leaving." I glanced over to Titus; his eyes were back on the crowd. "Do it tomorrow, or do it the day before you leave, but he needs to hear it from you."

I didn't understand Titus's request, I doubted Alexander would notice my leaving with his mistress around, but I nodded in agreement.

CHAPTER 46

I stood, staring at the bare room, the packed purple chests scattered around, the empty wardrobes, and the blank walls where decorative tapestries used to hang. All of it had been packed for my departure tomorrow.

My carriage had been readied, my father had been informed of my visit, and I had said goodbye to everyone, everyone except Alexander. The one goodbye that allowed me to leave. Yet it was the one I could not bring myself to make.

It had gotten easier to be in the same room as him; to see him escorting Veronica at the parties, watching him watch her as she walked around the room mingling with the other nobles, but we still hadn't talked. Alexander had tried before, but I always made excuses to leave or straight out ignored him. The pain it would cause was not worth it.

"The room looks so empty." Anna stood in the middle of my chambers, holding the diadem that had accidentally been packed away too early.

"The offer still stands if you want to come."

Anna offered a melancholy smile. "I wish I could but—"

"I understand." I smiled back, assuring her I wasn't angry before heading over to the vanity to pull a couple of strands from my bun to frame my face.

I had offered to take Anna with me when I told her I'd be leaving. Not just because of the sadness in her eyes but because she had turned into my confidant here in Modare. My friend. I would miss her, but things had progressed between her and Samuel. She hadn't told me so, but I saw the way they exchanged glances with one another. She couldn't leave him behind. I wouldn't leave a man who stared at me like that behind. I looked forward to seeing how their relationship progressed in the time I was gone.

Half a year. Enough time to rid my heart of Alexander.

I stood up. It was time for the final party to begin. "Shall we?"

"Of course." Anna straightened her back, following me out.

I paused as I stepped out, coming face to face with Alexander's door. Somehow, I still hadn't seen or heard Veronica coming and going from his quarters. Perhaps they were doing their nightly visits elsewhere?

The ballroom was decorated in its normal fashion. The raised table at the back, the two long tables on the outer rim of the dance floor—exactly how it had been decorated for our wedding. I headed straight for Titus, passing the long line of women in front of him.

"They're not shy at all anymore, are they?"

Titus rolled his eyes at me, trying his best to greet the next lady with the same enthusiasm as the last.

I motioned for both our glasses to be refilled, a gesture Titus greatly appreciated. Matching season tired him more than any war.

I stared out into the crowd as each woman made the same speech. I cringed as I realized that my own introduction had been like theirs when I first met Titus.

Titus and I finished our wine as the last woman came up. I summoned a servant again. At least Titus and I had bonded during this whole ordeal with drink, our dislike for Veronica, and the painfully repetitive introductions forced upon Titus. These fond memories could be a preventative to him breaking the treaty one day.

"Thank goodness that's over," Titus grieved, summoning an additional servant to bring over an amber-colored liquid, whisky. "Would you like some?"

"No, just wine."

The foul smell wafted over to me as it filled Titus's cup. My nose crinkled as I watched him take a sip, bringing forth old memories of when I had divulged in the devilish drink.

I had just turned sixteen and the Prince of Ula had come to visit. I was given the responsibility of keeping him entertained while our fathers had a private meeting. Back then I was so naïve, thinking no one could do me wrong. I had taken the prince to the gardens where we had a picnic. It was a rather lovely time as we were allowed to divulge in some wine, back then my father didn't permit me this pleasure often.

After some time, the prince pulled out a flask, urging me to drink. The contents had a strong vile smell, but I drank it anyway, afraid I would insult the prince. After a few sips, my head felt light, and my words came without thought. I looked to the prince, wondering if he felt the same but only found him slyly smiling, his face approaching mine, his hand sliding around my waist. I didn't know what was going on, but it made my stomach twist.

Without thinking, I punched him square in the jaw. My hand stung in agonizing pain. I fell back in the grass, clutching my jammed knuckles. The world was spinning. After that, the memories were hazy.

I awoke the next day with a throbbing headache. I was told Griffith had found me lying on the ground next to a wailing prince, whiskey fresh on my breath. My father scolded me for my brutish behavior, told me I could have ruined our relationship with Ula if it were not for Griffith explaining to the King and Queen of Ula the state he had found me in. The state I was in because of *their* son. It was then I vowed never to drink that vile liquid again as only a few sips made me numb to my wiser senses.

A distant voice carried over to the dais, "They do make a stunning couple."

"If only they wed," a male's voice replied.

I searched the crowd for the voices' owners. A couple, years younger than I, stood close by, eyes glued to Alexander with Veronica on his arm. She and the prince strode around the room in sync, greeting every lord they passed.

I chewed on the inside of my cheek. I hated that this affected me still. I had ignored his presence, burned all the gifts—the reminders of him in my room—yet he still would not leave my heart.

"Have you told him yet?" Titus inquired, feeling my rage.

"Not yet," I gritted out as I watched Veronica throw her head back in laughter.

"Remember our deal. If you don't, you're not permitted to leave."

I bit my lip. "I know," I hissed with spite but not at Titus, at myself.

I couldn't understand why I had delayed this one simple task. All I had to do was tell him.

Titus hadn't specified how I had to do it, simply that I had to tell him. I could've written a letter, had it delivered. I could've shouted it across the hall then locked myself in my room. I could've done it in so many ways—ways that allowed me to shield my eyes from the joy he would show upon hearing the news.

I was more scared than I thought.

Once I tell him, it would become all too real. No amount of distancing or the lies I told myself could prepare me for the heartbreak, for Veronica's victory and my loss. She would have Alexander to herself without my presence looming over them. By me leaving, it gave them permission to parade their love in more than just balls. But if I wanted the hurt to stop, I had to let this happen, I needed to leave. I would tell him tonight, but first, some courage was needed.

"I think I will partake in *that* drink tonight."

Titus raised a brow in surprise but still summoned a servant to bring a glass. I brought the cup to my mouth, chugging the contents, ignoring the vile scent as the liquid burned down my throat.

A cluster of women stood in a corner, giggling, attempting to draw Titus's attention. I rolled my eyes at their shrill voices. They wanted to be queen, to be royalty. A *stupid* dream. I'd much rather be a lady than a princess. At least the outcome of their marriages didn't affect treaties. They could leave without leaving a trail of destruction behind them.

I looked at Titus. I wonder if he planned to marry any of these ladies or if he had plans to attempt to wed another princess. If it was the latter, I'd hope he spare her from the misery of watching him dance with his future mistress. The mistress he would choose when he got bored of the woman who desired him so much.

Titus sat up in his chair, straightening his crown, flattening his ruffled hair. His eyes were focused on something. I followed his intense gaze to the group of women. There was commotion amongst them, a little shoving. I watched with curiosity as they pushed a rosy-cheeked woman from their circle. Strands of her black hair fell from her braided crown as she came into full view. She turned back to the group, shaking her head in embarrassment, but they shooed her away, facing her toward the dais. She bit her cheek in forfeit. Slowly she made her way to us, to Titus.

She bowed timidly. "King Titus, Princess Estelle." Her voice was like the delicate morning dew." I am sorry it has taken me half the ball to introduce myself."

She was adorable, innocent, and sweet. She shouldn't face the horrors of being queen, royal. She should enjoy her freedom.

Titus made conversation with her as I continued to watch their interaction. He smiled, even blushed. He wanted her, this sweet lamb.

She needed to be protected.

She bowed once again, a smile on her face before departing.

"Make her your mistress if you fancy her," I slurred out when she was out of ear's reach.

"What?" Titus sneered, disgusted with my suggestion.

"She's too sweet, she doesn't deserve to be stuck with you when your head turns to another." I let out a yawn, my head feeling light as I took another sip of the amber liquid. "She'll be mad at first—"

"I think that's enough drink for you."

Titus reached for the glass in my hand, but I was quicker. I let the liquid slide into my mouth and in one gulp I devoured all the contents. My face warmed.

Titus's eyes narrowed as I placed the empty glass on the table. "Now, as I was saying." Titus summoned a servant, whispering something in his ear. I waited for the man to leave before continuing. "She'll be mad at first, but she'll thank you for it in the end. The heart is so fickle. It changes who it loves so often, leaving the other hurt. Now, if she's your wife she can't leave, but if she's your mistress, at least, she can find another to warm her. I would say that's a much better fate." I rubbed my eyes trying to clear the blur in them.

Alexander's solemn voice came from behind, "Such depressing words."

I turned, glaring at him. Of course he decided to show up now. I stood with crossed arms. He had no right joining this conversation.

"Words I speak because of you." Alexander's face hardened. It was time for us to finally talk, fight.

The doors slammed open. Three women ran in, followed by two men swirling around a chain of fire. A thrilling song erupted from the musicians that now stood in front of the table. The crowd's attention, even the group of women, focused on the performing troupe.

"Get her out of here. She's drunk," Titus whisper growled.

I hastily turned my head. "I am not. I'm quite content to stay." My body swayed, the speed of my turn confusing my balance. I reached for the chair, but my hand missed. I was falling. Alexander's arm wrapped around me, preventing gravity from taking me further down.

"I would argue that." His voice was filled with concern. Fake concern, no doubt.

I pushed away.

"Get her back to her room. Carry her if you must."

I scoffed. It was my last night. I would go when I wanted.

I sat back down; eyes fixed on the performance.

"Have it your way," Alexander grumbled.

I turned to face him then Titus, nose crinkled. They wouldn't dare humiliate me, themselves, in front of the court.

Alexander stepped toward me. Titus's eyes filled with annoyance.

My pupils widened. I was about to be carried out. This wasn't an empty threat.

"I can walk myself out," I spat, bracing my arms on the chair to help me stand.

Carefully, I descended the stairs and made my way out. I had walked about ten paces out the door when the world began to spin. I leaned against the wall, praying to the gods to make the dizziness stop.

Damn that whiskey. I knew better.

"Lean on me," Alexander whispered, his voice gentle, his hand already wrapped around my waist.

"I'm fine." I pushed him away, retreating back to the wall, the coldness of it oddly helping my head.

"By the gods, why do you have to be so stubborn?" he angrily asked.

I will make it on my own.

I took a step forward, my hand sliding against the wall, helping me to keep my balance. My head throbbed as I looked up at the steep ascent I had to make.

Had the stairs always been this tall?

"Estelle, let me help."

I exhaled, shaking my head. I didn't *need* him.

I lifted my foot, placing it on the first step. Not so hard. I took another step, my palms clammy. I clutched the railing tighter, but it wasn't enough. My hand slid and gravity took me.

I was too drunk to brace myself. I let my body fall, ready for the hard floor, but only felt Alexander's calloused hands. He steadied me before repositioning so one hand was on my shoulder and the other under my knee. Effortlessly, he picked me up, holding me close to his chest. My body began to curl into him. His warmth, his smell so inviting.

No, I can't do this. I can't…

His steps bounced me in his arms as he carried me up the stairs. This would be the last time he would hold me. I closed my eyes.

I didn't sleep, just enjoyed the rhythmic sway, his scent swirling around me. I was still in love with him. I couldn't be. This had to end. These feelings had to end.

A door creaked open. I had mere moments till he put me down on the bed.

My head softly met the silk pillows as Alexander laid me on top of the sheets. I kept my eyes closed. I couldn't look at him, not in my current state. I waited for the sound of his boots to make their way to the door, expecting him to leave immediately instead I felt the bed shift. I felt his warm hand support my ankle as he took off my heels.

He was still so caring.

I almost felt bad for the death stares I had given him this month.

The bed creaked as he got up. The sound of his footsteps grew distant as they got closer to the door. I felt the tears well up. I buried my face in the pillows, accidentally breathing in some dust.

There was a tickle in my throat. I needed to cough, but I needed to remain quiet for a few more seconds.

The doorknob rattled. He was almost gone, but the tickle in my throat grew. I sat up, releasing a violent cough.

I heard the knob untwist, the sound of his boots returning. "Are you alright?"

"Yes. I just need water," I uttered out, reassuring him I was fine, hoping he'd leave.

"One second."

"I can—"

Alexander lit a torch, illuminating the room. "What? What is this?"

His eyes grew wide as he saw the packed chests, the empty wardrobes, and my riding cloak hanging on the changing screen.

My head cleared instantly.

I guess this was one way of telling him.

"I leave for Isara tomorrow," I replied, keeping my voice monotonous, hiding my emotions, as I readied for him to jump for joy.

"No," he gritted out, touching the biggest chest. "You're not allowed. The treaty—"

"I have permission from *King* Titus. I leave at first light."

"Titus knew about this?" His voice was faint, but a terrifying undertone began to form.

I remained quiet. I had given him the information I promised Titus I would tell. I did not need to say more.

Alexander opened the doors of the wardrobe wider, fully examining the empty space. "Who else knew?" he growled out, clearly annoyed I hadn't answered the last question.

I gulped nervously, confused by the hostility in his voice. "Does it matter?"

"So, I was the last to know." I remained quiet at his fury-filled whisper.

I bit the inside of my cheek, not knowing what to say.

Alexander rushed over to a purple chest, swinging it open, revealing the neatly packed dresses. He stared for a moment as if in shock. Then, all at once, he sunk his hands deep in the chest, pulled out a massive heap of clothing, and threw it back into the wardrobe.

"What are you doing?" I yelled, swinging my legs off the bed, storming toward him.

"You're not leaving," he declared, moving on to the next chest.

I grabbed his arm that held the next pile. "I'm not allowed to leave? What gives you the right to keep me here? You aren't king. You don't have that power."

Alexander threw the dresses down on the ground, turning toward me, fire in his eyes. I let go, taking steps back.

"You. Are. My. Wife." He closed the space between us with each word till our noses almost touched.

I stood my ground, glaring back into those fiery eyes. "You have a mistress now. You don't need me to keep your bed warm."

I stepped around him, heading for the dresses on the ground, throwing them back into the chests. I wouldn't let Anna see her hard work ruined.

"She isn't my mistress."

I laughed at his declaration.

"Estelle," he gently pleaded, begging for me to look at him. I continued repacking. "Estelle, listen." I didn't reply. "Estelle," he said again, this time more sternly, his hand on top of mine as

I knelt on the ground. "This fight, we've misunderstood each other for too long. We've been stubborn for too long. Please, listen." His broken voice, filled with heartbreak, taunted me to look. He had glossed over eyes of a broken heart. My heart sped.

"Estelle, I love you and only you."

I pulled away my hand. I wouldn't fall for his honeyed words, not again.

"Then explain the kiss."

"That kiss, it meant nothing. Nothing at all. I didn't even want it. I pushed her away as soon as her lips met mine." I looked away. This wasn't enough. "Veronica has been gone from my head, my heart since I took you to Asla. You have rid, no, healed me of her in every way.

"I've been stupid, stubborn. I should've talked to you sooner. I was mad. Mad and afraid after I saw you running to him. To Griffith. I couldn't be hurt like that again. I didn't want to hear you say you were leaving me for him. I was so stupid. If I had just explained to you, if I hadn't been a coward then you would know. Estelle, you have my heart now and forever."

His words were like hammers breaking down the wall I had built to keep him out. I wanted his words to be true. I wanted him. But it didn't explain why he clung to her this past month.

"So, you've used Veronica to get over me?"

His eyes were bewildered. "No, absolutely not, I could never go back to her."

I scoffed, "Then why have you been by her side for every party, every ball?"

"Estelle, I've been trying to find her a husband, without my help she will never marry."

I bit my lip. "So, you still care for her?"

"No, Estelle, I could care less about her. But that night, of the spring festival, when I met with Lord Leon, he begged me to help find her a suitor. I couldn't say no. Lord Leon, he's done so much for me, he's the only reason I'm still alive. If it was anyone else, I would have said no. I would have let Veronica suffer." Images of Alexander's scars flashed in my head as I remembered the talk Titus and I had at the tournament. "I should've told you about it that night, but I didn't want to complicate things between us, not with you finally opening up. I see now that was a mistake." I bit my lip. "Estelle, I'm trying. Please stay."

His voice broke as he pleaded, tears flooded his eyes. I stared deep into them, Aeson's words resonating in my mind. *You're just as stubborn as him. It will be both your downfalls.* Alexander was telling the truth. We had both feared the same thing, and neither of us wanted to be hurt again. I clutched Alexander's hand.

"Let's just promise to tell each other everything from now on."

Alexander stared in shock at my hand as if it wasn't real. I caressed his cheek. "I said terrible things as well, for that, I'm sorry."

"Estelle, you have nothing—"

Gently, I lifted my finger to his lips. "Remember, miscommunication is our downfall, let me finish.

"I've been an idiot too. I've been avoiding you, wanting to flee to Isara. You tried to talk to me, but I shut you down each time. I'm just as guilty, if not more."

Alexander smirked, the smirk I had missed so much. "So, you won't be leaving anymore?"

I chuckled. "Yes, it was just a big misunderstanding. I have all this packed so I can move into your room," I joked, trying to rid the somber air around us.

"I'd like that."

My eyes widened. "You would?" I asked timidly, my brows pressing together, my nose wrinkling.

"I could reach across and hold you every time I got the urge without having to cross the hall."

I breathed in deeply, a blush forming across my cheeks.

"When do you want it to happen?" I asked, biting my lip, moving closer. It had been so long since we had touched each other.

He stood. "Let me get some servants now."

"Alexander, they're all busy with the party." He froze before turning on his heels.

"Damn it."

I examined his perplexed face. "You still need to help Veronica?"

"It's the last night. I have a feeling, with the right persuasion, she and a lord far in the eastern territory might make a connection." He bit his lip, his leg shaking, clearly not wanting to go.

"Go. Come back to me when it is done." I kissed his cheek. "I think Titus has had enough of me for the night. I'll wait for you."

"Promise?" Alexander tenderly kissed my hand.

"Promise." I brushed my finger under his eyes, wiping away the tears that stuck to his cheek.

I plopped onto the bed, flailing my arms in happiness. We had both been so stupid. We had almost given up our love due to our stubbornness, our fears, but now we had overcome them. We were going to live happily ever after.

But first, I had to sleep off this whisky.

CHAPTER 47

I wiggled in the bed as warm lips pressed against mine. I reached up, eyes still closed, wrapping my arms around Alexander's back, pulling him closer. I moved my hands upward to his hair but where my fingers should have become entangled, I felt fabric. My eyes flashed open.

Blonde hair filled my vision. This wasn't Alexander. I pushed on the mystery man's shoulders, kicking as I tried to squirm out from under him. He grabbed my wrists, pinning them above my head, as a liquid passed from his mouth to mine. I wedged my tongue where our lips met, creating a barrier, but the liquid still seeped in.

The man pulled back, still pinning my hands down, revealing his mask-covered face. I glared, my lips puckering as I tried to spit out the liquid. His other hand pinched my nose.

I couldn't breathe. I had to swallow.

I closed my eyes, composing myself. After I swallowed, I could yell for the guards. It would be brief but maybe they would hear.

Please, someone, hear.

I swallowed, letting out a shrilling noise before the man's hand clamped down on me.

"Sleep, sweet girl," a familiar voice lulled.

The world began to spin, my sight blurred, and I could no longer fight against my heavy eyelids. The world went dark.

CHAPTER 48

ALEXANDER

Lord Leon shook my hand, a wide smile on his face.

"He's already asked about a dowry."

"Glad to hear it."

"Thank you again. I don't know what I would've done without your help." Lord Leon's voice was solemn. His face pivoted down to the floor as nobles walked by, judgment apparent on their faces.

I grimaced.

I wished I could do more for him.

Veronica had not only shamed herself, but she brought it upon Leon as well. Leon knew it too, that's why he had summoned me the night he had arrived. He had begged for my help, begged me to help him and his daughter have a decent life. He knew that no one would want Veronica, not after everything she had done, that people would blame her behavior on her upbringing. They would be cast out of society. Life would be hard for them.

Leon didn't deserve that, not after all the things he's done for Titus and me. For Modare. For the war. I owed him my life. But the help I had already given had risked my happiness. I had almost lost Estelle. I would do no more.

I nodded to Leon as I had no further words for him. I turned, passing Veronica. Her hand reached out for my tunic, but I quickly dodged her grasp. I knew what she wanted. Lord Hamlin was not the richest lord nor was he rich in power. He was far below *her standards.* She wanted more. She wanted me. But she had used me far too many times. She had destroyed me, and Estelle was the one to mend the pieces that remained.

"Alexander," she called familiarly.

I froze as my blood boiled. "*Prince* Alexander," I hissed. "You will address me as someone of your standing should." She opened her mouth, attempting to speak, but I cut her off. "The niceness I have shown to you this past month was at your father's request and only his. I was generous and helped him achieve what he could not on his own because of the sacrifices Lord Leon has made for Modare in the war. But now, his goals have been reached. There is no need for my assistance anymore. Do not speak to me again."

Veronica's mouth dropped at my tone, shocked, defeated. She wouldn't bother us again.

I turned on my heels, heading for Estelle's room. My beautiful wife.

We had both been idiots. We had acted like children running from their fears, their insecurities. We had played games with one another, but we would do this no more.

Aeson was right when we talked a month ago. Talking fixes all. But tonight, I had no intention of using words to show her the depth of my love.

I gently twisted the doorknob in case she had fallen asleep. I wanted to wake her gently with kisses, not with the booming sound of a knock. Stepping inside, I was met, unexpectedly, with the night's crisp air. My brow crinkled, and my hair stood on end. She hadn't slept with the window open since the attack.

"Estelle," I called out in the darkness. No answer, no groan in annoyance.

My adrenaline flared. My stomach twisted as I raced to light a torch.

She was gone.

Her trunks remained. Her traveling cloak still hung. She wouldn't leave without these things. She had promised she'd be here when I returned.

I raced to her bed, lifting the sheets as if she was merely hiding underneath. The sound of glass hitting the marble floor rang in my ears.

I spied a small empty crystal bottle on the ground. I held it to the light, revealing a green discoloration on the bottle from the liquid it had contained. I brought it to my nose, my eyes widening. A sleeping draught and not one of Aeson's.

She had been taken.

I pulled the rope beside her bed, then raced to the doors, screaming for guards.

"Shut the gates. No one leaves. The princess has been abducted. I need Kenric in the throne room, now," I roared out before fetching Titus. Somehow, I still had enough sense to not subject a servant to his anger.

"We've searched the entire castle, the town. There is no sign of her," Kenric, Captain of the Guards, reported. "We need to start searching outside the gates. I've prepared four parties, all of them trained to be discreet."

I ran my hands through my hair, trying to remain calm. I should've been with her. I should've—I kicked the stairs leading to the thrones.

"Send them," Titus calmly ordered, waving Kenric away.

"I'll go too," I announced, following Kenric's steps.

"You are needed here," Titus said with a slight growl.

"You expect me to stay in these walls when my wife is missing?" I asked, my voice rising with each word.

"The delegate from Isara will be arriving soon. I need you here"

I clenched my fists.

Estelle's request to return home, not even after a year of being married, had already raised suspicion among the Isarans. Her lack of presence, when the delegate arrives, would reek of foul play.

My hand tightened on the hilt of my sword. We needed to handle this with care; we needed both our skills, I knew that. But what good was I when all I could think about was Estelle? My fear, my anger, all of it clouded my better judgment.

"They will find her Alexander." Titus rested his hand on my shoulder, grounding me, helping me to remember the collected and calculated general I had been in the war.

I nodded at Kenric, allowing him to go without me.

I sat on the steps below the throne where Titus was waiting for news or the delegate to arrive. If the latter came first, I prayed it would be Griffith.

Perhaps, if it was him, I could convince him that it was not us behind Estelle's disappearance.

She had told him that she loved me. They had tension between them because of it. At least that's what I inferred when I saw her necklace missing at the spring festival. If Griffith took her words to heart, he would see I could never harm Estelle, never let harm come to her.

Or would he see this as an opportunity to seek revenge for the love I stole from him?

The doors creaked open. I jumped to my feet.

Finally, some news.

"Kenric, did you," my voice trailed off as a middle-aged, brown-haired man, wearing the crest of Isara on his chest entered with Leo slightly behind him.

"I have come to collect Princess Estelle." There was calm hostility in his voice.

Titus adjusted in his throne, straightening his back. I glanced a look of warning as Leo squeaked in fright.

Where was Griffith? He would have jumped at the opportunity to be alone with Estelle.

Titus rubbed his temple, stalling for a minute more as a last hope Kenric would run in with news.

He never did.

"There was an attack." Titus licked his lips as the words struggled to come out. "Princess Estelle was the target," Titus flatly reported, there were no emotions to decipher, only information. "We believe she has been abducted, alive. We have guards—"

"Abducted?" the delegate yelled. "By whom?"

Titus looked at me, silently telling me to answer. "We are unsure, but we suspect it is the same person that was behind the first breach. But I can assure you—"

"You assume?" he roared through the chamber. As much as it pained me, I held my tongue, yelling back would only make matters worse. "My king will not take this matter lightly as you are doing."

"I can assure you"—my teeth ground at the rage burning inside me. How dare he think I take this lightly—"we are doing everything we can to bring her back home."

"But you have no leads as to who has taken her?"

I pushed my tongue against my cheek before replying with a simple no.

"With the rumors of Modare being an impenetrable castle, surely there was some evidence on how she was *taken*."

I looked to Titus, silently asking permission to show the delegate the bottle. He nodded.

The delegate held the bottle to the light before sniffing it. "A sleeping draught?"

"That was all that was found in her room."

"Sleeping draughts can be used daily to aid in sleep." The delegate handed the bottle back to me. "Last I heard the princess was suffering from night terrors."

"The smell of this one is stronger than a normal potion."

"I smelt no difference," he snarked. "Do you have any other clues?"

"No," I growled out.

"I see." He smacked his lips, thinking. "Could I see her room? See the signs of the struggle? Perhaps there was something you missed."

I took a breath. Estelle's room had been in perfect condition. There were no signs of struggle. It would seem as if she was betrayed by someone she was supposed to trust.

"After the guards fully examined the room, it was cleaned," Titus responded.

"*How diligent of your maids.*"

"We do not like mess in our castle," Titus replied flatly.

I sucked in my lips, trying to think of anything more to add, the tension in the room rising as the suspicion worsened.

The delegate raised his brows, his foot taps echoing in the silence. "I will return to Isara. I will tell the king of this *tragic* news. I will tell him of the bottle you found. I wish you luck in your search. I hope, for all our sakes, that the princess is found, *alive.*"

He turned, his cloak dramatically flowing behind him. I waited for the doors to shut before turning to Titus.

"Leo, bring me Kenric. We must prepare for war."

"War? Titus, it was just a conversation," I raged.

"Alexander, you aren't thinking clearly. He does not believe us. You could hear it in his tone, see it in his actions. Isara will declare war on us."

Kenric opened the doors. "King Titus?"

"Pull back the search parties, assemble the troops and prepare them to march."

"Pull back the search parties? Who will look for her?" I climbed the stairs, a fire burning inside me.

"Our best men are out there looking for a princess that we will never find. We need them here, ready to defend. I cannot have them weary."

"And how do you know we will never find her?" I roared.

"It's been a day and we've found nothing." His voice grew soft as he placed his hand on my shoulder, comforting me. "Alexander, I fear that they've—"

"You haven't sent me out yet," I growled, making my way to the iron doors.

"As your king, I forbid you to leave." Titus's words echoed through the throne room signaling the guards to cross their spears, effectively blocking the exit.

My brows furrowed together, my gut twisted, and a heat rose in my chest. It was rare for Titus to give me orders as my king, but when he did I normally obeyed, knowing that it was my duty, his right. But this—this I would not let him decide what was best, even if that meant going against the monarchy.

I turned, grabbing the hilt of the dagger I had strapped to my thigh. Titus didn't even have time to process my motions before the blade was at his throat.

"You will let me leave," I whispered, death in my voice.

I hated the cold stare Titus gave me. He knew what I was choosing, what I had chosen. I had chosen her over Modare, over him. But the truth of the matter was that they would both be ok without me. I had given the new defense plans to Kenric, foolproof strategies on how to protect the castle if war were to happen again. Modare would be safe. And Titus, he may not believe it himself, but he was the king Modare needed. He could rule on his own. He had believed that it was me who pulled us out of our losing streak during the war, but his grief had blocked him from seeing that it wasn't a losing streak. We were winning all along.

"I've seen you put that dagger to many men's throats, but never did I think it would be on mine."

Kenric took a step forward, sword unsheathing, following the oath he had taken many years ago. I grimaced, knowing the odds were against me, but Titus waved him off. This was between him and me.

"You've never given me an order that I didn't agree with." Titus ground his teeth. I lowered my voice so only he could hear as I spoke, "Titus, let me go to her, please."

"You need to protect Modare."

"Titus," I whispered upon seeing his hard expression falter, a flicker of fear in his eyes. "You can protect it without me, I promise, you are ready."

"We've always protected it together," Titus mumbled. His voice was weak, void of the persona he played in front of the court, in front of the guards. Fear had overtaken him and now he was just my brother.

"I know, and Modare has been blessed by the gods to have two protectors, but Estelle, she only has one. Me. She is mine to protect and if you do not let me go to her…Titus, do not make me fight you, fight Modare. Please." I pressed the dagger harder on his throat, allowing a bit of blood to spill, making sure he knew my words were real.

"Let him go." The guards looked at one another puzzled but lowered their spears.

"Thank you," I whispered, dropping the dagger from his neck revealing the broken skin.

Titus only nodded as I silently made my way to the door.

I entered the stables. A group of young guards were watering their horses. They looked at me in confusion as I mounted Shadow. I paid them no heed, knowing their confusion stemmed from the orders that I had just heard in the throne room, but those orders no longer included me. I mounted Shadow when one finally spoke.

"Prince Alexander, King Titus has ordered all of us to return."

I rolled my eyes, not wanting to take the time to correct him, to tell him that I wasn't a part of those orders but as I twisted my neck, I couldn't help but eye the young man and his companions. There were four of them, all young and inexperienced. They wouldn't be missed if Isara attacked.

My gut twisted at what I was about to do, but I would need help to rescue Estelle.

"He has, but I've found that some orders aren't meant to be followed. Don't you agree?"

I squinted, waiting for their reaction. Boys like them were dying to go on an adventure, and if they had heard the stories from the war, they'd jump at the opportunity to go on a mission with me.

They looked at one another, eyes wide as they realized my words were an invitation. Quickly, they mounted their horses.

I smiled; glad they accepted my invitation but the sight of their unmarked bodies made me grimace. They were so young and underqualified for this mission. They had not experienced any of the horror I had that led to the scars on my back, marks I did not wish for anyone. But I needed them. If they survived this, I'd make sure they never wanted for anything.

We rode around the perimeter of the castle for hours looking for any sign of the kidnappers. I had almost given up until I found a single broken branch with a minuscule piece of purple fabric.

Estelle.

I had found the start of the trail. From here it was easy to track. We raced on.

I leaned back in the rundown wooden chair, my finger circling the rim of my glass, my leg shaking.

I should keep going.

I watched as the young guards quietly filled their bellies, struggling to keep their eyes open. They needed rest. We had been traveling for a day and a half with one or two breaks. The speed I drove them at was brutal, even for the most experienced riders. They never once asked to stop, but as we entered what was previously known as Astra territory, I saw the youngest—Will—begin to slip from his horse. I had pushed him, all of them too far. I slowed my pace, finding the nearest inn with half the mind to leave them behind, but I knew I needed them and even Shadow had his limits.

But being in this tavern, the dim lights, the harlots dancing around potential clients…it reminded me of her, the night we first met. I needed to find her, not just because of the impending war but because she was everything to me. I had wasted the precious time I had with her on stupid mistakes. I needed *more* time with her.

The tavern doors burst open. A man stood on the threshold, one hand resting on the frame, bracing himself as he caught his breath. We all stared at him in silence.

"Isara. The treaty," he huffed through his nonsensical words. "Isara has declared war on Modare. They march in three days."

Silence followed, then mumbles, bickering, and finally, panic.

I stood up, hand on my hilt. The group of guards followed suit as we made our way out of the tavern. This was all the rest we could afford.

CHAPTER 49

I felt the rhythmic bouncing first as the potion wore off, then something pushing into my hips as my head and feet were pulled down by gravity. My forehead wrinkled as I forced my heavy eyelids to open. Below me was overgrown grass, slowly getting trampled on by brown hooves. I braced my hands on the horse's side, trying to push myself up. I needed to see my surroundings, but my bound hands were like butter, causing me to slip back down with a thump.

"Looks like someone's awake," a voice boomed from behind.

"Aye, looks like it," another voice spoke ahead of me.

"Release me," I yelled, thrashing my bound limbs in an attempt to sit up and see my captors.

About three or four different laughs sounded at once.

I raised my leg high and brought it down in one fell swoop, hoping it would help me get off the horse. Instead, my feet only hit the poor creature in the side. The horse, startled, stood on its back legs, sending my body to the forest ground. I wheezed, trying to regain the breath I had lost on impact.

"Fuck, is she still alive?" asked one of the previous voices.

I let out a groan as I tried to sit up.

"Looks like it! I guess princesses aren't porcelain dolls after all," a voice replied, followed by a cackle of laughter.

"Get her back on the horse. It's almost dark," came a third voice, not amused by the other two.

The man behind me groaned, the stirrups clattering as he dismounted his horse. "Up you get." He grabbed my upper arm, pulling me to my feet with sheer force.

My eyes darted from him to the men ahead. There were three, all of them wearing a black silk mask, the same mask the blonde man had worn and the assassin—the one that came many moons ago. My heart stopped.

"Move your feet," the man yelled, pushing on my back.

I had to escape.

I inhaled, collecting all the strength I had, and slammed my heel into his foot. With the man distracted by his pain, I pushed him aside and made a run for it.

I had only made it a couple feet when the sound of hooves caught up to me, then I felt a searing pain on my scalp. I shrieked, grabbing the base of my hair which was being pulled taut by scarred hands.

"Not a very smart one we have here." He pulled my hair backward, forcing me to look up at him. He leaned down, his disgusting breath hot on my nose, his beard scratching my cheek. "Horses will always outrun a human."

Using my hair like reins, he moved me side to side, con-fusing my senses before throwing me to the other two men who both took one of my arms. They gripped so firmly that I expected bruises to form immediately. They placed me back on my horse, thankfully, in a normal seating position, tightly tying my hands to the reins.

"Now, if you try to get off again, you'll find yourself being dragged. And trust me, Princess, that isn't a pleasant experi-ence," the bearded man sneered.

I kept my eyes forward, showing no emotions, no signs of worry. Each member trotted in front of me, the last one taking the reins of my horse and tying it to a rope, allowing him to lead me but remain with his companions.

Once they were all ahead, I examined my surroundings, hoping to see any clues as to where we were or where we were headed. As far as my eyes could see, there were only trees and foliage. The sun shimmered through them.

The sun!

When I was taken it had been night. Now, the sun was directly overhead. It was midday. Alexander had to know I was missing by now. No doubt, there were already search parties. A flicker of hope sparked in my chest, but as the sun peaked through a tree, blinding me, the hope quickly vanished. Modare had some of the best trackers I had seen. If they hadn't found me by now—my breathing hastened.

I must be calm. I must be calm.

If I were to escape this, alive, I needed to think strategically. I looked at the four men in front of me. All of them were heavily armed. A sword at one's hip, a mace on another's back, and daggers attached to all their thighs.

Daggers.

If I could get one, I could put Alexander's lesson to use, but there were too many of them to take on by myself. I could maybe kill one of them if I caught him alone and by surprise. An almost impossible task, but one I had to attempt. But first, I had to figure out how to steal a dagger without getting noticed.

"Let's stop here," the bearded man, whose name I recently learned was Elric, ordered. He seemed to be the leader of the party, but he wasn't the boss. No, the boss was waiting at their hideout, at least that's what I gathered from their conversations.

"I'll get the wood," the slender red-haired man stated as he tied his horse to a low hanging branch.

"Goose and Gust, tie the princess to that tree then go hunt." Both grunted as they dismounted, tying their horses off as well.

Goose, the younger of the two, untied me from my horse's reins. Gust, before I had the opportunity to move, grabbed my arm, yanking me down. I yelped as I felt the muscle in my shoulder stretch.

"Careful with her! The boss says we bring her unharmed." Elric stormed over, his face inches from Gust's.

"It's only a little bit of pain. I'm sure she's fine."

Elric grabbed my arm leading me to the tree across from the horses. "I'll tell him you said that if he finds her *wellness* not to his liking."

Gust clenched his hand into a fist, sneering at Elric. Goose quickly hauled him away into the woods before things could escalate further.

I was wanted alive.

My mind raced back to the night of the assassination attempt. He had worn the same mask as these men, the same outfit as the man who drugged me. They had to be from the same group. Why did they want me alive now? Or was it that the first never meant to kill me?

Elric pushed me down onto the ground, wrapping a rope around my waist and the tree trunk. He tied the rope tightly, making sure I couldn't escape as he cut the ropes off my wrists. They burned in pleasure at the freedom.

Elric unlatched a wineskin from his belt and poured the contents of it on my skin. I whimpered as the liquid seeped into the invisible cuts from the ropes. Elric covered my mouth as he took a swig from the container.

Liquor, a vile liquid, but I was thankful I wouldn't have to worry about an infection.

Elric used his forearm to wipe his mouth before carefully applying some bandages to my wrists. Whoever these men worked for wanted me in peak condition. Elric pulled out leather handcuffs from his horse's satchel, clamping them tightly around my wrists. I winced at the tightness, but it was superior to having my hands bound together by rough rope. At least now I could catch myself, stretch my wrists, *grab items*.

I eyed Elric's thigh as he knelt and tied a rope to the center of the cuffs then knotted it to the tree. There were two daggers, one on each of his thighs. With how my hands were tied, I could grab it easily. I just needed him to be distracted.

"Tell me where you are taking me." I straightened, trying to make my frame appear bigger as he pulled on the rope, checking his knots.

Elric unsheathed one of his daggers. With cold eyes, he admired the blade then me. I shivered as he tucked a strand of hair behind my ear.

"So demanding."

I gulped but pressed on. If I could get him to talk, to be invigorated by conversation, I could steal a blade.

"Tell me," I growled.

Elric laughed at my sad attempt to be intimidating. "That's for us to know and you to find out." He slashed the rope that tied my waist to the tree, allowing me to stand while still being bound.

I took deep breaths, calming myself from the sight of Elric caressing the dagger.

"If I will find out eventually then there's no reason for you to keep me in anticipation."

Elric smiled, showing his tarnished teeth. I grimaced, looking away from the site.

"Don't like the look of my smile, Princess." He brought his face closer. I pushed my head into the tree trunk, trying to distance myself from him. "Guess you're used to seeing only pretty men, aren't you?"

"And what do you know of the men I see?" I sneered out, still looking away, my breathing ragged.

Elric put down the dagger, grabbing my face with his thumb and forefinger. "You'll look at me when you talk to me."

I recoiled as his hot breath assaulted my nose. He was getting angry. I could use this to my advantage. "From the way you look and smell, I would think pretty things hide from you."

Laughter came from behind Elric. "She's got you there," Goose stated, his voice accompanied by the ruffling sound of leaves.

Elric stood on his feet quicker than lightning, his voice booming like thunder, "Shut up, you idiot."

Elric stormed to Goose as Gust stood close by with a rabbit in hand, foolishly leaving his dagger behind. I eyed all three of them, their attention was wholly focused on one another.

This was my chance.

I extended my leg, firmly planting my foot on top of the weapon. My eyes never leaving the sight of the men, not until I had the blade in my hands.

I frantically looked for a place to hide the item. I had no pockets. The leaves would move with the wind. I looked down to my skirts, at the many layers. I wouldn't be able to move or stand, but the dagger wouldn't be found if I placed it between them.

"Just cook the rabbit and keep your mouth shut," Elric growled, storming off to unpack his sleeping materials.

My eyes flashed up, making sure none of them saw me lifting my dress.

"What are you looking at?" Goose yelled at me.

I looked away, trying to look as meek as possible.

I needed to avoid confrontation till nightfall, wait for them to sleep.

The sun began to set, and the woods grew quiet apart from the crackle of the fire and the occasional chirp of a cricket that wasn't scared by the smell of burning rabbit.

"You've burned it again," whined the fourth party member, Jacob. A man of few words and wit but made up for it in strength as I had witnessed him rip off the rabbit's head in a single motion.

"Well, you can cook it next then," Goose yelled.

I rolled my eyes. For a group of men who had kidnapped me from the castle, they were barely self-sufficient.

Goose and Gust always had something to complain about but didn't have any skills to offer when it came to setting up the camp. Both were slender in build and could barely hold their own swords. However, they were quiet, fast. It was clear they were trained for a silent murder. They were the party's stealth. Elric, the leader, kept everyone in line and was the most decorated with weapons. Jacob had the least, but I doubted he needed one. Not only had I seen him rip the rabbit's head from its body with his bare hands, but he had effortlessly cleared the camp of boulders and tree trunks that had fallen. A true beast of a man. I worried what he could do if his hands ever found their way onto a human neck.

If I were to have a chance of killing anyone, it had to be Goose or Gust keeping watch tonight.

Elric picked apart the rabbit, piling a small portion onto a plate. "Eat." He placed the metal plate next to me. I glared at him through my lashes, waiting for him to leave despite the raging hunger in me, making me think I had been asleep for more than just a night and half a day. He smiled, enjoying the anger he stirred in me. "Goose and Gust, you're on watch tonight."

Both?

I looked down, hiding my growing eyes. I could only handle one of them. The other would see me kill the first, if

I succeeded, and come after me. I didn't have the skill or the strength to win a fair fight.

I leaned against the tree trunk, looking up at the stars, rethinking my plan. The snores of Jacob and Elric filled my ears, but the noise wasn't loud enough to block out the eerie sounds of Goose and Gust sharpening their knives. Occasionally, they tested the sharpness by running their forefinger ever so lightly down the blade. They seemed only satisfied when they accidentally drew their own blood. They were fiends. A *wonderful* reminder that I needed them separated if this plan were to work. But how? I gripped the knife from the outside of my skirts.

Think, Estelle, think.

"What are you grabbing at?" Goose's whiney voice came from the fire. Gust's eyes glued to my hand.

Damn it. They hadn't looked at me once. Why now?

"My skirts. That should be apparent, even from there." I tried to sound unafraid, sound like I had nothing to hide, use the tongue I had sharpened over months of teasing with Alexander.

"Why are you holding your skirts? Seems like an odd thing to do"

"Nah, it looks like she's holding something."

Elric sat up, groaning, "What are you two blabbering about?"

"She keeps holding her skirts."

Gust smacked the top of Goose's head. "No, she's clearly holding something in her pockets."

Elric's eyes met mine. I loosened my hand, trying to hide any outline of the dagger.

Elric stalked over to me, crouching down. "What were you doing that interrupted my sleep?"

"Nothing," I spat.

Not convinced, Elric's hand slid to my waist, smiling as it drifted down to where mine had been. His touch lingered far longer than need be.

"Your employer said not to lay a finger on me," I muttered out, as my gut twisted in disgust.

"I'm sure he'll forgive me for a necessary search."

Elric squeezed the middle of my leg through the fabric, then my inner thigh. I grinded my teeth. Every ounce of me wanted to retch, scream as he smiled in pleasure. His grip became tighter, but I couldn't let him find the dagger that rested on my outer thigh. If this kept him from finding it, I'd endure.

Elric raised a brow, surprised I hadn't done anything. He bit his lip, eyes full of mischief. His hand trailed upward. "Could you be hiding something up here?" He smiled up to me, making it clear he wasn't going to stop.

"Don't you fucking touch me," I screamed, loud enough to wake Jacob as I jumped to my feet.

Elric, still squatting, eyed the ground. The sound of rustling leaves echoed in my ears, and my heart sank knowing what he was about to find. "When did you get this?" He stood, allowing the blade to caress my cheek. "You're starting to be quite the handful." He grazed the dagger against my skin, creating a small line that ended between my breasts.

My nostrils flared as my breathing heightened. I couldn't get enough air. Elric had found the dagger and like that, my plan had failed. He pushed his face closer, his hot breath so close I could taste it. Panic filled me. I kicked up my knee, slamming it into his gut.

He wheezed, clutching his stomach, slowly regaining his composure. "You'll regret that," he mumbled, his eyes murderous. "I think it's time we taught you a lesson." His forehead pressed against my throat, as he breathed in my scent.

"He said not to touch me, not to lay a hand on me," I angrily reminded, trying to hide the shaking in my voice.

Elric laughed into my neck. "He won't be able to see this lesson. Will he boys?"

A nerve-racking cackle came from the rest of the party. Elric, keeping the dagger at my chest, reached his hand down, pulling up my skirts.

"I'll scream." The blade of the dagger broke my skin as I pushed further back into the tree, the bark cutting into my back.

"Scream all you want, no one will hear you. You said pretty things hide from me, and because of that, I shouldn't know what they look like. You're only half right." His thumb wedged between my lips, opening my mouth. "Pretty little things, like yourself, do run, but I always catch them, and I make them show me their pretty little selves."

Tears filled my eyes, a sob escaped my mouth, and my body shook, uncontrollably.

Alexander, where are you?

Elric's eyes danced with amusement as he continued to raise my skirts, proud of the tears he caused. "I make them show me their pretty little sounds too. Shall I show you how?"

I shook my head, silently, begging him to stop. He let out a single laugh before his eyes filled with terror.

Hot liquid splattered onto my face as an arrow flew by and sent Elric's head backward. His limp hands released my skirt. His knees buckled, and he fell to the forest floor. The ground around him was stained with blood.

I choked on the air in my throat as Elric's cold, dead eyes stared up at me, a blue feathered arrow sitting between them.

Modare had found me.

Battle cries rang in my ears as four men came from behind, racing toward the remaining three kidnappers who desperately reached for their weapons.

Gust and Goose stood back-to-back, protecting each other's blind spots as two guards sprinted at them. Their swords clashed again and again like a synchronized dance.

All four were evenly matched, the battle seeming impossible to end. The two guards looked to one another, nodding before trading opponents. The switch confused Gust and Goose. Taking advantage of this, the guards rushed forward once more, determined to break their defenses.

The guard facing Goose held his sword high, bringing it down with exceptional force, breaking through Goose's stance, slitting his throat. Gust turned, wailing as if his own life had been taken. He reached for the dagger on his thigh, throwing it into the guard's chest. Blood splattered out. Gust smiled at the fallen body. Too distracted by his victory, he didn't see the second guard running at him, didn't see the sword aimed at his heart before it was too late. Gust's body fell and joined the other two corpses.

The guard, fighting the urge to grieve his fallen comrade, let out a scream as he ran toward Jacob to aid the other guards. Jacob—drenched in blood due to the gushing gashes caused by the guards—moved like a deranged animal.

Jacob let out a deafening scream as he lunged forward. The three men struggled for breath, their swords dragging on the reddened ground. None of them had the energy or skill to deliver the final blow.

My breathing hitched. They were so close to saving me. They just had to kill once more. I clutched my dress, giving up hope when a blue shimmer blinded me. A blue like sapphires, sapphires from Alexander's sword.

I squinted, looking past the guards, past Jacob, to the edge of the woods. Alexander, sword raised, rushed toward the final villain and plunged his sword into Jacob's back. Jacob thrashed, trying to pull out the sword but it only dug deeper. He looked up to the sky, his legs bending, his breathing halting, then his face fell into the dirt.

The guards knelt on the ground, catching their breath as Alexander's eyes met mine.

He had come.

My legs raced forward, but I was pulled back by my bonds. Tears began to fall as Alexander raced forward to cut the leather cuffs.

"Alexander." I threw my hands around him, holding him tightly.

"Careful," he groaned out.

I pulled back, my eyes frantically examining him. There was no sign of blood, but his face was filled with pain.

"Shoulder."

"It still hasn't healed?" I asked, grazing it as if my touch could heal it.

"Only a little. I'm still supposed to be taking it easy."

"Alexander, you shouldn't have—"

He gripped my waist tightly. "I couldn't call myself your husband if I allowed someone else to rescue you." He kissed my forehead, caressing my cheek.

"Prince Alexander, we should go."

Alexander turned, his hands leaving my waist. "Yes, but one of ours has fallen."

My eyes flickered to the lifeless body laying between Gust and Goose. One of the guards knelt beside him, closing his eyes so the guard may rest.

"We need to bring him home." The men nodded in agreement, their eyes grieving for their fallen friend. "Build a cot and carry him back to Modare. Tell Titus what he has done, that he deserves a knight's funeral."

"Your Highness, that will lead away from our destination," spoke one guard, his voice grievous.

"He deserves better than to be laid to rest in these woods. The princess and I will travel alone. I refuse to allow Will to be left behind."

The men stared at one another then Will. Kneeling to the ground, they thanked their prince. Alexander silently nodded before picking me up and placing me on Shadow.

"Alexander, can't we stay with them, help in some way?"

His heels nudged Shadow's side. "We have a different destination than them."

I looked up at him, puzzled. I thought we'd be going straight home. "Where—"

I couldn't finish the words as Alexander quietly spoke, "Isara."

CHAPTER 50

"We've made it," I muttered, seeing the purple flags a few feet away from Modare's. We had finally made it to the border.

Alexander slowed Shadow whose breath was heavy. I stroked his neck, showing my appreciation for him and his strong legs and to apologize. It was hard enough for any stead to carry two people for this long, not to mention the pace we rode at, but it was all necessary. We had two more days till my father's men began their march. Time was running out.

"There's a stream up ahead. We'll stop there for a couple of minutes," Alexander mused behind me.

I simply nodded. Worry taking my words.

I loved both kingdoms. If there were to be a war, if we didn't make it in time to stop the bloodshed—I shuddered at the thought. I would grieve for both sides.

Alexander's soft lips brushed my shoulder. "We'll make it," he mumbled into my skin.

"Are you certain?"

Alexander pulled on Shadow's reins and dismounted him. The river babbled in front of us.

"Absolutely. Shadow is fast, and you are a surprisingly good rider in the wild." He smirked as he placed me on the ground.

"Alexander." I loved his smirk, his teasing, but now was not the time.

Alexander let out a sigh. He led Shadow to the river before coming back over and squatting. He picked up a stick and drew an odd shape in the dirt then an x and a circle. "The castle is in the middle of the country"—he pointed the stick at the x he had drawn—"we are at the border. If we traveled leisurely, assuming we rested here and took off at sunrise, we would be there in a day. Now, if we travel like we've been, we'll be there in half the time." He placed his hands on my arm, rubbing my anxiousness away. "Trust me, we'll make it."

I offered a small smile. I trusted him, but time was moving too fast.

Alexander kissed my forehead, understanding my silent worries. I stood still, watching him fill his wineskin with river water next to Shadow who hadn't stopped drinking.

Alexander turned to me, holding out the container full of water. "Come, drink. You'll need to be hydrated for the ride."

I took a step forward, wobbling as pain shot through my legs. Alexander's hand was on me faster than I could regain my balance.

It had been a while since I rode, my legs were out of practice.

"You need rest." Alexander swept me off my feet, gently placing me down on a boulder.

"I'm fine, just sore." I took the container from his hand, taking a long drink.

"Estelle, you won't be very useful to me or Isara if you show up bowlegged." He stroked my cheek with his thumb. "Remember, those arrival times were based on us traveling tomorrow. We still have much daylight left today."

I lowered the wineskin, my eyes glancing down at my shaking legs then Shadow whose eyes looked as if they would close any minute. Alexander was right. We needed rest. Shadow needed rest. We hadn't stopped moving, hadn't talked, since Alexander had rescued me. I nodded, reluctantly.

"Good." Alexander raised my hands to his lips. "If we follow the main road, we should come along an inn. We'll rest there tonight."

We followed the beaten path, a slower pace than before, for an hour till we came across a small inn. A young stableboy raced out upon seeing Shadow, grasping the reins as Alexander dismounted.

"Give him the best care and I shall reward you the same amount when I leave." Alexander dropped ten pieces of silver into the boy's hands, his eyes widened, it was more than he would make in a month. Alexander grabbed my waist, setting me carefully on the ground. He looped my arm through his, taking some of my weight, to lessen the pain in my legs as we made our way into the inn.

The scent of alcohol flooded my nostrils as the door shut behind us. A soft melody could barely be heard over the chatter of the drunk, unsightly customers. Alexander took a step heading to the barkeep, me at his side.

The barkeep dried a mug as he talked to another man. My stomach flipped as I stared at his broad back. The man twisted upon hearing me and Alexander approaching. I released Alexander's arm, jumping behind him.

"Estelle, what's wrong?"

I shivered as Alexander's body shielded mine.

"It's Elric. He's alive." My breath hastened as memories of his tarnished teeth, his hot breath, and his hands on my waist flashed in my mind.

I closed my eyes, feeling Alexander's body turning to examine the man by the bar. "Estelle," he whispered in my ear, "it's not Elric. It's alright."

I opened my eyes to see the bearded man and the barkeep looking at me with a raised brow. It wasn't Elric. They looked nothing alike except for the beard and the black clothes.

I hugged Alexander's arm, trying to rid myself of paranoia.

He kissed the top of my head. "I'll never let anything bad happen to you again." I nodded allowing him to pull me forward despite my pounding heart. "One room, please, preferably on your top floor."

"We have one left, but it's rather small," the barkeep explained.

"That's fine." Alexander unhooked his leather pouch from his belt. "Will Modarian money be acceptable?"

The man with the beard cocked his head to Alexander. "What's a Modarian doing here with a war coming on?"

Alexander ignored the man, eyes focused on the barkeep. "I'll pay double."

The barkeep's eyes bounced between the bearded man and Alexander, debating which customer's favor he'd rather have. "Double it is. Leave the man alone, Lucas." Lucas sneered and left the bar, heading to a table where men played cards, as the barkeep took the money. "Best not mention you're Modarian." Alexander raised a brow. The barkeep leaned in, his voice barely audible as he whispered, "There's been a band of men searching for a Modarian male traveling with a woman." I pulled my hood closer as the barkeep's eyes flashed to me.

I could feel Alexander's body tense, but he remained expressionless as he slid a couple more coins on the bar. "For two platters and your silence."

The barkeep nodded, placing enough food to feed four people on a tray along with the keys to the room. "Best to leave once you're rested, can't promise protection with this crowd."

Alexander bowed his head in thanks, grabbing the tray of food, gesturing for me to walk in front of him.

CHAPTER 51

The room was small and dusty, but it was better than the overcrowded bar downstairs.

Alexander sat the tray down on the small table that stood in the corner of the room. "Come eat." He pulled out one of the worn-down chairs, motioning me to sit.

I obeyed, the chair creaking as it took my weight. My legs shook uncontrollably, finally accepting the soreness from today's riding.

Alexander pushed a plate toward me before checking that all the windows and doors were securely bolted. I picked at the bread, trying to gain an appetite, knowing that Alexander would scold me for not properly feeding myself, but worry filled me.

"They're searching for us, for me."

Alexander unfastened his sword from his belt, placing it next to the bed, satisfied with the bolts before speaking. "I know." He sat across from me, rubbing his temple.

"Why?" I stammered out. "They've lost so many men. Why do they keep coming?"

Alexander picked at his lips with his thumb.

"Alexander, if you have a theory, I need to know."

He sat up, letting out a sigh. We both knew better than to keep each other in the dark now. "At first, I thought it could be a king with a vendetta against you, against Modare. That they wanted to scare us, influence us into making a decision that would be in their favor, or perhaps break the treaty. However, the second time they came they could have easily killed you. That could've ended the treaty right then and there instead they kidnapped you.

"Kidnappings happen all the time to lords and ladies. Not often does a thief try to steal a royal, but if they did, the money would be well worth the trouble. You just need to find men with the courage to do so."

"So, we're dealing with an overambitious kidnapper?"

Alexander shook his head. "No, after we took down the four men, it should have ended. Word would have reached his future employees about the deaths. No one would be foolish enough to accept the job again. Unless an absurd amount of money was offered and given before the mission was complete," Alexander paused, the silence deafening. "Whoever we are dealing with, they have a substantial amount of power and wealth. They want you for more than a princess's ransom. I just don't know what exactly."

I clutched my dress. They wouldn't stop, not till their leader was caught. My shoulders trembled.

"Estelle"—Alexander knelt before me, wrapping his hands around mine—"everything will be fine. Once we get you to Isara, we'll speak to your father. Isara and Modare will join forces. We'll find whoever this is. I promise you'll be safe."

I looked into his eyes. They were strong, soft, full of love for me. We had been together just shy of a year and only had a few happy memories due to all the incidents. Now, our lives were at risk. I would be hunted by this elusive villain, never knowing when he'd strike again. I needed to live as if each moment were the last.

I leaned down to find Alexander's lips with my own. Gently, he kissed me back, but I wanted more. I pushed my lips to his, tangling my fingers in his hair.

"Estelle"—he pulled away—"are you sure?" I titled my head in confusion. "When I found you, Elric was—"

I shivered at his name, at the thought of what would've happened if Alexander had shown up a minute later.

"Estelle, we don't have to." He ran his thumb over my cheek, wiping away tears that trickled.

I brushed them away, sternly, commanding them to stop. Elric had scared me but the thought of not enjoying every moment with Alexander, letting Elric haunt me from beyond the grave was horrifying. I wanted this. I wanted Alexander. I wanted to have control of my life.

I stood up, pulling Alexander to his feet with me. "I want you to touch me, touch me everywhere he did, erase him from my memory." Alexander's eyes stared deep into mine, making sure I truly meant what I said. That I was ready for him. "Alexander, please. I need you."

My words were true. I needed him, not just to rid the memories of Elric but so I could feel as though I had a choice. That I could control what happened to me, what I would go through, despite all the odds against me. Despite the murderers, bandits, kidnappers, whatever they called themselves. And right now, I yearned for Alexander's body against mine and nothing would stop that.

I pushed my body against his, feeling the hardening bulge in his pants. He took a breath calming himself. "But if you want to stop—"

"I won't." I smiled, untying my cloak.

Alexander stared at my body, teeth digging into his lip. His yearning was just as strong. "Promise you'll tell me if it gets too much for you."

"I promise." The words brushed over my lips as I pulled my hair to the front and turned, giving him access to my dress's laces.

Alexander's lips caressed one side of my neck, his fingers trailing the other side, making his way down to my laces. The softness of his touch sent shivers down my spine. Tantalizingly slow, he freed the ribbon from each eyelet, biting the flesh that was revealed to help him suppress the urge to ravish me immediately.

He was halfway done when I became tired of waiting. I spun around, hands pulling at my sleeves, wiggling out of the dress.

He smiled. "Impatient, are we?"

"You're teasing too much," I accused, a red blush forming as his eyes delighted over my naked body.

"I'll show you teasing." He picked me up and threw me gently on the bed then kissed my lips and neck. My fingers laced into his hair, pulling him to me, my legs wrapping around his hips. He chuckled into my skin. "What happened to my shy little princess?"

"Shut up," I breathed. My body knew what pleasure his lips would give, I wouldn't wait any longer.

Alexander obeyed, not lifting his lips as he moved down to my navel, his tongue coming out to play. I squirmed under his expert touch, gasping as he threw my legs over his shoulders, his tongue trailing down to my inner thigh.

"Alexander," I panted.

I wanted him, needed him in me now. Any part of him.

His possessive eyes met mine, his fingers replacing his tongue as he spoke, "Not yet, I need to lick you clean."

My head jolted back as he slid his head downward, his tongue grazing down with him, his teeth leaving lovingly placed marks. Tension raised in my stomach as he made his way back up, biting my flesh. I never knew pain could feel so good.

He was mere inches away from my entrance. I closed my eyes ready to feel his tongue instead his lips stayed on my thigh.

He had kissed away the foul memories so why did he hesitate?

His nails clawed at my waist. His manhood pushed against me. He wanted me. I was sure of it, but he wasn't sure I was ready.

I wasn't the delicate princess he had met so long ago. He needed to know that.

I sat up, taking my legs off his shoulders.

"Estelle," he whispered, his voice filled with concern, wondering if he had pushed me too far. "Do you need to stop?"

I said nothing as I pushed him onto his back, mounting him.

"Estelle," he groaned, his hands clamping to my hips, his head ramming into the pillow as I put him in me.

I winced as I lowered myself. There was more pressure than anything I had experienced. It was tighter, a bit painful, but still, the tension between my legs rose, telling me not to stop. I continued to lower myself, taking all of him in me, resting my bottom on the heels of my feet. My hands rested on his chest, grounding myself.

Alexander's nails trailed down my spine. "How does it feel?" he cooed, clearly enjoying himself but still concerned for me.

"Different," I breathed out, wiggling, trying to get used to the position.

"Do you want to change?"

I shook my head. It was a bit uncomfortable, but as I sat on top of Alexander, pinned him to the bed, I felt in control. In control of the pleasure, of my life, my body—something I never thought I'd have. I pressed off my thighs, rising so only the tip was in me then slowly I came back down. It felt good. I did it once more, this time a tinge faster. Then again and again till I was bouncing. Both our breaths became ragged. I looked down at Alexander. His eyes closed. His head was tilted back as his lips formed an O. I was in control of his pleasure and mine. I didn't know how badly I needed this. After all the things that happened; the arranged marriage, the attack, Veronica, then Elric, I had felt the world spinning. I had felt that everything that happened to me was not in my power, but this, I was in control of this. The pleasure, my time with Alexander, it was all mine. He was mine, and I was his. No one would disrupt our lives again.

"Estelle, I'm close." Alexander's eyes met mine, his nails digging into my thighs, trying to contain himself, denying his own pleasure till I had my fill.

"I am too," I muttered. I sped up, using all my strength to bounce faster, harder but it wasn't enough. I wanted more. I cursed, if only my legs weren't sore from riding.

Alexander's hands cupped my backside. I sank into his palms as he helped throw my body up, catching me as I came down.

Together, we'd do this together.

My entrance tightened around him, the tension between my legs ready to explode. He growled my name as I came around him, his manhood twitching in defeat.

Alexander lifted me up, sliding himself out of me, then gently placed me beside him as if knowing my strength had been depleted. I curled into him, intertwining my legs with his. His fingers ran through my hair, lulling me to sleep.

CHAPTER 52

Fingers trailed down my back, gently waking me from my deep slumber. My eyes fluttered open to find the room dimly lit by a single candle. I turned in question seeing Alexander fully dressed, sitting on the bed.

"We should leave before the sun rises."

I made a move to sit up but only groaned in response to my aching body. A body still sore from the riding I had done all day, then late into the night.

"Sorry, I brought you here to rest but I think I just made your legs worse." He softly smiled as he brought me my dress.

I rolled my eyes, grabbing the clothing from him, grimacing at how long it would take to put it on. But as I turned over the dress, I smiled. Alexander had loosely redone the laces, all I had to do was just throw it over my head and tighten the ribbons.

I dressed quickly as Alexander hastily gathered our belongings, packing them in our satchels. His speed, highly contagious.

"Ready?" He draped the cloak he had brought with him from Modare over my shoulders, tying it tightly.

I nodded.

After today, everything would be fixed. Sure, the band of kidnappers would still be out there, but after last night, I knew I could be in control, that I was powerful if I chose.

"One last thing." He knelt before me, hiking up my skirts.

"Alexander, I thought you said we needed to leave." I bit my lip, gripping his hair with devilish intent.

He chuckled into my skin, his calloused hands running up to my thigh. Tingles ran through my body. I gripped tighter to his hair but released when I felt cold metal and rough leather wrap around my flesh. I looked down to find the matching dagger to his sword given to me on our wedding night. I looked at him, puzzled.

"Precautions. I don't want you to use it but if you must, do you remember how?"

I nodded as he dropped my skirts. My hand reached out to his throat. "The neck"—my fingers trailed down—"the chest"—Alexander smirked—"*and the navel*." I licked my lips as my eyes darted lower than necessary on the last word.

Alexander let loose a heavy sigh as he readjusted his pants. "When did you become like this?" I shrugged, feigning innocence. He looked at me with lustful eyes, wishing he could touch me as he did last night, but he knew better than to delay our departure. He kissed the top of my head, hoping it would satisfy his needs for a bit.

Alexander took my hand, leading me down the dark stairs into the empty tavern apart from the barkeep who rested his head on the bar.

"Is he asleep?" I whispered as Alexander tiptoed to him.

"I think so. I'll leave the keys beside him." I nodded in agreement.

I remained five steps behind Alexander, worried the sound of our combined feet approaching would wake him. But as Alexander got closer, his steps slowed.

I called his name, tentatively. He softly hushed me as he brought the light closer to the barkeep, revealing dried blood on the table.

There was a loud bang as a wind whipped through the tavern. The sound of unsheathing metal rang in my ears as Alexander jumped in front of me. "Conceal your dagger, use it only when necessary," he whispered, careful not to let the three masked men blocking the door hear.

"There, just like I said, a Modarian and a woman." Lucas appeared from behind the men. "Give me my reward."

The man in the middle turned his head slowly, his blonde hair shining in the darkness. The same blonde hair that I had awoken to the final night of the matching season. The blonde man dropped a couple silver coins in Lucas's hand.

"That's it?" he blabbered, grabbing the masked man's wrist. "I ought to get more than that. You killed my favorite—"

Blood dribbled from his mouth as the blonde man's blade pierced his gut. I gripped Alexander's arm, throwing my free hand over my mouth, muting my gasp. I wouldn't let them know I was afraid.

The blonde man took a handkerchief from his pocket, wiping the steaming liquid from the blade before sheathing it. Silently, he glanced at the other two, cocking his head toward Alexander and me. They drew their swords, running full speed for Alexander. He held his sword high, the clanging of metal ringing through my ears. Sparks flew, briefly revealing faces in the darkness. I couldn't tell who was winning.

The sound of metal meeting wood echoed through the room then grunts of struggle, *Alexander's grunts.*

"Estelle, run!" Alexander screamed.

I stood my ground, shivering. I would not leave him. I would fight.

I began to pull up my skirts, but the sound of a match stopped me. A candle illuminated the room, revealing the details of the shadows I had watched.

My breathing stopped. One of the men had their knee pressed into Alexander's lower back, effectively pinning him down as the other man bound Alexander's hands. I looked on in terror at their quick work. I gasped as the man on Alexander's back yanked his hair and pulled him to his knees then held a dagger to my husband's throat.

They would slit his throat before I could draw my dagger. I let go of the fabric, concealing the weapon I hoped they hadn't noticed. Alexander groaned as blood began to dribble from his neck. They were slowly cutting him.

"Stop!" I cried, running forward. The second masked man raised his sword, stopping me a foot in front of Alexander. "Please, I'll do anything. Just let him live." Tears began to fall. I couldn't lose him.

The floorboards squeaked as the blonde man moved from the door. All eyes turned to him as he slowly approached me. Without a word, he held out a glass bottle containing a green liquid. My eyes flickered to it, no doubt, this was the same potion he had used in Modare.

"I drink it and he stays alive?"

The man nodded.

I reached for the bottle.

"Estelle, no, don't—" Alexander's body fell to the floor.

A gasp slipped from my lips. My eyes rushed over his body. *No blood, good.* I watched his chest move up and down as if he was sleeping. I let out a sigh of relief.

The blonde man pushed the bottle toward me again. My hand hovered over it.

I'm sorry.

I pulled the cork off and drank the contents.

The room began to spin. My feet went numb. I took a step back, fighting the potion, but soon enough it took effect on me, and I was falling.

Giant hands caught me before I hit the floor. My vision blurred as I looked up and found a pair of blue eyes staring at me from behind a mask.

CHAPTER 53

My heart was racing as my eyes fluttered open. They had captured me and Alexander. My eyes shot around my surroundings expecting to see bars of iron. Instead, I found satin sheets, a chestnut wardrobe, and a table filled with food.

I jumped to my feet. Had we been rescued? There was only one way to know.

I placed my hand on the doorknob, taking a deep breath.

Please open.

The door creaked open, revealing a brightly lit hall. I froze before taking a step forward, turning my head left and right checking for signs of our captors or saviors. My steps echoed through the hall, not a picture nor decoration graced the walls. There were only burning torches.

I passed several doors, placing my ear to them, listening for any signs of life. I listened for any clues as to where I was, where Alexander was. I didn't dare open any doors, not knowing if friend or foe waited on the other side.

I had almost reached the end of the hall when I heard a voice, one known throughout my life.

"Lock him up. I don't want him in sight when she wakes."

I beamed, peeking down the stairs. Down in the foyer stood Griffith. He had saved us.

"Griffith," I shouted from the top of the stairs.

He spun to me with wide eyes. "Princess Estelle, I didn't think you'd be awake so soon." He bowed deeply.

I ran down the stairs, hands reaching for him. "Stop that, after everything I need a hug from a friend."

He was slow to hug me back, no doubt, because of our argument, but I was happy to see him, happy he had come to rescue us. No matter what, I could always rely on Griffith.

"How did you find us?"

He pulled back from me. "I was traveling back to my estate when I came across a group of masked men. I went to question them, their masks a clear indicator that they were up to mischief, when I saw a bit of lavender fabric under the cloak of one of the riders.

"I didn't know if it was my mind playing tricks on me or that the desire to see you was that strong, but I thought it was the same fabric as one of your dresses.

"I demanded the rider to reveal their face, but they didn't answer. The men stated she was finally in a deep sleep after a long night, and I shouldn't wake her. I persisted, then they attacked me and my party. We fought, killing every one of them. I pulled the cloak off and saw you.

"You laid so still, so quiet, I thought—I imagined the worst."

I reached for Griffith's hand, comforting him as he stumbled over his words.

"I raced you to my estate and summoned a physician. He told me that you were under the influence of a sleeping draught and that you were still alive. Then, he gave you something to make you wake quicker. I've never thanked the gods so much."

Griffith brought my hands to his lips, kissing them in relief. I allowed it, knowing it brought my friend comfort but was torn as I knew the sight of this would wound Alexander. My stomach turned, realizing Griffith had not once mentioned him.

"What of Alexander? Where is he?"

Griffith stepped back, his eyes narrowing. "*The Modarian Prince.* He, like a coward, ran upon seeing our colors. He, no doubt, is already in Modare."

Wrinkles formed on my forehead. Alexander had no reason to run from Isaran soldiers, and he would never run from a fight.

"Griffith, you said the men were masked, that's what made you question them. If Prince Alexander was with them, wouldn't that have drawn your attention first?"

Griffith tilted his head, rubbing his temple, struggling to find words. "He was wearing a mask as well."

Unconvinced, I continued to question, "Then how did you recognize him?"

Griffith laughed, trying to hide his nervousness. "It fell." He nodded aggressively as if he was trying to convince himself. "I cut it off, just before he ran." Griffith turned from me and headed to a pitcher of water, ending our conversation.

I followed, still confused. Griffith was an excellent swordsman, if he cut off Alexander's mask then he should've been close enough to strike him.

Griffith turned, handing me a cup, his eyes meeting mine.

Blue eyes.

My cup clanged against the floor, water splattering as I stepped back in horror.

How had I not seen it?

Griffith had been trying to separate me from Alexander since the rose garden. He had tried to convince me that Modare was a treacherous country. He had asked me to spy. He had information about the castle, about my schedule, when I would be alone…because of my letters.

"Before I called out your name, you were ordering one of your men to lock someone up. Who was it?" I questioned, my volume rising.

"Princess?" Griffith stepped toward me, an arm reaching out. "Are you well? You seem pale."

"You said, 'lock him up. I don't want him in sight when she wakes.' Who do you not want me to see Griffith?"

"One of your kidnappers. Seeing them would only upset you and—"

"You said all of them died, Griffith. So, I'll ask once more," I roared so ferociously Griffith stepped back, "who do you not want me to see?"

Griffith was silent, his forehead wrinkling in irritation as he realized what I had figured out.

"Estelle," a voice thundered. I turned, eyes widening as I raced to the room that it came from.

I pulled open the door. The two masked men from the tavern lay on the floor, blood sputtering from their chests. Alexander stood over the corpses, clutching his shoulder.

My heart raced as my arms wrapped around him, tears pouring out as I listened to his staggered breath.

Thank the gods. He was alive.

"Estelle," he murmured into my neck, breathing in my scent. "You're ok." He pressed his forehead into mine, holding me tight.

"And so are you." I kissed his lips.

"Apart from this inept shoulder, yeah. Aeson, he's going to kill me."

A laugh escaped my lips as I continued to sob. Aeson, Titus, they were never going to let Alexander outside again.

"Estelle, you can't trust Griffith he's the—"

"I know." I looked up, meeting his eyes. "I just figured it out. But I don't understand why."

"We'll figure it out once we get to your father but for now—"

"Well, isn't this a *disgusting* site," Griffith's treacherous voice came from behind.

Alexander grabbed my waist, pushing me behind him, sword ready.

Griffith leaned on the doorframe as he continued to talk. "It's not too late, Estelle. You can still be with me."

"What?"

"Come with me to the castle. Tell your father it was Modare that kidnapped you, mistreated you. Tell him that I rescued you." I gripped Alexander's tunic as Griffith edged closer. "We can be together, you and me. We can be the next King and Queen of Isara like you've always wanted."

"So, that's been your plan? Start a war, become the hero, gain power," Alexander spat out.

"I wasn't talking to you." Griffith pulled out his sword. "Estelle, you can trust me," Griffith cooed, the gentleness in his voice sickening. "I kept him alive as promised. I'll keep all my future promises if you just be a good girl. It would be no different than when you heeded my advice for all those years."

Griffith stepped forward, reaching out a hand so he could caress my cheek. Alexander rested the point of his sword on Griffith's neck in warning. Griffith froze in response, glaring at Alexander.

"Estelle," he murmured my name, pushing for an answer.

"Why would you do this, Griffith? We've been friends since I was little. You've always been loyal to my family, to Isara."

"And it's gotten me nothing," he roared out. "You were supposed to be mine. I played the perfect lord for you. I protected you, was your confidant. I was there for you in every way." He took a step forward with each sentence, not caring that Alexander's sword drew blood. "I was supposed to marry you, become king. It was decided until your *idiot* father opted to marry you to some foreign royal for peace."

I gulped, wondering how different my life would have been if Modare didn't take Ula and Astra. I would have been married to Griffith, once the love of my life. Would I have been happy?

Pain, jealousy, and hunger took over Griffith's serene blue eyes. He, like Veronica, was power-driven but far worse. There was no sign of the man I once loved.

No, that man never existed. I was too naïve to know better. I was a fool to his play.

"Back away," Alexander growled.

Griffith cynically laughed. "Or you'll do what?" he asked, a corner of his lips moving upward, his head cocking in challenge.

Alexander lunged forward to pierce Griffith's throat, but Griffith was faster. He spun away, barely dodging the blade while a bead of sweat ran down Alexander's forehead.

"Now, I care about you, Estelle, I really do. So, let me point out the obvious. Little Prince here, seems to have a damaged shoulder. Now, if I remember correctly, one of your letters stated he was a fair match to me. I doubt that's still the case now, with his little injury and all." Griffith held his sword up, admiring the glimmer as he trailed on, "You can make the choice to play along with me, become my bride—it would make the accession to the throne a lot easier—or I can kill you alongside him. I can bring his head with me, tell your father I was too late, but I made sure his death was slow and painful." Griffith grinned ear from ear, his eyes filled with insanity.

"Estelle, you should—"

I knew what Alexander was going to say. He would never want to see me suffer but living with Griffith, pretending I was his, that was true suffering. I'd rather be dead.

"You're a monster, Griffith. My father will see through that," I yelled out.

"Have it your way then," Griffith growled before holding up his sword and charging.

Alexander threw me back, my bottom smacking on the cold floor, as their blades met. In a daze, I watched them fight. Griffith smiled brighter with each clash as Alexander's shoulder trembled uncontrollably.

Griffith advanced, pushing Alexander toward the wall. He would be cornered soon. I knew little about battle strategy, but from the duels I had seen from tournaments, once your back was against the wall there was little you could do, and it was certain you'd lose.

I had to do something. I couldn't let Alexander fight by himself. I had to—I gripped at my skirts only to feel something hard strapped to my leg.

The dagger. I had forgotten about it.

I lifted my skirts, wielding the beautiful blade. The blade that matched my husband's. I raced forward.

Alexander's back was already against the wall, his sword pressing into him as his strength waned. I didn't have time to hesitate.

I took my dagger to Griffith's neck, slashing it open. Blood splattered onto Alexander. I stumbled back as Griffith fell to his knees, his eyes growing cold as his hand tried to reach for me.

It was over.

It was finally over.

CHAPTER 54

My body rocked back and forth as the carriage wheels hurriedly spun to our destination. I looked out the window, smiling at the peaceful greenery, the busy marketplace, the people walking in unpredictable patterns—all the things that would've been destroyed. They were all still here, untouched.

We had saved Modare, Isara, and all the people who would have been affected by the war with only a few hours to spare.

I had run up to the gate shouting that the Princess of Isara had arrived, to stop the march. My father came sprinting out, tears rolling down his face as he clasped his arms around me.

He hadn't been mad at me, he hadn't ignored me, not once this year. Griffith had been stealing our letters, making my father question how safe I was at Modare. Griffith had been whispering in his ear, much like how he had whispered in mine, that Modare was plotting to take my life and betray the treaty. All the tension, the mistrust was caused by him.

It had been a long month as all three of us told our stories, searching for answers, trying to piece together the information so we could truly know what happened. We even had Griffith's estate and his room in the castle searched in hopes of filling in the missing parts of our stories. We found nothing apart from a letter he had failed to hide. The penmanship of the letter was almost identical to Lord Visimar's, but the evidence from this was far too little to accuse Vropan of aiding Griffith's sinister plan. We'd have to keep a closer eye on them from now on in case they found another way to wreak havoc on the continent, but that was a problem for another day. For now, we'd focus on the happy things in life.

I leaned into Alexander, his warmth spreading through my body as he wrapped his arm around me. The guards opened the gates revealing Leo, Samuel, Anna, and even an apologetic Titus, waiting for us in the courtyard. I knew Titus had forbidden Alexander to search for me. He had said so in a letter and apologized for it, apologized for everything. He told me that I was, indeed, a very useful princess, despite my feelings getting the better of me. That now, he would do everything he could to protect Alexander, Modare, and *me* in the future. He told me that his family had finally grown. Little did he know how much it had, I thought, rubbing my swollen stomach.

"Are you excited to be back in Modare?" Alexander softly asked, pulling my attention away from the welcoming party.

I looked at everyone's smiling faces.

I laughed thinking of the first time I came through these gates. I was so terrified, pretending to be strong, thinking that this was punishment, that this was the lion's den. Now,

I wanted nothing more than to swing open the carriage doors and embrace those who waited outside.

"No." Alexander raised a brow. I let out a chuckle as I responded, smiling, "I'm excited to be back home."

Acknowledgments

Writing a book had been an exhilarating, crazy journey. It is one adventure I never thought I'd take and even when I did, I didn't think I would finish it. It was supposed to be a hobby to pass the time as I tried to find a new job that made my heart soar. However, the more words I wrote, the more I realized this was it. This was what I had been looking for, but I wouldn't have realized it, nor would I have pushed through if it weren't for the many wonderful people who cheered me on along the way.

David, my best friend and husband, you were the first person I told about this book. You were the first person who said I needed to follow my heart and write my stories despite it not being the most conventional job. You were there for every cry session, every small victory (even though we were in different countries some days) and it made all the difference. I know I've said it before, but I'll say it again. Thank you for believing in me and my dreams. Thank you for never letting me give up.

JayLynn, my writing buddy, where do I even begin? Thank you for making this journey full of laughter. Thank you for the late night skype writing dates, for the calls, and snapchats where we just rambled about our stories. And thank you for being one of the first people to read my story in its entirety, for all the feedback you gave.

Sake and Inari, my fur babies, I know you guys can't read but that won't stop me from being a little crazy and giving you a shout out. My little fluffballs, thanks for keeping me company in the study, for warming my feet as I wrote, and all the cuddles when I got stressed. Thanks for making sure I took breaks by asking for all the walkies and bringing me your toys. Love you, little ones!

To all the friends who let me tell them about my book, regardless of how long we have known each other or if we met in real life or bookstagram/booktok, thank you. It may not seem like a lot but even if you gave one encouraging word or liked a post about my writing journey, it kept me going. It kept me believing that someone out there would eventually read my novel and enjoy it. You guys gave me hope.

And finally, thank you, the reader. Without you, this book would only have stayed in my head or in a drawer collecting dust. It is the joy we see in your eyes that gets writers through the bad days, the days when we want to give up. It is the idea that one day a reader will come along, pick up our book, love it, and possibly be the book they needed. That idea keeps writers going. So, thank you, readers. Thank you for giving my debut book a chance.

Always follow your heart,
Renee Palstring

ABOUT THE AUTHOR

Renee M. Palstring has not always known she wanted to be an author, in fact, she originally started out on a completely different path. She earned a Bachelor of Science in Mathematics and Computer Science and set off on an adventure to become an engineer/programmer. However, after marrying and moving to Hawaii during the pandemic, she realized that her passions were somewhere else, she just didn't know where. She finally realized this when she started reading again, to keep her occupied as she job searched, this sparked the creative writer in her. She started writing as a fun hobby which ultimately turned into her debut book, A Misplaced Love.

When Renee is not busy chasing her newfound dream to become an author, she can be found doing a variety of activities ranging from lounging near the garden to trying to survive a three-hour hike. She'll jump at the chance to travel and experience another's culture, but she also loves the comforts and familiarity of home.